NIKKI SOARDE

Cerridwen Press

A Cerridwen Press Publication

www.cerridwenpress.com

Mortal Wounds

ISBN #141995332X

Edited by Sue-Ellen Gower.
Cover art by Syneca.

Electronic book Publication June 2005
Trade paperback Publication April 2006

Cerridwen Press is an imprint of Ellora's Cave Publishing, Inc.®

Acknowledgement

MORTAL WOUNDS is set in two very diverse worlds. The world of the conservative Mennonites is one that is very familiar to me, and didn't necessitate a lot of extra research. However, war-torn Bosnia in the former Yugoslavia was indeed very strange and unknown territory, and in order to lend realism and texture to this part of the book I needed to do extensive research.

I was very fortunate to come in contact with two local police officers who had served in Bosnia with INTERPOL and who were so kind as to share their detailed knowledge of the country's history, geography and social climate. Many thanks to Waterloo Regional Police officers Inspector Dan A. and Sergeant John S. Thanks to them for putting up with endless questions and for sharing their experiences and insights, not to mention their photographs, with me. *Mortal Wounds* wouldn't have been possible without them!

Trademarks Acknowledgement

~

The author acknowledges the trademarked status and trademark owners of the following wordmarks mentioned in this work of fiction:

Celica: Toyota Jidosha Kogyo Kabushiki Kaisha (Toyota Motor Co., LTD.)

Converse: Converse, Inc.

Dom Perignon: Chandon Champagne Corp.

Firebird: General Motors Corporation

Glock: Glock, Inc.

Klaxon: Klaxon Independent Quality Assurance Pty. Ltd.

Kleenex: Kimberly-Clark Corporation

Lincoln Continental: Ford Motor Company

Poison Perfume: Parfums Christian Dior

Scrabble: Hasbro, Inc.

Part One: Wounded Heart

Chapter One

June 1987

A single bead of sweat pearled between Veronica's shoulder blades. It slipped down to tickle her back in the precise spot that had tortured humanity with unreachable itches since the dawn of time. She wriggled against the hard wooden pew but only succeeded in plastering her dress to her sweat-dampened skin.

She was hot. She was cranky. She was bored. And the air in this tiny church was so thick and stagnant she could barely breathe. *Thick and stagnant.* The words reverberated inside her brain. It struck her that, in too many ways, those words summed up her life.

To distract herself from her discomfort, she tried to concentrate on the sermon but it was futile. The heat, together with the rhythmic rise and fall of the pastor's voice, began to lull her to sleep. Her head began to droop but a sharp jab from her mother's elbow snapped her back to attention.

Restless, she stole a peek at the congregation seated around her. At Silas Lapp, with his sun-weathered face and the scar on his left cheekbone where a cow had kicked him two years ago. At Eva Brubacher, with her hair pulled so tightly her center part had begun to widen under the strain. Neither of them acknowledged her gaze but sat still as stone, like statues, unblinking and uninspired.

Veronica sighed. How she longed to see a flicker of humor or a spark of emotion in these eyes that she loved and knew so well. Sunday service, however, was not the place for laughter or excitement, for tears or applause. Church was for prayer and reflection, for silent and reverent worship. Unfortunately Veronica had never been much good at silent and reverent.

She focused on the man behind the pulpit and tried to hide an impertinent smile when she noticed the sweat that trickled down his nose and dripped from his chin. His straight-cut black jacket, cotton shirt and simple black trousers hung on him like damp rags. In fact, he looked almost as miserable as Veronica felt.

Time slowed to a crawl and fatigue pulled on her eyes but she managed to keep her head erect and her eyes focused. At last, the second sermon of the morning drew to a close, completing a full hour of hell-fire and brimstone theology. The final sermon, which promised to last between an hour and an hour and a half, would begin shortly. But first they would enjoy a moment of musical respite.

She should be relieved, she knew. It would mean a break in the monotony and give her a chance to stretch her legs and exercise her voice. However, as they stood and flipped through their hymnals, all she felt was dread.

Veronica loved to sing. She often took long walks in the fields and forests near their home and sang out loud, casting her voice unabashedly to the heavens. Music welled up from within her until she ached, and only when she could release herself in song did her spirit soar. Her voice echoed across the fields, its tones rich and sweet. It was a gift from God and one that she longed to share. But not like this.

The plodding notes grated on her like the drips from a leaky faucet. This wasn't singing. The notes barely spanned a single octave and the rhythms lacked any trace of imagination.

They had just begun the final stanza when Veronica felt a tug on her sanity. She had to get out of there.

"Mom," she whispered. "I'm feeling a bit nauseous. I think it's the heat."

"All right, dear." Her mother patted her hand. "Go out and get some fresh air. Don't bother disturbing everyone by coming back in. Just wait outside under one of the maples."

Veronica nodded and quietly slipped out of the pew. She headed toward the back of the church, meeting no one's gaze, her eyes low. Not that there was much to see.

No crosses or carvings adorned the walls of this tiny church. No gold or silver gleamed from the altar. In this House of God the members chose to worship the Lord and His faithfulness, they did *not* worship His gifts.

She ignored the disapproving glances that she could feel burning into her back as she exited the sanctuary.

She stepped outside into bright sunshine, breathing deeply of the lilac-scented breeze that tugged at her skirt and evaporated the sweat from her skin. *Freedom.* Out here she could taste it.

Unable to abide it a moment longer, she reached up and pulled off the small piece of white netting that adorned the head of every female member at all times. The covering symbolized humility before God and men. Perhaps that was why it never seemed to fit her quite right.

She crumpled it up and stuffed it into her pocket.

A glance at her watch told her that she had plenty of time before the service let out and she had no intention of wasting it napping under a maple tree. She set off at a brisk pace that would clear her head, and possibly give her an opportunity to spill a little bit of her soul in song.

She strolled along the side of the gravel road. Her eyes scanned the horizon, taking in the endless fields of sprouting corn that characterized the rolling farmland of Wellesley Township in Southern Ontario. Her only companions were the chattering starlings and the occasional crow that soared overhead, crowing aspersions at her invasion of its domain.

A car sailed past. Its excessive speed stirred up enormous clouds of dust and threw stones at her bare legs. She scowled at it as it disappeared around a curve.

The breeze picked up and dispersed the dust and debris. It billowed her skirt about her legs and teased the few strands of hair that had escaped her bun. In another burst of rebelliousness she pulled the pins from her hair. Thick auburn waves that had never felt the sting of scissors tumbled over her shoulders and fell below her waistline. It tickled her face and arms as it swirled and flirted with the breeze. Veronica would pay dearly when she faced the hairbrush that night but the pleasure far outweighed the pain.

She rounded a curve in the road and was just considering which song would be the most pleasing to her irritable, feathered friends when she noticed a car stopped a short way ahead. The hood was up and steam belched out from beneath. She noted with smug satisfaction that it was the same car that had screamed past her just a few moments ago.

She smiled. The driver was obviously paying for his recklessness.

But as she approached, fascination gradually displaced contempt. This car was a far cry from the matte black vehicles that stocked the Maple Grove Church parking lot. She reminded herself once again that she had reason to be grateful. At least their particular sect of the Mennonite Church had graduated from buggies to cars and the members were allowed limited access to electricity and telephones. But for her a radio in the barn was no substitute for a television in the living room, or—God forgive her—a trip to a movie theater. And sometimes her eyes ached to feast on this kind of color.

The car glistened fiery red in the intense morning sun. With its wide sunroof and sparkling chrome, the beast was as alien to her environment as a sleek, black panther. Seemingly of their own volition her fingers reached out and caressed the warm, gleaming metal as she passed.

"Goddamn, stupid, fucking bastard…" She heard a muffled voice from beneath the hood.

The curses halted her in her tracks and her eyebrows arched. She had heard those words before but her experience with them was extremely limited. And she had certainly never heard them strung together with such emphatic enthusiasm. But rather than afflicting her with the vapors, the words and their spirited delivery intrigued her.

She poked her head around the front of the car. "Problems?"

A man bent over the engine straightened up too quickly and bashed his head against the oily underside of the hood. "Fuck!" he roared. "Where the hell did you come from?"

Veronica blinked. He was about her age, maybe a year or so older, but definitely no more than twenty. His disheveled black hair clung to his forehead in damp tendrils but his cool, blue eyes sparkled. A white T-shirt with rolled-up sleeves and a pair of faded blue jeans sheathed his body from shoulders to ankles and left little to the imagination.

Butterflies fluttered in her tummy.

This man bore little resemblance to the men she knew. Most of them trained their hairline around a sturdy steel mixing bowl. Their wardrobes consisted exclusively of button-up shirts and loose fitting black pants. And while most of them could sling a sixty-pound sack of feed without batting an eye, their clothes revealed little. And even on the hottest days, they rarely removed a shirt—and never in front of a woman.

"Sorry, I didn't mean to startle you," she said through lips that suddenly felt quite dry. "I was just out for a walk and thought maybe I could help."

He rubbed the bump on his head as he studied her. Dark brows furrowed in concentration as he evaluated his visitor. He chewed on a wad of gum. "You from that church up the road?"

"Yes."

His eyes roved over her from head to hips to toes and back again. His audacity astounded her. "You don't look much like the other chicks I've seen gettin' in and outta those sorry-excuse-for-cars you folks got."

"I'm not a *chick,*" she said as she threw her shoulders back.

He smiled with half of his wide mouth. "Sorry. *Women.*"

"Why?" she asked, her face growing hot. "What makes me so different?"

"Well, for starters, I thought you had to keep your hair up and wear that doily thing on your head."

She had forgotten about her unkempt appearance. "The bun was too tight," she shot back. "And it's called a covering."

"Oh. Sorry." But his expression was less than apologetic. "For another thing, you're a hell of a lot prettier than any of the others I've seen around here."

Veronica's face burned with embarrassment and an unsettling irritation. She took a step back. "Would you like me to go back and call someone from the church for you? We do have phones, you know."

"Hey, hey! Don't run off." He stepped toward her. "I didn't mean to scare you away. I don't need to call anybody, I just gotta wait 'til this thing cools down. I got some water in the trunk. My buddy Lenny said he fixed the leak but I should've known that son of a bitch didn't know what the fuck he was doing."

"Were you born in a gutter?"

He stared at her, blinked as understanding dawned. "Oh." He chuckled. "Sorry about that. I live with a brother, two cousins and my dad. I guess we do get kinda comfortable with the swearing. I have to remind myself to tone it down when I'm with *women.*"

"Oh." She licked her lips to try and replenish the moisture. "Well…I guess you don't need any help then." She continued to back away, but halted in astonishment when his hand whipped out and grabbed her. She stood, frozen, unsure what to do as she gazed down at the grease-stained fingers latched about her wrist. Perhaps she should have screamed or, at the very least, rebuked him for his boldness but all she could think of was how strong and warm his hand felt against her skin.

Just as suddenly he let go. "Sorry. I didn't mean to frighten you. But really, you don't have to go." He ran his fingers up and down the metal rod that kept the hood of the car from slamming down on his head. Finally he relaxed and leaned back against the front of the car as he wiped the grease off his hands with an old rag. He cocked an eyebrow at her. "Were you leaving 'cause you're scared of me?"

She considered the question. "Maybe. A little."

He nodded. "Smart girl. Honest too. I like that."

"Well, I live for your approval."

He rewarded her sarcasm with a wry grin. "You know what? I'm kinda scared of you too."

She raised her eyebrows and looked him up and down. He was easily six foot tall, and must have weighed a hundred and eighty pounds. His hands were large and strong, and his thighs—

She dragged her gaze back to his face. "How could you possibly be scared of me?"

"Don't you know how dangerous beautiful women are? Women like you pack more punch than an H-bomb."

She chewed on the inside of her cheek to keep from smiling. "Is that so?"

He nodded.

"You really think I'm beautiful?" Compliments like that were unheard of in her house.

"You're kidding, right?"

She shook her head. "No. No one's ever told me that before."

"Well, that's a fucking crime." He winced. "Sorry. Old habits, you know."

She looked back down the road. "I really should get back." Veronica couldn't say why but she really didn't want to. She thought she *should* be afraid of him—seriously afraid. Even in her sheltered little world she had heard stories of abductions and rapes. This was an ideal scenario for such a crime and he certainly would have no trouble overpowering her. But, inexplicably, she felt no fear.

He took advantage of her hesitation. "Why? You got lots of time. I drive by here Sunday mornings all the time and I figure it's at least an hour before they let outta there." He tilted his head. "Besides, you don't really want to go."

"You're a mind reader now?"

"It doesn't take a mind reader to see the way you're lookin' at me."

Veronica set her jaw. "And how, exactly, is that?"

"Like you'd like to eat me up."

The heat crept into her face again and her stomach knotted at the image his words evoked. She refused to acknowledge the truth of it, and was furious with him for pointing it out. "I've never looked at anyone like that in my life. I don't have the faintest idea what that kind of *look* looks like."

"The hell you haven't. And you just have to look at me to know what it looks like."

"You're something else, you know that?" She was sure she was a bright crimson by this time but still she couldn't tear herself away.

"So they tell me. Now, tell me honestly, do you really want to go back to that stuffy little church? Or would you rather stay here with me?" His expression left little doubt that he knew the answer to that question all too well. "I thought maybe, once I get this thing cooled down, you might like a ride. I got a set of awesome woofers in the back of this thing. They could blow your ears off. I'd lay pretty good odds you've never heard anything like it."

"Woofers?"

He laughed and the tension drained out of her. It was an easy laugh and his eyes danced with mischief. She couldn't help but smile in response.

"Right. I guess you're not exactly up on the latest lingo. Woofers are speakers, you know, for a stereo. The woofers give off the deep bass sounds and the tweeters are for the higher ranges."

Veronica brightened. "You like music?"

He looked at her like she was from another planet. "Sure. Don't you?"

She peered around to try and see inside the mysterious vehicle. "What kind of music?"

"Rock and roll, of course. But I don't mind a little blues and even some of the pop stuff is okay."

The temptation was just too great. She had listened to some of the popular music, but only very occasionally when she could slip a radio into the barn and listen secretly. She had certainly never had her *ears blown off*. "I'd like that."

"Which? The ride or the tunes?"

She smiled. "Both." She watched him tentatively tap the radiator cap to see if it was cool enough to remove. "By the way, what's your name?"

"Jesse Ward. How 'bout you?"

"Veronica."

"Hmm. That's quite the handle." He gazed off into space for a moment. "Can I call you Ronni?"

She chewed on her lower lip. "Um, I guess so."

"Great." He refocused his attention on the engine. "I think it's cool enough. Would you mind grabbing the jug of water outta the trunk? It's not locked."

She nodded and headed to the rear of the vehicle. "What kind of car is this?"

"Toyota Celica. I always liked the name. You know, *Celica* kinda sounds like *sleek*. I got it custom painted. Notice how the paint sparkles in the right light?"

On her way back with the jug, Veronica peered at the paint. He was right. At certain angles the red sparkled into a thousand other iridescent hues. It was a startling effect. "Wow. That's very pretty."

He scowled at her as she reached him. "Pretty *cool,* you mean."

"Cool?"

"Man, are you outta touch."

She propped her hands on her hips and glared at him. "Now there's a shocker. I don't suppose you'd know the meaning of words like humility and chastity?"

"Huh?"

"Man, are you outta touch."

Chuckling, he poured the water into the radiator. "Okay, I get your drift."

Veronica decided to let that phrase pass. She wasn't familiar with it either, but got the general idea.

She watched in silence as he worked. Out of the corner of her eye she caught a glimpse of her reflection in the polished chrome. What had he said? That she was beautiful? Had he been teasing? Or were his words sincere? She studied herself in the distorted curvature of the sideview mirror.

Her eyes were wide and a deep, jade green, but she had always thought her cheekbones stood out too crisply and her lips were too full. Her father had once called them 'thick' and she'd never liked the sound of that. But perhaps the overall effect wasn't completely displeasing.

She glanced back at Jesse as he poured the water into the radiator and decided that she believed him. Perhaps her family considered her beautiful but they never spoke it out loud and, she had to admit, it was very good to hear. Perhaps, coming from a stranger, it meant even more.

Finally, Jesse replaced the cap on the radiator and tossed a glance at her over his left shoulder. He arched one eyebrow. "Ready?" He slammed down the hood and sauntered around to the passenger side. He opened the door and motioned for her to slide in.

Veronica hesitated only briefly before seating herself on the velvety bucket seat. He didn't close the door immediately. She glanced up and caught him staring at her legs. The hem of her dress had ridden up past her knees and she self-consciously pulled it down again. As if withdrawing from a trance, he dragged his gaze away and slammed the door shut. Veronica caught herself smiling.

A moment later he slid in behind the wheel.

"I have to be back by the time the service is finished." Veronica had no intention of explaining her whereabouts to her parents.

"No problem. But we gotta get off this gravel and onto some hardtop. I wanna show you how this baby can fly."

Veronica was enjoying his unique way of expressing himself. Unlike the plodding words of the sermon she had just escaped, he danced with the language, turning phrases and meanings in unexpected and colorful ways. For him the words came alive.

He turned the key and the motor hummed. He revved the engine a couple of times and flashed her a grin. "Purrs like a kitten."

Veronica didn't exactly agree. She might not be terribly familiar with cars and all their quirks but she definitely knew cats. There had to be at least twenty of them that roamed about their barn, hunting mice and rats, and slurping up the milk that spilled out of the huge automated cooler. She knew how a purring kitten sounded and the noisy engine on Jesse's *Celica* didn't exactly fill her with the same sense of contentment. But she just nodded, not wishing to shatter his inflated image of his crude machine.

He pulled away slowly and they drove in silence for about a kilometer. When they reached a crossroad Jesse turned onto the paved highway and floored the accelerator. Veronica was pressed firmly back into the cushions of her seat. The wind screamed about her ears and whipped her hair about her face and up through the sunroof. She gathered it together and held it tightly in a clenched fist.

Scenery flashed by in a blur. Isolated farm houses, wide open pasture land and small clusters of pine and ash trees came and went almost before she could focus on them. The endless corn fields that had just begun to sprout became a solid green haze. The dotted line on the center of the highway blurred together as they tore down the gentle slope of a long hill and started to climb the next rise.

At first she was annoyed with his apparent attempt to impress her but soon the thrill of acceleration and speed seeped through the protective layers. She was surprised to find herself smiling.

"Feels good, doesn't it?" he asked.

She nodded, closed her eyes, put her head back against the headrest and relished the sensation of speed and freedom.

"There's nothing like tearing down the highway at a hundred and twenty clicks," he continued. "I know it can be risky. I've gotten nailed by the cops a couple of times. But there's nothing like it to work out the kinks."

"Kinks?" She cracked open an eye.

"Oh, I get in fights with my dad and my brother sometimes. They're okay, but the house is so crowded, and with no woman around to keep the peace, sometimes things get kinda tense. So, when that happens I take off in my stress buster," with that he patted the dash, "and tear down a few highways until I feel liberated again."

Veronica nodded mutely. He no doubt lived a very different existence than anything she had ever experienced or could even imagine. The thought at once disturbed and fascinated her.

He broke into her thoughts. "What do you do to blow off steam?"

"I sing." Her own mouth had betrayed her. She'd never shared that with another soul and yet she hadn't even hesitated with that response.

"No kidding?"

She shifted in her seat and turned her gaze out across the fields. "You mentioned music?"

"Right. Nearly forgot." He popped in a tape that was sticking halfway out of the slot in the stereo. As the music began, Jesse laughed out loud. "I couldn't have picked a better tune if I had planned it."

Veronica looked at him questioningly.

The music blared through the car. Guitars screamed and drums pounded, the voice that accompanied them was rough and raunchy and yet strangely appealing as it sang of freedom, adventure and youthful rebellion.

A smile trickled across her face as Jesse sang along, "Born to be wi-i-i-ild!" He listened and tapped the beat. "Is that you, Ronni? That's me. I bet you're just itching for adventure, just like me. That's why I'm heading out west. I'm going to university in Vancouver in the fall. I'm sure to find some adventure out there." He turned to look at her. "Where you gonna find it?"

"I think I just did."

He raised his eyebrows and wordlessly turned up the stereo a few more notches.

The music was loud. Louder than anything she had ever heard in her life. But she didn't cover her ears. The beat and the rhythms were insidious. They crept into her psyche, tugging at deep, delightful places she never knew existed.

Jesse spoke over the music. "So how do you like rock and roll? That's Steppenwolf. Great band. You got anything like that in that prissy little church of yours?"

Veronica knew she should be offended but she wasn't. How could she deny such a blatant truth? She shook her head. "No. Our music is a lot different than this."

"I'll bet." He paused as the next song came up. The beat and rhythms were completely different, much slower and more melodic. "This is *Take it to the Limit.* It's by the Eagles. They're one of the biggest bands of all time. You know the secret to Rock and Roll? You gotta close your eyes, crank it up and let it soak into your soul. I love to sing along but usually I've got it so loud I can't even hear myself."

Veronica was watching him, spellbound by him.

"Go ahead. Try it."

She closed her eyes and put her head back. She noticed the music got a little bit louder again. He must have turned it up a couple more notches. He was right. She could feel the beat in her bones, in the pit of her stomach, in her soul. Of course, that was the reason her church banned this kind of music. Her elders were afraid that its relentless, pounding beat would somehow corrupt the innocence of their youth. But this didn't feel like corruption. It certainly felt decadent, but not in any depraved sense of the word. It assaulted her senses and filled her with contentment. By the second verse she found herself singing along with the chorus. She wasn't sure exactly what the words meant but somehow they touched her.

When the song ended Jesse pulled to the side of the road, popped out the tape and turned off the stereo.

She looked at him suspiciously.

He twisted in the seat to face her. "You weren't kidding."

"About what?"

"You sure can sing. That must've been the first time you heard that song but you were right on the tune and the rhythms and, honey, you got a voice like Diana Ross."

"Who?"

"Trust me, it's a compliment."

She sat up, leaned forward. "Really? You really liked the way I sing?"

"Shit, yeah!" He flinched. "Sorry. But you should join a band or something." His fingers tapped rapidly against the wheel and his eyes glittered. He blinked. "Hey! I might know somebody. There's this group of guys I used to hang with. They've got a band. It's just a hobby but they play weekends in some bars and the occasional wedding. Their lead singer's okay but he's got nothing on you. Maybe I could talk to them. I bet they'd love to have you." He cocked his head and looked her up and down. "'Course you'd have to lose the dress. They'd probably want you in tight leather and sequins or something."

Veronica had momentarily lost herself in his excitement but now reality reared its ugly head. She shook her head. "Thanks, Jesse. But I could never do something like that."

"What?" He was incredulous. "You're just gonna waste talent like that?"

She swallowed against a lump in her throat. "Can we just drive and listen a little bit more? I was really enjoying that."

He studied her and she could see the disappointment in his eyes. For some inexplicable reason it cut her deeply.

He sighed. "Sure. We've still got some time. This is one of my best tapes. I put together a bunch of my favorites. I think you'll like the rest of the tunes just as much. Don't hesitate to sing along." He pulled out onto the highway. "I like it."

They drove for another half an hour, the stereo blasting and the wind blowing through their hair. Jesse was right. This was the embodiment of freedom. She tried to let the music soak into her soul, as he had suggested. Who knew when she would have an opportunity like this again? She kept her eyes closed much of the time, and occasionally sang along when the tune and the words became familiar enough.

Every once in a while she would catch Jesse watching her out of the corner of his eye, a hint of amusement glinting in those blue depths. He was obviously gleaning great pleasure from helping her experience her first real taste of the *sins* of the world. He displayed no remorse for the role he was playing in leading her down the road to ruin.

She probably should have been irritated with his arrogance and casual disregard for the values and principles with which she had been raised. But he was so good-natured, and so obviously taken with the music and with her talent, that she couldn't bring herself to feel annoyed. In fact, several times she caught herself smiling back. Those twinkling blue eyes and that mischievous smile were just as beguiling as the pounding beat and intricate rhythms of the music that swirled around her ears. Maybe even more so.

The husky tones of a Bryan Adams love song were washing over Veronica as Jesse turned the car back toward the church. She closed her eyes and allowed herself to float on the vivid images and emotions that the passionate lyrics evoked. But a moment later she lost her focus on the music.

She felt an odd sensation close to her head. She stiffened, held her breath and willed her heart to stop its furious pounding against the inside of her chest. Jesse was touching her hair. He was stroking some of the errant strands that lay over the back of the seat.

She remained still, afraid to open her eyes and unsure what to do, but hoping desperately that he wouldn't stop. Eventually his fingers worked their way up until they rested against the back of her scalp. At last he laced his fingers through the thick mane and cupped her head gently in his palm.

The Earth dipped out from beneath her and Veronica's stomach rose to her throat. From head to toe, she was a trembling mass of gooseflesh, and hardly noticed when the car slowed to a stop. All she was aware of was the massage of his strong fingers against her scalp, and then the incredible heat as his other hand touched her cheek. She opened her eyes just as his lips joined with hers.

Chapter Two

Veronica was eighteen years old and had been kissed before. Twice. The first time had been behind her family's barn after a particularly grueling harvest session. She and her sixteen-year-old co-conspirator had both been sweaty and tired, and dismally inept at the task. The second time had been somewhat more satisfying. It had occurred after a strawberry social. She and Jonathan Erb had gone for a long evening walk amidst cool spring breezes and subtle aromas of lilacs and honeysuckle. That kiss had been notable. But it couldn't compare to this.

His lips caressed hers, sending shock waves down to her toes. Instinctively her hands moved up to his shoulders. His tongue tickled her lips, which seemed determined to part regardless of her wishes in the matter. When his tongue dipped into her mouth, ran along her teeth and challenged her senses to a hopeless duel, she conceded defeat and a low moan of surrender escaped her throat.

Just as her tongue initiated its own assault, he drew away. But not far. He still held the back of her head, his fingers laced through her hair as he rested his forehead against hers. "I better get you back now or you'll never get there."

She noticed he was breathing hard and, oddly, that pleased her. She licked her lips, still tasting him. "Yeah. They'll be getting out very soon."

His eyes had focused on the motion of her tongue. He groaned. "Can I see you again?"

"Yes. I'm just not sure—"

"Which farm is yours?" Abruptly, he released his hold on her and sat back.

"Two concessions over. We're dairy. The name's on a sign out front. It's Lichty."

"You probably don't want them to know about me?"

She hesitated, suddenly uncertain of where this was leading. "You're assuming an awful lot."

His gaze penetrated her, searching… "Am I? Am I wrong?"

She closed her eyes for a moment. She couldn't believe what she was about to do. "No, you're not wrong." It had been a feeble attempt to call a halt to the proceedings. "Them knowing about you probably wouldn't be a good idea."

"Can you get out of the house? Late, I mean. You know, around midnight?"

She nodded silently, an odd combination of euphoria and misery coiling within her. She was giddy at the prospect of getting to know Jesse better. He was exciting and charming and adventurous. He embodied everything her life seemed to be lacking. In an ironic twist of fate he was the answer to her prayers.

But she was about to deceive her family, willfully. She loved and respected her parents. As long as she could remember they had been loving and supportive—a solid, reliable influence in her life. They had sacrificed and provided for Veronica as well as her brothers and sister, Anna. They had rarely, if ever, disappointed her. But she was about to disappoint them. And she couldn't seem to stop herself.

"Okay, how about Tuesday?" he continued. "I'll be waiting at the end of your lane."

"All right."

He cupped her jaw, and ran the pad of his thumb across her cheek.

His hands were warm and slightly rough. She closed her eyes again, and concentrated on his touch. She allowed it to wash away all traces of doubt.

"God, you're beautiful." He kissed her again. This time it was urgent, almost feverish, but brief. "We better get going." He gunned the engine and tore down the road toward the church.

Veronica felt lightheaded, like part of her was floating in some surreal dream world. But this was all too real. Wonderfully real. How could she possibly get through the next forty-eight hours before seeing him again?

Her reverie was shattered when he skidded to a halt in front of the simple little building with the big maple trees out front. Maple Grove. That was the name of their church. *Her* church, she reminded herself, as if it had suddenly lost relevance to her life. She put a hand on the door handle but, before she got out, on an impulse she turned back to him and touched his face. Her fingers found just a trace of stubble. She ran a thumb longingly across his lips.

He quirked a sad smile and turned to kiss the palm of her hand. "You better get outta here before I ravish you in the back seat."

She heeded the advice and quickly jumped from the vehicle, slamming the door behind her.

He spun his tires in his haste to make a clean getaway. Barely a minute later the doors to the church were flung open and the throng spilled out into the delicious shade of the ancient maple trees.

Normally Veronica was starving by the time the service let out. Her mouth would water at the thought of the roast beef, mashed potatoes, gravy, pickled beets, jellied salads, green beans, fresh baked bread and fruit pies that would adorn their dinner table at home. But today, she wasn't sure if she would be able to choke down a single morsel. Her stomach had other things on its mind.

* * * * *

Veronica picked listlessly at her plate. The beef was fork-tender and the potatoes light and fluffy but, as predicted, everything tasted like cardboard. The lead-winged butterflies that fluttered about in her stomach had completely robbed her of her appetite.

"Are you still nauseous, Veronica?" asked her mother.

She attempted a weak smile. "Just a little."

Her mother stood and began clearing the table. "Why don't you take a break from dishes today, then? Anna and I can handle it. Do you want to go in and lie down while we have dessert?"

Veronica's mother bustled about the bright country-style kitchen, stacking plates and clinking glasses. The shy smile that stretched at her tiny rosebud mouth softened the severity of the hairstyle and never failed to warm Veronica's heart. Her short, ample frame strained at the fabric of her dress and Veronica considered that her mother hadn't always been so well-endowed. The last ten years had added several inches to Verna's waist and graced her with an extra chin but perhaps she had earned the extra padding. Years of cleaning, gardening, sewing, cooking and canning, not to mention bearing and raising five children and enduring three miscarriages, should count for something, even if it was only a second piece of pie with her coffee.

"Go on now," urged Verna as she shooed Veronica away from the table.

"Okay. Thanks, Mom." Veronica pushed her chair away from the crowded dinner table and headed for the privacy of the family room. A beige sofa and armchair and an old wooden rocker welcomed family and visitors alike. The decor was old and worn but comfortable and homey in muted, earthy tones that were consistent throughout the house. In fact they were common to every house that Veronica had ever encountered. The layout of the house also followed time-honored tradition.

A white-washed porch wrapped around the box-like farmhouse and shaded the main floor windows. The back door opened onto a mudroom where the working men stripped off their grimy overalls and washed up before coming in through the family room. On cold winter mornings they would often warm their fingers and toes at the ancient cast iron woodstove which sat against the far wall before heading through to the kitchen for their coffee and a hot breakfast.

Just after Veronica left the kitchen she heard the familiar whine of her sister, Anna. "I have to do everything."

Verna promptly shushed her youngest child but Veronica knew Anna would continue to pout right up until the last fork was dried and put away.

In many ways Anna resembled their mother. She had the same nutmeg-colored hair, close-set eyes and small mouth. Luckily, however, she still had the slight figure of a typical seventeen-year-old.

Veronica reclined on the couch. From her position just outside the doorway to the kitchen she could overhear the dinner activities clearly. Her mother poured the coffee and placed the pies on the table, allowing the guests to help themselves. Just like every Sunday, the house buzzed with company and the table was filled to capacity. Sundays were days for visiting and eating and general lazing about—the Lord's day of rest was taken quite seriously.

"Everything was delicious, Verna. Every time I come you manage to outdo yourself." Eli Martin, a distant cousin of her father's, supplied the requisite compliment for her mother's cooking.

"Ach, Eli. Just shush and eat your pie."

Veronica suppressed a smile. Her mother loved the compliments but could never accept one without a fuss.

Today Eli and his family had helped the Lichtys polish off a nine-pound pot roast. Eli's three children were still young, all under the age of six, so the five of them plus Veronica's family of seven, with her parents, three brothers and Anna, made for a very full dinner table.

"You better watch yourself, Glenn," Eli chided her father. "Too many pieces of this pie and you won't be able to bend over to hook up the milkers."

"Eli!" lamented her mother. "That's enough now."

She heard her father's deep chuckle. "So, are you planning to participate in the Lot next spring?" said Glenn in an attempt to distract Eli from his teasing.

The *Lot* referred to the method by which a given church selected a prospective pastor. The eligible men chose Bibles from a stack. One Bible contained a slip of paper with a significant verse printed on it. Whoever was left holding that verse was deemed to have been chosen by divine intervention as the next pastor. Eli was currently serving as a Deacon, or Elder, in their church. He was highly respected and was known to have a keen ability to speak.

"I'm definitely considering it," Eli said carefully. "Nothing would give me greater pleasure than to be able to minister to the congregation on a more regular basis."

"I certainly can't see any objections despite your age."

Eli's tender age of thirty-two years made him a somewhat unlikely candidate for leadership. Potential pastors usually surpassed the age of forty before being called to such a ministry. But Eli had some special gifts. He was charismatic and personable. He had a winning smile and a countenance that angels would envy. Veronica had often heard the women chat about him during Sewing Circle, where they stitched their intricate quilts and talked—*never* gossiped—about their fellow believers. With his blond hair, blue eyes and strong, square jaw he was widely regarded as one of the most attractive men at Maple Grove. It was a sure-fire combination for success. However, the Lot could not be ignored. No amount of popularity could guarantee being chosen by such a seemingly random method.

"I just hope people don't think I'm getting too big for my britches," responded Eli. "I don't want to be regarded as overly ambitious or prideful."

"Ach," chided Veronica's mother with the guttural inflection of her Pennsylvania Dutch heritage. "That's nonsense. No one would think that of you, Eli. You've done too much for this community for anyone to have anything negative to say about you."

"You're too kind, Verna."

"Now, why don't you menfolk go and join Veronica in the family room while Anna and I clean up." Chairs scratched on the worn pine floor as the men vacated the table. Then her mother's voice reached her again. "No, Mary." That was Eli's wife. "Don't you dare pick up a dishtowel. You've got those youngsters to watch and you look like you're ready to drop in a dead faint. You need your rest." Mary was seven months pregnant with their fourth child. "Anna and I can handle it just fine. Why don't you take the children out to the swing set and sit a spell while they play."

"Thank you, Verna. I think I'll do that." Veronica could hear the fatigue in Mary's bell-like voice. Soft-spoken and fragile, Mary tended to wither in the shadow of her dynamic husband.

"There's a lounging lawn chair propped up against the house."

Veronica opened her eyes and watched as Mary shooed her youngsters out the side door and waddled after them. Veronica screwed her eyes shut to block out the image. Mary had barely had six months between pregnancies and number four probably barely marked the mid-point of her maternal adventure. Veronica silently pledged to never be put in such a position. There were ways to prevent pregnancy and many of them were easily achieved beyond a husband's, or the church's, watchful gaze. Veronica wanted children. She didn't want a litter.

A callused hand rested gently on her forehead. "How are you feeling, Frany?" 'Frany' was a common German abbreviation for Veronica but only Eli got away with the endearment. She didn't particularly care for it but Eli's genuine affection and concern for her welfare made her irritation seem petty, so she kept her objections to herself.

She opened her eyes. "Better, thank you. Maybe I should go to my room and let you men talk."

"Don't be silly. Stay right where you are. Maybe our talk about farm business will bore you to sleep." He smiled and removed his hand then headed to his favorite wooden rocking chair beside the woodstove.

Besides being her father's second cousin, Eli was a partner in his dairy business. They helped each other out and covered each other's chores when one or the other took a much-deserved vacation from the farm or, heaven forbid, illness struck. Eli's farm, just one concession over, was close enough to make such a liaison convenient.

Veronica allowed her eyes to drift closed once more. However sleep was far from her mind and no amount of boring chatter would bring it any closer. Instead, images of that morning with Jesse kept flitting through her mind—the vivid color of the car, the thrumming beat of the music, the impudence of his smile, the warmth of his lips…

Her heart quickened at the thought of that kiss. Surely, that was a little taste of paradise.

"Hey!" exclaimed the middle brother, Roy. "That's the third time that car's driven past in the last half hour."

Veronica's eyes cracked open just enough to see the men all sit up and peer out the window toward the road.

"That's a hard one to miss," mused Veronica's father in his deep baritone voice.

Glenn's voice enhanced the sense of authority and power that hung about him despite the fact that he barely topped his wife's five and a half feet. Silver threaded his thick chestnut hair that had only recently begun to recede at the temples. And while time and gravity had taken its toll on his physique, his steely gray eyes were as alert and intense as ever.

Veronica's eyes popped open wide and her breath caught in her throat. *A hard one to miss?* It couldn't be.

She noticed Stephen, the youngest brother, looking very pensive. "I've seen that car before." He tapped a finger on the wooden armrest of his chair. "I know! He hangs out down at the Elmwood Tavern sometimes." That was a local establishment that even the conservative Mennonites and Amish frequented. Such activities weren't exactly condoned but most of the congregation chose to ignore those who indulged and simply pretended the problem of members staggering home in drunken stupors didn't exist.

Stephen pursed his lips before adding, "Yah, I'm sure of it. I think he's one of the Ward boys."

"Weren't those the boys that the police picked up a couple of years ago for smoking marijuana?" Glenn's words cut through her like a butcher knife.

Veronica squeezed her eyes shut and wrapped an arm across her stomach. *Marijuana?* Jesse had done drugs? What had she gotten herself into?

"Yah," said Stephen. "Both he and his brother got hauled in. Their dad had to go down and bail them out. Somehow he finagled them out of it."

Roy chimed in. "He's gotten into a couple of fights down at the Tavern, too. Both of those boys are troublemakers."

Fights? Drugs? Veronica moaned to herself. Could it get any worse?

Thankfully, Cliff, the oldest and most righteous of her brothers, was absent. He had headed out immediately following dinner to meet with his fiancé.

"Where does he get the money for a car like that?" asked Eli as he rocked and sipped from his mug.

"I think he works at a garage pumping gas. He must pump every penny he makes into that infernal machine." Stephen sniffed.

"How old is he?" asked her father.

"I don't know. Maybe nineteen or twenty," said Roy.

"What a waste," lamented Eli. "Just think what a boy like that could accomplish with a decent family and a supportive community behind him. He obviously needs a firm, guiding hand to keep him from ending up in jail or a gutter somewhere."

Now Veronica really *was* feeling sick to her stomach. She sat up on the couch. "I really think I should lie down upstairs."

"I'm sorry, Frany," consoled Eli. He ceased his rocking and fixed her with a concerned gaze. "We shouldn't talk about such things in front of you. We've obviously upset you."

"No." She shook her head. "It's not that. I just think I need a nap." She dragged herself from the couch and plodded out of the family room toward the back stairs. No matter how much she would welcome sleep, she was sure it would elude her. Her stomach was a mass of knots and her head was pounding. Jesse had taken drugs and gotten into fights. His future lacked ambition and commitment. Even if he changed, this was a mistake. With such a history her parents and family would never accept someone like that. This relationship was destined for failure before it even began. To pursue it was to invite disaster.

She lay down on her bed and stared at the tiny pink and green flowers that adorned her walls. When he came on Tuesday night she would put a stop to it. This whole thing was crazy anyway. She didn't know what had come over her in the first place.

She rolled over and buried her head beneath the pillows. Yes she did. It was those blue eyes and bulging biceps, that reckless charm and enchanting interest in music. He had appreciated her talent, had told her she was beautiful. He was witty and exciting and…fun. He represented a world she longed for but could never have, at least not without sacrificing things she wasn't prepared to sacrifice. The fact that he could kiss like the devil himself didn't exactly help matters.

She resolved to do what was necessary come Tuesday night. She had to. It would spare them both a much greater heartache down the road.

As long as he didn't kiss her again, she'd be fine.

* * * * *

Veronica awoke to a gentle shake of her shoulder.

"Veronica, wake up!" whispered Anna.

She rolled over, and noticed that the sun streaming in her window cast long shadows across her floor. She had slept, and she had slept long. "Why? Is it supper time already?"

"Actually, you slept through supper. Mom thought we should let you rest." Anna's voice squeaked with excitement. "But there's a boy here to see you."

She sat bolt upright, all traces of sleep eradicated from her eyes. "Who?" Surely he wouldn't have come to the front door asking for her.

Anna bared her teeth in an annoying, little grin. "Myron. He's asking for you."

She flopped back onto the pillows, relief flooding through her. Myron was their hired hand. He was just about Veronica's age, and had been hired on for the summer to help with planting, harvesting and general farm chores. His parents were old acquaintances of the Lichtys and they were experiencing some financial strain so Glenn had offered to take him on. Myron was staying in a spare room over the garage.

Veronica had noticed him watching her, but had tried to ignore it. He seemed nice and his fine features and big, hazel eyes were pleasant enough to look at. But he didn't exactly make her knees weak and her heart flutter. Then she reconsidered. In light of what she had found out about Jesse, maybe that wasn't what she should be looking for anyway. Maybe she needed someone more down to earth, someone she had more in common with.

She swung her legs off the bed, and planted her feet on the floor. "Okay. I'll see what he wants."

She straightened her clothes, and checked herself over in the mirror. She tidied up her bun and pinned her covering back in place before heading down the stairs. She found him in the family room chatting with Stephen while he awaited her arrival. His face lit up when he saw her.

"Hi, Myron. You wanted to see me?"

"Uh…yeah." He dropped his gaze to the floor, shuffled his feet and studied the fascinating patterns in the dark green carpet. He cleared his throat. "Uh…I was wondering if, maybe…maybe you'd like to go for a walk. It's a nice evening…and…well…"

Veronica interrupted the torturous monologue. "Sure, Myron. That sounds very nice."

His eyes popped up to hers, his expression suddenly as bright as the sun. He really was attractive, she persuaded herself. Thick dark lashes rimmed the widely set eyes. And his startlingly blond hair was swept off his face in a style that put most of his peers to shame. Myron was definitely a catch. So why didn't Veronica feel the slightest thrill when she looked at him? She shrugged mentally. She had no right to judge him on physical merits alone.

He opened the screen door and followed her outside. The heat had dissipated and a silky breeze caressed her cheeks. The sun was just about to slip below the horizon and a sliver of moon nudged the treetops.

"Would you like to walk along the road?" he asked.

"That would be fine."

They set off in silence, Myron politely matching his strides to hers.

At first the silence was pleasant and comfortable. Veronica's ears picked up on the regular scuffle of their shoes across the gravel. A cow mooed in a field nearby and a killdeer scuttled from its nest amongst the stones, trying to lure the intruders away from its eggs. Veronica smiled at the skinny-legged bird, and hazarded a glance at Myron. But apparently he hadn't noticed.

They continued walking and soon the silence stretched, beyond awkward, heading toward unendurable. She finally took the plunge. "Do you have a big family?" she asked, instantly scolding herself for such an inane question.

"Yeah. There's seven of us kids. I'm the second-youngest."

"Mmm." She waited but he said nothing else, so she tried again. "What kind of farm does your family have?"

"Eggs, mostly. But my dad also raises a few beef cattle, and even some goats."

"Oh. Goats aren't that common anymore."

"No. I'm not sure why."

"Yeah, I wonder." Again that intolerable silence. She kicked a rock and listened with satisfaction as it thunked against a telephone pole. "Do you ever think about traveling?" She pinched her eyes shut. Jesse had obviously been on her mind.

"What do you mean?"

"Nothing. Forget it." But her thoughts rambled on. *Don't you ever think about what's beyond these fields and hills? What about exploring and meeting new people? What about adventure?*

He startled her when he spoke. "I really enjoy driving the big tractors, and working on the engines though."

"Uh-huh." Her thoughts remained on Jesse.

"I might take a mechanics course some day. I thought it would be good to save money on those big repair bills."

"Yeah, I guess it would." *Oh brother! This is absolutely fascinating. He has yet to ask me anything about myself.* But she continued murmuring encouragement for his riveting narrative about the joys of trucks and tractors, and all their intricate workings. She very quickly came to regret not following her instincts. Myron was a nice boy with a cute face and a passive nature but he was boring as dust.

Finally they turned around and headed back toward home. As they turned in the lane, Veronica was astounded to feel his hand slip around hers. She fought the urge to tug it away and let it lay lifeless in his rough, callused fingers, hoping that would be discouragement enough. However, he seemed immune to such subtle signals.

When they reached the back door he was beaming, apparently assured that he had made a favorable impression and the walk had been just as enjoyable for her as it was for him.

"That was nice. Maybe we could do it again." Myron's wide smile revealed a small gap between his two front teeth.

"Mmm." She nodded and returned the smile uncertainly. "I should get in. I have to work at the restaurant early tomorrow."

"Yeah, I have to get up for milking." Then her astonishment peaked when he dipped his head and kissed her. Actually, kiss was a somewhat optimistic label for his feeble attempt at affection. It was more of a peck. He poked at her cheek with rigid lips. Then said his good-byes and ambled around the side of the house toward the stairs to his little apartment.

Veronica shuddered as she stepped inside and allowed the screen door to slam behind her. That little outing paled in comparison to her brief encounter with Jesse. It was going to be very difficult to go through with her intentions on Tuesday night. How could she say good-bye to Jesse when the likes of Myron awaited her, oblivious to the fact that they couldn't hold a candle to a reckless heathen with questionable morals? But she had to do it. Continuing with Jesse was pointless and risky.

Or perhaps that was exactly what attracted her to him.

Chapter Three

Veronica eased open the back door off the mudroom. It tended to squeak but she hoped it was far enough away from the second floor bedrooms that no one would notice. She pulled the inside door closed behind her.

The night air was cool and a million stars glittered above her. Crickets chirped and a dog barked in the distance. The sound was lonely yet somehow comforting. The sweet, rich scent of drying hay blew in across the fields and settled over her senses. That too never failed to comfort her. The fragrance of fresh cut hay drifting in through an open bedroom window could lull her to sleep more surely than a mother's lullaby. Except tonight.

She was amazed at how easily she had managed to drag herself out of bed despite her exhaustion after a typically busy day. She had spent the morning at her part-time job waitressing at a local restaurant, and the afternoon weeding in their huge garden. She had helped her mother and sister pick several baskets full of beans, then snapped them and stored them in bags for the freezer. After an early supper the men had headed to the barn for the usual session of milking while the women cleaned the kitchen and tidied the house.

Veronica was grateful that there were three men to handle the barn chores. Many of her friends were expected to help out in the barn, despite the fact that it was seen as mainly a man's domain. Veronica found no joy in washing udders or shoveling manure. Barn chores constituted one instance where she was grateful for the sexist stigmas.

She hazarded a glance at the barn. A light still glowed in the milking parlor, the room which housed the gleaming stainless steel cooler, and the milking equipment and sinks. But that wasn't unusual. Glenn was a stickler for turning out lights but unfortunately his sons weren't quite so conscientious. She confirmed, however, that the rest of the century old structure was dark. That indicated that her father hadn't been summoned from his bed to tend to a sick cow, or possibly one that was in the process of giving birth.

Reassured, she strode quickly down the short lane. As she approached the road, a pair of headlights flicked on and bathed her in blue-white light. A figure got out of the car parked about thirty meters away and Jesse's long strides met her in a matter of moments. Before she could object he swept her up in an embrace and her worst fears were realized. He was kissing her again.

She knew she should pull away but his lips were so delicious and his tongue touched her in places that had never been touched before. To her disappointment he withdrew first, setting her down, but still holding her tightly against him.

"God, Ronni," he breathed into her hair. "I dreamed about that for the last two days straight."

She said nothing but allowed him to hold her. Her cheek brushed his chest and every inch of them seemed to be touching in some sinful way. With difficulty, she found the strength to separate from him and focus on the task ahead.

"We have to talk, Jesse." She stared at the center of his chest.

He remained quiet for a long time, until she finally raised her eyes to his. She could just make out a crease between his dark brows.

"I don't like the sounds of that. Whenever women say that, it's never good news."

Veronica chewed on her lower lip. "Could we sit in the car?"

He grabbed her hand and led her back up the road, opening the door for her as she slid into the passenger seat.

He rounded to the driver's side, plunked down in the bucket seat and slammed the door, his expression dark. "You're backing out on me, aren't you?"

She shook her head. "I can't do this. It feels so—I don't know—wrong."

"The hell it does! I've never been with someone who felt so right in my life. And I think you feel the same way. You don't really want to go back home. What happened?"

She swallowed her uncertainty. She couldn't just break off their date without an explanation. She owed him that much. "Did you smoke marijuana?"

He glared at her. "Where did you hear that?"

"My father and my brothers were talking about you on Sunday after they saw your car drive by a couple of times. Is it true?"

"Yeah, it's true. So I'm an evil sinner, is that it? A good-for-nothing low-life who isn't fit to lick the pot you piss in?"

"Jesse, please!"

"Well, what is it then?" He was obviously working hard to contain his temper.

"They also said you've gotten into some fights down at the Tavern."

"Anything else?"

The edge to his voice could have cut stone but Veronica felt an odd need to tell him everything. "And my father questions how you afford such a nice car. He wonders if you spend all your money on it. That seems like a poor way to prioritize your life."

Jesse gripped the steering wheel and stared out the windshield into blackness. "I guess they didn't mention that I also pour a hell of a lot of money into my savings account so I can afford to go to University in the fall. That's why I've been working the past two years, sometimes holding down two jobs at a time.

"I don't suppose they also happened to mention that the couple of times I got into fights it was started by a couple of members of your own church who were pawing at my car out in the parking lot. It looked to me like they were thinking about hopping inside." Now he turned and his eyes bored into hers. "And I don't suppose they mentioned that the time my brother and I got arrested for possession was the week after our mother died. We were both sick with grief over it, and looking for anything to fix the hurt, even if it was just a little. Our dad was no help. He barely got out of bed after the funeral."

Veronica's mouth had gone dry as he systematically demolished each of her suspicions as surely as if he were swinging a hundred-pound wrecking ball.

Oblivious to her discomfort, he continued, "Unfortunately, the dope didn't help me at all. I got a little bit of a buzz but then I was sick to my stomach and ended up throwing up my toenails. It was just what my dad needed though. That call from the cops got him out of bed and woke him up. He figured out, then, that he had a couple of kids who needed him. After that things got a lot better again." His jaw muscles worked as he continued to rest accusing eyes on her. "So, did they? Did they happen to include all that with the rest of their juicy tidbits about me?"

Veronica felt shaken. She shook her head in one brief, vicious gesture of remorse. "I'm sorry, Jesse. I had no idea." She couldn't think of anything else to say.

"Obviously. And another thing—isn't gossiping supposed to be some kinda sin or something? I've never been to Sunday School but I could swear my mom used to say something about how it wasn't good to talk about other folks, especially when you don't have all the facts."

She didn't speak. She was treacherously close to bursting into tears.

He seemed to notice and at last his tone softened. "I'm sorry I got so riled but I'm kinda touchy about the pot thing." He gazed out the windshield again, his gaze far away as if reliving the fateful night. "Sam and I were sitting down in the river flats, smoking away. We couldn't believe it when they flashed their lights on us. I still don't know how they knew what we were up to down there."

She lifted her eyes and regarded him cautiously.

He sensed the movement and met her eyes. The green glow from the dash cast his features in relief, but even considering the eerie illumination and his harsh tone of a moment earlier, his eyes were soft and forgiving. Considering what he had just told her, she wasn't sure if she deserved that kind of grace.

She glanced down at her hands resting in her lap. "So you never did it again?"

He chuckled and just like that the mood shifted. "Nope. I got no interest in making myself sick for a fleeting moment of bliss." Then he got serious again. "So am I back in your good graces again? Did I manage to redeem myself?"

"You don't understand, Jesse. It wasn't that I was passing judgment on you." At least that's what she tried to tell herself. She was furious with herself for letting her opinion of him be swayed so easily. He was right. Her family had been gossiping and there was no excuse for it. But even considering that, there were still problems.

"No? Then what exactly was it?"

"No matter what your reasons or your plans for the future, as far as my family's concerned, you've got a black mark against you. They'd never accept you and me being together."

"What if I found *Jesus?* Then would it be okay?"

Now it was her turn to feel the heat of anger rise to her face. "Don't make fun, Jesse. I know you don't mean it and—"

"Okay," he conceded suddenly. "Sorry. That was a low blow. But what does it matter anyway?"

"What do you mean, *what does it matter?*"

He sighed in frustration. "Does it really matter so much what they think? We can keep it a secret as long as you like. Who knows, in three weeks we might hate each other's guts and break up anyway. But for right now I'm happy with a few stolen moments, if that's all you can give me." He scooped up her hand and drew it to his lips sending a parade of goose bumps trekking up her arm. He murmured into her hand, "So, what do you say? We can meet late like this and I can play you some tunes and you can sing for me, and maybe we can even grab a cup of coffee at an all-night coffee shop. I don't ask for much."

His grin was infectious. How could any sane woman turn away from that smile? "How did your mother die?"

He lowered her hand and cradled it on the console between them. "Drunk driver hit her. Son of a bitch took off. We never did find him. There was a witness that said he was weaving all over the road. That's why the cops figure he was drunk." A note of regret crept into his voice. "That was four years ago and I still miss her."

Veronica fought a lump in her throat. She couldn't imagine losing a parent like that and she had a large extended family and a church community to rely on. It sounded like Jesse and his family were pretty much on their own. Not only that but he had obviously cared deeply for his mother. Her heart ached for him. "What are you going to college for?"

"Electrical engineering. I know there's a good school right close by but I wanted to get out of here." He grinned again, his grief already tucked safely away. "You know, *'looking for adventure'*. I don't really have a lot of ties here and I wanted to see some of the world." He raised her hand to his mouth. "How 'bout you, Ronni? You gonna see some of the world some day?"

"I'd like to." She felt a fresh set of goose bumps shimmer up her arm as his lips tickled her knuckles.

"Well, maybe you can come visit me out west."

"Maybe." She tugged weakly at her hand but he refused to relinquish it. "But for now I'd be happy to see some of the countryside around here, with some nice background music."

"So, we're a go?" He raised his eyebrows hopefully.

She nodded.

"Okay, but you gotta do something for me."

"What?"

He dropped her hand and reached for the key. The engine roared to life. "Let your hair down or I'll do it for you. That bun makes you look like a goddamn…sorry, like a grandma."

She laughed and pulled out a few pins. "How's that?" she said as her hair fell loosely about her shoulders.

He ran his fingers up the back of her scalp. She closed her eyes and took a deep breath.

"Much better. God, I'd love to see you in a pair of Levi's with a tight little T-shirt. But I guess I'm a dreamer."

"I guess you are."

He granted her a half smile and revved the engine. They pulled out onto the road and soon the music of Eric Clapton was blasting through the interior of the car as the wind whipped through their hair and the stars winked down on them through the sunroof. This time Veronica reached for his hand, laced her fingers through his and held onto it for a long time.

She didn't question the kinship she already felt with this man with whom she had barely spent two hours. They came from cultures as disparate as the Old West and Victorian England and yet they connected, deeply. It wasn't just the music or the quest for something beyond the horizon. The bond defied categorization or definition. But it was as real and strong as the hunk of metal and glass that was hurtling them down the highway. Maybe more so.

They eventually did stop at an all-night coffee shop. Jesse headed to the counter to buy them each a coffee and a doughnut. He had suggested pie but she doubted the pies at this place could hold a candle to her mother's flaky creations and she promised to bring him a piece the next time they got together.

Veronica found a booth in the corner and seated herself on the worn vinyl bench. A cheap silk rose in a plastic bud vase adorned the chipped Formica table. The shop was almost empty. Only one other couple shared their secret and they were huddled together in a booth at the back, whispering quietly over steaming mugs of coffee and bowls of soup. It boggled Veronica's mind that there were actually other people in the world who would be out and about at two o'clock in the morning.

She focused on Jesse as he chatted amiably with the woman behind the counter. Platinum bleached hair topped her dark roots and an ample figure attested to the variety of fried treats that she likely sampled on a regular basis. She was hardly what Veronica would call attractive and she had to be twice Jesse's age but he took his time, leaning on the counter and shooting the breeze as if they had been friends for years. Veronica mused that Jesse was probably comfortable just about anywhere, and could strike up easy conversation with just about anyone. He was at ease with himself so he put those around him at ease. She felt a brief pang of jealousy for the assortment of strangers who would encounter him in her absence and then chuckled at herself for entertaining such a ridiculous notion.

He sauntered over to their table with a tray and soon they were sipping from steaming mugs.

"So what's it like?" he asked over the rim of his cup.

"What?"

"Growing up Mennonite."

"I don't know. What's it like growing up *not* Mennonite?" She batted her eyes at him.

"Okay, okay. How about this?" He bit into his day-old donut. "Do you sometimes wish you had some of the stuff like the rest of us have?"

She contemplated the dark brew that could likely strip the paint off Jesse's car. "Yeah, sometimes. For me, I just wish I could have a good stereo, and be able to sing like I want. The rest of the stuff isn't so bad. Television and flashy cars," and she tossed him a grin, "aren't all they're cracked up to be." She broke off a piece of her cruller and popped it into her mouth. "I bet I've got stuff that you don't."

"Oh yeah? Like what?"

"I've got brothers and sisters and aunts and uncles and cousins coming out my ears. I've always got a gang of youth to do stuff with on Friday nights if I want. If me or anybody in my family gets sick there's lots of people to look after us. If, God forbid, somebody dies, or a house or barn burns, suddenly dozens of offers of help come pouring in. People either offer to make a meal, clean the house, weed the garden, bring in the hay or help rebuild the barn. Have you got a network like that?"

He shook his head. "No, you're right there. Me and my brother and my dad are pretty much on our own. We got those cousins living with us but they sponge off us all the time. They hardly pay Dad a dime for all the pizza they eat and all the beer they guzzle. My dad's been complaining about them non-stop for the last month. He's on the verge of kicking them out." He took a sip of his coffee and his Adam's apple bobbed slowly. "Maybe stereos and televisions are a poor trade-off for what you're talking about."

"Maybe." She considered the question carefully. "But there's also a lot to be said for deciding your own destiny. I'm expected to be a farmer's wife. I could work at waitressing or cleaning houses but the idea of me going to college and having a career would give my mother a heart attack."

"Would you like to do that?"

Would she? No one had ever asked her that before. She shrugged. "I guess I've never really thought about it. But you talking about that band really got me thinking. That sounds like a lot of fun."

"Well, the offer's still open. I could give you their number."

She smiled at his casual persistence. "Thanks, I'll keep it in mind."

He checked his watch. "Maybe I should get you home. It's two o'clock. And I do have to get up early to pump gas at that dead-end job that's putting accessories on my flashy, red car," he said with a wink.

She grimaced. "Okay, okay. I feel bad enough."

"Bad enough to sleep with me?"

She froze.

"Hey! It was a joke." He set down his mug. "Sort of."

"Oh." Her insides had coiled into knots.

He grabbed her hand and hauled her to her feet. "Take it easy, I'm not gonna molest you or anything."

"I know," she said defensively as she trailed him out the door.

Once they were on their way again he asked her quietly, "So, I take it you've never done it before?"

"Of course not!" she said haughtily.

"Sorry! I'm afraid most of the other girls I've dated wouldn't exactly fall into the virgin category."

"I take it you took advantage of their *good nature*."

"On occasion." His eyes remained riveted to the road.

"Well, I'm not so easygoing." Veronica was grateful for the cool breeze that washed over her through the sunroof and the open windows. It made the heat in her cheeks a little less oppressive.

"I got that impression. Don't get your panties in a knot. It was a simple question."

"No, it wasn't."

He reached for her hand. "Okay, it wasn't. You gotta understand, us guys think about that every twenty seconds, you know. I read that in *Cosmo* once."

"*Cosmo*?"

He rolled his eyes. "Forget it." She thought she caught a soft chuckle but she couldn't be sure, and she didn't know what to make of it anyway. "Just don't worry about it, okay? I'm not opposed to sliding between the sheets but I'm not gonna push you into anything. Okay? Truce?"

She relaxed her shoulders and decided to believe him. "Okay. Truce."

This was uncharted territory for Veronica. While premarital sex wasn't exactly unheard of in her circles, she would never discuss it so openly with a boyfriend from within the church. The question of sex before marriage would never be asked outright. Her answer would be a foregone conclusion. That didn't mean things couldn't change in the heat of the moment but such an encounter would never be discussed or, heaven forbid, actually planned ahead of time.

Too soon they arrived at the end of her drive. He got out and came around to open her door. As she got out, he asked, "How about Friday night again?"

"Sounds good to me. I'm not terribly picky. Most of my evenings after midnight are pretty open."

"Right." He laughed.

"I should go." But she didn't move.

He picked up on his cue and wrapped her in his arms. "Not without a goodbye kiss you don't."

"Well, if you insist."

This one lasted much longer than any of its predecessors. Veronica was so lost in the exquisite pressure of his arms around her and the caresses that his mouth was lavishing on her, she hardly noticed when his hand covered her breast through the fabric of her dress. Heat sizzled through her and she sucked in her breath in surprise.

He pulled it away, and murmured against her lips, "Sorry. Reflex."

"No, it's okay. It just startled me."

His eyes registered surprise and he took advantage of her apparent concession. But he didn't push it. He kissed her softly as his hand gently kneaded her breast.

She thought her knees were sure to buckle any second and every inch of her felt thick and tingly.

She allowed herself those timeless moments of sinful pleasure before finally pushing him away. After she caught her breath she whispered into the darkness, "I really should go."

"Right. Friday."

"Friday."

She steeled herself and turned to walk, somewhat unsteadily, back toward home. She felt his eyes on her all the way down the lane.

* * * * *

Once she'd disappeared into the darkness, Jesse climbed into his car and burned rubber as he sped away. He was cursing himself.

He had a hard-on that threatened to burst through his ridiculously tight jeans. It was so bad he reached down and undid a button to relieve some of the pressure. But the release was minimal. If he was near metropolitan Toronto, or maybe Detroit or New York, he would seriously consider finding a willing companion to help ease the tension. But that wouldn't be an easy task around here. Hookers didn't exactly hang out on the corner of the Town Line and Concession Fourteen. It was too late to go to a bar, so his options were limited.

Besides that, he already felt an odd loyalty to this girl he had only spent a few hours with and he would probably hate himself for doing something like that anyway. He decided to drive for a while, with the music blaring, until the pressure against his fly diminished enough to allow him to at least consider sleep.

As he drove he continued to rant silently at his own stupidity. What the fuck did he think he was doing? Why was he letting himself get involved with someone like that? He had only had one serious relationship in his life. That had lasted for six months and just when he allowed himself to fall hopelessly in love, she had ended it. Just like that—without warning or explanation. The break-up had been so abrupt and mysterious that it had left him reeling, left him feeling completely betrayed and vulnerable. He didn't like feeling that way. So he had sworn never to let someone do that to him again.

Yet here he was, pining away for someone who probably thought he was the scum of society and, compared to most of the people she associated with, he probably was.

On top of that he was leaving in less than twelve weeks for a stint at a University that might as well have been on the other side of the world, for all the likelihood that he would come back before he finished his four-year degree. Even then he held out slim hope that he would return here. He had hoped to make British Columbia, or perhaps Alberta, his home. The mountains and the sea screamed out adventure and excitement. He'd seen enough corn stalks to last a lifetime. He was ready for a change.

He should nip this in the bud right now. He should cut it off at the knees before he wound up so miserably infatuated with her that he considered throwing away his one opportunity to ditch this crummy community and make something of himself. He just couldn't allow that to happen. He had scrimped and saved and worked like a dog for two years in order to have enough money to make this a reality. He would load up his car, drive out west and likely not return, except to visit his brother.

But, despite his silent turmoil, he knew he wouldn't stop seeing her. Even if it was only destined to last for a few weeks, there was no way he could stop the momentum that was carrying him forward in this crazy, shit-for-brains affair.

There was just something about her. Maybe it was her innocence. Maybe it was those fiery green eyes or that damn red hair that he longed to see spread out on a pillow beneath him. Maybe it was that voice that sent shivers through his gut and made him want to cry. Maybe it was all of that. Not that it mattered.

Even if he never pinpointed the exact source of his dementia… Even if he did, he knew he couldn't stop now. Maybe he could in ten weeks when the crunch came. But not now.

Chapter Four

August 1987

"You seem awfully tired this morning, Veronica," commented her mother.

Ronni moved over to the coffeemaker and poured herself a huge mug full. She couldn't say when, exactly, she had started thinking of herself as Ronni. It had been so gradual, she had hardly noticed. But one day, out of the blue, her family's label for her seemed all wrong. She didn't want to answer to Veronica anymore. Ronni seemed natural and right and she loved hearing it fall from Jesse's lips.

"I didn't sleep well last night," she lied. Well, maybe it wasn't exactly a lie. The truth was she had hardly slept at all, but not because she had tossed and turned in her bed. The truth was she and Jesse had played into the wee hours. Exhausted, but glowing, she had flopped into bed at four a.m. that morning.

That was the third night this week. This time they had driven for an hour until they got to a secluded beach on Lake Huron. They had walked hand-in-hand beneath the moon and the stars, their bare feet splashing in the warm, shallow waves and their toes sinking into the silky sand. It had been idyllic but now she was paying for it.

She hoped, maybe that afternoon, to have the opportunity to feign illness and take a nap. Lately deceptions had become second nature but she refused to dwell on that.

At least she had the option of napping occasionally. She didn't know how Jesse did it. He had to be at the garage at seven a.m. and work until five. Mind you, when he got home he didn't have to cook dinner. He probably flaked out until eleven-thirty, or slept right through on the nights that they didn't meet.

Their rendezvous had been becoming more frequent. In the last two weeks they had seen each other eight times. Neither of them acknowledged it out loud but they both knew why. In three days he would pack up his car and speed out of her life. He would be leaving for Vancouver and they were furiously trying to cram in the hours together before the inevitable farewell scene.

He had hinted once at the possibility of staying back and waiting another year. He was sure he could get in again if he applied next year or maybe he could apply to one of the local universities. But she had vehemently rejected that option. She had no intention of being the cause of him abandoning his dreams. What if he ended up resenting or, worse yet, hating her for it? He had sullenly agreed with her logic.

Even now, she could picture his pouting lips.

The thought of not resting her eyes on him again for close to a year, or possibly longer, brought the sting of tears to her eyes. Her exaggerated fatigue didn't help matters and she was unable to contain the flow.

"What's wrong, dear?" asked Verna from her seat on the other side of the table.

"I'm just tired. I had a bad dream that bothered me." She wiped impatiently at her eyes.

"You've been tired an awful lot lately. Maybe you should see a doctor."

She shook her head. "No, no. I'll be fine. Maybe I'll take a nap this afternoon."

"Yes, that's a good idea," agreed her mother. "Let me make you some toast to go with that coffee. I think you've lost some weight. You haven't been eating well either." The guilt squeezed Ronni's heart like a vice. Here she was, deceiving her mother regularly and remorselessly and in sweet ignorance her mother continued to dote on her. Ronni's mother didn't deserve to be treated this way. But that didn't mean anything was going to change.

Ronni was about to make a feeble explanation for her weight loss when Eli's voice rumbled through the stillness of the kitchen.

"Is Glenn around? I need to talk to him about some breeding stock." Eli stood in the doorway, his mere presence subtly commanding their attention. He often consulted with Glenn about the breeding experiments that he was conducting at his home farm. Some saw his cross-breeding scheme as risky and foolhardy but he was convinced it could eventually blossom into a gold mine. If, that is, he could just work out a few kinks and convince the other farmers of the merits of his mixes. He had sunk a considerable amount of money into the enterprise.

He noticed Ronni hovering over her mug. "Are you all right, Frany? Your eyes are all bloodshot."

Her mother answered for her. "She's just tired. She had a rough night."

He walked over and tipped up her chin with a rough finger. "Is that right? Is that all it is?"

She nodded and granted him what she hoped was a radiant smile. "Really. I just need a nap and I'll be good as new."

"I don't know, Frany. You've looked some the worse for wear this last month. Even I've noticed the change." He ran a thumb across her cheek. "You should take care of yourself. You need to find a man to look out for you." He dropped his hand from her face and stuffed it in the pocket of his work pants. "When are you going to find somebody to date seriously? Half the girls your age are already engaged or even married."

"I'm in no rush." How she longed to tell her family the truth about her involvement with Jesse. But his name had come up once more at the dinner table and the conversation had been far from complimentary. Stephen had seen him again at the local tavern, in the company of some men that he deemed to be the dregs of society. They played in a rock and roll band, of all things. Later, out in the parking lot, one of the motley crew had demonstrated some of his talents on a very noisy electric guitar that he had plugged into an outdoor socket. It had just about burst Stephen's eardrums.

Jesse, however, had quite enjoyed the show and that little incident had merely confirmed Stephen's low opinion of the *Ward boy*. Her father had grumbled his agreement and Veronica had gritted her teeth as she stared in silence at her pickled beets.

"Well," Eli was saying, "I guess you're right. You've got lots of time yet. I just want to see you happy, Frany. You're a very special girl and will make some man a wonderful wife."

"Thanks, Eli. Do you want some coffee?"

"No, I'll just go out and find Glenn. Is he choring or out in the field, do you think?"

Ronni's mother spoke over her shoulder as she buttered Ronni's toast, "I think he was going to check on Maria. She's pretty close to calving." All the cows, all one hundred of them, were known by name.

"Okay, I'll check her stall." He glanced at Ronni as he headed out the door and cocked a finger at her. "You get some rest, young lady."

She smiled and nodded as he headed toward the back door. She certainly intended to get her rest. She hoped to take a long nap that afternoon, and then get to bed early so she was sure of a full night's sleep. Because tomorrow night, Jesse had informed her, was going to be very special indeed. He had a surprise in store for her. Again, he hadn't said it but the words had hung, unspoken. *Because it will be our last night together for a very long time.* She wanted to be fresh and have lots of energy for whatever he had in store.

* * * * *

Ronni straightened up and stretched out aching back muscles. She glanced at Anna, crouched at the far end of the row of beans. Her fingers darted in and out of the vines as she picked her way toward Ronni. They were harvesting a late variety of yellow beans, the last of the season. Their mother planned to use these to prepare mustard beans, and would be putting up several dozen jars of the bright yellow condiment. Picking was hot, sweaty, grueling work and Ronni would rather be just about anywhere else in the world. Actually, one spot in particular came to mind but that would have to wait another day or so.

She was just about to bend back to her task when a cacophony of honks intruded into the peace and calm of the summer morning. Ronni and Anna looked up just in time to see the bright red streak as it churned up billowing clouds of dust in its wake. Anna shook her head in dismay as she returned her attention to the beans but Ronni smiled as she bent back to her work.

Occasionally Jesse took an early lunch break and headed to the Macton Diner where they made burgers and fries that swam in month-old grease. And, since the Lichty farm was right on his route—or only about five kilometers or so out of his way—he would take that opportunity to cruise past and discretely advertise his undying devotion.

She crouched there watching the dust settle and quietly humming *Revolution* by the Beatles. She was pretty sure that was the tune that had been blasting from his speakers as he sped by. Her knowledge of the music and the bands had increased exponentially since her first meeting with Jesse. He hadn't limited her experience to his own tastes, but had exposed her to everything from Buddy Holly to Led Zeppelin, from the

Bee Gees to ZZ Top, from Blues to New Wave. He encouraged her to find her own tastes and wanted to cram as much into their limited time together as possible.

Her mother's voice jolted her out of her reverie.

Verna motioned to Ronni from the back door of the house. It was an answer to prayer—any excuse to escape the blazing heat and the back-breaking position that bean-picking demanded. She strolled between the rows, her shoes kicking up clods of the heavy clay-like soil.

As she came closer her mother called again, "Could you take this thermos out to the fence by the old elm? Your father and Myron are fixing a broken post out there. I thought they might be thirsty."

Ronni accepted the large thermos jug and the plastic glasses, and headed dutifully into the field. As she approached she squinted against the sun and gradually realized there was only one figure working at the cracked fencing and broken post. As she walked, she clung desperately to the hope that she would find her father hammering merrily at the white-washed pine fencing but her dreams were dashed when the man bent low to the ground unfolded himself and stood at her approach. Myron waved enthusiastically and Ronni gritted her teeth. She had been set up.

Eli's concerns over her lack of a man must have spurred her mother's matchmaking urges. Her mother often commented on what a nice boy Myron was, how he would be a good provider and a steady companion. Ronni had nodded agreement. He would be steady all right, as steady as a post driven twenty feet into solid clay. Immovable and unbendable, without imagination or excitement.

She reached him and forced a smile. His hair was matted to his scalp and sweat dripped from his chin. He obviously needed a drink and that was exactly what she intended to provide him with.

"Veronica!" he exclaimed, accepting a glass. "You're an angel of mercy. I was dry as dust."

Ronni silently agreed as she filled his glass. "My mother thought you might like a drink. Was Dad with you?"

He shook his head. "No. He sent me out here on my own."

Her suspicions were confirmed.

She watched him drink in silence, not wanting to encourage him in any way. Physically he was an exceptional specimen. His sleeves were rolled up to the elbows and sweat had plastered his white, collared shirt to his chest. He was young and strong, probably stronger than Jesse. She silently scoffed at the comparison, because in every other way, there *was no* comparison.

"You know," he said in a voice that heralded doom, "there's a pie social tomorrow night at the church. Would you maybe…wanna go?"

His perseverance continued to astound her. She had put off his advances numerous times over the summer but he never seemed to get the hint. "I'm sorry, Myron. I have plans tomorrow night." That was the truth.

"Oh." He refilled his glass. "Too bad. Maybe another time."

"Mmm." She scanned the horizon and thought of the plate of greasy fries she wished she were sharing with Jesse.

She wasn't watching Myron, so was startled to realize that he had sidled up a little closer. He was close enough that she could smell the familiar scent that resulted from hours of hard work in the intense summer sun. He hadn't touched her but he was close enough to make her uncomfortable. She stepped back.

"You know," he purred. "I really like you, Veronica. You're one of the prettiest girls I know."

"Oh…uh…thank you, Myron. That's nice, but—"

"I was really hoping that maybe we could get to know each other better this summer. But you've been so busy with work and chores, I hardly ever seem to see you."

Feeling cornered and hopelessly unprepared for such a development, she stammered, "Yeah, well…I…" She didn't want to hurt his feelings. How could she be any more plain without coming right out and telling him that he bored the hell out of her. *Oops.* She was thankful neither he, nor her parents could read her mind.

His hand stole out and stroked her arm. His fingers were strong and callused, the feel of them not completely unpleasant. Too bad they were attached to a man obsessed with tractors and grain augers. She stepped out of reach. "I better get back. I'll leave the thermos with you."

A pout tugged at the corners of his mouth as she turned to go.

She scurried back toward home, mopping sweat from her forehead—sweat that had nothing to do with the heat.

She slipped inside the cool sanctuary of the house and the moment the screen slammed her mother called, "Veronica? Is that you?"

Ronni strode into the kitchen, wisely tamping down the fury she felt toward her mother. She headed to the fridge for some lemonade of her own.

"Did you leave the thermos with them?" asked her mother, as innocent as a lamb.

"Yes, Mother. I left it with *him*. Dad wasn't there."

"Oh really? Was it just Myron?"

Ronni sucked in a calming breath. Restraining her sharp tongue was taking its toll on her already frayed nerves. "Yes, Mom. But you knew that, didn't you?"

"Hmm?" Verna arched her eyebrows.

"Mom, I know you mean well but I just don't like Myron. Can you please stay out of it?"

Her mother sighed heavily. "Why? I just don't understand it. He's such a nice young man."

"I don't know, okay? We just don't have anything to talk about. We don't have anything in common."

"That's ridiculous. You have everything in common. And I think he's very nice looking as well."

"Yes, you may be right about that but I don't want to see him, okay? Please?"

Her mother turned back to the cupboard where rows of jars waited to be washed and sterilized in preparation for canning the beans later in the day. The rigid set of her shoulders announced her exasperation all too clearly. Ronni knew she had always been something of a puzzle to her family. Her mother, of course, felt the disparity between herself and her daughter the most keenly. Veronica was her oldest daughter and they should have shared something special. But lately all they shared was confusion.

"Oh, all right," huffed Verna. "I just wish you'd be a little more open-minded. Sometimes I don't know what you want. You're never going to find the perfect man, you know. He doesn't exist."

Ronni stalked from the room in silence. She reined in her tongue but she was just itching to assure her mother that nothing could be farther from the truth. Well, maybe Jesse wasn't perfect. He certainly had his faults. He drove too fast and refused to wear a seat belt. He was far too outspoken and had a mouth that could make a construction worker blanch. But to Ronni even his faults were endearing. He had injected color into her life, had opened her mind to things she had never dreamed of before. Maybe he wasn't perfect in the traditional sense but he *was* perfect—for her.

* * * * *

"Veronica?" asked a soft voice.

"What, Anna? I'm very tired. I'd like to get to sleep." Ronni had managed to take a nap that afternoon but her hopes of turning in early had been dashed with the unexpected arrival of her mother's sister, Salina. Salina was a good deal older than Verna and her children were all grown and married off. Her husband had been killed by silo gas a number of years ago, so she had developed the habit of dropping in on family, unannounced and expecting to be fed and put up for the night. Therefore, Anna had relinquished her room, and was bunking with Veronica in her double bed.

"Can't we just talk for a minute? You're always tired lately and you never want to talk anymore."

Ronni yawned and swiped the tears from her eyes. Her sister was right. Ronni had been neglecting her younger sibling. She and Anna had a somewhat rocky relationship. Knock-down-drag-out arguments were invariably followed by reconciliation, unquestioning devotion and the sharing of intimate secrets. Until, that is, the next clash of wills started the process all over again. Their relationship vacillated between kindred spirits and mortal enemies. The last few weeks had hovered somewhere in between, owing mostly to the fact that Ronni just didn't have the energy for anything else.

"Okay." Ronni stifled another yawn. "What did you want to talk about?"

"Do you ever think about…you know…*it*?"

"It?"

"Oh come on, you know what I mean."

"You mean sex?"

Anna's elbow nudged Ronni's ribs. "Shh, Mom will hear you."

"What? You think they've never heard the word? They've got five kids, remember. I kinda doubt they've only done it five times."

"Yuck!"

Ronni laughed, her fatigue suddenly forgotten in the face of her sister's endearing innocence. "Honestly, Anna, where did you think we came from?"

"I know, I just don't like to think about them like *that*, okay?"

"Okay." Ronni rolled onto her side and faced Anna's creamy complexion. The moonlight that filtered in through the window gave her skin an almost ghostly glow. "Of course I think about it. Doesn't everybody?"

"I guess."

"Has Mark been putting the thumbscrews to you?" Mark and Anna had been going steady for almost six months. Ronni was suspicious that wedding plans were already in the works.

"Huh?"

Oops! That was a Jesse-ism. "I mean, has he been pushing you to do it?"

"Kinda." Anna averted her eyes. "Well, he doesn't come right out and, you know, *ask*. But sometimes…" She shrugged. "Sometimes I just can tell that's what he wants, you know?"

Ronni knew. Oh, how she knew. "What are you going to do?"

Anna giggled. "I can't believe you asked me that. Isn't it obvious?"

Ronni shrugged. "Is it? I could name at least a half a dozen women from church who had babies a little short of the nine-month mark after the wedding. And one of them is Pastor Herb's wife."

Anna caught her breath in consternation. "You're kidding."

"You can do the math. Just think about it. Their oldest is almost thirty but just think about their anniversary date and his birthday. It doesn't jive." She cringed. Her mouth was definitely going to get her into trouble. "I know nobody talks about it but that doesn't mean it doesn't happen."

"Yeah, I guess. But at least we don't have single mothers around here. That would be horrible."

"Come on, Anna. Don't you know why that is? The only difference is that here, as soon as somebody finds out they're pregnant, they immediately run to mom and dad or the deacon and a wedding is arranged, post haste."

"You're talking awfully funny lately."

Ronni smiled to herself. That last phrase had nothing to do with Jesse. Her sister just never read anything more complex than a cookbook. "Am I right?"

"I guess so. But I think I'd rather have it that way than end up all alone with a baby."

"What if you ended up with somebody you didn't love or, worse yet, didn't even like?"

"Why would I sleep with somebody like that?"

"Your body and your heart can play funny tricks on you, Anna. Sometimes you do things you never thought you would."

Anna was silent and Ronni realized she had probably said too much.

Anna turned a puzzled gaze on her sister. "What's going on with you?"

"Nothing. I've just been reading too many stupid books. Go to sleep."

Anna seemed to accept that at face value. She rolled away from Ronni and was soon breathing softly.

But, despite fatigue and her good intentions of going to sleep, Ronni lay awake for a long time. She stared at the ceiling and considered the last few weeks.

Who would have ever thought she could be so deceitful? But when she was with Jesse it just felt so good and so right and so free. She knew she would do whatever it took to maintain this relationship. Then her thoughts turned to his kisses and caresses and Anna's original question.

She was thankful that Jesse had never pressured her. He didn't need to. Her body was making demands all on its own and they were very hard to ignore. Even now, just thinking about him and the way he touched her, her center felt thick and heavy. If she could hold onto her virtue through tomorrow night she would be safe. The spring might bring about more changes but, for now, she just had to get past tomorrow night.

The trouble was, she wasn't sure that she wanted to.

Chapter Five

"So what's the big surprise?" The wind screamed about Ronni's ears but for once the radio remained mute as they cruised along the back roads of Perth County. As usual, only the moon and the stars were witness to their transgressions.

"Now, if I told you, it wouldn't be a surprise, would it?"

"You're just plain mean." She feigned a pretty good pout.

"Yeah, so mean, you can't stand to be apart from me for more than a day."

"I'm a sucker for punishment." She continued to pick up on his favorite phrases and idioms. They were fun to use but she knew she had to keep a constant vigil or she was sure to *blow her cover*. Making slips with Anna was one thing. Doing it in front of her parents would be quite another.

In response, he cupped a hand around the back of her head and pulled her over for a quick, deep kiss. He never lifted his foot from the accelerator as his lips melted to hers and his tongue plunged into her mouth. "How's that for punishment?" he teased as he returned his eyes to the road, the grin on his face unrepentant.

"I told you I was a sucker for it."

He took his punishment a step further and dropped his hand to her shoulder, and then lower still, to her breast. She made no move to stop him. This was a familiar ritual, which she endured gladly. He even reached inside the open neckline of her dress. That too, was not exactly uncharted territory but, when he dared to slip his fingers beneath the fabric of her bra, that was new and it elicited a sharp breath from her. "Jesse!"

"Does that mean you want me to stop?"

She closed her eyes and rested her head against the seat back. She said nothing.

He took her silence as acquiescence and caressed her gently, brushing a fingertip across her nipple. That sent shock waves through her and she instinctively reached up to clutch at his arm. Her fingernails dug into his flesh but he said nothing. To both her irritation and relief his hand remained right where it was until he decided it was time to end the encounter.

The car slowed and he hesitantly returned his hand to the gear shift. "We're here."

She opened her eyes and watched with fascination as they left the gravel road and headed across a grassy field. It surprised her that he would endanger the shocks on his precious vehicle with such shoddy treatment. After a few good bumps and one startling bang he stopped the car just inside a thick grove of spruce trees.

She got out and surveyed his handiwork. The river flats stretched out before them. Clover and patches of thigh-high weeds and scrub dotted the landscape. Water gurgled less than twenty meters away. He must have mowed the area, because there in the midst of Queen Ann's Lace and cheerful buttercups that glowed in the moonlight, was a neatly trimmed circle. In the center of that circle he had spread a blanket. Nestled on the blanket was a wicker picnic basket and an ice bucket. A mysterious bottle peeked out of the top of the bucket and Ronni's mouth curved into a smile.

He came up beside her and grabbed her hand. "So? Whatcha think?"

"A midnight picnic by the water? What woman wouldn't love it?"

"Will you try the wine?"

So she was right. "Are you trying to get me drunk?" Despite the fact that many of her male counterparts patronized the Elmwood Tavern, the consumption of alcohol was severely frowned upon and Ronni herself had never tasted it.

"Maybe."

She tugged on his hand and kissed his cheek. "I'll try it."

He led her to the blanket and they settled down side by side. He opened the basket and laid out the assortment of goodies. There was a fresh loaf of French bread, cold chicken, two kinds of cheese, grapes and fresh strawberries. Where he had gotten strawberries this late in the season was a complete mystery to her.

Suddenly he jumped up. "Oops, I almost forgot."

She watched as he dashed back to the car, opened the windows and did something mysterious inside. Soon the soft strains of a Beatles love song drifted toward them. He rejoined her on the blanket and surveyed the scene. "I think that's everything."

"You went to a lot of trouble."

He shrugged. "You hungry?"

"Would you do something for me first?"

"Anything."

She smiled because she knew he meant it. "Dance with me? I've never done it before and I figure you're just the guy to teach me."

His mouth quirked into a grin. "I thought Mennonites weren't allowed to dance."

"We're not allowed to cavort around the countryside with pot-smoking fugitives either. But that doesn't seem to be stopping me."

"Good point." He stood and with a flourish, extended a hand. "I'd love to be the first to share a dance with you."

She took his hand and followed him to the edge of the clearing. He wrapped his right arm tightly around her waist, and took her right hand in his left. Soon they were swaying gently to the sensual rhythms of a lone voice accompanied by only an acoustic guitar and the gurgle of the brook.

Like a breeze across the water,

Like a breath of spring-fresh air,

Like silk across my senses,

Your tender whispers show you care.

She settled her head against his shoulder and whispered, "What is this one? I don't recognize it."

"A friend of mine wrote it." He bent low and kissed her cheek. "Especially for tonight."

She raised her head, blinked in surprise. "What?"

"Shh. Here comes another verse." He smiled at her, eyes twinkling and lips twitching and she couldn't help but be caught up in the music and the mood.

You touch my soul in ways,

I never thought I'd feel,

And your life entwined with mine,

Has made it all so real.

The voice was a little rough, the riffs a little uneven, but the singer had heart and he poured it into his music. And he had written the song for her. For her and Jesse. That knowledge wrapped around her heart and squeezed.

With you I'm free to live,

Free to love,

Free to see.

With you I'm free to be the one

I was always meant to be.

The verses began to repeat and she felt a growing pressure in the back of her throat. "Oh, Jesse. I—"

"Look at you, Ronni. Drinking and dancing," he teased, cutting off words that couldn't begin to express the depth of what she felt. "You're bound for hell in a hand basket, for sure."

"Probably." She found her smile again. "But you're worth it." She touched his hair. "You're definitely worth it."

In response he nuzzled her hair against his cheek.

It was ethereal, magical. The moon glittered off the gurgling water, the crickets chirped like a thousand tiny violins. His cologne was dizzying. She removed her hand from his and wrapped it around his neck. He pulled her in more closely and his mouth descended to her throat. He brushed his lips against bare skin.

She closed her eyes and returned the gesture. Her initiation of intimate contact was so rare, it must have shocked him. She felt his body tense very briefly but, after a few moments, he relaxed again and they continued to sway.

As the song blended into another, he began to nibble on her neck a little more insistently, then laced his fingers through her hair. She always wore it down for their dates, knowing how much he loved to run his hands through it. Soon his mouth found hers and she lost herself in the kiss, her tongue now as experienced and aggressive as his own.

She hardly realized when her feet contacted the blanket but he must have been purposefully heading in that direction because he didn't hesitate. He stopped the rhythmic movements of his body and started to lower her to the soft oasis of wool amidst the dewy grass.

She made no move to stop, or discourage him. It never even occurred to her. Then he was lying beside her, his lips gently coaxing and distracting her as his hand slid to the front of her dress. He opened the buttons to the waist and slid his fingers beneath her bra again. She moaned and drew him closer.

He nudged his hips against her and she became keenly aware of his arousal. Spurred on by desire and frank curiosity, her hand moved down to the front of his jeans.

He hurriedly undid the button and zipper.

She was shocked at her own blind acceptance of what was happening but that shock did nothing to dissuade her from continuing.

She found his ridge and when her hand caressed him firmly through his briefs, he uttered a soft curse. "Jesus Christ."

She had become jaded to his profanity, but wasn't jaded to the next phenomenon she encountered. He reached down, still beneath her dress, and slid a hand beneath her panties. She was swollen and wet and the pressure of his fingers on her center just about sent her rocketing skyward. A moment later, as his fingers dipped inside her, something *did* rocket through her. Something new and intensely exciting. His fingers remained inside as she pulsed around him and fought to regain her breath.

His breath coming hot and fast, he whispered in her ear, "I can make it happen again, Ronni. Can I make love to you?" She didn't answer right away and he took the opportunity to manually slide her hand beneath his briefs. She was fascinated by the strong, smooth length of him.

His breathing became choppy. "Please, Ronni. This is killing me."

For some reason, that phrase jolted her back to reality. She snatched back her hand and rolled away. When she looked at him she could see evidence that he was having trouble returning from the alternate universe he had just been inhabiting. "Are you saying you'll actually die if you don't have sex with me?"

"What?" He managed to sit up and stare at her.

"You heard me. Are you trying to tell me that if you don't have sex with me tonight you'll actually die? Because that's a really tired line, Jesse. I won't fall for it."

"Jesus, Ronni. It's an expression for God's sake. I know I won't die if I don't get it. It may feel like I will but I know it's an illusion." He stopped and she could see the temper flare in his eyes. "You were certainly enjoying it though. Were you just leading me on so you could get a taste of your first orgasm? Then drop me, leaving me hanging?"

Ronni's mouth dropped open. "That's a terrible thing to say!"

He plowed his fingers through his hair and rolled away from her. He stood and zipped his fly. "Well, I'm sorry. But I'm leaving in two days—actually more like twenty-seven hours—and I want to be close to you so bad it hurts. Who knows when we'll see each other again." He returned to the blanket and knelt beside her. "*That's* what's killing me." He cupped her face in his hands and studied her as if truly seeing her for the first time. She could have drowned in those deep blue depths. "Come with me, Ronni."

"What?"

"I know it's crazy and I don't know how we'll make it. I've barely got enough money to pay my tuition and live on. I don't know, we could both get part-time jobs or something. We could manage somehow." His hands dropped to his thighs and he rubbed his palms back and forth in a way that suggested they had grown damp. Ronni didn't think she had ever seen him nervous before. About anything. "Don't tell me you haven't thought about it."

"Yes, I've thought about it," she conceded. His anxiety squeezed her stomach like a cold fist. "But I didn't think you'd actually ask."

"Well, I just did. So what do you say?"

"Oh Jesse, I can't!" She had a terrible time wrenching those words from her throat. "I know I don't have a perfect life here but I love my family, and even my church. I can't bear the thought of leaving them." She looked away. Suddenly the shame of the past few months came crashing down on her head with the weight of the moon. Hadn't she done enough? Midnight trysts and white lies were one thing but abandoning her family was quite another. How could she possibly consider such an absolute betrayal of everything she had ever loved and believed in? But she loved Jesse too. She felt like she was being torn in two but the answer couldn't be denied. "I just can't. Not even for you. At least not yet."

"Shit!"

"I'm sorry." She was fighting a hot flood of tears. She had known there would probably be a confrontation like this but nothing could have prepared her for the reality of the disappointment on Jesse's face and the hole it bored into her heart.

He shook his head. "No, don't be sorry." But his voice lacked its usual conviction. "I knew you wouldn't want to go. I shouldn't have asked and put you in a spot like that. I was just—" She heard him swallow and his eyes met hers again. "I'll try real hard to come back next summer. Maybe by then things will have changed."

"Maybe." She wiped at her eyes.

He leaned in and pressed his mouth to hers again, then mumbled against her lips, "Now that that's out of the way, can I make love to you, for real?"

She smiled wistfully. "You know, if I weren't scared to death of getting pregnant, I'd actually consider it."

"I got condoms in the glove compartment."

"You always come prepared, don't you?"

"Always."

But she shook her head mournfully. "I guess that's not the only reason. It's been drilled into me since birth that that's a sin. I can't ignore everything I've ever been taught about what's right."

"Would it make a difference if I was a virgin too?"

She cocked her head in bafflement.

"Does it matter that I've had some experience? You know, I'm a fornicator, a sinner. Would sleeping with me somehow make you evil too?"

"It's not sleeping, Jesse."

"You didn't answer the question."

"No, that has nothing to do with it." She couldn't evade the problem no matter how much she wanted to. "Part of me wants it just as much as you do. But I can't get past that nagging feeling that it's wrong and I should wait until I'm married." She chewed on her lower lip. "Can you understand that? Please don't hate me."

He leaned over and brushed her cheek with his lips. The touch was as soft as the moonlight and it sent a shiver down her spine. "I could never hate you, Ronni. It's okay, I'll live. But you better do up your dress or I'll have a hard-on all night."

Blushing, she did up a few buttons. "How about the picnic?"

"You got it, babe. You divvy out some food and I'll pop the cork."

* * * * *

Ronni leaned back in the plush bucket seat as the wind whipped her hair up through the sunroof. She closed her eyes and basked in contentment, refusing to think of the goodbye that loomed.

Two glasses of wine had left her with a fuzzy, warm haze of satisfaction. Her fingers were laced with Jesse's as he drove lazily toward her lane for what would likely be the last time for a long while. It was four-thirty in the morning. They were cutting it awfully close to the wake-up call for milking but neither had been eager to leave their little paradise. She had idly hoped he might suggest seeing her briefly again that night, but he had said nothing.

As if he had been reading her mind he spoke, "You know I'd love to see you before I leave, but if I don't get some sleep tonight I'll fall asleep at the wheel tomorrow. I'd like to get there in one piece."

She squeezed his hand. "I know. Tonight was perfect. It'll last me until the spring."

They stopped at their usual spot about thirty meters from the end of her lane. They sat there, silent and motionless, as if willing time to stand still and allow them to savor the moment just a little longer.

Jesse broke the silence. "I've got something for you."

Surprised, she looked at him. "What do you mean?"

He reached beneath his seat and pulled out a small, gift-wrapped box.

"Another surprise?" she said in delight. "You're just full of surprises tonight."

He grinned. "Yeah, I'm full of it, all right." He waved impatiently toward the box. "Go on, open it."

She tore into the package, and eventually pulled out a small tape player and headphones. Another small box in the package revealed an assortment of a half a dozen tapes. She chewed on her lower lip and tried to hold back the tears.

"Here," he said gruffly, holding out a small package of batteries. "I had it all wrapped before I realized you would need these too." He wouldn't let her say anything. "You've got to promise me to take this on some long walks and sing along. I picked out what I thought were some of your favorite groups, and a couple of new ones I thought you might like. You learn the words and sing 'em for me when I get back."

He was about to continue when she placed a finger to his lips. "Thank you," she said quietly. "It's the perfect gift. I wish I had gotten you something."

"That little scene on the blanket was gift enough for me." Mischief danced in his eyes and across his lips.

She mused how she would miss his smiles, his mouth, his hands, and found herself fighting tears again. She gazed at the end of her lane, and was startled when she felt her door being opened.

"Come on, Ronni. Let's get this over with."

She got out of the car and immediately wrapped her arms around him. He tipped up her chin for a long wet kiss. After a few moments of incredible heat, she murmured against his lips. "I think maybe I made a mistake."

"What do you mean?" He stroked her hair.

"I think I should have said yes. I'll regret that for the next nine months until you get back."

"It'll just make it that much sweeter when we get together again."

She nodded weakly.

He couldn't quite bring himself to let go yet, so bent down for another kiss. This one seemed to stretch out to infinity. Their tongues courted and their bodies molded together. He fondled her breast and nestled himself in her cleft as she tipped up her hips and ground against him. She had never felt such a desperate need to be close to someone as she did at that moment.

"Frany?!"

She almost jumped out of her skin. They ripped apart and she turned to see the unmasked rage of Eli Martin bearing down on her. Reflex overcame panic and she quickly did up the top button of her dress.

"What, in the name of heaven, is going on here?"

She couldn't form a reply. This couldn't be happening. There was no proverb, no Bible verse, no Sunday School lesson that fit such a situation. She floundered for words that wouldn't come. But she wasn't alone.

Jesse wrapped an arm protectively around her, and replied for her. "Just a private little strawberry social. None of your concern."

Eli glowered at him, then shifted his fiery gaze back to Ronni. "Frany! Answer me! Have you been seeing him all summer? Is that why you've been so tired?"

Jesse's arm tightened around her shoulders and she finally found her tongue. Barely. "I'm sorry, Eli. I didn't mean for it to happen, but…well…"

"But…well…you love him, right? Is that it? Did you sleep with him, Frany?"

She cringed at the shock and disappointment in his eyes. But she shook her head vigorously, suddenly grateful again that she didn't have to lie about that. "No," she whispered as she dropped her eyes to the gravel beneath her feet. "Of course not."

But Eli wasn't convinced. "How can I believe you? You've been lying to everyone for months. How can I ever believe anything you say again?"

"Hey!" shouted Jesse. "Give her a break. She was just trying to avoid this exact scene. You're a bunch of self-righteous bastards! I should—"

"Jesse!" rebuked Ronni. Then more quietly, "Let me handle this."

He closed his mouth but his silence was stony. She felt his fingers grip her dress.

Eli clenched his fists. "Jesse Ward, right?" he said with contempt. "The car's a dead giveaway. Come on, Frany. I'll have to tell your parents about this. It's one thing to be seeing someone outside the church but it's quite another to pick a juvenile delinquent and then sneak around behind everyone's back and lie about it." He turned a steely stare on Jesse. "And you're not to set foot near here again. You leave her alone."

"I don't take orders from anyone." Jesse's voice was low but deadly. "I'll leave her alone when she tells me to."

Ronni turned to him and pulled him down to whisper in his ear. "You better go. I'm sorry we have to say good-bye like this."

He laced all ten fingers through her hair and touched his forehead to hers. He held her eyes. "Are you sure you don't want me to come in there with you? I don't mind. I can stand up to them."

She bit her lip to ward off tears. "No, you go and don't give me another thought. I'll…I'll be fine. I'll see you in the spring."

Jesse hazarded a glance at the undisguised rage seething just a couple of meters away. He flagrantly wrapped his arms around her and kissed her hard. When he pulled away he whispered in her ear, "I'm here for another twenty-four hours. You've got my number if you change your mind about coming with me. Okay?"

She nodded.

Then, even more softly he whispered, "I love you."

A tear squeezed out of her eye.

He reluctantly loosened his grip and walked around the front of the car. As he passed he knocked shoulders with Eli. It was no accident.

Eli remained rigid, stewing silently until Jesse had slammed his door, started the engine and pulled away.

Ronni watched his taillights retreat from her, and suddenly felt very alone. "Why are you here, Eli?"

"Maria was having trouble calving. Glenn called me from the barn to come give him a hand. Good thing I found you. Who knows how long this could have gone on." He grabbed her hand and dragged her back to his car.

Ronni was astounded that neither she nor Jesse had heard him pull up. His headlights must have swept across them and yet they were completely oblivious to it.

She sat in silence until he pulled up beside the house. He sat motionless, staring straight ahead as Ronni tried to melt into the upholstery.

"Do I smell liquor on your breath, Frany?"

"It was just a glass of wine."

She could see his hands grip the steering wheel. "You go on in the house. I won't say anything until the calf is safe and sound but then there'll be a reckoning. You've got some explaining to do."

Ronni said nothing, but trudged into the house, clutching her Walkman and tapes tightly in her fist.

* * * * *

"Have you completely taken leave of your senses?" blasted Glenn Lichty. Late morning sunshine streamed in the family room windows but nothing could lift the oppressive atmosphere of that room.

"He's a good person, Daddy. Really. You just don't know him." Ronni had lain in bed for the last five hours. With heavy eyelids and a heavier heart she had stared at the ceiling and waited for the inevitable confrontation. She had come up with no speeches and no excuses. All she had was her faith in the love of her family. She prayed that would be enough.

"Huh," grunted her father.

"Did he force you to do anything?" asked her mother quietly.

"Mother! Of course not. Jesus! What do you think—" Too late she realized her incredible misstep.

Glenn's face flushed bright red. "Yeah, he's such a good person, he's taught you how to swear. And Eli, here, says you were drinking wine and he was mauling you when Eli drove up." Glenn stood stock-still, the clenching and unclenching of his fists indicating his level of anxiety. "Have you got some fancy explanations for all that?"

"No." Now Ronni's temper flared with a righteous indignation fueled by her father's hypocrisy. "But what's the big deal about a little wine? Lots of the menfolk go drinking and nobody seems to care. Nobody ever says a word. Why is it so different for me?"

"Because you're my daughter, that's why. I expect better from you."

Better from his daughters, but his sons could frequent the Tavern without judgment or guilt. Ronni seethed in silence.

"Did you do drugs too?" It was Eli's soft voice from the rocking chair.

"No! He only smoked pot the one time and he hated it. He was grieving for his mother. He hasn't touched it since."

"Huh! And you believed him?" Glenn had begun to pace.

Now she stood up to face her accusers. "Yes, I did! He never gave me any reason to doubt him. And for your information, Dad, he doesn't live for that car. He takes care of it but he's been saving for school this fall. He sometimes worked a second job to make enough to go to university."

Glenn considered that development, but that didn't change the result. "Well, I suppose that's commendable but it hardly redeems all his other faults."

"They're not faults," she said haughtily. She just wouldn't tolerate them talking about Jesse like he was some reprobate.

"Well, no matter what you think of him, you're not to see him again."

Ronni sat down again, defeated. "It doesn't matter anyway. He's leaving for Vancouver tomorrow. He'll be gone until the spring."

"Well, thank the Lord for small favors," said Glenn.

"You're sure to forget about him by then," contributed her mother. "Maybe you'll come to see that Myron is the one for you."

"Don't count on it," she muttered through clenched teeth.

"You're young, Frany." Eli rocked slowly. "You'll bounce back quickly."

Glenn nodded agreement. "Yes. All you need is a little time to really look at this. We raised you right, Veronica." *Just who is he trying to convince?* wondered Ronni. Himself or her? "You know what's right. You just need a little distance from this in order to find it again."

Ronni bit back her response. Right and wrong had nothing to do with her feelings for Jesse. Or maybe it did, but not in the way her father was thinking. No amount of time or distance could change how *right* their time together felt. Her parents didn't have a clue what they were talking about. Even she, herself, had no idea what Jesse meant to her until she was faced with nine months without him. May seemed like an eon away. At least she had the tape deck he had given her. That would feel like a little piece of him. She had stashed it safely up in her room, under her pillow.

"What do you want to do with this?" asked Eli as he held up his prize to Glenn.

Ronni was astounded to see that he was holding the very tape deck and box of tapes. Fighting an unparalleled panic, she vaulted from her seat once again. "Where did you get that? You had no right to go into my room!"

"You're in no position to cast stones, Frany."

"Stop calling me that! My name is Ronni!"

"Veronica!" exclaimed her mother. "You don't talk to your elders that way."

"Well, he had no right to take that. Give it back!" Panic was melting into desperation and rage

But instead Eli handed it to her father. Glenn glanced at the tapes, his face turning red with fury. "You know how we feel about this music. It's the devil's own."

Ronni couldn't keep her eyes from rolling back into her head. "It's just *music,* Daddy. It's not going to corrupt me or possess me or anything. It just makes me feel good."

"Well, maybe the music won't corrupt you but he certainly has." He sifted through the tapes. He paused at Meatloaf's *Bat out of Hell* album and his color deepened. The vivid depiction of a demon on wheels and the opening to the gates of hell was all the excuse he needed. He dropped the Walkman to the floor and ground the heel of his work boot into it. The plastic cracked and shattered under the pressure.

"What are you doing?" she screamed. "You can't do that!" He may as well have stepped on her heart. The pain in her chest was just as intense. Just as real.

"I just did. Trust me, *Ronni*. It's for your own good."

She stared at the bits of debris that were all the remained of the most precious gift she had ever received and didn't bother to meet her father's eyes. He didn't deserve that kind of respect. Not anymore. Without a word, she whirled around and fled up to her room. When she reached it, she slammed the door closed and flung herself on her bed, her face already drenched with tears.

* * * * *

"Are you all right?"

"Go away," said Ronni, her words muffled by her pillow.

Eli ignored her and seated himself beside her on the bed. He rested his hand on her back. "I'm sorry you're hurting so much. But you've got to understand we're only thinking of you."

She sat up, her eyes fierce. "No you're not. You're all just worried about what everyone will think when they hear I was hanging around with someone like that. You're afraid it might affect your chances for the Lot next spring because you and my dad are partners. They might think you were partly responsible for the *error of my ways.*" She shot those last words at him like tiny pellets of scorn.

Eli didn't flinch at her words. "You know that's not true, Frany."

"I told you to stop calling me that."

He closed his eyes and took a deep breath. "Very well…Ronni." The word peeled off his tongue like a stubborn stamp. "But like I said, you know that's not true. You're upset and looking for someone to lash out at. I'm happy to be your target. Your parents are upset enough.

"You know I've always held you in high esteem, sweetheart. When I saw you out there with…him, I may have lost some objectivity. I'm sorry if we all overreacted a little."

She flopped back down and stared at the ceiling. "He's not what you think he is."

"I doubt that he is what *you* think he is either, but the point is moot since he's going away anyway. Take the next several months to really look at this." His hand moved up to her shoulder and he squeezed it gently. "I'm sure by the spring you'll see things differently."

She rolled over and muttered into the pillow. "You just don't understand."

"Us adults rarely do." With that he stood to go and stuffed his hands into his pockets. "I know I'm not exactly your favorite person right now, but if you need a shoulder to cry on, I'm willing." He stood there silently for a moment before his feet thudded heavily on the worn pine floor and she heard the door close behind him.

Ronni pulled the pillow over her head. Eli had always been incredibly good to her. Ever since she could remember he had a special smile and a hug for her when he came to visit. He always said she reminded him of his mother who had died before Ronni was born. She had confided in him numerous times about things that she wasn't comfortable to tell her parents, merely because they were too close to the situation. He had always been objective and tried to be supportive and helpful. But tonight—tonight she hated him. And she hated herself for hating him.

She hadn't really believed what she had said to him. He was right. That was an ugly accusation. But she did believe that they were all being incredibly unfair and judgmental. Not to mention hypocritical. They were passing judgment on someone they knew virtually nothing about, based solely on idle gossip. Their hypocrisy over drinking alcohol grated on her as well.

Certainly, she held some responsibility. She had been less than honest and she had probably let things go further than she should have. But premarital pregnancies were hardly unheard of in their church. They were hushed up but they weren't exactly a rarity. Even devout Christians had active libidos. She often questioned whether the image of Christ himself as a celibate icon bordered on naive. The Bible itself presented him as a man with human weaknesses and, from what Jesse had said, that was the ultimate male weakness. There were other things in the Bible that she questioned.

But now was not the time for a theological self-examination. Her faith had very little to do with her feelings for Jesse and her current antipathy toward her parents. Her father's destruction of her prized gift was unforgivable. She was eighteen years old, an adult in the eyes of the outside world and that had been her property. *No*. She would never forgive him for that. *Never.*

Her eyes were just beginning to droop when she heard the phone ring and her father's angry voice reached her from the kitchen. Jesse. No doubt worried about her, he'd called and that made her smile but her father's adamant refusal tore the smile from her lips.

His exasperation came through loud and clear. He hated having to deal with Jesse—an outsider, an unwelcome intruder into his sanctimonious little world. She gleaned some small satisfaction from her father's discomfort. It wasn't nearly enough but it was something.

She finally fell asleep on a damp pillow.

* * * * *

Ronni eased open the back door. She had slept through much of the day and now sleep eluded her. It was just after midnight, and she had an irresistible urge to walk out the lane. Maybe…just maybe he would be waiting out there for her. Maybe, considering the events of last night, he would come by to check on her.

She could have called him and asked him to come but he needed his sleep and she didn't want to pressure him into anything. It was wishful thinking but she couldn't resist the urge to see for herself.

She ambled slowly down the lane. The ritual was so familiar but the end result had always been assured before. The uncertainty tugged at her heart. The crickets chirped and the breeze blew. Her hair was down and she savored the feel of the wind casting it about her face. She imagined Jesse's fingers massaging her scalp and combing through the strands. She reached the end of the lane and dragged her mind away from her fantasies. She looked longingly up the road.

Empty.

She knew it would be. It was an idle fantasy. In a few short hours he would be hitting the highway, driving thousands of miles all alone, facing a new world—without her. She could still call him. She knew, even if the phone rang at two a.m., he would rush here to pick her up at a moment's notice.

She was tempted. Very tempted.

Dejected, she turned around and headed back down the lane. She wouldn't call. She just wasn't ready to take that step. She didn't have the free spirit that Jesse seemed to. He had tapped into a taste of it but she didn't have the hefty dose of it that he did. He was the essence of spontaneity and adventure. Maybe that was what she loved about him. He had awoken feelings in her that she never knew she had but that was only part of it. There were so many other things about him to love as well.

For the thousandth time that day she relived their moments on the blanket. She dreamed of what it would have been like to share herself with him—to know him completely. Perhaps she could have held onto that for the next nine months. Perhaps those dreams could have kept her warm through the long winter months to come. No one could have taken that gift away from her.

She sighed, trying to banish those thoughts. It was over and nothing could change those events. The fact that she had made the *right* decision was a comfort, albeit a small one.

She had reached the house but wasn't ready to go back inside yet. She set off without destination, shuffling her feet and gazing at the ground, not really aware of her direction, and finally found herself at the door to the barn. She hadn't been inside for weeks. She used to love petting and talking to the cows and cats that inhabited the warm, humid old building. Perhaps a visit was long overdue.

She went in and was greeted by the familiar hum of the cooler. It was programmed to mix the milk every twenty minutes. Tomorrow morning the milk truck would come and drain it, taking the milk to some nearby dairy. It came every other day, come rain or shine, steadfast, predictable…boring. Maybe that was the greatest gift Jesse had given her. His quest for adventure had lifted the haze of monotony from her life.

She walked through the cooler room and entered the milking parlor. She strolled between the rows of sleepy cows, savoring the musty smells of warm bodies, manure and hay. She patted sleepy, velvety noses and reacquainted herself with old friends. She found Maria's new calf. He was currently with his mother but, likely the next morning, they would be separated. He would be fed from a bottle so that her milk production could be closely monitored, and not be interfered with. She stroked the tiny nose. "We're both losing somebody special, aren't we?" His only response was to blink his big wet eyes.

She eventually worked her way to the opposite end of the barn where the stairs to the loft beckoned. She climbed the creaky steps, flicked a switch and the big, empty space was illuminated. A cat skittered out of sight and stirred up a small cloud of dust. Bales were stacked on the far side of the room. There would likely be one more cutting and those bales would barely fill a third of the huge room. She breathed deeply.

Fresh hay brought back happy memories of playing hide and seek in here, cuddling newborn kittens, swinging from ropes that hung from the rafters and flying into a huge pile of loose, fluffy straw. She'd had a good life. She had always felt loved and wanted and happy. Despite her present misery, she had to acknowledge that.

She strolled to the door at the far side of the room. It opened directly to the outside, onto a huge ramp of earth that allowed the tractors to drive in and out of the mow with their loads. As she reached for the light switch she felt a presence behind her. Strong arms wrapped around her waist and her heart leapt to her throat in excitement.

"Jesse?" she exclaimed with glee as she turned around.

The light flicked off and, as callused fingers caressed her cheek, she knew instinctively that nothing would ever be the same.

Chapter Six

Winter, 1987–1988

Ronni gazed out the window. Snow swirled around skeletal trees, tiny particles of ice blasted against the glass pane and the wind whistled faintly in the chimney. In the washed-out glow of the moon on the snow she watched the old tire swing, now empty and forlorn, as it swayed and banged against the trunk of the ancient oak in their backyard. That swing should have brought back happy memories of summers full of laughter and bustling activity. Her brothers used to push her on that swing until she flew so high she was sure she could touch the sky. But now, set in the midst of such a bleak and foreboding landscape, the swing only reminded her of everything that she had lost—or was about to lose.

It was three weeks until Christmas and, for the hundredth time, Ronni wondered what it would be like to decorate a Christmas tree and watch its twinkling lights and glittering tinsel every night as the holiday drew near.

The only decoration was a nativity scene that graced a small corner table. The scents of hot apple cider and cinnamon filled the room and the fire crackled in the woodstove on the far wall. She should feel happy and content. But all she felt was empty.

"So what's this all about?" asked her father.

She turned around slowly. "Where's Eli?"

"He's just getting himself a cup of cider from the kitchen."

At that moment her mother ambled in and seated herself on the couch with her sewing basket. Ronni watched her work at patching a pair of overalls that had seen better days. Frugality was another virtue that required constant diligence and sacrifice. *Sacrifice.* She had sacrificed too much.

Ronni blinked away a tear. "I want to wait for Eli. Is everyone else in bed?"

"Yes," responded her mother.

Finally Eli strolled in with a steaming cup, and seated himself in the rocking chair.

"Okay." Glenn's foot tapped impatiently. "Now, why the meeting and why all the secrecy?"

Ronni paced to the corner of the room and seated herself in a large armchair. "I just wanted to tell you privately. Everyone else will find out soon enough but I thought you should hear it first without the rest of the family." She clasped her hands in her lap.

"All right," said Glenn with an exasperated air. "You've built up the suspense, now out with it. Are you planning on leaving us and flying out west to live with the Ward boy after all?"

Ronni almost laughed at the prospect. That question had never been more ludicrous. "No, that's not it. I wish that was all it was."

"Honey," said her mother, "you're scaring me. Are you sick?"

"No, at least not in the conventional sense of the word." She listened to the crackling of the fire and gazed at the carpet. "I'm pregnant."

Silence hung in the room like a physical presence. A piece of wood popped in the stove and it echoed through the stillness like a gunshot. The wind howled outside, mirroring the desolation Ronni felt in her heart.

She heard her father draw an exaggerated breath; certainly he was attempting to calm himself. It didn't seem to be working, however, because when he finally spoke his deep voice trembled. "I thought you said you didn't sleep with him."

Ronni remained silent. She felt so heavy she feared she might sink through the floor.

"Didn't you at least take precautions?" It was Eli's voice.

Now Ronni looked up and met his gaze. She set her jaw. "I guess I wasn't thinking straight."

"Obviously," ranted her father. He paced like a caged bull.

Ronni heard her mother sniffle, but decided against looking directly at her.

Glenn scrubbed his face with his hands. He swept his eyes across the bleak landscape outside the window and then rested his gaze on his daughter. "Well, you'll just have to face the music," he said with conviction. "You'll stay here. We certainly won't kick you out. But I don't know how you'll find a husband now. Especially once the identity of the father gets out. Even Myron doesn't want anything to do with you anymore and he's only heard rumors."

She remained silent and stared pointedly at her father.

Glenn studied her and Ronni willed herself not to be hurt by the disappointment in his eyes. "Well, do you have anything to say for yourself?"

She blinked against the sting of tears. She waited, hoping someone in the room would say something else, anything, but the silence was relentless. The choice had been made for her. "I'll stay, but only until I have the baby. I'll give him to you and Mom for adoption if you'll have him. I won't be able to give him a decent life and I know you'll love him like he was your own."

"Ronni," sobbed her mother. "What are you saying?"

"Isn't it obvious, Mom? I can't—no, I *won't* stay here. I won't live in a hive of hypocrisy. I'm giving up the baby because I love it." Already, she loved it so much the pain of it twisted around her heart like razor wire. But she had to do what was right for this baby, had to give it the best life possible. And at this point in her life she knew she couldn't do that, not on her own. Not yet. "I don't want to raise a child without a husband. My baby deserves better. I can't stay here and I certainly can't provide for it…out there. I've done a lot of thinking the last few months and I've come to some realizations and some decisions. I don't belong here." *Maybe I never did.*

"I suppose you belong with *him*." Her father's tone was icy.

"Where I go is none of your concern."

"Ronni, how can you say that?" whispered Verna.

"Will you take the baby?" she asked, her voice even despite the knots in her belly.

"Yes, of course," said her mother into a handkerchief. "I just don't understand why you feel that you need to leave us."

She didn't respond, just stood and walked across the room toward the stairs. Her legs felt as fragile as stalks of wheat.

She heard her mother implore, "Eli, talk to her. She always listened to you."

"She's made up her mind, Verna. There's nothing I can do."

Ronni ran through the kitchen. She stumbled up the steps, barely able to see them through the tearful haze. She had made the right decision, the *only* decision. That was painfully obvious to her now.

After she gave birth she would contact Jesse. But not before. She wouldn't let this interfere with his studies and she certainly wasn't going to saddle him with a baby. She was sure he would insist on assuming the responsibility but she wouldn't have it. A baby would make continuing his education impossible. She knew it would be difficult to carry through with her intentions but there was no other way. The baby would have a good life here, much better than she could do for it on her own, with no education and limited resources. Maybe, if she and Jesse ended up together, once he finished his degree, they could come back for the baby. But not before.

The other option, to stay here, was unthinkable. The encounter a few moments earlier had firmly reinforced that decision. She no longer had a place here. She would be outcast, and even if she wasn't, she had lost all respect for the people around her.

She slammed her door and flopped onto her bed, which had recently become her one refuge—her safe haven in a house that used to be filled with nothing but love. An odd twist of words struck her and she laughed mirthlessly at the irony of it. Perhaps she *had* made her own bed and now she must lie in it. But no matter how true that was it didn't lessen the pain that she felt or change the trials that she faced.

Unconsciously she placed a protective hand over her belly.

The next few months would be difficult but she could get through it; Jesse's return glimmered like the light at the end of the tunnel. With a little luck, the baby would be born before he arrived home, as she wanted to have given it to her parents and moved out before she saw him again. That way he couldn't talk her out of it. In Jesse's words, it would be a *done deal.*

She gazed at the ceiling, feeling his absence like a fist in her stomach.

What if he found someone else while he was out there? She couldn't rest all her hopes on him. He had implied a commitment but he was only twenty years old. She knew how fickle young men could be. Or at least she had heard. But surely he was different. He had said he'd come back to see her and she believed him.

She had to hang on to that. It was all she had.

* * * * *

"Thanks for coming, Herb."

Herb Brubacher watched Verna pour three mugs of coffee and set out the fresh cream.

"Where is Veronica now?" asked the balding pastor.

Silver flagged his temples and the remaining hair circled his head in a mousy brown wreath. Herb was short with an expanding middle, owing in no small part to his wife's incredibly rich cooking as well as the goodies that his parishioners plied him with whenever he visited. But that part of his life was drawing to a close. His pastorship at Maple Grove had lasted for more than fifteen years but his retirement was imminent.

"She's in her room," answered Verna, settling herself heavily at the table. "She spends an awful lot of time there these days."

Herb nodded knowingly.

"Well," said Glenn as he stood, staring blankly into his mug. "You know the story. Do you have any wisdom to impart?"

"This Jesse character, do you think it likely he may cause a stink when he comes back and finds out the situation?"

"I sincerely doubt it but I don't really know the family." Glenn set down his coffee without tasting it. "I can't imagine him *looking* to take on that kind of responsibility but, then again, he might just do it out of spite, to make us pay for interfering with his plans for Veronica. Trouble seems to follow that family like a dark shadow."

"Yes, that could be the case. You say she's determined to leave after giving you the baby?"

"Yes." Verna's voice wavered. "That's why I asked Glenn to call you. I don't see the need for it."

"I don't know, Verna. I think that may be the wisest thing she could do. Do you really think she'll have a place here? She has made no effort to hide her situation."

"She's hardly talked to anyone and never goes into town."

"True, but she goes out to the market and to church, strutting around like her belly is some sort of badge. She does nothing to deny accusations and rumors that they were having a torrid affair throughout the summer." Herb shook his head ruefully. "What man would want her after that? She'd be sentenced to spinsterhood, not to mention the effect on the congregation if she stayed. I hate to say it but she would be a black mark against us."

Verna said nothing, but merely dabbed at her eyes with a tissue.

"No, my advice is to let her go." Herb sipped from his mug. "Help her through the difficult time of giving up the baby, then don't pressure her to stay. As for the Ward boy, if he shows up I would advise you to have as little contact with him as possible. I haven't had any direct dealings with the family but I've heard rumors that the father isn't to be trusted. Who knows what they might be capable of?" He nodded thoughtfully. "Yes, I definitely think it's best if they have as little contact with our community as possible. Hopefully, if Jesse has designs on the child, he'll give up if there's enough of a cold shoulder. We'll have to stand together to protect that child."

"I just hate to lose a daughter when this is all said and done," murmured Verna.

"It seems to me you've already lost her. Jesse Ward stole her from you."

Color flooded Glenn's face. "Thank you, Herb. I'm sure that's all very good advice. We'll take it to heart."

Herb stood to go. "I should get home. I've been out almost every night this week. It's just been one crisis after another. Pastor or no, I better show my face at home or Elsie will have my hide." He nodded to a tearful Verna and walked with Glenn to the back door.

He and Glenn said their goodbyes and Herb slogged through the deep snow to the driveway. He slid in behind the wheel of his black Lincoln Continental and drove out the lane but, less than a mile from the farm, he pulled over to the side of the road and reached beneath the seat. He pulled out a small silver flask and impatiently twisted off the cap. He drank deeply.

He wiped his mouth with his sleeve and muttered to himself, "Nope. Can't have those Ward folks gettin' too nosy, now can we? They start pokin' around, who knows what they might turn up?"

He mopped his brow with a handkerchief, wiping away all evidence of the nerves he'd been battling ever since arriving at the Lichtys'. He hoped he'd been convincing. If things took the wrong turn and the Wards had too much contact with him and his church it could become very sticky indeed. He was close to retirement from a long and blemish-free career as pastor of a well-respected church. This could very easily undo all that hard work, not to mention the possible ramifications with the outside community as well. This way was best anyway. Veronica Lichty had made her choices; there was no reason to take her pastor down with her.

He took another long drink and stuffed the flask back under the seat before driving carefully away.

* * * * *

Ronni lay on her bed and gazed out the window at the stars that glittered like crystals of ice against the harsh blackness of the December night. One hand absently stroked her abdomen. She was trying desperately not to fall in love with this child but even she knew it was a losing battle and that the moment of truth would likely be the most difficult task she would ever be faced with.

"You've just got all the answers, don't you, Herb Brubacher?" she whispered to herself. Ronni had been listening to the conversation from a secluded spot on the stairs.

Herb's position had hardly come as a surprise to her. He was widely known for being extremely concerned with appearances, both the congregation's and his own. Her sordid tale would definitely be a blot on his good name. She should be grateful. She had heard of other young people who had decided to leave the church. They had been allowed to go, but only after a heated discussion with Herb in which he had warned them that such a decision would likely land them in Hell.

Ronni didn't need the warnings. She was already there.

She smiled without humor. It wasn't like Herb's attempt to bury the issue and shoo her away would erase the distasteful events. Even once she left, the damage would have been done. The whispered gossip and pointed questions were already circulating through the congregation, touching young and old alike. But she knew that the youth were the elders' prime concern. The next generation should be shielded from such barbaric influences at all costs. Veronica Lichty had become a liability, a rebel, a risk. What if she began leading their youth down the garden path? What if she sparked their interest in the evils of the outside world? What if they saw in her the same excitement and allure that she had seen in Jesse Ward?

She grinned sardonically at her new status. She had read the story of the Pied Piper of Hamlin once. But despite their suspicions, she possessed no magic and had no desire to lead anyone astray. One lost soul in the community was definitely enough.

However, she harbored little remorse over the anguish she was putting her family and so many of her fellow believers through. They had turned their backs on her in so many ways—in ways even they didn't understand. She hadn't thought her loved ones capable of such a flagrant betrayal but she had learned her lesson, hadn't she? She would have no regrets at leaving these people behind and hopefully starting a new life with Jesse. She only hoped he wouldn't have forgotten about her come spring.

As if in answer to her doubts the phone rang downstairs.

* * * * *

"Well, then where is she?"

Jesse frowned at the response from the other end of the phone.

"*Out*. She's always *out*. When do you think she might be *in?*"

Again he paused. His fingers tapped impatiently on the cheap plywood end table beside him.

"Well, you know what I have to say to that—fuck you!" He slammed down the receiver. "God dammit!"

"I don't know why you bother. It's been four months of this. You try once a week and they never let you talk to her. She must be somethin' else to go to all this trouble." Jesse's scrawny roommate, Tom, lounged on their tattered sofa. An open pizza box lay across his lap. The apartment was small and sparse but it was all they could afford considering the outrageous rents in Vancouver and the surrounding districts.

"She's something else all right. She's got the body of a goddess and the voice of an angel."

"No kiddin'," sniffed Tom.

Jesse continued glaring at the phone as if he could send his thoughts by ESP through the phone lines. Tom was right, it was hopeless, but he kept trying anyway. How was it that she never happened to answer the phone? And why didn't she try to contact him? She had his dad's number. Surely she knew she only had to call and ask him for Jesse's new address and number. Did they have her chained to her bed for chrissake?

It was useless to speculate. He really didn't have time for this. His studies and his part-time job were taking up all his time. He was doing well but it was a grind and he often stayed up past midnight poring over texts and notes.

"That was that Eli character. He's over there constantly."

"Eeelie?" Tom drew out the name like it was made of taffy. "What the hell kind of name is that?"

"Mennonite."

"Oh yeah, I forgot. Horses and buggies and shit."

Jesse didn't bother to correct him. It was pointless. "That was the guy that caught us out on the road. There was something about him. I didn't like him."

"Well that's hardly a shock considering he practically ripped her out of your arms."

Tom was well versed in this story. Poor Tom had heard it ad nauseam, forwards and backwards, in scattered bits and pieces, from beginning to end. But despite the fact that Jesse knew Tom was tired of it, despite the blank look that would descend over Tom's eyes whenever the subject came up, Jesse just couldn't seem to stop himself from reciting it all, chapter and verse, over and over.

Tom never protested, never complained, never told him to shut up, but it wasn't because Tom was a selfless, supportive friend, and a fantastic listener. It was simply because Jesse scared Tom shitless and Jesse had no intention of doing anything to alter Tom's impressions of him. Why throw away a perfectly good, free therapist?

Tom took advantage of Jesse's silence. "I know at least a half a dozen chicks that would give their eyeteeth for a roll in the hay with you. Maybe that would ease some o' your tension."

"Thanks, but no thanks." Jesse had never told Tom this but, about a month before, Jesse had succumbed to his libido…at least partially. He had been studying with an ardent coed and her advances had been so blatant, he had kissed her. But it went no further. It was like he had acquired a taste for Dom Perignon, and anything else tasted like flat Pepsi. The kiss had been insipid, sickeningly sweet and syrupy. There had been no fizz, no excitement, and her taste had soured his senses. And then he had promptly started hating himself.

He hadn't slept at all that night. He had wallowed in guilt and self-loathing into the wee hours of the morning. Only when he had taken a pledge of fidelity to Ronni, had the guilt been assuaged. But even that had been an incomplete penance. Only confessing to Ronni could purge his demons. And that didn't appear likely to happen any time soon.

Tom shook his head with puzzlement. "You're nuts. Think you could shove a few of them my way?"

Jesse grinned. "I kinda doubt it works that way."

"It was worth a shot." Tom munched. "You want a piece?" he asked, pointing to the pizza with the works.

"No, thanks." Jesse was sick of pizza. Pizza and macaroni had rapidly lost their appeal. He had lost weight, partly because he never felt like cooking for himself, and partly over worrying about Ronni's fate. Their refusal to let him speak to her was a constant source for concern. His mind focused elsewhere, he sauntered over to the couch and grabbed a slice of pizza. He stuffed it absently into his mouth.

Tom grinned and shook his head. "Man, you got it bad."

"Huh?"

"Nothing."

* * * * *

Glenn watched as the suds slipped down the slippery exterior of the steel cooler. He rinsed off the last of the bubbles and dried the metal with a clean rag. He glimpsed his own reflection in the gleaming surface, but immediately turned away.

Lately he couldn't look at himself without wondering who he was and questioning every decision he had ever made with regard to his home and his children. His world had been turned upside down and inside out, and no amount of pastoral advice or prayer or self-examination seemed to be able to turn things right again. He couldn't even talk to the source of his anguish and try to sort things out with her. They sat across from each other at the dinner table and she wouldn't look at him. She refused to even acknowledge his existence.

Outside the snow whirled and twisted—at the mercy of a wild, senseless wind. But in here it felt warm and humid and comfortingly familiar. In here Glenn felt like he had some control over his environment and his destiny. The cows and the equipment, even the cats and the mice, followed a routine that he understood and could control to a certain degree. Unlike his daughter.

It was late and he really should be in bed but he knew sleep was not going to come easily so he had decided to do something productive with his time. So he had come out here and proceeded to scour and clean things that had already been scoured and cleaned.

Herb's advice had made sense but that was hardly a surprise. Herb had been a strong support and guiding hand to him and his family on many occasions. Glenn hated the thought of letting Veronica go but Herb was right. She had betrayed them with her flagrant disregard for everything she had ever been taught. Glenn's other prime source of support, Eli, seemed to be in agreement with Herb's evaluation of the situation and Eli had always had a special fondness for Veronica. If he felt it best to let her go without a fight, then surely that was the correct path to take.

If only Glenn could shake the feeling that he had let her down somehow. If only he could dispel the images of her out in that huge scary world all alone, without her family and community to support her. But then the image of Jesse Ward's insolent face invaded his thoughts. Glenn had seen him around the county, and once at that garage where he pumped gas and washed windshields and displayed his body in tight jeans and grease-stained T-shirts.

Well, Veronica wouldn't exactly be alone, now would she? Jesse embodied the arrogance and recklessness of youth. He embodied everything that Glenn had tried to avoid for his children. And Veronica had embraced him with total disregard for her upbringing. That thought sent his blood pressure skyrocketing again. The thought of her with the likes of him—the image of the two of them laying together in sin—made Glenn's blood boil. It renewed his resolve.

Veronica was free to make her choices but no grandchild of his would be exposed to such unsavory influences as the Wards were sure to provide. Perhaps he had lost his daughter to them but he fully intended to reclaim his grandchild. He would do whatever it took to make sure that happened.

Chapter Seven

May 1988

"Is there anyone you want us to call, honey?" The portly lady in the dull green scrubs bent over Ronni's bed and checked the readout on the fetal monitor.

Ronni shook her head. "No. My midwife should be here soon. I called her and she said she'd only be about twenty minutes."

Ronni was grateful that no one here had bothered to ask about the father of her baby. She suspected that this hospital saw enough single mothers and that such a common occurrence hardly warranted even a raised eyebrow, let alone embarrassing questions.

A contraction seized her and she gripped the sheets until her knuckles matched their pallor.

"Breathe through it," chanted the nurse. "In and out, slow and steady."

Ronni tried to comply, but was having trouble breathing through both the contraction and the tears that were threatening her at every turn. She was amazed there were any left. Surely she had cried herself dry in the last six months. Almost every night, she cried herself to sleep, but it was always worst on the nights that he called. She often overheard her father put off Jesse's inquiries and could tell by his expression after the fact that Jesse must have loosed some of his ample profanity on her father's frail constitution. Well, maybe that wasn't fair. Her father was anything but frail. But he certainly didn't take kindly to Jesse's lack of respect for his authority. Secretly, Ronni relished it.

In the beginning she had often made a dash for the phone, only to be thwarted in her attempt. But after her announcement she was almost grateful for her seclusion. She didn't want Jesse to know about the pregnancy and she was sure if she got on the phone with him it would all come spilling out like a tidal wave. She couldn't do that to him, especially over the phone.

The last four months had, as predicted, been hell but she had refused to remain sequestered in the house. She had quit her waitressing job but, other than that, had gone about her business and attended church as usual, flaunting her scandalous condition, almost begging for them to gossip about her. She took a strange pleasure in their shock and outrage. It didn't take long for the stories of her *affair* with Jesse to hit the rumor mill. And once they did, and were then reinforced by her bulging belly, the gossip spread like wildfire.

She never confirmed or denied anything. She would have loved to flagrantly admit to everything but, as long as it was unsubstantiated, the rumor was certain to stay within the church community. Ronni feared that if she was too brazen about it, it would get back to Jesse's father and brother. She flaunted her condition to the church community but tried to keep it out of the eyes of the rest of the public for that very reason. She had no idea how often Jesse had contact with his family but she couldn't take the chance that they knew about her connection to him and that they would draw the inevitable conclusion and forward the information.

Another contraction racked her body as the midwife entered the room. Viola subscribed to the conservative Mennonite philosophy, complete with covering and simple dress, but she was also a world traveler. She had practiced midwifery for twenty years, and had spent a good chunk of that time in Africa and South America. She and Ronni had become fast friends, despite Ronni's questionable past. Viola had seen too much to hold her ideals above anyone else's.

"Viola," breathed Ronni as she exhaled the last of the wave of pain. "I'm so glad you're here."

Viola grasped and patted her hand. "I wouldn't let you go through this alone, honey. Are you sure you don't want your mother here? She called me last week, pleading with me to let her know when you called me."

Ronni had moved out of the house two weeks earlier. She didn't want anyone from the family to have to drive her to the hospital and her departure was imminent anyway. She had found room and board in town, close to the hospital, and had called a cab when the time came. Her father had provided her with some cash to tide her over until she delivered the baby and could find a job but she had sworn to herself that that would be the last bit of charity she would ever accept from her parents.

"No, I don't want any of them here. When you figure the time is close for the baby to come, then you can call them. I want someone here quickly to take it away." She choked back tears. "I don't think I'll be able to look at it."

"Are you sure about this, Ronni?" A deep frown creased Viola's wrinkled brow. "It's not too late to change your mind. I know how much you love this baby."

"I'm more sure about this than anything in my life. I can't live with them and I can't look after this child properly. It'll be hell but I've got to do it."

"That's a very responsible attitude."

Ronni smiled without humor. "Yeah, I'm real responsible." She knew another contraction loomed and her time was limited. "How about that epidural? I don't know how much more of this I can take."

"Okay, but I have to remind you that once you get that you'll technically be under the care of the on-call obstetrician. I'll stay as your labor coach but he'll be calling the shots."

Ronni nodded. "I understand that. I just can't face this pain knowing what I have to face when it's over." She couldn't numb her heart but perhaps she could numb her body.

"Okay. I'll speak to the nurse. I'm sure it won't take long." Viola left the room, leaving Ronni alone for the first time since she had been admitted.

She took that time to indulge in a little self-pity and rubbed her abdomen affectionately. "I'm gonna miss you, Leah." During one of her ultrasound sessions she'd been fortunate enough to learn the sex of her unborn child. She'd always loved the name Leah, had dreamed of naming a little girl that someday and decided that a name was the one gift she could afford to give her daughter. It was a little piece of Ronni that would stay with her always. And, thankfully, her parents had agreed.

She blinked away a fresh swell of tears. "Maybe someday you'll understand. I sure hope to hell *I* will."

Chapter Eight

Jesse drove like a demon.

He had lost three days when his car had conked out in Winnipeg and he was trying to make up for lost time. He had been riding it hard and knew he was asking for trouble. His trip out west had put a lot of miles on her and he hadn't had the money to put into maintenance and service like he should have. He had just hoped to make it home, where a trusted mechanic could breathe new life into her. It hadn't worked out that way.

A hundred miles outside of Winnipeg he gave up hope. If he kept going he'd probably end up stranded at the side of the road somewhere. And if you had to pick a spot to blow out your engine you definitely wouldn't pick the middle of a Manitoba prairie. The prairies didn't boast a gas station at every corner or a friendly farmhouse just around the next bend. And even if they did, out there the corners were five miles apart and the farmhouses spread even more thinly. So, he had steeled himself and pulled into what looked like a reputable garage. Even so, it had taken three days for them to acquire parts and complete repairs. It had been the longest three days of his life.

Now he was so close he could smell it. The Lichty farm was just around the next bend and he could already taste Ronni on his tongue. He hoped she would be as eager as he was. He would flatten that father and that Eli character if they tried to stop him. He'd tear that place inside out if they tried to hide her. Nothing was going to stop him. They couldn't hide behind a phone any longer.

He saw the familiar sign. He stopped by the side of the road, at the old familiar rendezvous site. He didn't want to give them any warning. His car was too remarkable. If they saw him drive in the lane they might whisk her out the back door or lock her in the basement. He wanted to retain the element of surprise.

God, he hoped Ronni hadn't given up on him. Exams had finished the middle of April but he couldn't leave right away because he had to finalize the sublet for his apartment. There was no other way he could afford the trip home. He'd had someone lined up but the guy had stiffed him for the first month's rent so he had been forced to look for a replacement. It had taken two weeks before all the final arrangements were made. And then the crap with his car had just about sent him into orbit. It was like the gods were conspiring against him to make him wait longer than humanly possible.

But he was finally here. He trudged down the lane, trying to look inconspicuous, and knowing it was a losing battle. But apparently no one noticed his approach because the expression on Ronni's mother's face when she answered the door was one of blatant puzzlement.

She studied him through the screen. "Yes? Can I help you?"

Then he remembered, this woman had never seen him. She had no idea who he was. This promised to be entertaining. He spoke slowly and evenly so as to avoid any confusion. "I'm Jesse Ward."

She didn't disappoint, actually took a step back as her face fell. "Wha-what do you want?"

She was afraid of him! As if he were a rampaging rapist or a common thief bent on ransacking her house. But then again, maybe *thief* wasn't so far off. He was, after all, after their daughter. "I want to see her. She's nineteen years old, you can't hold her against her will. Where is she?"

Ronni's mother inched back another few steps. "I really think you should talk to my husband."

He had been distracted by the fear in her eyes but suddenly Jesse became aware of the cries of an infant. The soft wails echoed from somewhere within the house. She must be baby-sitting for somebody.

"Look, lady, I'm not gonna hurt you. It's a simple question. Where is she?"

Her eyes darted a glance over his shoulder, then behind his back. "Please, wait for my husband. He's in the barn. I'll just call him."

Jesse rolled his eyes. "This is ridiculous. Is she here or not? Mind you, if you say she's not I won't be likely to believe you and I won't leave until I get a tour of the house. So what's the answer?"

"I really have to tend to the baby." She reached out and latched the screen from the inside before hustling away.

"Goddammit," he yelled. "You really think that'll stop me?" He couldn't believe these people. Was this some kind of cult? Was she locked in the attic?

He knew this was a mistake, and probably illegal, but he wasn't inclined to stay within the lines anymore. He kicked at the door and the latch gave way easily. He was just about to step over the threshold when he felt a heavy hand on his shoulder.

"What do you think you're doing?"

He whirled around to see the blazing countenance of Glenn Lichty.

"I'm looking for my girlfriend. Your wife didn't seem inclined to help me so I thought I'd help myself. Unless you'd like to answer the question or, better yet, produce her."

"She's gone."

Jesse frowned. "Gone? What the hell does that mean?"

"She moved out, left, abandoned the family. Is that clear enough for you?"

Jesse smiled and snapped his fingers in glee. "Well, hot damn! Good for her. So where did she go?"

"I don't know."

The smile fell from his face. "The hell you don't! You're asking me to believe you have no idea where your own daughter is living?"

"That's right."

Fury gripped Jesse and he clenched his teeth as if that could keep him from exploding. This was obviously just another stall tactic. Something to throw him off the scent. He must be in the Twilight Zone. "You're a lying son of a bitch!" He kept his voice low and even. "I'm not leaving here until you either produce her or give me an address."

Glenn studied him. "Are you sure you're not here to lay claim to the baby?"

Now that one just about sent Jesse for a loop. "Baby?" he said vacantly. "What are you talking about?"

Glenn didn't have a chance to respond because Eli sauntered up behind him. "You need a hand, Glenn? I think the two of us could manage to throw this trespasser off the property."

"Thanks, Eli. I just might, at that."

Jesse was seething. "I don't know what the hell a baby has to do with anything. All I want is Ronni. Now, for the last time, where is she?"

"For the last time, we don't know. Now get off my land before I call the police."

Jesse ignored them and, to their shock, stormed into the house. He moved so quickly it took them a minute to gather their wits and pursue him. He was already at the stairs calling Ronni's name loudly when he felt a hand on his arm. He swung it violently sending its owner careening into a wall. He glanced back and confirmed with satisfaction that it was Eli.

He started up the stairs and heard Glenn's voice. "Just leave him be, Eli. We'll never get rid of him otherwise."

He called back down the stairs, "Which room is hers?"

"Last door on the left. It's empty."

His boots clicked on the bare pine floor as he stalked down the hall. He glanced in doorways as he went. A couple of the rooms obviously belonged to boys. He peered in another door and a startled figure gazed at him from her lounging position on her bed. *Anna,* he thought. Ronni had mentioned her. He reached his target and pushed open the door.

It had definitely been a girl's room. Flowered paper adorned the walls and frilly curtains hung at the window. The bed was devoid of sheets, however. He pulled open a few drawers and checked the closet. They were right. Empty.

He hesitated in the room that had been hers. Okay, so they weren't kidding. She was gone. But if she had moved out why didn't she call him? He shook his head. They *had* to know where she was.

A moment later he was bounding down the stairs. He passed through the kitchen and noticed Ronni's mother holding a very tiny infant. *Baby? Lay claim to the baby?* But that was ridiculous. He had to talk to Ronni and find out what the hell was going on.

He reached the front door where Glenn was waiting for him. Eli had disappeared.

"Satisfied?" asked Glenn.

"No. I want an address or a phone number. You can't seriously have no idea where she is."

"I'm serious about this… If you don't leave right now I'm calling the cops."

"Damn you! Who do you think you are?"

In response Glenn pushed open the door and glared at him. Jesse figured that, for now, he had exhausted his options. There were other ways to find her. He stormed out and headed down the lane, cursing liberally. On his way past the shed he noticed a black Lincoln Continental peeking out from behind the driving shed and wondered idly who it belonged to.

He got to the end of the lane, hopped into his car and slammed the door. He churned up a cloud of dust as he sped away from the Lichty Dairy Farm.

Damn fanatics! He would head home and consult a phone book. Maybe she had been gone long enough that she had a number listed. Or maybe he could just call directory assistance. Maybe his father had heard something. Jesse had recently related his story to his dad over the phone. His father had been understanding, if not completely sympathetic. Maybe he knew something and didn't even know that he knew. If not that, maybe he'd check out the Tavern tonight. That was always a source for juicy gossip. If that didn't get him anywhere he'd make an appearance at Maple Grove on Sunday morning. He smiled at the thought.

He'd love to see their faces when he showed up, preferably in black leather with a couple of days' worth of stubble, maybe with a switchblade in his pocket. They needed a good shocking. He would refuse to leave until somebody told him something.

The more he thought about that, the better he liked it. They had obviously made Ronni miserable enough to drive her away. They deserved to be a little uncomfortable.

Baby? But his thoughts were interrupted. He pumped the brakes but they weren't responding like they should. He had been driving in a rage, going a little faster than was probably advisable on this freshly grated gravel road. The curve coming up was sharp.

"Shit!" He knew he shouldn't have trusted a bunch of strange mechanics with his little red beauty. They had obviously fucked up. And now his car was probably fucked.

And, it seemed, so was he.

* * * * *

Oh God! Oh GodohGodohGod. If somebody would just get this damn hippo off his chest maybe he could catch his breath. He blinked. Again.

Things began to clear. His head pounded. Somebody was using it for batting practice. Slowly the haze began to lift from his eyes and his mind.

He laughed silently. It wasn't a hippo after all. It was the dashboard of his car. How was it that the dash of his car was barely six inches from the front seat? Then he remembered. *Oh God.* He looked around. *Yup. Definitely fucked.* His car was toast but he was alive.

He felt an intense pressure on his legs. He tried to move to relieve it. "ShitfuckdamnChrist!!" That had been a mistake. Spears of pain shot through him. Even after he relaxed they didn't seem inclined to abate. And now the batting practice on his head had moved from Little League to the majors. Babe Ruth himself must be swinging on him.

He tried to get his bearings. He was upside-down. Maybe. Everything was careening on an angle. He saw blue sky but it was in the wrong place. The sun was shining on his face. Ironic, he thought. Something tickled his cheek. Grass. If only he could breathe properly. The pressure on his chest was intolerable.

He closed his eyes, concentrated and tried to stave off the pain in his head and forget the pain in his legs. When he opened his eyes again he forced himself to take a good look around. At least there was no blood. He could feel a warm trickle on his cheek but he was sure that was superficial. If only he weren't so damn isolated. Nobody would ever find him on this godforsaken back road. He had picked the wrong spot to fuck up.

He had thought getting arrested for smoking dope was stupid. Well, he was just getting started. He was going to have to learn to control his temper or it would eventually kill him. Unless Ronni managed to do it first. He couldn't blame her if she did. She had every right to be furious with him and scold him like a stupid child. She could look forward to long days beside a hospital bed. He could count on that. If, of course, he ever found her. *Dammit!* That thought aggravated his blood pressure and that didn't help his headache.

And then he heard the rumble of a car. He heard the crunch of gravel as it slowed to a stop and then a door slammed.

Thank God! He had never prayed before but now he silently thanked the Almighty for small miracles. He was saved. They'd bring in the jaws of life and cut him out of there. He'd find Ronni and soon everything would be fine again.

A moment later a shadow blocked out the sun.

Chapter Nine

Ronni waited impatiently for the other end to pick up. She had finally broken down and dialed Jesse's father. It had been weeks since the winter semester had let out. Why hadn't he shown up, or called? She couldn't take it anymore. Surely his father would know where he was. Maybe he had decided to stay in Vancouver after all. If that was the case she'd fly out there. Her new waitressing job didn't pay a lot but she could save if she had to. She only hoped she would be welcome. She hoped he'd forgive her for the months without communication or contact. She hoped he'd understand. She hoped he hadn't forgotten. It had been a very long time.

Finally the other end picked up and a tired voice muttered, "Hello?"

"Mr. Ward?"

"Yes? Whatever it is, I don't want any."

"No, please don't hang up." She twirled the phone cord around her finger. "I'd like to talk to Jesse. Is he there by any chance?"

The other end was silent for a long time. She almost thought he had managed to hang up without her realizing it before he finally spoke again.

"Is this some kind of sick joke?"

Ronni blinked. "No, please, I really need to talk to him. Didn't he come home? He said he would try. If not, maybe you could give me his number out west."

"Who the hell is this?" The voice was angry and she could swear it cracked at the end of that phrase.

Her confusion mounted. "It's…uh… I don't know if he ever mentioned me. My name's Ronni Lichty."

"Oh God."

"What?"

"Just a minute." Then there was silence. This was the strangest conversation she had ever had in her life but she hung on as if her life depended on it. In a very real way, it did.

"Can you come here?" he said at last.

"What?" She sounded like a broken record and her confusion was shifting into anxiety. All she wanted was to talk to Jesse. Why did it have to be so complicated?

"I'd like to talk to you in person. Can you come out here?"

"Um…I don't see how. I don't have access to a vehicle. Why, what is it?"

"Shit! Where are you?"

"I'm living in Kitchener. It's not that far but there's no buses that run out there and I don't know how to drive yet."

"Dammit!" Agitation edged his voice and it grated on Ronni's nerves. She twirled the phone cord around her finger so tight that her fingertip turned blue.

"I wish I could come meet with you but my car's in the shop and Sam's disappeared on me. God knows when he'll turn up."

"Please, Mr. Ward. Can't you just tell me over the phone? I just want to talk to him. I'm sure he'll find a way to come see me, or vice versa."

"I guess I don't have a choice. I just hate to deliver this kind of news over the phone."

Suddenly Ronni's palms began to sweat and a knot of foreboding formed in her stomach. "What kind of news is that?"

"There's no easy way to say this, Ronni. I wish to God there were." He took a deep breath, and let it out slowly. "Jesse was in an accident. He's dead."

The words hit her in the chest like bricks, knocking the wind out of her and arresting the rhythm of her heart. They screamed in her ears like a Klaxon.

If Ronni hadn't been sitting down she would have fallen down. Her jaw went slack and she couldn't seem to find the strength to speak. Her vision blurred but she didn't cry. It didn't seem real enough for that.

His words echoed over and over in her mind and her thoughts ran on furiously… *There must be some mistake, Mr. Ward. Jesse can't be dead.*

You see, we had plans. I've waited for ten months to see him. I gave up everything for him. Dear God, I need him. I don't have anyone else. And I've missed him so. And he's only twenty years old. And…and there's something so important I need to tell him. Please don't take him away from me now. Please… pleasepleaseplease…

Jesse's father waited.

She finally croaked out the most inane thing she had ever said in her life. "What do you mean?"

"His car flipped. He wasn't wearing his seat belt." Mr. Ward's voice was laced with understanding as well as grief. He swallowed with audible difficulty. "They figure he lived for a while but nobody found him for several hours. It was a back road, very little traffic. He was dead when they found him."

"Oh my God. OhmiGod," she mumbled through the hand that had clamped over her mouth. Everything was running together. *Dead when they found him. Found him. Dead.* Dead.

Jesse's father kept talking. "We knew it had been hours because he had left your parents' place at about one p.m. He was found at four. I figure he was driving like a maniac. They told the police that he was looking for you. He actually forced his way into the house when they wouldn't tell him anything. Knowing his temper, he probably drove like a demon. The gravel was fresh and he must have lost control. He flipped and hit a tree."

Gradually, as Jesse's father spoke, an eerie calm had settled over Ronni. "They wouldn't tell him where I was?"

"That's right. *I* even approached them, thinking you would like to come to the funeral, but they swore up and down that they didn't have a clue where you were. I thought it sounded fishy but I got nowhere." He paused. "I'm really sorry. He told me about you about a month before he died. I knew you would have wanted to be there."

"Where is he?"

"River Meadows Cemetery. He was buried six days ago."

She swallowed but the lump continued to grow. It threatened to cut off her air supply but somehow she retained her ability to speak. "Thank you for trying, Mr. Ward. I appreciate everything you tried to do. I wish I could have been there too."

"I wish a lot of things."

"Was he doing well in school?" The attempt at pleasant conversation sounded ludicrous above the sound of the blood rushing through her ears. But she felt the need to talk about him.

"Yes. He finished the year on the honor roll. He was really enjoying it. But he told me he missed you like hell." He paused. "His words."

"Thank you for that." She had to ask. She needed to know. "Mr. Ward…was he…uh…" She swallowed dryly. "Do you think he suffered?"

Jesse's father uttered a strangled sound as if he, himself, were in agony. "Christ! I should probably lie to you about that, but…" He sighed in resignation, the weariness in his voice seeping out through the phone lines. "They told me later that his pelvis was crushed. Apparently that alone is extremely painful but he had a lot of other internal injuries as well. Even if he had made it, it would have been a hard road. But it wasn't those injuries that killed him. A shard of metal had nicked his carotid artery. It wasn't a large cut but it was enough. Essentially, he bled to death. It probably took a couple of hours before…"

"I see." Ronni blinked furiously. She had a horrible image of them pulling Jesse's lifeless body from the twisted, red wreckage. Red car. Red blood. Jesse's blood. She closed her eyes and burned the image on her retinas as if that could help make it real.

"He would have turned twenty-one two days ago. Did you know that?"

She struggled for the words. "No, I didn't. We never talked about birthdays."

"He was planning on a big party. He was gonna drag you there by your hair if necessary."

Ronni felt a smile but it didn't make it to her lips. At that moment she doubted she'd ever smile again. Then the silence stretched out and she felt awkward. "I should go."

"Stop in any time. I'd like to meet you and I think he'd like you to have some of his tapes."

"Yes, I'd like that. Very much."

Another awkward silence followed. He finally offered, "Goodbye."

He waited politely for the expected response but instead she heard herself blurt out, "Mr. Ward?"

"Yes?" At that moment she felt as if she had known this man her entire life.

"I loved him. I loved him very much. More than I can say." She closed her eyes and saw Jesse smiling at her, saw the twinkle in his eyes, felt the warmth of his love. He couldn't be gone. How could she never see him again? "I just needed for you to know."

"So did I, Ronni." She heard a hitch in his breathing. "So did I."

They bid farewell and Ronni gently set the phone back in its cradle. Her hand rested there for a long time. She pictured Jesse as she had seen him that first day—so cocky, leaning against the front of his pride and joy, teasing her with his eyes. Those beautiful blue eyes.

A voice reached her from the kitchen. "I heard you say goodbye. Was he there? Am I gonna meet this hunk?"

Rachel Erb, Ronni's landlady, was a warm, kindly woman. She and Ronni had hit it off instantly and Ronni had shared her story. The ample woman with the flowered apron walked into the living room and gazed at Ronni's still form, seated on the wicker chair by the little phone table, her auburn tresses hanging loosely about her shoulders. She wore jeans and a tight little T-shirt, just like any carefree teenager, but Jesse would never see her like that. She had wanted him to.

Ronni hadn't yet spoken, or even moved. "Well?" said Rachel with a smile.

Ronni forced her gaze up to meet the other woman's eyes. She had caring, compassionate eyes. Despite being active in her church, and having a deep personal faith, she didn't judge or condemn. She had accepted Ronni, sins and all, and had done everything in her power to help Ronni adjust to her new world. This house embodied Rachel's easy, casual charm. How could Ronni say the words in this house that had quickly become a comforting oasis for her in a sea of the unknown? Saying the words would make it real. Making it real would shatter the oasis. No matter how safe she felt here, she would be truly alone. She blinked twice to ward off the tears that she knew would come no matter how hard she fought them. "He's dead." She instantly dissolved.

It only took a moment for her words to sink into Rachel's befuddled brain. "Oh, dear Lord." She kneeled in front of Ronni and Ronni latched onto her as if her life depended on it. Sobs tore through her body.

It was a very long time before Ronni's breathing calmed and she pulled away. Rachel rushed away for a box of much needed tissues. She led Ronni to the couch and they sat down side by side. Rachel draped an arm over Ronni's shoulders and with halting phrases, Ronni related what Jesse's father had told her.

Then she added some information of her own. "They lied to him. They killed him as surely as if they had held a gun to his head."

"What on earth are you talking about?"

"They knew where I was." She drew a shuddering breath as she wiped roughly at her eyes. "Well, I didn't give them an address but I gave them a phone number with explicit instructions that they were to give it to him if and when he showed up."

"Why would they do something like that?"

She shrugged and shook her head. "I don't know. I knew they were judgmental but that was pure evil."

"Come now, Ronni, they had no way of knowing what would happen."

"Maybe not, but I hold them responsible just the same." She drew her gaze slowly to Rachel's. "Or maybe I do have an idea. What if they were afraid that once we were together again he would change my mind about the baby? They think he's—" She corrected herself. "They thought he was evil incarnate; they wouldn't want to let their grandchild have anything to do with him."

"I don't know, Ronni. Evil? That's awfully far-fetched."

"So is Jesse bleeding to death all alone in a ditch somewhere!" That brought on a new wave of anguish. She covered her face with her hands, and tried to hold just a little bit of herself together. She felt like she was coming apart at the seams. She had tried to fool herself, tell herself that she could make it without him. What if he had changed his mind about her? What if he didn't come back? But it was a feeble defense mechanism. And now she knew that he *hadn't* changed his mind. He had come back looking for her. Now she admitted to herself that everything had hinged on his return. There was nowhere to go from here. "Oh God, Rachel. What will I do? How will I ever get past this?"

"It'll take a long time, sweetheart, but it'll heal. I know it doesn't seem possible right now. But it will."

Ronni disagreed. This kind of wound could never heal completely. In fact she didn't want it to. She intended to harbor it, cultivate it, nurse it. She intended to hate her family, and blame them for Jesse's torturous demise until her dying breath. That was the least she owed him. Maybe she was as much to blame as anyone. That thought hurt more than a dagger in her breast.

She stood. "I'm going to my room for a while."

"Of course. Take all the time you need. Kent and I will drive you out to the cemetery whenever you like."

Ronni nodded and walked out.

There was a phone number she needed to find. There was something she needed to do first and then she would lie in bed and cry herself to sleep. She knew she could look forward to that for months. She had thought the tears were at an end when she had finally come to terms with separating from her baby. It had been a week of solid tears. It had been hell but it had been for the good of that beautiful little girl that she had never held. That anguish was starting to abate and so were the tears. But now she knew that it had only been a prelude. The tide on her own private ocean of grief had been at an ebb but now forces beyond her control were drawing in the tide. That ocean was gradually going to fill to the brim.

The tears had just barely gotten started.

Part Two: The Wounded Body

Bosnia, October, 1996

ഗ

Chapter Ten

Enormous and imposing, a tank on wheels, the mud-spattered Grizzly crept across the Yugoslavian landscape. Inside, the tiny compartment stank of diesel fumes and old cordite, but the occupants neither noticed nor cared. Bored to the breaking point, the four men sat and sweated and hoped for something—anything—to break the tedium of four hours of monotonous patrol duty. They were about to get their wish.

"I think I got something!"

Captain Wolf Mercredi looked up from the map he'd been poring over. "Well?" he barked. "Spill it, Neilsen."

Private Arnie Neilsen, his eyes glued to his binoculars, shouted above the roar of the engine. "On the horizon. A couple of trucks and jeeps and…"

"And?"

"And a personnel carrier."

"Full?"

"How the hell should I know?"

The inside of the Grizzly fell silent. Despite the drone of the engine and the labored breathing of four anxious men, there was the sense inside the vehicle that even the soft ping of a shell casing hitting the floor would have echoed like a rifle shot.

Neilsen felt it. He lowered the binoculars and looked at Wolf, immediately wilting under his commander's incisive stare. It was the kind of stare that pierced through Kevlar and cloth, through flesh and bone, directly to the soul.

Neilsen knew that stare well and after barely a moment's hesitation averted his eyes. "Uh…" He placed the binoculars to his eyes again. "It seems to be riding a little low, so…my guess is it's occupied."

"Dammit!" cursed Wolf, his subordinate's lapse already forgotten. He had other things to worry about.

Although the last two months had been quiet, Wolf had known it couldn't last. Since the NATO Stabilization Forces, or SFOR, had taken over from the UN Peacekeepers, the fighting had gradually declined. This owed, in no small part, to the military crackdown on all aggressions initiated by any of the three main factions in the former Yugoslavia. The Peacekeepers had been subject to ridiculous restrictions, barely able to defend themselves, let alone intervene in the local fighting or stop the atrocities. But things had changed.

Now, any military aggression, movement of arms or violent demonstrations of any kind were not tolerated. When SFOR troops showed up, they either lay down and surrendered their weapons or they were cannon fodder. Serbs, Croatians and Muslims were treated equally and none were immune to SFOR authority. Or their weapons.

That was what these patrols were all about. Wolf commanded a unit of thirty men, the unit being split into three patrols of ten men each. The rotating patrols consisted of three Grizzlies with three or four men in each, with each patrol taking its turn on recon missions into the countryside looking for any local troops who dared to defy the NATO directives for peace.

Wolf didn't personally command each mission but he tried to get out regularly to maintain a good rapport with his men and a feel for the climate of the war.

"Okay," shouted Wolf. "Radio over to Riley." Sergeant Riley Spencer was his second-in-command and led this patrol when Wolf was otherwise occupied. "Let's head 'em off at the pass." He grinned to himself. He had always wanted to say that.

Lyons floored the accelerator while Corporal Jackson radioed their intentions, and the location of the convoy they planned to intercept—just in case the look-out on the other Grizzly hadn't been as vigilant as Neilsen.

Neilsen was a screwup. He could barely fire his rifle, had a problem with authority and had trouble finding his nose with his finger but he had eyes like a hawk and Wolf capitalized on that. Wolf had been the only one to command Neilsen who could manage to keep him in line and realize any potential.

Wolf approached each of his men differently. He gauged their strengths and weaknesses, tapped into key personality traits and tempered hard-nosed authority with loyalty and understanding. Some of his superiors believed he had always been destined for command,

and if he played his cards right he would go far. The trouble was Wolf had gone as far as he wanted. Maybe too far.

Neilsen informed him that they were within a hundred meters of the convoy.

"Are they slowing down?" asked Wolf.

"Nope. Actually, they're veering away." Neilsen tossed Wolf a gap-toothed grin. "I think they're making a run for it."

Wolf sighed with profound regret. "They don't know me very well, do they?" He focused on Jackson. "Call in the birds, just in case." Then to the gunner, "Fire one, Lyons."

They were all thankful for their earplugs when the report from the cannon echoed through the interior of the vehicle.

"That got their attention," said Neilsen as he chawed on his wad of gum. They had hit about fifty feet in front of the lead vehicle and Riley's cannon had gone off mere seconds later, to make sure their intent was clear.

"Did they stop?"

"Uh…yup…but…ah shit!"

"What?"

"They're disembarking and looking mighty mean."

"Well, we'll just have to get meaner." He addressed Jackson. "Make sure the choppers are on their way. Lyons, fire off another round and aim for the lead vehicle," he paused. "Don't miss. Everybody else, load up." That meant rifles and rocket launchers as per pre-arranged assignments.

They emerged out the top of the Grizzly, weapons locked and loaded. They watched as one more round from the cannon flattened the lead jeep, long devoid of occupants. A couple of strategically aimed rockets from the four launchers and the arrival of the Hueys all combined to convince the Serbs in their sights that they meant business.

The Serbs had barely gotten off a round of ammunition from their AK-47s before dropping their weapons and, to Wolf's amazement, there had been no casualties. Now that SFOR troops were becoming more well-known as a force to be reckoned with, resistance and weapons-fire was becoming rare. Even so, however, it still astounded him that there could be such a confrontation without bloodshed.

Wolf tamped down the images that such thoughts brought to mind. There had been enough bloodshed on this soil to last for generations. Dead bodies and decay had contaminated the water supplies, mass graves were commonplace, and it was hard to find a child under the age of ten who hadn't had his life touched by the violent death of a loved one. Wolf had no desire to add to the body count.

Wolf's men held the Serbs at bay while their vehicles were inspected. From a distance he saw Riley climb out of the last truck in the line. The wind tussled Riley's hair as he locked eyes with Wolf and tossed him an impenitent wink. Wolf shook his head and sighed. The damn fool never wore his helmet, no matter how much Wolf ordered or nagged.

Riley held up a grenade and motioned toward the truck. Apparently it was loaded with them. The damn things were as common here as apples—even more so, since fresh fruit was almost unheard of since the war had started.

Wolf assigned a man to drive the confiscated munitions truck back to base and the Serbs, minus their weapons, were allowed to continue on their way. Unlike many of their Slavic counterparts, SFOR troops didn't follow the practice of lining up their enemies and exterminating them.

Although sometimes, it was tempting.

* * * * *

"Want some, Cap?"

"No thanks, Neilsen. Never touch the stuff."

"Huh? Whiskey or booze in general."

"Shut up, kid. Go to sleep."

Neilsen tipped up his flask for one final swig before quietly rolling over in his bunk. He knew better than to push his luck by trying to initiate more conversation with his CO. Lights out was one camp rule that Wolf enforced rigorously. Not all the rules, however, met with Wolf's favor.

Due to some embarrassing incidents in recent years, the bigwigs who parked their butts in the cushy seats of Canadian Parliament had taken steps to ensure that the spotless reputation of the Canadian military would never again be sullied by drunken antics or other inappropriate behavior. Canadian troops were limited to two beers a day, regardless of circumstances. Apparently it never crossed their minds that exposure to incessant cannon fire, land mine blasts, bitter cold and encountering the occasional maimed toddler might cause some stress in the typical GI, and that maybe a slug or two of whiskey might help to ward off the cold and the insanity of this godforsaken wasteland.

Captain Mercredi bent the rules when he thought they were unreasonable. And considering what they were dealing with and the conditions they were living under, he deemed that rule unreasonable.

Here in their barracks, where their unit had some privacy, Wolf allowed the flasks. At lights out, a shot or two from a hidden stash of whiskey or vodka seemed like a reasonable way to warm a homesick heart.

He had lied to his subordinate. He had drunk many a red-faced officer under the table but he wanted to preserve the illusion that he was a notch above. He believed it necessary to preserve respect and authority, especially considering the fact that he flagrantly flouted the rules occasionally.

"Uh…Cap?" Neilsen's whisper startled him.

"What is it? I thought I told you to go to sleep." Sometimes Wolf felt like he was in charge of a herd of rowdy twelve-year-olds. Sometimes just getting them to bed on time was a challenge. *Christ*!

"I…uh…" Neilsen stuttered.

Wolf reined in his temper and prompted, "Spill it. I'm listening."

"I just wanted to thank you for taking care of that shit with the colonel."

Pleasant surprise softened Wolf's tone. "You don't have to thank me, kid. That's my job. Just keep doing yours and we're square. Got it?"

"Yes, sir. Got it, sir." Neilsen rolled over once again and was soon snoring softly.

Safely hidden by the shroud of darkness Wolf allowed himself to smile at Neilsen's little show of gratitude. For Neilsen, it wasn't so little.

The day before he had run an errand for the man in charge of their two-hundred man division on the base. Wolf's immediate superior, Colonel Wilker, had asked Neilsen to deliver an urgent package to a neighboring base. Unfortunately, Neilsen had run over some broken glass, gotten a flat tire and had considerable difficulty changing it because the jeep had been equipped with the wrong lug wrench.

Neilsen had delivered the package two hours late and upon his return had felt the sting of Wilker's rage.

Already uncertain and fragile, Neilsen's self-image hardly needed the abuse, so Wolf had intervened. Neilsen had faded into the background while Wolf and the Colonel had waged their usual battle of wills. Wolf never yelled, never uttered threats and certainly never spoke inappropriately, but somehow, mysteriously yet consistently, he always ended up leaving his colonel a little more confused and a little less pompous and arrogant than he had found him. Invariably the colonel came around to Wolf's way of thinking and Wolf came out on top. And invariably that elevated him in the eyes of his men.

Wilker loved power for power's sake alone. He often targeted men for disciplinary action on the basis of personal grudges and bogus charges. To the General in charge of the base he was Col. Kiss-Your-Ass Wilker. But to the men he was merely *Asshole*. And it was a generally accepted fact that, despite the chain of command, he was intimidated by Captain Wolf Mercredi.

Wolf rolled over and pulled his blanket over his shoulders. In the distance he heard the rapid report of automatic weapons fire and knew sleep wasn't going to come easily tonight.

But maybe it wasn't just the gunfire that was getting to him. Maybe it was the futility of the whole damn war. He knew in much of the world, the situation was perceived as a simple good guy-bad guy scenario. The Serbs were the villains, responsible for the atrocities chalked up to ethnic cleansing and ancient hatred. But after living the conflict for close to eighteen months he saw things differently. Each faction bore responsibility for the atrocities. There were no good guys. There were no bad guys. Just a country full of intelligent, committed people who were all as stubborn as mules and hung onto grudges for generations. Some as long as eight hundred years.

He kept telling himself that their presence was making a difference. The fighting *had* waned in the last two years and some semblance of order had been restored. But then he heard the machine guns again and cursed silently because the SFOR units couldn't be everywhere at once.

Who was being shot at now?

Perhaps the Kosovo Liberation Army had finished their business with a group of women in some abandoned house and had decided to cover their tracks before Amnesty International got wind of their atrocities. Wolf had seen the bodies of too many women who had been used and thrown away like the wrapper from a cheap candy bar. Their rapists didn't always kill them afterwards but sometimes that wasn't doing them a favor in light of the views and stigmas surrounding the crime. The act brought shame not only to the victim, but to the victim's household and extended family. The rapist, on the other hand, rarely saw retribution.

Wolf shuddered at the vivid images that thought dragged back to the surface. He preferred to bury those images—deeply. No one had witnessed the events that haunted his dreams and threatened his sanity. He hoped that retirement would cure him of the cold sweats and vivid nightmares. Perhaps he hoped for too much.

More machine guns. The rounds rattled around inside his brain like so much shrapnel. Restless and hoping for answers, he cast off his blanket, grabbed his coat and rifle and headed outside. He nodded to the sentry on duty and scanned the horizon but the moment he stepped outside the shooting stopped. With a sigh and a shake of his head, he shouldered his rifle and set out, his boots crunching on the cold gravel.

"Wolf? Is that you?" yelled Riley. When they were out of earshot of the rest of the company the friends tended to dispense with formality. Eighteen months of sharing hardships and witnessing horrors meant something. And it meant a hell of a lot more than salutes and chain of command.

"I was trying to find some peace and quiet..." grumbled Wolf. "By myself."

"Dreamer. You know that's nigh on impossible around here." Riley sauntered over to join his commander, leaning against the one remaining wall of some unidentified structure. The base had been built around the shells of several buildings, the largest of which had once been a school.

The base housed over fifteen hundred men, boasted two dining halls, a hospital and even a small movie theater along with the barracks, officers' quarters and unit headquarters. Some barracks had taken over gutted buildings, some men slept in portable, metal containers and some in tents. Only the command elite slept in comfort.

Riley slid a cigarette between his lips and popped out a lighter as he leaned his short, wiry frame against the wall. Riley's small stature was deceiving. He had a strength of will and a keen sense of humor that shone through his expressive blue eyes without remorse. His light brown hair defied all efforts to comb it into a regulation style but the disheveled mop merely added to his carefully honed image of an unrepentant shit-disturber.

Riley took a long pull on his Player's Light. He exhaled slowly, blowing a smoke ring toward the stars as that shit-disturber grin made a covert appearance.

"Nope. Can't let you have too much time to yourself. You are the alpha male, you know. Can't shirk your responsibilities." Riley loved to tease Wolf about his name.

"If I'm the alpha male, what does that make you, Riley? An ass sniffer?"

"Depends whose ass we're talking about."

Wolf stifled a chuckle.

"You ever gonna tell me how you got such a quirky name?"

"Nothing to tell."

The set of Riley's mouth made it clear he didn't believe him. "Uh-huh. You know the rumor, don't you?"

"Nope. What's that?" Wolf propped his back against a rickety beam and set his rifle on the ground.

"What with the name and where you grew up and your coloring and everything, the guys think you're at least half Inuit."

"I'm dark, Riley. The Yukon Inuit are pale with almond-shaped eyes. I look more like a Plains Indian. Iroquois or Blackfoot."

"So you admit it. You *are* Indian."

"I admit nothing."

Riley made a sound of disgust and Wolf smiled into the darkness. It was common for people to mistake his high cheekbones, large black eyes and olive-toned skin for a connection to a Canadian Inuit heritage but it had never been quite so much fun.

"Jesus. You got some thing about keeping people guessing, or what?"

"Maybe."

"You gonna keep me guessing about when you're going home?"

"No guesswork there, Riley. Couple more months and my tour is done. What about you? You've got a wife at home and a baby on the way. I know you're anxious to get back to them."

"Anxious to get home and see them, sure. Not anxious to quit altogether and throw away a full military pension at the age of forty. You're only a few years short, Wolf. Why would—"

"I've got my reasons." He slid Riley a hard look that left no room for discussion. "And they're mine alone. Don't ask me again."

Riley averted his eyes, dropped his cigarette and ground it into the dirt with his heel. They'd been having this discussion a little too frequently lately to suit Wolf and he hated to take that kind of tone with his friend, but this was one area of his life that was *not* open to discussion.

Riley cleared his throat. "You coming in then? Tomorrow's another day. Gotta keep the locals from killing each other, you know. It's a dirty job… Well, you know the rest." He winked and the tension of a moment before evaporated.

"All too well." Wolf watched the cloud of his breath dissipate into the night. "You go ahead, I still wanna catch a few seconds of solitude."

"Dreamer." But Riley took heed of the hint and headed back into the barracks.

Wolf pulled his jacket more tightly about him, a meager defense against the nip of frost.

Despite the cold he considered going for a stroll. He suspected sleep would elude him, despite the cozy comfort of his regulation bunk and his regulation blanket and his regulation pillow. Maybe a brisk walk would warm his blood and clear his head.

He grabbed his gun and moved on, waving to the sentry on duty as he passed through the gate. Sand bags and razor wire marked the perimeter of the base. The only people allowed in or out were the base personnel, both military, and the few local civilians who had been hired as cooks or for other domestic duties.

He strode toward the Sarajevo city limits and could just make out the tattered skyline in the silvery starlight.

Sarajevo had once been an exquisite, thriving city. Spires and arches and the bell towers of magnificent cathedrals had once graced the skyline, their grandeur outshone only by the majestic mountain peaks that surrounded the city.

The population of the cosmopolitan city had reveled in its unique and eclectic mix of cultures. In all of Yugoslavia, only Sarajevo claimed the peaceful harmony of Serbs, Croats and Muslims living together. The cultures had resided side by side as friendly neighbors for as much as twenty years. But when war broke out Sarajevo's strength had become its greatest weakness. Neighbors had shot at each other across alleys and streets, laying waste to the homes and yards where their offspring had played together as children.

Now Sarajevo was a shell, an empty husk of a city. Streets once lined with bustling shops and markets were now littered with shrapnel and casings. The laughter of children and the friendly gossip of old men and busy mothers had dwindled down to a cold, empty silence.

He continued, breathing deeply the familiar scent of wood smoke. The war had used up fuel supplies, leaving families to scrounge for their own sources of energy. Wood was used for virtually all cooking and heating and the scent of smoke saturated the fabrics, clothes and hair of every man, woman and child who lived here. Wolf wondered absently if it had soaked directly into his skin.

He stopped and cocked his head, certain he had heard something. He listened and…there it was again. A faint whimper followed by silence.

This area of the city, once a busy market and business district, had retained very few of its former charms. Few buildings had all four walls intact and now the only ones conducting business here were the rats.

Wolf stood…still as death. He'd had a lot of experience with *still as death* in the last eighteen months.

The seconds ticked by but, at last, he heard it again and was able to narrow down its source. It came from a building just to his left. It was one of the more intact ones on this block but, even so, a gaping hole marred the west wall. It was just large enough for him to squeeze his six-foot-one-inch frame through. As silent as a cat, he stole up to the opening and peered inside. A dim light glimmered in the far corner. It silhouetted a collection of tattered furniture that had been arranged in a protective circle. He had a vague impression of wagons pulled in a circle and Indians whooping wildly as they circled the doomed settlers.

He shook his head and suppressed a private grin. He'd been hanging around Riley too much.

He stepped through the ragged opening and his boot tapped softly on the bare concrete floor. He had barely drawn a breath before the unknown occupant doused the light and plunged him into complete blackness. He froze, half expecting to hear a bullet whiz past his head but all he heard was the whisper of the wind through the walls.

His gut tightened but he forced himself on regardless. Fear was natural and necessary and he had learned to live with it, learned to use it. It made him cautious and kept him focused at times when he had no choice but to push forward. This was one of those times. Perhaps it was foolish and perhaps it was sentimental but the sound of that whimpering haunted him. And it would continue to haunt him unless he did something about it.

He pulled out his flashlight and leveled the rifle. "SFOR. Identify yourself," he said in his best Yugoslavian.

Silence. In the brief moment before the light was extinguished he had committed the layout of the room to memory and had no intention of turning on his flashlight. The last thing you wanted in a potentially hostile situation was to announce your position with a cheerful little light bulb. He continued forward slowly in the general direction of the little grouping of furniture. He repeated his request but received no response.

He stumbled over something in his path and heard the crack of a rifle shot. He dropped like a rock, his finger wrapped around the trigger. His nerves relaxed marginally when he heard a nervous murmur, "Oh damn. Oh damn," followed by a burst of quiet sobs. The tension drained away, leaving only concern. He was obviously dealing with a woman but her reaction to his approach puzzled him. Usually his reception by the females in the area was significantly warmer than this. The local forces never recruited women, so invariably the women were the victims, grateful for any intervention by international forces. So why had she shot at him?

He took a chance and flicked on his flashlight in a show of good faith. "Hello?" he said in the gentlest tone he could coax from his raspy voice box. "Ma'am, I'm from NATO. There's no need to be afraid. I'm here to help."

The sobs were stifled briefly and the light in the corner flicked on again. "American?" was all she said. It was little more than a whisper.

Wolf stood slowly, his rifle still at the ready. "No, Canadian." The Canadian label could still open a few doors that were closed to some other, less well regarded nationalities. He stepped forward far enough to see over the small couch that separated them. He made out a frail figure huddled in the corner. He couldn't see a weapon. In fact she hardly looked strong enough to lift one. She just gazed up at him with a hunted look in her eyes that tore at his heart. Wolf had never felt his name so acutely, had never felt so much the predator.

He was afraid to breathe too hard for fear she might whither from the heat of his breath.

He took a step forward, cautiously, trying to look as non-threatening as possible. No small feat for a two-hundred-pound officer with an automatic rifle over his shoulder. She remained still, only her eyes moved—following him. She had trusted enough in the SFOR title to turn on her light but fear and distrust lingered in her eyes. Wolf suspected that she had good reason to be wary.

Huge dark eyes and full lips were set in a face that was so thin as to be almost gaunt. The wide, frightened eyes reminded Wolf of a fawn caught in the sights of a prowling cougar. Her clothes hung on her in shreds and her dark brown hair fell limply about her shoulders. Her features suggested Croatian heritage and what was left of her western style clothing confirmed it. The Serbs and Muslims held to rigid custom, which dictated that the women wear the scarves and conservative dress which distinguished them, and reminded them of their place in the order of things.

With two more steps he breached her sanctuary and entered the circle of furniture. He scanned the area, confirmed that she was alone. Then he saw the source of the *shot* that had echoed through the empty chamber. Shards of glass from a shattered light bulb lay on the floor. She must have knocked it down as she retreated after flicking off the light.

He knelt down a few feet in front of her and tried to look sympathetic. "Are you injured?" he asked, again in his best Yugoslavian.

"I speak English," she said, again so softly that he could barely hear her. He could hardly discern an accent. If anything, she sounded more British than Slavic.

"Are you a national?"

She nodded. "Educated in London."

Well, that explained that.

"Injured?" he asked again.

She shook her head but her eyes immediately swelled with tears. *Dammit.* She had probably been raped. It was like an epidemic, all part of the design to completely undermine morale and the very fabric of the culture. It didn't hurt that the troops got a few kicks along the way, often as a reward or perk in the face of incredibly harsh conditions.

"Were you raped?"

She shook her head again, more vehemently this time. But that could be meaningless. Some women still viewed their victimization as somehow being their own fault and a reflection on their entire family, and would deny it with their dying breath. But this woman was educated internationally. Hopefully she didn't hold to such outdated conventions. Maybe she was telling the truth. He prayed she was.

"I should get you to a shelter. You have no blanket and it'll be getting cold tonight. There's no heat in this place." There was nothing like stating the obvious to fill in awkward verbal space. He held out his hand as he stood.

"No, I can't." Her voice gained in strength.

Wolf cocked his head in puzzled concern. "Why not? Surely this can't be home." He made a sweeping gesture around the gutted structure.

"You don't understand. I can't go anywhere until I find my baby."

Those few softly spoken words penetrated his gut as sharply as a sniper's bullet. He had grown up with a loving family who was always *there*. The constant, in-your-face reminders of families who were torn apart and destroyed so violently never failed to touch him.

He studied her and tried to remain objective. Okay, so she had lost a child. Very likely she had also lost a husband. Had the child been kidnapped? Unlikely. What would Serbian or Muslim troops or police want with a child or, as she suggested, an infant? The other two, more likely possibilities were that she had been separated from her baby, and another family had taken it in. Or, and unfortunately this was the most likely of the two, the infant had been killed in a raid or as an innocent victim of crossfire. No matter what the situation, the chances of reuniting her with her infant were remote, at best.

But he decided on compassionate diplomacy. "Well, you can't find her tonight." Why did he assume it was a girl? "Why don't you come with me? I know of a Croatian family in a safe part of town that would take you in for the night."

She shook her head. "No." Then she hesitated as uncertainty flickered in her eyes. "I wouldn't be safe there."

Wolf arched his eyebrows. "And you're safe *here*?"

"At least here—" She clamped her mouth shut, reconsidering what she was about to say. "I'll be fine."

Wolf blew out a breath and gazed at her through the warm mist. He couldn't stay here and he couldn't leave her. His conscience would gnaw at him all night.

The barracks weren't exactly cozy but they *were* warm. "Why don't you come back to our barracks? The base isn't far and you'll be safe there. I'll put you up on a cot with a nice warm blanket and maybe we can find a way to help you tomorrow." Strictly speaking this went against regulations but he knew the sentry would look the other way for him. Bill was one of his own.

She stared at him, still unmoving.

He unzipped his jacket and shrugged it off. Chivalry was not dead. "Here, you can wear this. It's a bit of a walk."

Nothing.

"Look, I can't make you come." Actually he could. She obviously weighed little more than a child herself. He could pick her up and carry her with little more effort than he carried his standard issue backpack. Even kicking and screaming she would hardly be a challenge. But that wasn't his style. "But you're a smart woman. Surely you see that it's pointless to stay here. And if you come along maybe we can help you. You shouldn't be out in this area of town alone and unarmed."

In response she reached behind her back and pulled out an enormous pistol. It was difficult to see in the dim light but he thought it was a .44 Magnum. His hand reflexively flew to the butt of his rifle but he was soon reassured that she hadn't intended to threaten him. It lay across her outstretched palms, a dull, dark reminder that here women toted weapons as readily as lipstick. He lifted his gaze to her face.

Her lips twitched into a smile. "I *am* armed."

"Yeah, no kidding. I'm surprised you can lift that thing."

"I can lift it. And I can shoot it. My father taught me when the war started."

"Smart man."

Her face fell. "Not smart enough."

Shit! He had stumbled into that one. But he decided to ignore the implications of those three words and move on. "So, will you come with me?"

She unfurled from her crouched position and stuffed the gun into a tattered leather knapsack at her feet. "Yes, thank you. You're very convincing." She smiled sheepishly. "And very kind. It would be nice to be warm again." After stuffing the remainder of her few meager belongings into the knapsack, she accepted the jacket graciously and slipped her arms in the sleeves. It hung almost to her knees, making her look like a five-year-old playing dress up with one of Daddy's sport jackets. She couldn't have been more than five-foot-one, small for a Croatian, and Wolf would have guessed her weight at ninety or ninety-five pounds.

He led her out of the hole in the wall and they began to walk back the way he had come. Wolf was thankful that the distant machine gun fire had finally ceased, leaving behind a hopeful silence. Only the steady crunch of their boots echoed through the cluttered streets.

"You said you were Canadian?" she asked, eyes forward, shoulders rigid.

"Yep. Born and raised in the Yukon. Ever hear of it?"

"Of course. I'm not ignorant like our Serbian neighbors." Bitterness and rancor laced her voice. It stood out like a sour note in a symphony but he couldn't say that it surprised him.

"Right. Sorry. In my experience, internationally educated women are a rarity here. How did you manage it?"

"My father was very wealthy and successful. He only had daughters—three of us. So he insisted that we all be properly educated. He didn't want us to have to rely on the right marriage to guarantee our future. He wanted us to be independent and self-sufficient."

"Like teaching you how to shoot."

She nodded.

"He sounds like a wise and dedicated father." She was silent and when he glanced over at her he saw a quick movement as her hand brushed across her cheek. So he continued, "My father was pretty great too. Both he and my mom helped us with our home schooling. It was me and my sister but he never treated us any different. He took us both fishing and taught us how to hunt. In the Yukon that's pretty much a foregone conclusion. Food up there is so expensive, it's in your best interest to supplement your freezer with your own meat. I used to think I never wanted to taste another morsel of moose or rabbit, but after spending a year and a half here, what I wouldn't give for a serving of hasenpfeffer." After a while the wild taste of game became addictive. It became a part of you—sank into your soul as surely as the fresh mountain breezes and pristine lakes.

"Doesn't your government provide you with decent rations?"

"Oh, they're okay and there's a pretty good variety, but it tends to be bland, and we don't tend to see a lot of juicy steaks." His mouth watered at the thought. But then he wondered if it was the steak or the thought of home that stimulated his salivary glands.

"I'm afraid you won't get a lot of sympathy here, Mr…"

"Mercredi. Captain Wolf Mercredi."

"Captain Mercredi. I have seen my people too close to starvation. I can't imagine complaining about the monotony of the food available when there are so many who have none."

Her words were clipped and her tone openly belligerent, but Wolf took no offense. "You're absolutely right," he conceded softly. "I guess we Canadians are pretty spoiled. We enjoy one of the highest standards of living in the world and I'm afraid we get pretty used to it. That wasn't very sensitive and I'm sorry."

She was silent for a time.

"What's your name, by the way?"

"Lubica. Lubica Saric."

"Mmm." He would have liked to say that was a pretty name but he knew so little of the culture. And, honestly, the sound of it wasn't particularly appealing to him.

"Wolf is very unusual. I'm not that familiar with North American names but I've never heard anything like that."

"My mother saw a wolf the day she went into labor with me." Somewhere back on base he was sure Riley tossed on his bunk.

"Really? That's fascinating. What kind?"

"Arctic. It was white as snow. She almost missed it against the drifts in our backyard. I was born in January. It was just sitting there, staring at the house. My mother could swear it was looking directly at her through the kitchen window. She said she got a shiver when she met its eyes." He shrugged. "She thought maybe it meant something. Even up there it's a rarity to see a wolf, especially all alone like that."

"They're noble animals. I've seen pictures."

"I agree. It's too bad they've gotten such a bad rap over the centuries."

"Bad rap?" she asked, looking at him for the first time since they had set out on their walk.

He chuckled. "You know, they've been accused of being pure evil, of killing livestock and attacking people when that usually wasn't the case. They were often a convenient scapegoat for other problems. Not to mention getting all the scut work in fairy tales. The Big Bad Wolf always met a gruesome end. I figure he was just misunderstood." He tossed her a grin.

She smiled back, a trace of mischief glinting in her eyes. "Are you misunderstood, Captain?"

He shrugged and turned his attention to the road ahead of them. "Isn't everybody?"

A clatter in an alley stopped them in their tracks. Wolf had already leveled his weapon, but soon relaxed his grip when a medley of barks and growls echoed down the alley to their ears. Wild dogs. They were everywhere. When food became scarce the cherished family pets had been liberated to fend for themselves. They had blended into packs and now roamed the countryside in search of food and—a high-pitched yowl erupted but was abruptly snuffed out—cats. Only a scant few remained to prowl the streets in search of scraps and anorexic mice. Most of them had ended up as hairballs in the guts of German Shepherds and Labradors.

He shook his head with exaggerated mournfulness. "There goes another one."

"You don't like animals?" she asked soberly.

"No, just cats. I can't stand cats. Sorry, if you're a cat lover."

"No. If there's one thing the last few years has taught me it's that animals are expendable. There are too many *humans* to worry about."

Wolf nodded approval. "I would have to agree." He kicked a tin can with his boot and it skittered across the street. "I wonder what those animal rights activists back home would think if they knew how the farmers around here clear their fields of mines." It was common practice to let a herd of cows loose on a field that was suspected of being mined. Once the cows had grazed for six weeks or so, the farmer could safely assume that the field had been cleared out. If a few cows ended up as hamburger, or minus a leg or two, it was of little concern. Better a cow than the farmer or a farmer's child. Three-legged animals of all kinds were common in Bosnia for that very reason.

She sighed heavily. "Yes, I got to know those groups all too well while I was in London. I would love to bring some of those people over here for a few months. Maybe they'd redefine their priorities."

"It has certainly made me reevaluate mine."

They had reached the base. He spoke briefly to the sentry, explaining the situation. The man on duty gave Lubica a quick once-over and the stupid grin on his face revealed his thoughts all too well. One quick glance at Wolf's stern expression, however, wiped away the smirk. Wolf wouldn't tolerate insubordination, spoken or otherwise.

Wolf led her to their barracks and pointed out his cot. "You take this," he whispered. "I'll get an extra blanket and flake out on the floor."

She grabbed his sleeve as he turned to go. "I don't want to put you out of your own bed."

"Believe me, Lubica, I've slept on lots worse. Don't worry about it." He disappeared as she sat down on the cot.

She was still sitting there, huddled inside his enormous coat, when he got back. "Do you really think you can help me?" she whispered quietly, gazing up at him with those fawn eyes.

"I don't know. Depending on the circumstances…maybe. But I have to tell you, my gut says finding a missing child in this mess is a long shot."

She hung her head. "I know."

He focused on arranging his blanket. He couldn't let himself get sucked into her grief. There was enough of it here to drown in—if you let yourself. "You get some sleep and we'll discuss it in the morning."

She finally shrugged out of his coat and lay down. She pulled the blanket up over her shoulders and allowed her head to sink into the pillow.

Wolf watched her in the darkness for a long time. How did people cope with this kind of horror? He had never had children but he could certainly imagine the kind of anguish she must be going through. And it was all too common in this country. It wasn't unusual for entire families to be wiped out, save one member. For a mother to lose husband and children, or a child to lose both parents and all siblings staggered the imagination.

Wolf had grown up in a tightly knit family. They had shared their hopes and their dreams alongside disappointments and laughter. They spent time together—both quality and quantity. It was fortunate that they got along, because they'd had little choice in the matter. Living in an isolated northern community definitely tended to lend itself to forming strong familial and community bonds. You had to rely on your family and neighbors because there wasn't the elaborate network of public services and community resources that were so readily available in larger centers.

The Yukon winters were rugged, harsh and cold—much like here. But unlike here, that landscape brought with it a feeling of peace and serenity, a feeling of being one with nature and in touch with your own spirit. Perhaps he didn't miss his home so much as the state of mind that went with it.

Lubica's breathing had fallen into a deep, regular rhythm. A vague sense of satisfaction accompanied the knowledge that she had finally succumbed to sleep. He didn't have a clue as to how to help her—not even where to start. But despite her frail appearance he got the distinct impression that she had the emotional strength of an ox, and a will to match. If anyone could survive this hell, and find a missing child, it would be her.

Chapter Eleven

"What do we have here?" slurred a heavily accented voice very close to Wolf's ear. He knew better than to move because he also felt the unforgiving pressure of cold metal against his cheek. He slowly cracked open his eyes.

It was just before dawn. The blackness in the barracks had given way to a dull gray, and the half-light lent an eerie hue to the butt-ugly mug hovering inches from Wolf's face. The ugliness of the face was exceeded only by the stench of his breath.

Serbian Police. It was obvious by the uniform—and the odor of stale whiskey.

How had he gotten past the sentry? Wolf cursed silently. He could usually rely on Bill Hipwell. But obviously Wolf's trust had been misplaced. Wolf would have his ass in a sling for this. He only hoped Hipwell's ass was still slingable.

The soldier-*cum*-cop prodded him with the gun. "Answer me, asshole." With that he grinned. Many of the locals took great pride in learning English swear words and using them ad nauseam. The offensive words were accentuated by the hideous smile. It was common for locals to lose teeth or even require dentures by the age of thirty or forty. Oral hygiene was a foreign concept to them. Even successful professional women who shaved their legs, applied makeup religiously and colored their hair, often had the teeth of an eighty-year-old.

"You've got one mean son of a bitch," growled Wolf. "I don't know how the hell you got in here but if you don't get outta my face and outta my barracks you're going to have a thousand very irate soldiers shoving their rifles up your ass."

His assailant laughed heartily and Wolf caught a glimpse of one of his cohorts standing behind him. Wolf suspected there were more located in strategic positions out of sight.

His assailant contained his mirth enough to speak. "You're either real brave or a real stupid son of a bitch." But he pulled the M84 automatic weapon away from Wolf's cheek and took a step back.

His assailant's casual attitude astounded Wolf. They were in the middle of a base that housed close to fifteen hundred armed soldiers. Surely this little escapade was insanity. Or maybe that was his answer. "Look, asshole, leave or one shout from me will bring a hundred men running."

The leader flashed him a grisly smile. "I don't think that would be wise." He indicated for Wolf to stand up and motioned to the area behind him.

Wolf slowly turned and saw his men gathered, huddled on the floor nearby, an assortment of weapons trained on their heads. But his attention was particularly riveted by the Glock semi-automatic .38 that hovered at Riley's temple. It was equipped with a very effective silencer.

Obviously gunfire would draw too much attention and they were holding Riley hostage to ensure Wolf's silence. But for what purpose?

Wolf's confusion was mounting. Such incidents were unheard of. The SFOR units weren't exactly immune to attack but usually the local forces afforded them a wide berth. Perhaps many of the natives resented them because of their interference in the war but their presence and firepower were generally respected and avoided. The purpose of such an ambush eluded him.

"What the hell is this about?" Wolf bellowed. "Remove the threat to my men and get the hell out of this unit." Suddenly something registered. The man holding the gun to Riley's head looked familiar. Wolf couldn't quite place him but he was sure he had seen that face before.

"Or what?" laughed the scarecrow. "You may call in the troops but by then you and all your men will be dead."

"And so will you," said Wolf evenly. "Surely you know the consequences for an unprovoked attack on NATO forces."

"Who said it was unprovoked?"

"What? Spit it out, you shithead. What's this all about?"

"You are harboring a criminal."

Wolf was incredulous. "What?" But then his thoughts turned to Lubica. She had momentarily been wiped from his mind by the threat to his men. But Lubica a criminal? That was ridiculous.

"One of my men saw you escorting a woman down the street last night. She was vaguely familiar to him, so he followed and was soon able to identify her. She is wanted for crimes against the state. You had better hand her over if you know what is good for you."

Wolf had no intention of turning her over. The threat was empty. But that raised a good question—where was she? When he had fallen asleep she was lying a mere three feet from him on his bed. He didn't want to hazard a glance at the bunk, which was behind him now. But if she was still there why hadn't they found her? And if she wasn't there…

He decided to stall with a little diplomacy. "Before we even discuss this you'll have to explain to me the nature of her crimes."

His assailant shoved the barrel of the weapon against his chest. "I do not have to explain nothing to you. You are trespassers, pure and simple. We should just blow the whole lot of you away for interfering in domestic business."

"But you won't because despite appearances even you aren't that stupid."

Wolf could see him gritting the few teeth that he possessed. Wolf knew he was just itching to pull the trigger but self-preservation was a powerful motivator.

Wolf continued, "Now why don't you tell me what she's done and then—maybe—we can talk."

"She is wanted for embezzlement and fraud and tax evasion, along with numerous other crimes against the government. So where is she?"

Wolf's confusion grew. These were certainly not crimes that the Serbian Police typically concerned themselves with. At least not to the extent of ambushing troops in search of the culprit. But he decided to play along. "I can see the reason for the manhunt. She obviously poses a mortal threat to society. But unfortunately she disappeared through the night. I have no idea where she is."

The next moment he was on the floor clutching at his side as blinding pain lanced through him. One of the men behind him had struck him with the butt of a rifle. He gasped for breath as he knelt on all fours. In the background he could hear the muted protests of his men. But then, above that, came the menacing whisper of the Toothless Wonder.

"You know, Captain, I do not believe you." He hovered over Wolf, breathing acrid ethanol-laced fumes into Wolf's already tortured lungs. "Maybe this would help persuade you of the seriousness of our intentions." He motioned with his head to the man holding the gun on Riley. Riley cast a confused glance at his friend.

Wolf had managed to regain his breath. "What the hell—" But his voice was drowned out by the muffled report of the weapon.

The breath rushed out of him and the floor dropped out from beneath him. But it was a reflexive reaction to what he had perceived to have happened. Riley still sat, pale and drawn, exactly where he had been. His eyes blinked furiously but he was unbloodied and very much alive.

In a singular, fluid motion, Wolf erupted to his feet and launched himself at their tormentor. He had his hands around the scrawny throat and had just gotten a decent grip when he found himself on the floor again, this time clutching at a gash on his head.

"Get out!" he croaked with more vehement certitude than he felt. It was true that with one spray of bullets this maniac could wipe out his entire unit. It would be suicide but that didn't appear to be a deterrent. "You have no authority here and if you continue this idiotic charade, there will be hell to pay. That woman is long gone and you're wasting your time, so unless you're planning on annihilating this entire unit and then digging your own grave, I suggest you get the hell out of my sight because we *can't help you!*"

That said, Wolf's energy was all but spent but he managed to keep up appearances and stare down his opponent with a dark, menacing glare that rivaled that of his namesake.

That toothless grin made another hideous appearance. "I'll say this for you, Captain, you got balls. We will go but if you are lying to us and you are harboring this criminal, rest assured there will be consequences." He paused in thought and Wolf swore he could hear long unused wheels, gummed up with alcohol, begin to turn in that petrified brain. Wolf knew what he was thinking. How could he and his men get out without repercussions? Then the light bulb flicked on.

The leader reached down and grabbed Wolf by his shirt. He dragged Wolf to his feet. "You will accompany us to the gates."

"Like hell I will."

Then Wolf felt the pistol with the silencer against his back. It threatened to gouge a hole right between his shoulder blades. "Oh, I think you will." The whisper was soft but menacing. But then he spoke more loudly, "And your men will remain silent, because if I see anything the least bit suspicious out there as we walk to the gate I won't hesitate to put a gaping hole in their commander." He paused and breathed in Wolf's face. "Is that clear?"

"Clear as a bell," said Riley.

"Shut up, Riley." Every muscle, every tendon, every fiber in Wolf's body screamed in protest. He had never taken well to threats and he had to fight the urge to tear his tormentor apart. But the danger to his men kept his reflexes in check.

The leader merely laughed and, with an arrogant swagger, led his men out of the building—a coat over the other man's arm, the gun at Wolf's back and the four men clustered about him, chatting casually as if they were old friends who had met at the commissary for a coffee.

Wolf gritted his teeth against fury the entire time, enduring the outrage in stoic silence. He felt the warm trickle of blood down the side of his face.

As they approached the gate his tormentor whispered to him, "When we get there and we let you go, I would advise you to keep your mouth shut until we reach our jeep just beyond the gates. I left one of my men outside with his sights trained on your sentry. One wrong move and he will pick him off and, I would guess, you would be next."

They reached the gate and Hipwell smiled and waved to them from his post. Wolf muttered curses under his breath but kept up the charade. Before they parted the leader whispered in his ear, "If you see her again you can tell her that we've got something of hers. All she has to do is march her bony little ass into our camp and she can claim it. But she better not wait too long. This thing has an expiry date. It won't be viable forever. Time is running out." With a wink and one last flash of his gruesome grin, he led his men out the gate.

Wolf stood stock-still and watched them walk away. He suspected the threat of a sniper was a bluff but he couldn't take that chance. When they had driven away he riveted his eyes on Hipwell, who returned his gaze with a stupid grin.

Hipwell tipped his hat back at a jaunty angle. "Ten more minutes and my shift's done."

Wolf glared at him.

Hipwell lost his grin. Then he started to sweat. "Uh…what's up, Cap?" He swallowed visibly under Wolf's continued scrutiny. Then he frowned. "You know you're bleeding?" The gash on the side of Wolf's head continued to drip

Wolf did nothing to stop it. He still didn't speak.

Hipwell tugged on his collar. "Something wrong?"

With a low growl, Wolf said, "Your shift's over *now*, Hipwell. Get the hell down from there, find your relief and meet me back at the barracks. We got something to talk about."

Hipwell's face was stricken as he climbed down from his sentry tower. He was obviously in shit up to his eyeballs and nobody liked to piss off Mercredi.

Wolf stalked back the way he had come and the moment he re-entered the barracks Riley and the rest of the men sprang to his side. Riley started barking instructions and soon someone was holding a clean rag to the gash on Wolf's head.

He tried to bat them away but everyone ignored him. "Will you guys leave me alone?"

"What the hell was that all about?" asked Riley, ignoring the scalding tone in Wolf's voice.

"The woman." Wolf looked up at Riley's confused expression. "The one that was asleep in my bunk." Before anyone could jump to the obvious conclusion, he added, "While I slept on the *floor*."

"Sorry, Cap. We didn't see any woman. We all woke up with guns to our heads. They woke everybody up real quiet and left you for last. They searched all the cots and every nook and cranny and didn't turn up anything. What woman are you talking about?"

"I found her—" But he didn't need to continue because a moment later everyone's heads swiveled toward a muffled groan coming from beneath Wolf's bunk.

The lot of them bolted to the bunk and pulled the big duffel bag out from beneath. Riley pulled open the strings at the top and, lo and behold, a dark head of hair peeked out at them from inside the canvas. She straightened slowly, gradually uncoiling herself from the fetal position she had been maintaining inside the bag.

The men helped her out of the bag until she stood, drenched with sweat and breathing heavily, beside Wolf's bed.

Wolf had remained silent, watching the activities from a few feet away. She finally met his gaze and visibly flinched.

He took two huge strides and grabbed her shoulders in a vice-like grip, his face mere inches from hers. "How dare you jeopardize my men with your little games!"

She shook her head and was visibly fighting tears.

Wolf was unmoved. Nobody fucked with him and nobody endangered his men. Above all he expected honesty and directness from everyone he dealt with. And that included homeless waifs with tearful eyes and a tragic past. "You must have known they were looking for you. I'm not saying I wouldn't have helped but I deserved a warning. They came *that* close," he held up his thumb and forefinger, a hair's breadth apart, "to killing Riley. And I took a beating for you. I think we deserved to know what the hell we were getting into."

The tears overflowed and coursed down her cheeks.

He heard Riley in the background, "Hey, Wolf, cut her some slack."

"Shut up, Riley!"

He shook her gently. "Get over the crying shit and answer me."

"Th-they killed my father," she stuttered.

"Tell me something I don't know. Why did they kill him? Obviously he wasn't the victim of a random raid."

"He was a very wealthy and very influential man in the Croatian community." Her voice had gained intensity but suddenly she stopped.

Wolf waited.

She blinked once, squared her shoulders, threw back her head and met his accusing gaze squarely. "Years ago he was a journalist, and later moved into management at a local newspaper. He eventually bought the paper. He had contacts throughout the government and was very vocal against the atrocities that the Serbian and Muslim forces were perpetuating. He even pointed the finger at his fellow Croatians occasionally. He was a man of honor who hated what the war was doing to his country.

"He used the paper and his influence to work toward getting many of the crimes investigated and eventually prosecuted. They hated him because he was successful and because he was a vital force in the fight against their campaign of terrorism and brutality. Branko Saric was assassinated while he slept." Unwelcome tears shimmered in her eyes again. Wolf's gaze softened but he didn't drop his hands from her shoulders. "They also killed one of my sisters who was sleeping down the hall. My other sister and I had gone to visit family unexpectedly."

"And you've been running ever since?"

She nodded.

"I still don't get it. You're father was the threat. Why all this trouble to eliminate you as well?"

"They're afraid one of us will take up where he left off. We're all just as educated and strong-willed as our father; we loved him and what he stood for. They know that. They don't want to take the chance. But of course, there is also revenge. They won't rest until everything that my father loved is in ashes."

"Where's your other sister?"

"I had gone looking for supplies and she was killed while trying to defend my daughter from those barbarians. They took my daughter to try and lure me into their camp. That's why she's still alive. She's the bait to draw me in."

Wolf let go of her and sat down heavily on the bunk. "Christ!" He took a moment to rub at his temple where a dull throbbing had taken up residence. He didn't bother to ask about a husband. He was obviously not in the picture. Either she wasn't married or he had been killed as well.

So it hadn't been random violence. Lubica's story involved social responsibility and activism. She and her family had tried to make a difference, had tried to make things better. Perhaps that didn't make her story any more tragic, or the thousand other stories like hers any less so, but it did tell him something about *her*. And he couldn't deny that it softened his judgment of her.

Hipwell walked in.

"You wanted to see me, sir?" The familiar *Cap* nickname had fallen by the wayside.

Wolf turned on him. His stance had relaxed while listening to Lubica but, at sight of Hipwell, hell's fury returned. He stood and spoke slowly. "Why did you let those bastards onto the base?"

"What?"

"Those four men who walked out a few minutes ago. You let them in. I wanna know why."

"They work here."

"What? Are you sure? Did you check IDs?"

Hipwell's eyes darted nervously around the room, seeking support, but all he found were hostile stares and eyes trained on the ceiling. "Well, I know the one guy real well. He's been a cook here for months. I just figured the other three were new."

Wolf dropped onto the bunk again. He closed his eyes and rubbed at his temples. He winced as he aggravated the gash that had been inflicted. He felt like a father with an errant child. "Go to your bunk, Hipwell. I'll deal with you later."

Hipwell skulked away with an uncertain glance at his commander.

Wolf turned back to Lubica. "It's a lost cause, you know. You'll never find her and both get out alive. I'm sorry to say it but it's the truth. You should just go into hiding until you can find a way to take up your father's cause again. Either that or get out of the country."

He looked up at her, and was startled to see a deadly stare that rivaled his own. Her eyes shot daggers into his. "You've obviously never been a parent, *Captain Mercredi.*" She virtually spat the words. "I'll get my daughter out of there or die trying. Would you do any less for one of your men?"

Wolf glanced at his ragtag band of charges who were watching the proceedings with undisguised fascination. Then he turned back and faced those brown eyes that blazed with maternal fervor. She was so thin he thought he could almost see through her but, knowing her now, frail was not a word he would use to describe her. Her thinness merely accentuated the noble cheekbones, fine chin and huge fawn eyes. He wondered what her hair looked like when she was scrubbed and clean. Now it was limp and matted but its deep chestnut color still managed to glimmer through. He shook his head trying to dispel these less than appropriate musings. "Yes, you're right."

She nodded with satisfaction. "I thank you for your hospitality, Captain, and I extend apologies for any inconvenience but I will be on my way."

She had barely taken two steps when Wolf's fingers snaked out and latched around her upper arm. He stopped her in her tracks and she looked up at him in surprise.

"Hold on there a minute, little lady." He'd definitely been watching too many old movies lately. "You go out there by yourself and you're sure to get yourself killed."

"I can't ask you to help me. I doubt this is within the mandate of the SFOR directive."

"'Course it is. An innocent child's life is being threatened. We're here to protect and preserve, and what better way to do that? But we're not rushing into anything. I need to know what I'm dealing with." He paused and couldn't deny he was pleased to see a smile twitching at the corners of her lips. "Got that?"

She nodded. "Yes, sir." A hint of shy gratitude replaced the fierceness in her eyes. "I don't know how I can thank you."

His face was grim. "You can start by telling me how you managed to lace up the strings on my duffel bag from the inside."

"Old family secret." She grinned.

"Uh-huh." He allowed himself to smile back. "All right. Let's eat some breakfast and then I want to know everything you know about these guys. It doesn't matter how insignificant. I want to know if they have hemorrhoids and, if so, how big. We don't make a move on them until we know *everything*."

Chapter Twelve

"How's the coffee?" asked Wolf through a cloud of caffeine-laced vapor.

Lubica sat across from him in the base commissary, her tiny hands wrapped around a steaming mug of coffee that she had yet to taste. She appeared to be making a production of savoring the aroma first.

"Wonderful," she breathed.

"You haven't even tasted it."

"It's hot and it smells good. So far it's wonderful." She raised it to her lips, blew across the creamy surface and finally took a sip, keeping her eyes closed as she savored and then swallowed slowly.

"I take it it's been a while." Wolf took a strange pleasure in sharing her little ritual.

She nodded. "I love good coffee. It's been weeks since I've had it."

"I can't quite see labeling this crude oil as *good coffee*."

She shrugged. "I guess I'm not quite so picky as I used to be." She repeated the ritual and another swallow made it to the hollow pit that she called a stomach.

"Captain Mercredi!" bellowed an abrasive voice from the other side of the room. The echo bounced off the high ceilings and tiled floors of the old school cafeteria.

Wolf rolled his eyes as the portly man with the bushy mustache and the bow-legged waddle approached. Tiny reptile eyes glanced from Wolf to Lubica and back again.

"Yes, Colonel Wilker?" asked Wolf, his words clipped.

"What the hell do you think you're doing?"

"Having breakfast, sir." Wolf glanced at his superior with a sigh and a look that communicated his complete boredom.

But Wilker was far too dense for such subtle signals. He turned to Lubica. "Who's this? And what's she doing in the camp? You know fraternization is strictly prohibited."

Wolf's gaze took on a new dimension. "Yes, sir. I'm perfectly aware of that. The question is…are you?"

Wilker froze, eyebrows arched, jaw slack. A muscle in his cheek twitched. His face was a study in confusion over the implications of those few words.

"Now, me," continued Wolf, "I wouldn't dream of undermining regulations. I'm by the book all the way." His tone was casual but his gaze was deadly. "I would never be one to rock the boat. I just look out for my men and do my job. I don't pay attention to what others may be doing around me." He set down his coffee and stirred it absently. "If I were to see or hear about something that wasn't completely appropriate, well, I would just figure it was none of my business. I worry about my own unit, nobody else's."

Wilker still said nothing. His eyes darted about furiously as he attempted to gauge exactly where this was going and what Wolf may or may not be implying.

"This lady here is Lubica Saric and she came to me for help. She's having a few difficulties with a band of Serbian Police and I was sure it was within our mandate to offer our assistance." He paused and took a leisurely sip from his coffee, then drew his eyes back up to his superior. "I knew you would be anxious to help someone in need. Isn't that right, Colonel?"

Wilker withered visibly under Wolf's accusing stare. "Yes. Yes, of course. As long as she's not here for too long."

"No more than a couple of days."

"Good, g-good," Wilker stammered.

"Was there something you wanted?" asked Wolf, suppressing a smug grin.

"Yes. Yes, there was. Hipwell. I wanted to know why he's out digging a trench around the perimeter."

"Discipline."

Wilker met his gaze briefly, trying to read his subordinate and discern how far he could push him. But, obviously, the answer was *not far*, because a moment later Wilker dropped his eyes. "Oh, I see. Well…whatever you deem necessary."

"Thank you, sir. I appreciate the vote of confidence."

Wilker addressed Lubica. "Nice to meet you, ma'am. You're in good hands with Captain Mercredi. I'm sure he'll take good care of you."

Lubica dipped her head graciously. "Yes, I'm sure he will."

Wilker turned on his heel and swaggered out of the room.

"Was that your commanding officer?" asked Lubica.

"Technically."

"What do you have on him?"

"Nothing." Now he grinned without derision. "It was an educated guess. I let him fill in the blanks."

"I'm glad you're on my side."

He raised his eyebrows. "You should be."

She returned her attention to her cup. "I'm sorry I couldn't be more help with regards to that band of police."

"You have a good idea as to where they might be holding your daughter. That's a start. But we'll have to move quickly. Even if they don't intend to harm her, I don't trust that they have any idea of how to care for a one-year-old."

She nodded grimly. "I worry so much about her." She set down her mug as if it had suddenly lost its appeal. "It's been three days. I couldn't believe it when I fell asleep on your cot."

"I don't get it. Why?"

She met his gaze. "How can I sleep peacefully when my child is in danger? It's like I'm betraying her by being warm and safe and comfortable. I know it mustn't sound logical to you but that's how I feel."

Part of his heart ached for her, no matter how much he fought against it. "No, I think I can understand feeling that way. But you have to remember that you're no good to her if you're a walking zombie. You have to take care of yourself so you have the energy to help her."

"I know. I know." She traced a slender finger around the rim of her mug. "I keep telling myself that but it doesn't really alleviate the guilt. The only reason I fell asleep when I did was out of sheer exhaustion. That, and feeling safe for the first time in a very long time."

He snorted softly. "You may have felt that way but obviously you weren't. It was only your quick wits that kept you from getting dragged away. Lot o' good we did you. Maybe you'd be better off on your own after all."

She shook her head very slowly. "No, I'm better off here." She lifted her eyes from her mug. "I'm not sure how I know that. But I do."

Unexpectedly, Wolf felt uncomfortable under her penetrating gaze. He started visibly when he felt a hand on his shoulder.

"Sorry, Cap. Didn't mean to scare ya."

Wolf turned to look up at Riley's shit-disturber grin. "You didn't scare me," he muttered impatiently.

"Right, I forgot," conceded Riley. "Nobody can sneak up on a wolf."

Wolf rolled his eyes. "Did you want me for something? I haven't even finished my first cup of coffee yet."

"Brooks is back."

"What? Already?"

"Yup. Want me to send him in here? I bet he could use a coffee too. His lips were purple." The morning had dawned bright but chilly. That would have been tolerable but the wind had picked up and it could bite through the sturdiest mid-weight jacket.

Wolf nodded and Riley headed out of the hall.

"Is his being back already good or bad?" asked Lubica.

Wolf shrugged. "I'm not sure. I'm just surprised, that's all."

A few moments later Brooks walked in with his usual crisp, clipped steps. He helped himself to a coffee and plunked himself down across from Wolf.

Brooks should have been an Indian. He could move like a predatory cat, hardly making a sound, and was able to stay immobile for an astonishing period of time. These skills came in very handy when his sniper skills were called for, but they also came in handy for the occasional recon assignment. He was so young, barely twenty-three, with tousled blond hair and dancing green eyes. A boy next door who could pick you off from a half a mile away without batting an eye. But his innate skills had also made him cocky to a fault. Wolf sometimes worried that he wouldn't make it to his twenty-fifth birthday.

Just as Riley had said, Brooks was shivering. He wrapped his hands around the mug and took a large scalding swallow before looking over at his commander.

"So?"

Brooks shook his head mournfully. "It's not a good scene, Cap. There's at least thirty of them in the camp. It's built around an old, abandoned farm outside of town. They're holed up in the house, the barn and a whole bunch of tents. It's not exactly a fortress but there's so much activity, people coming and going all the time, it would be a nightmare to try and sneak in there." He paused and took another sip. "No, let me rephrase that. It would be fuckin' impossible. That's why I came back already. I was afraid of getting spotted. They were everywhere and there's hardly any cover, no place to hide. I can't figure why they decided to camp way outside the city like that, when there's tons of abandoned buildings here in town. Be a lot warmer than those lousy tents."

"Probably for the exact reasons you just listed, Brooks. In town there's a lot of places for enemies to hide. Out there they can see you coming a mile away."

Lubica rested a hand on Brooks' arm. "Did you see my daughter?"

He shook his head. "Sorry, ma'am. But there was one tent that I saw a couple of women go in and out of. I wondered if maybe that's where they're keeping her. But it's right in the middle of everything." He turned his gaze back to Wolf. "I'm afraid it'd be suicide to try and get in there, and then try and get out with a screaming kid."

Wolf was silent. He downed the last of his coffee and gazed, unseeing, at the empty cup. Lubica started to say something but a motion from Brooks warned her to keep quiet. It was several minutes before Wolf broke the silence.

"No, I think there's a way."

"This I gotta hear," said Brooks as he sipped from the mug he had already replenished from the old percolator at the counter.

"The activity could work to our advantage. We'd just have to get our hands on a couple of uniforms—"

"Wait a goddamn minute there, Cap. I know where you're going and I don't like it."

"I don't recall asking your opinion, Corporal. If I were to ask anyone's opinion, I certainly wouldn't pick a wet-behind-the-ears, green-off-the-tree, sorry-excuse-for-a-pea-shooter like you, now would I?"

Brooks set his jaw and remained silent. He had been reprimanded but Wolf's words held little sting. The insult had been half-hearted at best.

"If we can blend in well enough we should be able to slip in there unnoticed. It sounds like the camp is big enough and busy enough that a couple of unfamiliar faces would hardly be cause for alarm. As for the child, we might have to sedate her so we can hide her in a knapsack or duffel bag but I think it's at least worth considering."

Lubica was beaming. "Yes, and I could pose as a—"

"You won't pose as a anything. Anything happens in there and you'd be toast. You're the one they want. If we get caught we at least have the SFOR name protecting us. It might not do us any good but I doubt they'd execute us on the spot. You, however, wouldn't be so lucky."

"But—"

"No buts. You want our help, that's the deal."

"You can't seriously be considering going in there yourself." It was Riley's voice. He approached them, swung his leg over the bench and seated himself beside Wolf.

"Of course I am. Say around ten or so, when it's dark but there's still activity to cover our movements. I'm planning on asking for a volunteer, since this is sort of outside the usual scope of our duties. But I couldn't ask anyone to attempt something this risky if I wasn't willing to take the chance myself."

Riley looked hard at his friend, his mouth an uncharacteristically grim line. "Can I talk to you alone for a minute?"

Brooks didn't wait for further instructions. He instantly swept up his coffee cup and headed out the door. Lubica, a little unsure of herself, didn't move at first.

Wolf directed his words to her, but kept his eyes on Riley. "Lubica, why don't you help yourself to the bathing facilities. By this time of the day everybody's pretty much done what they need to do. You should have all the privacy you need."

She rose somewhat hesitantly. "Yes, thank you. I'd like to get cleaned up." But before she left she placed a hand on his shoulder and said softly, "I can't tell you how much I appreciate this, Wolf."

He remained still and silent until she disappeared through the doors. "I know what you're going to say, Riley."

"Really? Well then either you're a mind-reader or I'm right on the money."

"There's a third option."

"Yeah? What's that?"

"You're way outta line and you got no business questioning my orders."

"Dammit, Wolf, I'm not questioning your orders, I'm questioning your sanity. Not to mention your motives."

"You think I'm doing this because I've got feelings for her."

Riley crooked a finger at him. "Right. But actually, *hard-on* was the phrase that came to mind."

Only Riley could get away with speaking to him like that. Their friendship, Riley's savvy attitude and his blind dedication had earned him liberties that were denied the others. The fact that he was treading painfully close to the truth had little to do with Wolf's tolerance of his insubordination. "I'm not following my cock, Riley. But essentially you're right."

"Huh? I didn't expect you to admit it."

"Admit what, exactly? Admit that I've got compassion for a woman who's lost everything? She's lost her home, her parents, her siblings, likely a husband, and now is on the verge of losing her child. What kind of unfeeling bastard would I be if I *didn't* have some feelings for her and her situation."

"But this kind of thing happens every day over here," bargained Riley. "We don't go risking life and limb to this extreme for every sob story we hear. If we did we'd all be dead by now. Or at the very least playing with our toes in a rubber room somewhere."

"But in this case, there's a hope of saving this kid. Usually we come on them after the fact, after they've had bullets or shrapnel rip through their bodies or they've already succumbed to the elements. This one's alive and healthy, just begging us to save her. I can't turn my back on that." He touched a finger to his temple. Thanks to a hefty dose of Tylenol and codeine, the throbbing had settled down to a dull ache but the spot beneath the bandage was still tender to the touch. He winced but then a half smile teased at the corner of his mouth. "Besides, we don't have any patrols scheduled for tonight. I'd be bored."

Riley didn't take the bait of humor intended to distract him. He silently studied his CO. "You sure you don't have *other* feelings for Lady Lubica?"

"You mean sexual feelings?"

"Something like that," grinned Riley.

"Good God, man, what do you think I am, made of stone? I haven't been with a woman in almost two years. Of course I have a *sexual* awareness of her. But I would never let that interfere with my judgment. You know me better than that."

"Maybe. I just got a funny feeling, that's all."

"Well, keep your humorous impressions to yourself. We've got uniforms to dig up and a volunteer to recruit."

On cue, they both swung their legs over the bench and stood.

"Oh no, you don't. You actually think I'd let you risk your ass with anybody else?"

Wolf slapped him on the back. "You're gonna risk your life for a skirt?"

"She's a baby."

"Eventually, she'll be a skirt."

Riley added softly, "I'm not risking my life for *her*."

Wolf accepted that in silence, the sentiment unspoken but clear. Riley was referring to an incident almost a year earlier in which Wolf had braved hostile crossfire to carry an unconscious Riley to safety. The two of them had come upon a skirmish unexpectedly, driving only a jeep and carrying nominal firepower. The battling factions had been completely oblivious to their presence. Once Riley was safe, they had retreated and allowed the two sides to all but annihilate each other. Any attempts at intervention in that situation had been pointless.

Other than the concussion, Riley had been uninjured but he most certainly would have been dead within minutes if Wolf hadn't carried him to safety.

The two men exited the building in companionable silence.

* * * * *

Lubica lounged back in the cramped tub. She could have showered but the tub had called out to her, reminding her of happier times when she would spend hours soaking in the enormous spa tub that her father had installed in their luxurious home a number of years earlier. This portable tub had no massaging water jets and she could barely straighten her knees. But it felt luxurious just the same. After five days of living like an animal, her hair and skin were finally clean, scrubbed pink from her zealous efforts. Now she merely relaxed and tried to let the water leech the emotional toxins from her system.

Like a private slide show, a series of faces flashed across the backs of her eyelids: her father, her sisters, her grandparents—thankfully long dead—and of course her sweet Anja. They had been such a close family, their deaths had cut her deeply, torn apart the very fabric of her life. But she hadn't really allowed herself to grieve yet.

She couldn't indulge in that luxury until her baby was safe. Once she had Anja safely back in her arms again, and they were far out of harm's way, then she would lay her child down to sleep and allow herself to cry the river that was currently being blocked by an emotional dam the size of the Hoover.

Then another face wheedled its way into her psyche. The nose was crooked and the lips thin, but the jaw was strong and the eyebrows expressive. Those black eyes, however, tended to outshine every other feature, and hold their audience captive like an invisible tractor beam. It was like gazing into pools of liquid midnight. Like the night sky, they seemed to go on forever, and hold just as many mysteries.

His short-cropped hair was almost as dark as his eyes but, despite the fact that he hadn't yet hit thirty-five, a touch of silver already dusted his temples. Somehow, considering his namesake, that seemed appropriate.

Lubica considered the story he had told her and wondered. Did the sighting of a lone wolf on the day of your birth hold some mystic significance? If so, what? Wolves were predators but he certainly didn't strike her as predatory. They were also hunted and persecuted, just as he had said. They were often wrongfully accused of crimes and just as wrongfully punished.

Lubica hoped desperately that Wolf's life wouldn't follow such an unjust path. She hoped she wouldn't be a facilitator for such a tragic fate. He was about to take great risks on her behalf. She hoped she would prove worthy and that the great risks would not result in great sacrifices.

* * * * *

"Wow!" whistled Riley. "You clean up pretty good." He allowed his eyes to rove briefly over her slim figure and rest on her hair. The limp, lifeless tresses had transformed into a thick, lustrous mane.

Lubica blushed slightly at the compliment, saying nothing as she sat herself across from him with her lunch. The dining hall already buzzed with activity.

He smiled. "Sorry, didn't mean to make you uncomfortable. I guess a bunch of guys like us can be pretty intimidating."

She shook her head and her hair swished softly across her cheeks. "Not at all. Actually you're the least intimidating group I've encountered in a long time."

"Right." Of course, her experiences with the military and men in general had given her a very different perspective from that of the typical Vancouver housewife. No doubt a group of gawky, but well-intentioned, Canadian soldiers couldn't hold a candle to some of the Neanderthals she had encountered.

Riley knew he had a tendency to speak without thinking and invariably that habit landed him squarely in trouble. Whether it was harmless embarrassment or hot water with the brass, Riley had a knack for ending up in places he never intended. So he never took for granted those friends who ignored his run-off-at-the-mouth tendencies and well-meaning jibes. When he found someone like that he hung on for dear life and cherished the friendship as dearly as pure gold. Wolf Mercredi was one such *animal*.

He grinned at the play on Wolf's name. He'd have to remember that one.

"Thank you for the compliment though," said Lubica graciously. *Gracious*. He thought that word fit their guest quite nicely. "It's been quite a long time since anyone's said anything like that to me."

"Well, that's a crying shame." Riley had to make an effort to wrench his eyes from her. Now that she was freshly scrubbed, lacking the previous layer of grime and sweat, she sparkled. Her hair was her crowning glory. Its chestnut waves rippled with golden highlights.

Riley silently chided himself. Wolf could afford to admire a beautiful woman. He had no one waiting back at home. But Riley had a wife and a kid whom he loved dearly, and even noticing Lubica's becoming features felt like cheating to him. So, instead he concentrated on his lunch.

"Where's Wolf?" she asked.

"He had some stuff to look after. He should be along shortly."

"Have you known him long?"

"The eighteen months since we both got here."

"He seems to hold you in very high regard."

Riley played with a ball of potato. "We've been through a lot of shit together. Plus he knows I can take his crap, and vice versa. He's a good CO because he cares about his men. He holds us all in pretty high regard. It shows."

Lubica's eyes were focused on the food in front of her. "Yes. He seems very competent."

"Yep, he just oozes responsibility." There was no way Riley could pass up such a plum opportunity. "That's why I can't figure out how it is that no female has managed to snag him yet."

"So, he's not married," said Lubica with a knowing glance and a twinkle in her eyes.

"Nope. Hardly even a nibble. Darnedest thing. Handsome, sensitive and responsible. I always thought that was a woman's version of a walking wet dream. But somehow he's still single."

Riley told himself he was doing this just to irritate Wolf. His attempt at matchmaking wasn't exactly subtle and Wolf rarely welcomed interference in his personal life. It was a practical joke. Or that was what he would tell Wolf if he confronted him. Honestly, Riley thought Wolf could use some female companionship. Maybe Bosnia wasn't the best place to find it but guys in this situation couldn't be too picky.

"Walking wet dream?" asked Lubica.

"Uh…" Riley squirmed. "Never mind."

"Are you teaching her how to talk dirty, Riley?" asked Wolf as he seated himself beside their guest with his tray of salad greens and a roast turkey sandwich.

Riley smiled innocently. "Who? Me?"

Wolf ignored him and turned his attention to Lubica. "How do you like the food so far?" Then he did a double take. "Wow! You clean up pretty good."

She laughed. "Do you guys rehearse this routine?"

"Routine?" said Wolf with a questioning look at Riley.

"Long story. I'm done. I gotta go track down our Halloween costumes. See ya." Riley scuttled out of the commissary.

He could feel Wolf's eyes boring into his back like laser beams.

* * * * *

Wolf narrowed his eyes at Riley's retreating back. "Yellow," he muttered.

"Yellow?"

"It means he's a chicken. I know him too well. He's done something he doesn't want me to know about and he's worried I'm gonna figure it out. That's why he's running." He squinted at Lubica. "So, what were you two talking about?"

"You."

"Dull subject."

"I don't think so."

"What did he tell you?"

"That he thinks you're a good commanding officer."

"He damn well better say that," said Wolf with a grin.

"And that you'd be a good catch for some lucky lady."

Wolf's eyebrows arched. "Oh, so that's it. He's playing matchmaker again." He stuffed a chunk of tasteless tomato into his mouth.

"Again?"

"About a year ago we were stationed briefly in this little village. He ran across this woman with legs up to her neck and hair down to her ankles. He tried to nudge us together. Trouble was she had the IQ of a stump. He just can't stand it that I'm still free and unfettered. He's married so he thinks the whole world should be just as tied down as he is." He tried to hide the conspicuous twitch of his lips as he related his concocted opinion of marriage.

"Is that how you view marriage and children, Captain? As the proverbial ball and chain?"

"No, not at all. You can't fuck a ball and chain." He was pushing her—with a humorous edge, but pushing her just the same, and he wasn't sure why. Maybe he was testing her. Maybe he needed to see what it took to push her away. But the profanity and the implied insult didn't faze her. At least not outwardly.

"You're level of sensitivity is admirable, Captain." He was strangely pleased to notice the corner of her mouth twitch as well.

"He said I was sensitive too?"

She chuckled softly. "You two are scary, you know that?"

"It's hard to be in this situation and not get to know each other more intimately than is probably advisable in a heterosexual male friendship." He speared a wilted chunk of cucumber. "You know I was kidding, right?"

"Yes. It was all too obvious."

Wolf decided it was a good time to broach a difficult subject. "Was your husband killed, too?"

"I wasn't married. He skipped out the second he found out I was pregnant. We had been together for two years. He had been hesitant about marriage but I truly thought he would propose when he found out we were going to have a baby."

"I take it he wasn't wild about the idea."

"Not exactly. He left that night and I never saw him again. It still astounds me. I thought he was a decent person, with a sense of responsibility and honor. But obviously I was wrong. He abandoned a decent job and a home. I guess with my father's reputation, and our standing in the community, he didn't think he'd be able to stay in town and manage to shirk his responsibilities. His only escape was to vanish without a trace."

Wolf shook his head and blew out a slow breath. "I can't imagine doing something like that."

"No, I'm sure you can't." She fiddled with her fork and he noticed that she had barely touched her lunch. "So how is it that you aren't married? You're obviously not afraid of commitment."

"Married to my career, I guess."

"Do you plan to stay in the army your whole life?"

"Actually, no. When I finish over here, I'm retiring. I've been doing this since I was twenty. Riley can't figure me out because I'm giving up a full military pension but I'm losing my taste for it. Honestly, I'm getting tired of being so responsible." He took a bite of his sandwich. *And I'm getting tired of looking in the mirror and not knowing the person I see.* "I like having a position of command but I'm ready to just look after me for a while."

"Well then, you better not become a parent."

"Somehow, I think that would be different."

She smiled. "Somehow, I think you're right."

They ate in silence for a time. It struck Wolf that this was the longest conversation he had had with a woman—or any civilian, for that matter—since he had arrived in the war-torn republic. It amazed him that the words and ideas flowed between them so easily. Even he and Riley hadn't hit it off so quickly, or so thoroughly. And he and Riley had come from similar backgrounds, similar cultures, with an assortment of common reference points ranging from hockey to politics. It was hard to imagine having any *less* in common with a woman and yet they seemed to share common ideals and perspectives. He felt as if he could sit here and chat with her all day. Even the silence was agreeable.

And that made him very uncomfortable.

"What was your major in University?" asked Wolf finally.

"Political Science."

He raised his eyebrows in surprise. "So maybe you're just as much of a threat as the your enemies seem to think."

"I would have been before I had my daughter. But right now her safety is my only concern. I would never do anything that might put her at risk. Even if it meant taking a stand for my people. She's…" She struggled, her expression intense. "She's *everything* to me."

Wolf's heart swelled a size or two. If only the rest of the world prioritized their life with their family and their children ranked number one. If that was the case there'd be a hell of a lot less war. And a hell of a lot less pain. "Well, I hope we can do you some good."

"I hope you don't get yourself killed."

"You're confidence in our abilities is overwhelming."

She gave him a withering look. "Aren't you worried that they'll recognize you?"

"There were only four of them here this morning. Plus they won't be expecting us to show up in the middle of their camp. They don't think we're that stupid." He winked. "Plus we'll be dressed like them and Riley is even going to get his hands on some fake facial hair." He stroked his upper lip. "What do you think of me in a mustache?"

"I think, with those eyes and the rest of your aura, you'd look positively sinister."

"I have an aura?"

"Yes, Captain. *You* definitely have an aura." She pushed away her tray.

He frowned. "You're finished? I know it's not exactly gourmet fare, but it's not that bad. You barely touched it."

"My stomach's in knots. I can barely think about food."

He pointed to his own tray, which was almost clean already. "You're going to have to get over that or you're going to fade away to nothing. You don't have a lot of body fat to sustain you. You have to train yourself to eat no matter how nervous you are."

"You're nervous about tonight?"

"I'd be crazy not to be." A day rarely went by that Wolf didn't experience some form of anxiety. Not only for his own safety but for that of his charges. After dropping twenty pounds he had finally learned how to focus on the hunger instead of the butterflies.

Lubica combed her fingers through her hair. "I need some fresh air. I'd like to go for a walk."

"You're crazy. It's only seven Centigrade out there. I'm amazed we didn't have frost last night."

"The chill will help clear my head."

"All right. If you insist." He stood, grabbed her disposable tray along with his own and tossed them in the garbage.

"You're coming along?"

"You think I'd let you get killed after all the trouble we've gone to on your behalf? I'm protecting our investment."

"Your selflessness is admirable."

"Yep, responsible to a fault, remember?"

They grabbed their coats and exited the hall together. Wolf retrieved his rifle and, as they headed toward the gate, he noticed Riley occupied with a cigarette off to his left. Riley offered him a mocking salute accompanied by a cheeky grin. He obviously thought his matchmaking efforts had been successful.

Wolf scowled. Riley's ego would fill the entire barracks if allowed to grow unchecked. Perhaps some shaving cream in his bunk tonight would do the trick. He grinned at the thought.

"What's so funny?" asked Lubica.

"Just plotting a little prank on Riley."

"I like him."

"I think it's mutual."

They continued to walk in silence, their breath visible in the crisp autumn air. They soon approached a more populated section of town and the traffic on the streets picked up. Ironically that was the most dangerous thing about `Bosnia. The locals drove like maniacs with absolutely no regard for the most basic rules of the road. Drivers and pedestrians alike took their lives in their hands when they ventured onto the streets. More SFOR soldiers were injured in traffic accidents than by gunfire and land mines combined.

But just before they reached the busiest sections, Lubica veered away toward the outskirts of the city. Wolf allowed her to lead him but kept a watchful eye, and one hand on his M16.

After about fifteen minutes they left the last of the houses behind and came to a band of trees. They found themselves at the foot of one of the numerous low mountains that surrounded the city.

She gazed up the hillside, her eyes wistful. "Beautiful isn't it?"

"Definitely. But I'd appreciate it a lot more if it weren't a mine field."

"This area isn't mined."

He regarded her suspiciously. "How do you know?"

"I just know." She held out her hand. "Do you trust me?"

He hesitated. Certainly, he trusted her. He didn't believe she would intentionally harm him and she certainly wouldn't intentionally place herself in danger. But all his training and his gut instinct told him to stay away from that hillside. The cardinal rule around here was "Don't step off the pavement". The one exception being if you were preceded by a trusted local who knew the area.

He decided that she fit the bill. He took her hand and stepped beneath the heavy pine boughs and winter dead limbs of oak and ash. Her hand felt so fragile in his own. It was hard to imagine that hand pulling the trigger on that .44 Magnum but he had no doubt that she could do it, and possibly already had.

They climbed steadily. They ducked low branches, and shuffled through the dead leaves and rich mulch that had accumulated over decades, or possibly centuries, on the forest floor. Finally they reached a clearing and he could hear water bubbling over a rocky stream bed not too far away. In the distance they could see the mountain peaks that had once boasted some of the finest ski slopes in the world. World champions had shushed down those hills to the rowdy cheers of a hundred nationalities all joined together in a celebration of international competition and sportsmanship. But the 1984 Olympics seemed like a century ago. It was a different city, a different country, a different world. The site of those past glories had been reduced to rubble by the pursuit of ethnic singularity and unadulterated hatred.

"How does a country survive something like this?" he reflected. In the still of the clearing his words echoed back to him. Even the usual cacophony of birds, insects and wildlife had been unnaturally stilled, scared off by the constant background noise of automatic weapons fire, tanks, low flying helicopters and exploding grenades.

"It will take time to rebuild but we're a strong people. If only we could get past the hatred and the fighting. I'm afraid a million NATO troops couldn't put a stop to it though. It's inside." She covered her heart with her hand. "The cure has to come from within as well."

At that moment Wolf realized that he was still holding her hand. The realization startled him and he tugged on her hand as if to pull away. But she only gripped him more tightly.

"When I saw you last night," she continued, "at first I thought you were an apparition. I was so terrified. I almost thought I had died and you were the angel of death coming for me." She smiled. "It seemed appropriate to me that the angel of death be wearing army fatigues and carrying a machine gun."

He chuckled and tugged on his cap with his free hand. Not knowing what else to do with it, he then stuffed that hand deep into his pocket. "Yes, I guess it would. The scythe is a little outdated."

"But when you knelt in front of me I saw something I didn't expect."

"Oh?"

"I saw strength and compassion. I instantly knew I could trust you."

"Maybe you trust too easily."

"I don't think so. You're the first man I've trusted since Anja's father left."

Wolf felt the tentative squeeze of delicate fingers. The air between them crackled with energy. Every nerve ending tingled as those fawn eyes drilled into his soul, beckoning to him, drawing him in. He resisted. This wasn't the time to become emotionally attached to anyone, least of all a hunted Bosnian refugee. A relationship like that was just begging for heartache. Tragic heartache. Wolf was used to protecting his heart.

He had gotten burned once, years before, by a fellow officer who had decided her career came first. Wolf always learned his lessons well and this one was no exception. He didn't let someone in easily and, when he did, he had decided it would have to be someone with whom he at least had a snowball's chance in hell of building a future.

Lubica hardly fit that category and he refused to open himself up to that kind of pain again.

That was why he was amazed when he realized that he was kissing her.

Chapter Thirteen

He had to flex his knees, and bend at the waist to a ridiculous degree in order to reach her but none of those bodily discomforts registered in his brain. All he was conscious of was her tiny body pressing into his and her slender arms reaching around his neck as his encircled her waist.

He finally lifted her feet from the ground as his tongue dipped deeply into her mouth. She tasted like mint and he wondered fleetingly how the hell she managed that in this desolate place where mouthwash and gum were as hard to come by as ambrosia.

She offered no resistance as his lips caressed hers. She withdrew slightly, but only enough to nip playfully at his lips with her teeth. It was crazy but he found that to be incredibly erotic and when he covered her mouth with his again, and her tongue challenged his own, the sensations were too much for his starving libido to withstand. He set her down and drew away.

He turned and walked away several steps, taking that time to build up his waning courage before he faced her again.

When he did, he found her smiling at him. Smiling in that irritatingly smug, feminine way that said she had him and she knew it.

He plowed his fingers through his hair. "I'm…uh…sorry about that."

A hint of a frown dimpled her brow. "Sorry? Why? I'm certainly not."

"I…I just don't think this is such a g-good idea." *God!* He had never stuttered in his life.

"What's the harm in a kiss?"

"Nothing, I guess." He felt like he was sixteen and had been caught on the front porch with his hand under the boss's daughter's blouse.

"Well then, we're in agreement." She took a step toward him.

He stepped back. He'd never run from anything in his life either. And here he was, quaking in his boots before a five-foot-nothing wood nymph. Add embarrassment to the list of new sensations. "No, we're not. There may be no harm in a kiss but there's plenty of harm in what goes with it. This is not a good time to start up a…some sort of…" he faltered.

"Relationship? Affair? Meaningless encounter?"

He relaxed marginally. "Yeah, that last one."

"I'm not trying to trap you into anything, Wolf. But I felt something for you from the moment you stepped into that gutted-out building. I think you did too. The way things are here I can't be too picky about where I find love and affection. I've lost my entire family, I haven't felt cared for in a very long time. Even if it only lasts a few hours I'll take what I can get." Her eyes caressed his face and shoulders. He felt their touch as surely as brush strokes from a feather. "If that makes me an easy lay, or cheap trash so be it. But I've been living with the fear of not seeing another sunrise for too long. I refuse to deny myself what little morsels of humanity I can glean out of this hell."

He remained silent, trying to decide how to respond and whether he could ignore the patches of heat that her probing eyes had left behind.

She continued, "Having said that, though, and despite the fact that I've only known you for a day, what just happened here felt anything but cheap or easy."

He shook his head. "No. No, you're right. It didn't. I guess I'm just wary of letting myself in for a huge letdown." Then he grinned. "Not to mention the fact that I would hate for Riley to think his matchmaking attempts were actually successful."

She stepped close enough to grasp his hand. Icy fingers entwined with his own. "We can keep it quiet if you think it will interfere with how the men see you."

"Oh no, it's not that. Actually the men are always bugging me about being so damn celibate. I just can't stand to see Riley get a big head. He gives me a hard enough time as it is." He paused and sandwiched her hands between his own. "But I guess I can put up with him if I have to. Now, we should get you back. You're half-frozen."

He wrapped an arm around her as they started down the hill. He told himself he was just trying to warm her but he couldn't deny the pleasure he took from her intimate proximity. And gradually he let himself acknowledge that maybe they had more in common than he had initially suspected. And perhaps her future was tenuous but no one, no matter where they lived or how rich they were or who they knew, could definitively count on seeing another sunrise. And what she lacked in certainty, she made up for with tenacity and hope. And really, wasn't hope all that mattered?

They reached the edge of town and started back toward the barracks. They walked several blocks, hand in hand, as Lubica pointed out some landmarks and recounted some childhood memories for him.

"I'm afraid I can't relate to growing up in a city of this size," mused Wolf.

"I can imagine you have plenty of pleasant memories of growing up in such a beautiful and isolated region."

Wolf was just about to agree with her when he found himself kneeling on all fours, struggling for breath. His rifle was ripped from his shoulder and the muzzle of his own gun was being rammed up against his temple.

"Hey, Vlad, look what we got here!" taunted his attacker.

Struggling to catch his breath, Wolf took stock of his assailant. He couldn't be more than sixteen and yet he was obviously already well versed with the operation of a sophisticated automatic weapon. Unfortunately, here few boys his age lacked that particular skill.

"Yeah," grinned his equally juvenile compatriot. "That's one o' those smart-ass soldiers from the base." He held Lubica firmly, with an arm encircling her waist and a hand clamped over her mouth. "What you think he's doing out here with a mangy Croat, Milan?" He snickered like a typical teen but it sounded surreal considering the situation. "They were holding hands. What do you bet he's fucking her?" Vlad was apparently pleased with himself for knowing the proper usage of such a renowned English four-letter word.

Milan nestled the gun more firmly against Wolf's temple. "Is that right? You fuckin' her?"

"Why don't you boys give me back my gun and we'll be on our way. You've had your fun but you don't want to get into something over your heads."

Both of the boys roared at the joke.

"You think you can take us both, Mr. Soldier Man!" said the one who held Lubica. "You're the one on the ground with a gun to your head."

Milan squeezed the trigger a little more firmly. "BOOM!"

Again they both laughed at their incredible wit.

Wolf hadn't yet moved. At that point he merely sighed at his inane tormentors. He was more concerned for Lubica than himself. He really doubted these kids would be stupid enough to kill an SFOR officer. But, then again, he had often been surprised at the stupidity that plagued the human race.

"What do you boys want? You just looking for some action? Can't find any innocent little kids to torment? Maybe you ran out of hand grenades to throw at hapless animals, so you thought you'd bag yourself a Captain."

"Who says we're after you?" Milan's gaze turned to Lubica, held captive against the young, but physically substantial, Vlad. "What do you say, Vlad? You want first go?"

"You little bastard!" growled Wolf as Vlad took his cue and began fondling Lubica through her clothes.

"Shut up!" laughed Milan. "Jealous? Maybe you didn't get any yet. Tell you what, when we're done, if there's anything left, she's all yours."

Wolf moved too fast to give him a chance to pull the sensitive automatic trigger. He bashed the gun away from his head and, although it went off, it only succeeded in taking out a few windows in the building across the street. Milan lost his hold on the weapon and it went skittering along the concrete. Wolf surged to his feet and his fist sank deeply into Milan's gut. His knee connected with a particularly vulnerable spot as his elbow cracked against the boy's face. Milan was prone by the time Vlad had flung Lubica to the ground and lunged for Wolf. He landed a solid blow to Wolf's back, but soon joined his friend, clutching at a bloody gash on his lip and trying in vain to catch his breath, which had been brutally knocked out of his body.

Wolf quickly retrieved the rifle and approached Lubica. "Are you all right?"

She nodded weakly.

He helped her to her feet, and told her to stay put as he walked toward the two youths who were making a weak attempt to regain their feet. A couple of sound kicks incapacitated them again.

Wolf trained his gun on them, and growled, "See what happens when you try to take advantage of innocent women? Just remember that the next time you get the urge to join in the fun like your Serbian buddies and rape a few defenseless women. You never know who might be waiting around the corner." Wolf slung the rifle back onto his shoulder and turned back to Lubica.

He wrapped an arm around her again and headed back toward base. Behind them they heard the sound of four feet running briskly in the opposite direction.

"Stupid little shits," he muttered. "That's one thing I'll never get used to, the systematic use of rape like some sort of legitimate weapon in this sorry excuse for a war."

She hugged him tightly with her right arm. "Thank you."

"Hell, you don't have to thank me for that. It's not like I could have stood by and let them do it."

"Yes, you could have."

"No," he said softly. "I couldn't."

They entered the base and he felt her begin to withdraw her arm from around his waist. But he gave in to an unusual surge of recklessness and grabbed her hand and held it where it was. Why not give Riley a thrill? Let him brag and gloat. He'd pay for it eventually. Wolf would see to it.

As they approached the barracks he realized that the supper hour was approaching. They had been gone longer than Wolf realized. It seemed that time had lost its significance during their hike. Usually Wolf was so bound by his watch, bound by schedules and shifts and rotations, he rarely went more than a half an hour without checking the time. But he realized he hadn't looked at it once since they had left the base. And he hadn't missed it.

They stopped outside a tent that Wolf had asked Riley to erect next to the barracks. They had moved Lubica's bag and belongings in there to afford her some privacy. He'd arranged for a cot and a portable heater, and planned on posting a guard outside after she retired. Assuming, of course, that was where she chose to sleep that evening.

He pulled her around to face him. He unzipped his jacket and snuggled her in tight, drawing the Goretex about her. He hooked a bit of her hair around her ear so he could see her face better.

"I have some things I should tend to before supper. Would you like to freshen up and meet me at the commissary for an evening of fine dining? I hear the baked beans are exquisite there, rivaled only by the meat loaf." He kissed the tips of his fingers in the elegant gesture reserved for haute cuisine.

She giggled and the sound settled around his heart like a fuzzy blanket. "That sounds wonderful. Maybe I can actually eat something." But then she dropped her eyes and seemed to be studying his chest with intense interest. "Do you really think she's okay?"

"Yes…for now. But I can't make any guarantees about tonight. I hope you understand that." On an impulse he tipped up her chin. He had to smile at the awkward angle of her neck. He had also vowed years ago, that any woman he took an interest in would have to be at least five-foot-nine or taller. He was tired of awkward embraces and having to adjust his pace for short little legs. So much for that. Another one of his self-imposed ideals shot to hell.

Just a hint of a smile flitted across her face and he was about to ask her why, when he heard the sound he had been dreading. "Well, well, well. Isn't this a sight for sore eyes? Now, who do you have to thank for this cozy little scene? Hmm?"

Wolf pretended not to have heard Riley's taunts. Instead he raised his eyebrows briefly, in silent query to Lubica. She just continued smiling at him as he bent to kiss her. This time he didn't question what he was feeling, didn't hold back because of self-doubt and didn't care that Riley was looking on with a stupid grin on his face from only a few meters away.

Their lips connected and slowly, languorously his tongue plumbed her mouth. She pressed herself against him, more insistently than before, and gripped the hair at the nape of his neck in a desperately possessive gesture. He groaned, so softly that only she could hear, before breaking the kiss and separating himself from her.

Then, to his chagrin, he heard a series of bawdy whistles and applause. Too late he realized that Riley wasn't alone. At least a half a dozen others had joined him for the show.

"So, he's human after all," teased Brooks, the cocky sniper. He also had a reputation for sampling the local feminine wares whenever possible. And according to him, the wares were available quite readily to someone of his obvious appeal. Wolf questioned how much of that was based in fact and how much in Brooks' inflated opinion of himself.

"Yeah, but only halfway," chimed in Riley. "The other half's pure wolf, no question. I always suspected as much. Now I know it's true."

Wolf refocused his attention on Lubica. He grimaced. "Sorry about that."

"I can take it. Besides, they're not teasing *me*. See you in an hour?"

He nodded and let her go, nudging her in the door of her tent. Once she was out of sight, he slowly and deliberately turned his eyes and his attention to the rowdy group that was still sharing a few bad jokes at his expense. When his eyes locked with Brooks' however, Brooks lost his grin.

"Oh shit!" Brooks took a step back. "I just remembered, I got…I don't know…but I got something real important to do." He turned and ran, complete with tail between his legs. Most of his cohorts followed his lead, leaving Riley to fend for himself in the face of Wolf's wilting glare.

But Riley held his ground. "That was quite a show," he smirked as Wolf sauntered in his direction.

"I couldn't disappoint you, old pal."

"Don't try and scare me with that *old pal* crap. It's obvious you were thoroughly enjoying every minute."

"Granted, but if I end up on the short end of Cupid's arrow I'm gonna hold you personally responsible for any injured cardiac tissue."

"Hey! I didn't exactly hold a gun to your head, now did I? It was obvious that you two had a connection from the moment you brought her in here. I just added my vote of confidence."

"Whatever. Let's go check out the stuff I know you dug up while I was gone. We got a busy evening ahead."

"Yep. And you've got a busy night."

"Shut up, Riley. You don't know shit."

"Oh, I may not know much but I know shit. After all, I'm full of it."

Wolf had to chuckle at that. "Never a truer word was spoken."

Chapter Fourteen

Wolf stuck his head under the tepid spray that trickled from the showerhead and reviewed his little meeting with Riley. The uniforms and accessories were adequate and their discussion of what should transpire that night was short and to the point. They could only lay limited plans, since so much would depend on what they encountered once they entered the camp. But Wolf had faith in his friend, and knew they made a good team.

Wolf was anxious about the events, but not overly so. He had confidence in their ability to handle any situation that presented itself. And if his confidence was misplaced, or they encountered elements that surpassed their ability to handle them…well, there was no point in dwelling on that. He preferred to dwell on Lubica.

He poured shampoo into his palm and lathered his hair, barely aware of the smile that curled his lips when he thought of her.

Riley's revelation that he had sensed a chemistry between Wolf and Lubica had come as a shock. How had he been so blind to it at first? He had definitely thought her attractive, but hadn't attributed any special significance to it until they were alone in that clearing. At least not consciously.

But when the truth had finally been revealed it had hit him suddenly and completely, with a blinding and mind-numbing clarity. But what man wouldn't find her intriguing? He admired her beauty, intelligence and eloquence. He respected her unwavering dedication to her beliefs and her child. Her independence and strength set her apart.

A country at war with itself tended to separate the wheat from the chaff, so to speak. The chaff was blown away with the wind, either abandoning long-held principles in favor of a 'look out for number one' mentality, or it was mowed over by stronger forces. The wheat managed to survive against the odds, while keeping principles and morality intact, using the adversity to build and strengthen character rather than erode it.

He dried himself off and slipped into a fresh set of fatigues.

Was Riley right about his potential activities that evening? He had known Lubica for little more than a day. Wasn't that rushing into things? Then he recalled what she had said about grabbing onto the little bit of warmth her current life had to offer. Maybe that was good advice. This time tomorrow she might be reunited with her child and Wolf might be helping her to find a safe hiding place or, better yet, a way out of the country. He might never see her again. That was a very good reason to not take this any further. *And* it was a very good reason to throw caution to the wind.

He muttered and cursed at himself for his indecision. He was a commander, used to making split second decisions that affected the lives of dozens of men. This shouldn't be that difficult. Maybe he would leave it to the last minute and treat it as the kind of decision that was made in the heat of battle. The more he thought about that, the more he liked it. It was pretty damn close to the truth of the situation.

There was just one other factor that weighed heavily on his mind. He usually bunked with his men, shunning the idea of separating himself in some private haven. He didn't want to take too many special privileges solely because of his rank. So, if he decided to take advantage of his rightful access to private quarters tonight, it would be all too obvious to everyone as to why. Could he put up with the stories and teasing that were sure to follow? Or was there another way around that particular obstacle? That would take some thought but time was running short and his options were limited.

Whatever he decided he had to do it fast. But the more he thought about it the more he realized that he desired to encounter more of her. All of her, in fact. Could he really pass up the opportunity to feel her body beneath his? To confirm that she wasn't as fragile as she appeared and that his weight wouldn't crush her? To see what lay beneath those tattered clothes she wore? Did she bear scars from her adventures?

He slipped a comb through his damp hair and tried to clear his thoughts. Torturing himself over these questions served no purpose. And it didn't help that his stomach had begun to growl and protest the sorry state of affairs in his hunger-ravaged gut.

He hustled out the door. She was expecting to meet him and he didn't want to disappoint her.

* * * * *

Wolf ambled into the commissary only a few minutes late. Riley was seated with Brooks and Neilsen, already stuffing his face. Wolf stopped at their table before heading over to fill his own tray.

"What's on the menu?"

Riley picked at the mound of food. "Not sure, really. Does it matter? It all tastes like cardboard anyway."

"You're too picky, Riley. Gotta be grateful for what we have. Don't be such an insensitive clod."

Riley harrumphed. "You been hanging around with the locals too much." His eyes twinkled.

Wolf scanned the room. If Lubica were here he would have expected her to sit with Riley, pending his arrival. "Have you seen Lubica?"

"Nope. Not yet."

Wolf shrugged and headed over to the lineup. Several minutes later he swung his leg over the bench and seated himself across from Riley. His gaze rested on the doors again.

"Something eating you, Cap?"

"Huh?" asked Wolf absently. He finally acknowledged Riley's *shit-disturber* grin, but was too distracted to do anything about it.

"No. Nothing."

Neilsen and Brooks chuckled as well. They were apparently enjoying this glimpse of their CO's human frailty.

Wolf ate in silence for about five minutes, his eyes roving to the doors every few moments. Although the roast beef was actually quite tasty tonight, the food gradually lost its appeal. More than half of it remained on his plate when he abruptly stood and addressed the men. "I'm going to check on her. I don't like it. She was supposed to be here twenty minutes ago. It's not like she's got a ton of cosmetics to fuss with to make her late."

The notable lack of a grin on Riley's face indicated that he had begun to share Wolf's concern. "I'm done. I'll come along."

They both strode outside and headed toward her tent.

They called but received no reply. They stepped in but found it empty. The cot looked like it had been slept in or, at the very least, laid upon. Perhaps she had taken a nap. There was a damp towel tossed across the foot of the cot and her clothes were gone.

Her knapsack lay in a heap with half its contents strewn across the floor.

A giant fist wrapped around Wolf's gut and twisted. He and Riley locked eyes. Almost in unison they said, "Shit!"

"How the hell did they get in here unnoticed?" exclaimed Riley.

"I'm not sure but I bet those kids who attacked us have something to do with this."

"What kids?"

"No time to worry about that," growled Wolf with as much feral intensity as his namesake. "I guess this moves the timetable up a bit."

Riley laid a hand on his arm. "Are you sure it's worth it, Wolf? We're likely already too late."

The fist gripped Wolf's gut a little tighter but he refused to accept such a possibility without a fight. "Maybe so, but I'm not taking any chances. You don't have to come. I'll do this on my own if I have to."

Riley shook his head. "Are you kidding? If there's even a remote chance that the first woman to get you fired up in two years is still alive, I'll do everything in my power to help get her back. My motives are purely selfish. Maybe getting laid would mellow you out a bit."

Wolf appreciated the attempt at humor, but couldn't work up a smile. "Shut up, Riley. We've got work to do."

* * * * *

"What are we waiting for, Dimitri?"

"I just thought we'd have some fun with her first," said the gaping grin and the beetling brows.

His cohort instantly brightened. "Oh, I never thought of that."

Dimitri scowled. "Of course you didn't. You're an idiot."

Lubica couldn't help but think the ringleader had no right to cast stones. He hardly struck her as a tactical genius and she found it hard to believe that he was the one in charge of this entire outfit. But she had yet to see anyone who remotely resembled the true leader of this little group of rogue militants.

She sat, shivering with cold and anxiety, huddled in the corner of the tent. They had ambushed her just as she was about to exit her new sleeping quarters. It was an incredible stroke of bad luck that no soldiers happened to be in close proximity when they had assailed her, tossed her in the back of a garbage truck and shipped her out with the trash.

But perhaps it was her own fault. She had been late in leaving the quarters, having taken an inordinate amount of time to make herself attractive. She didn't have much to work with, but had managed to put her hair up in what she thought was a reasonable French braid. She had even allowed herself to entertain thoughts of Wolf helping her to loosen the strands from the complicated arrangement. If she hadn't allowed herself the luxury of vanity she mightn't be in this situation. If she had left for supper on time there would have been more troops in the vicinity and her assailants wouldn't have had such a clear shot at abducting her.

She took in her surroundings. The tent was part of a group of shelters situated between the old farmhouse and barn. She could smell the distinctive odors of hay and manure, and could hear the occasional *moo* from a pasture behind them. Obviously this little group had made themselves quite at home here. They were probably milking the cows, taking eggs from the chickens and helping themselves to whatever stores of food the previous owners had left. Then she wondered what had happened to the owners. The buildings seemed to be in good repair, so she doubted they had been abandoned for a long period. The answer was all too obvious and she chose not to dwell on it. She thought of Wolf instead.

She regretted the fact that he would be disappointed when she didn't show up for dinner. She regretted that she would likely never see him again. She regretted a lot of things. She thought, maybe, she had found something special. But she seemed to have a knack for losing the things that mattered to her the most. That thought goaded her into action.

"Where's my daughter?" She threw down the question like a gauntlet. "I insist that you let me see her, before you… " She couldn't complete the thought.

The ringleader sneered at her. "You're in no position to make demands, my sweet."

"Don't call me that, you Neanderthal."

That gave him pause. He obviously had no idea what the insult referred to. But he soon regained his composure and called to someone outside the tent, "Send in those two boys." He granted her his most vile grin. "I believe you have already made their acquaintance."

In walked Milan and Vlad.

Lubica retained her poise. "Didn't you boys learn your lesson from the Captain?" She turned to Dimitri. "Did they happen to mention how he gave them a sound thrashing and that they ran away for fear of their lives."

The leader wasn't fazed. "That hardly matters, does it? Your bodyguard isn't here, and isn't likely to make an appearance. If he does he will be dealt with severely. These boys provided us with some key information that led us directly to you. I like to repay loyalty." There was that repulsive grin again. "I thought the least I could do is let them finish what they started."

Lubica hazarded a glance in the boys' direction. To her surprise they had lost the cocky self-assurance of their earlier encounter. In fact she thought they looked a little scared. This was probably not exactly what they had in mind. Essentially, they were going to be asked to perform, in front of much older, more experienced men. Lubica wondered if their anxiety would completely inhibit their ability to perform. She almost felt sorry for them. They were only boys, caught up since their birth in a world that no child should be exposed to. They were coping in their own way, just as anyone would. They had no role models, other than the likes of the men in this camp, on which to draw. In the truest sense of the words, they really didn't know any better.

"Maybe I can be of assistance." Dimitri turned to Lubica and pointed his rifle at her chest. "Remove your clothes."

Though her heart crashed against the inside of her chest, outwardly she didn't move. "I'll do nothing willingly. I'll fight you to my last breath."

"Is that so? Perhaps we can persuade you otherwise." He yelled out the door, "Dragan! Bring in the child."

Lubica's breath caught in her throat. A moment later in walked two uniformed men. One was carrying the squalling Anja. Dragan handed her to the leader.

Lubica stood, caught up in a whirlpool of emotion. Rage, indignation, fear and relief swirled about her but, somewhere in the midst of the vortex, she found the eye of calm. And there she found her voice.

"Leave her alone! She's no threat to you. You've got me." She jutted out her chin and donned her pride like a protective cloak. She drew herself up to stand tall and straight in the face of what she knew would come. "Just as you said, I'll be anything you want me to be if you'll just let her be!"

"I may just consider that, if I'm assured of your cooperation." He pulled a pistol from his belt and held it to Anja's head. "Let's try this again. Remove your clothes."

Lubica knew he wasn't bluffing. Killing children was well within the repertoire of the Serbian forces. With trembling hands but a firm resolve she slowly began to unbutton her shirt, now stained with filth and garbage.

"Faster! There's a lot of men who want a turn and I don't want to be here all night." He laughed at his own extraordinary wit.

But his laugh was cut short when the few remaining, intact teeth in his mouth were shattered by a gut-wrenching blow from the butt of an M16 rifle. Anja had already been ripped from his arms and he found himself writhing on the floor, moaning in pain and staring up at the muzzle of that same rifle.

Dragan glared down at him. "We meet again, my friend," whispered Wolf. Then, more loudly, "I would advise the rest of you to remain where you are unless you would like your esteemed leader to meet with a grisly end." He frowned thoughtfully. "Not that I'd have any objections. Please, feel free." He smiled, revealing a mouthful of blacked-out teeth. Still sporting his grisly grin he glanced over at Riley, who was handing Anja to a dumbfounded Lubica.

She was still reeling from the sudden turn of events but sight of his teeth brought a smile to her lips. She shook her head in wonder. "How did you—"

Wolf waved away the question. "We'll tell you all about it later. Right now we've got to get out of here in one piece."

Riley hustled the boys and the one remaining compatriot over to a corner of the tent where he proceeded to bind and gag them. "Now what, Einstein? Sure, we tie 'em up, but what about the kid?"

"Come on, Riley. Give me a little credit." He pulled out a syringe, and a rolled up duffel bag from beneath his coat. "I'm a good Boy Scout; I always come prepared."

Lubica eyed his equipment warily, but decided she had no choice but to trust him.

Wolf noticed the concern in Lubica's eyes but could also see faith, trust and perhaps a touch of something else that he hesitated to name. He shook himself mentally and refocused on the task at hand.

"You son of a bitch," hissed the leader through bloody lips. "You think you'll survive after this outrage?"

Wolf regarded the vile piece of human flesh huddled at his feet. "You're in no position to make threats, old buddy. Don't tempt me. It's taking every ounce of self-control I possess not to blow your head off your shoulders. The thought of your slimy hands touching her makes me want to retch." Wolf nudged the Serbian scum with the muzzle and sneered. "Go ahead, make my day." He grinned at Riley. "I always wanted to say that."

Riley rolled his eyes. "Are you just about through? I'd like to get out of this hellhole in one piece."

"Nag, nag, nag," muttered Wolf. Then he turned to his victim on the floor. "Just one more thing…" With that he swung the butt around again and it connected soundly with the side of the leader's head. He toppled to the side, and lay motionless. Satisfied, Wolf then headed toward Lubica.

"Jeez, Cap. I hope you didn't kill him."

"Yeah, yeah, whatever." He knelt beside Lubica and the wide-eyed toddler. He was touched by the fierceness with which Lubica was holding her, clutching her. The baby had quieted once she was in her mother's arms but he doubted that would last once she found herself in the duffel bag. "I'm sorry, Lubica. But I don't know how else to do this."

She swallowed dryly and nodded.

Without ceremony, he plunged the needle into Anja's arm. She just continued gazing up at him with the same wide eyes that he had come to adore on her mother. She even reached up to touch his nose. He had purposely chosen the tiny syringe with the finest needle he could find, hoping to cause her minimal discomfort. Her unfazed response encouraged him but, a moment later, the sensations registered. Her face screwed up in pain and a scream welled up from her tiny lungs. Despite the circumstances he couldn't help but smile. Even screaming bloody murder, there was something endearing about a baby's cry. Unfortunately, a small swell of tears in Lubica's eyes told him that she wasn't able to share the sentiment.

Having completed his task, Riley joined them. "This better work fast. Somebody's gonna get suspicious soon."

He needn't have worried. Within moments, Anja's cries subsided and her eyelids began to droop. A moment later her head lolled against her mother's shoulder.

Wolf brushed a tear away from Lubica's cheek. "She's going to be fine. Now let's go." He extended a hand and helped Lubica to her feet then, as Riley held open the duffel bag, he gently lay Anja in the bottom. The bag was made of a loose weave canvas but, not wanting to take any chances he had punched a few holes in it a few inches from the bottom. He carefully swung the bag over his shoulder and Riley handed Lubica a large coat with a hood. She slipped it on and drew the hood up over her head, pulling it forward to cover as much of her face as possible.

Wolf squeezed her hand briefly before heading to the entrance of the tent. Riley checked outside and motioned for them to follow. The farmhouse glowed with lights and off to their right a campfire blazed brightly. A large group of people were gathered around it. They were involved in boisterous drinking and bawdy jokes appeared to be flying back and forth. Obviously Lubica's capture had only concerned a very few, selected individuals. Contrary to what Dimitri had implied, there was no lineup of men waiting anxiously for a crack at Lubica.

The trio slunk away into the night and no one gave them a second glance.

Once they were safely out of earshot, Riley sighed. "Wow, that was easy. Almost too easy."

"Don't look a gift horse in the mouth, Riley. Let's get a move on."

They kept to a narrow road lined heavily on both sides with trees as they headed back toward the jeep that they had left at the main road. Riley led the ragtag group of subversives and Wolf brought up the rear.

They had gone about twenty paces when Wolf heard a soft thud. He was instantly on alert.

He grabbed Lubica's coat and snatched her back, throwing her into a bush off to his left. He gently dropped the duffel bag beside her. But as he whirled around his rifle was ripped from his grasp and he barely had time to deflect a knife descending toward his chest.

He wrestled with his assailant and called out for Riley. There was no answer. His attacker was large and remarkably agile—a disturbingly even match for Wolf's skills. They continued to struggle, grunting and grimacing, as they tried to break the stalemate. Wolf eventually found himself backed up against the trunk of a large tree. He aimed a kick at his opponent's crotch but the sentry dodged Wolf's foot and laughed at the desperate attempt. Wolf was still gripping the wrist of the hand that held the knife as he grappled for the advantage. He was just starting to feel like he might be able to get the upper hand when the other man rammed the full force of his massive body against Wolf, crushing him against the tree.

The blow exceeded Wolf's tolerance. Starved for breath and energy he lost his hold on the knife hand and crumpled. As he tried to catch his breath he could envision that knife driving toward his chest. Resignedly, he looked up into an evil grin. The knife was poised, ready to strike, but it never fell. Instead, he heard the crack of a rifle shot and the huge man toppled forward, a look of stark surprise on his face.

"Riley?" he croaked as the sentry thudded to the ground a few inches away.

"No, but I think he's okay."

"Lubica?"

"Who else?"

"Remind me to say a little prayer to thank your dad for teaching you so well."

Her hand grasped his and tugged. "Come on, let's go." She gave Wolf the rifle, then quickly retrieved Anja while Wolf found Riley. He was groggy, but otherwise intact.

"I knew it was too easy," he muttered as he clutched at his head.

"He must have been patrolling the perimeter."

"Thanks for the news flash, Einstein. That gorilla leveled me like a domino."

Wolf was relieved that his friend was as crabby as ever.

Once they had safely cleared the farm's perimeter, Lubica removed her daughter from the bag and carried her sleepy form close to her breast until they reached the jeep. They made it back to base without incident.

Once they were within the confines of the base, Wolf and Riley exchanged some quiet words and Riley split off.

"Where's he going?" asked Lubica.

"He's going to have a medic check him out and then he has something to do for me." He grasped her hand. "Come with me."

He led her into the barracks but then headed down a small hallway that was tucked unobtrusively behind a pair of bunks. They reached a door, which he opened to reveal a full-size bed, complete with sheets, blankets and pillows.

She gaped at the sight.

"I thought you and Anja deserved a little more privacy and shelter than that tent provided. Technically these are my quarters, I just hadn't used them for a while. There will be a guard outside all night in case those morons get any more bright ideas."

Lubica gently laid her daughter on the mattress and tucked a blanket around her. "I'd like to give her a bath."

"I could have someone bring a portable tub right in here if you like."

Lubica remained seated on the mattress as she stroked Anja's satiny cheek. She looked up at him and tears glistened in her eyes. "Thank you, Wolf. I really wasn't sure if I'd ever see her again."

He shrugged. "Ah, it was nothing," he drawled in an attempt to lighten the moment. He'd never been much good at dealing with blatant gratitude and outright adoration.

But she wouldn't have it. She stood and crossed over to him. She reached up and stroked the mustache. "I was wrong. Even that lousy mustache can't make you look sinister."

"Darn, I was—" But his words were interrupted by her fingers, which had moved on to his lips. "Please, let me thank you properly."

"Your being here, safe and sound, is thanks enough for me." He glanced at the sleeping child. "By the way, she's beautiful."

"I know."

A smile twitched at his lips as he returned his eyes to hers. "I should go see about that tub."

"What do I have to do to get you to kiss me? I'm too short to reach all the way up there on my own."

Wolf finally surrendered to the battle he had been fighting ever since entering the room. He crushed her lips beneath his own, but they were chilly, and when she reached up to link her hands behind his neck, her fingers were like slender icicles. He pulled reluctantly away.

Disappointment haunted her features.

"Don't worry, I'm not finished. But I feel it my duty to warm you up. I'm going to get a tub in here and fill it with scalding hot water, then you and your daughter are going to get in and have a good long soak until it penetrates right through to your bones." He kissed her fingertips. "Is that understood?"

"Yes, sir. On one condition."

"Yes?"

"You have to join us."

Shock robbed him of the power of speech. "But...well...we..."

She interrupted, "That's the deal—take it or leave it."

"We'll never fit." Christ, that was lame.

"You're not *that* big and Anja and I are rather small. Besides she won't stay in long. Once she's clean I'll wrap her in a nice fuzzy blanket and she'll drift right off." She smoothed a hand across his chest. "Next objection?"

"The men—"

"Won't care. Next?"

He hesitated.

"Then it's settled."

"You're one pushy broad. You should have been a commander."

"Tell me something I don't know."

Chapter Fifteen

"Lubica?" Oddly, her name had recently taken on almost musical qualities. It was one of the most beautiful words in his vocabulary.

"Hmm?"

Wolf moved his hand from its resting place on her breast and, with a feather touch, brushed his fingertips across her tummy. A fine smattering of goose bumps saluted the touch. It beat a GI salute any day. "Are you warm now?" His breath ruffled her hair.

She snuggled herself more firmly against him, nesting the curve of her bottom against his fuzzy middle. "I'm warmer than I've ever been in my life."

Nearby, nestled on a bed of pillows, a sleeping Anja cooed her affirmation of her mother's testimonial.

At first Wolf had been self-conscious about making love with a child in the room but Lubica had soon laid his fears to rest. A freight train could have run right through the middle of that room and Anja wouldn't have stirred.

The bath had been a tantalizing experience. Lubica had nestled between his legs and Anja had gurgled and splashed playfully in front of her mother, totally oblivious to the glaringly male presence in her private sanctum. When she was clean and warmed through, Lubica had taken her out, clothed her in a diaper and one of Wolf's soft, well-worn undershirts, then swaddled her in one of the stack of blankets Wolf had brought in along with the tub.

Once the baby was snoozing contentedly she had rejoined Wolf in the bath. They had soaped each other, and washed each other's hair, exploring intimately in a provocative prelude to what occurred the moment they hit the mattress.

With towel-tousled hair and dewy skin, they had slid between the sheets and continued the erotic adventure. Wolf was gratified to confirm that she was, indeed, warm and toasty from head to toe. He had confirmed it with his hands, his lips and his tongue, exploring every inch until she was begging him to end the torture and bring it to its logical conclusion.

When he sheathed himself inside her, he thrilled to discover how deeply the moist warmth penetrated. Despite her tiny frame she accepted him completely, over and over until they both lay quiet, spent and content. Wolf had bitten back the moans of satisfaction that welled up. After all, there *was* a guard just outside the door. No doubt he had a pretty good idea as to what was going on but Wolf saw no need to advertise the fact.

Wolf's awareness of the guard outside was suddenly emphasized when a familiar voice from the other side of the door jolted him out of his private utopia.

"Where the hell is Mercredi?" growled the Colonel.

"I'm afraid I couldn't say, sir," replied the guard in clipped tones.

There was a lengthy pause during which Wolf could just picture the Colonel sizing up the guard, trying to figure out why he was standing there, unmoving.

"I'm not sure I believe you, Private. Isn't that his private quarters? Who's in there?"

"I'm not at liberty to say, sir."

"Are you guarding the occupants?"

"I'm not at liberty to say, sir."

Wolf smiled. He knew his men and there was no way the colonel was getting in, short of driving a tank through the door. If he did manage to find Wolf in this compromising position it would mean his immediate dismissal, and shipment back home in disgrace. The guard knew that and would protect his commander with tenacity. Although, at that moment, Wolf was having trouble finding the energy to care one way or another. Suddenly, losing his career and even his reputation came in a distant second to the warm flesh and blood that was snuggled up to him.

Wilker continued his tirade. "What if I ordered you to step aside, Private?"

"I'd have to take that up with my commander, sir. I answer to him." *This boy has potential.*

"You're treading on thin ice, boy."

"Yes, sir."

But Wilker's stamina appeared to be wearing thin. He muttered a few unintelligible curses before conceding defeat. "All right. But if I find out anything illicit was going on here, or that Mercredi was a part of it, rest assured his ass won't be the only one in a sling."

"Yes, sir. Ass in a sling. Got it, sir."

Wolf chuckled quietly.

"Shut up. And if you see Mercredi tell him I want to see him ASAP."

The Private remained silent and Wolf heard retreating footsteps.

Lubica stirred. She had been dozing and had missed the fun. She drew his hand up to her breast.

He cupped it gently, and mumbled into her hair. "I'm so glad you've never had to be subjected to this against your will." He shuddered again at the thought of that animal laying his hands on her tender flesh.

"I have you to thank for that," she said sleepily.

He wrapped his arms around her slight waist and hugged her tightly. "And I have you to thank for a lot of things."

She turned to nuzzle his stubbled cheek. "You're definitely welcome."

There was a soft tap at the door.

Wolf tried to ignore it.

But it persisted and then he heard a familiar, raspy whisper, "Wolf!"

Wolf rolled his eyes. There was only one man that the guard would allow this liberty. "He's the one who tries to get me in bed with you and then he's the one to drag me out of it." He drew back the covers.

"Come back soon. I'll start to get cold again."

Those few words brought on an unexpected and primal surge of possessiveness. If he had anything to say about it, she would never be cold again. She would never know fear and she would never know doubt. He made a solemn oath to himself toward just that end and Wolf always took his promises seriously. As if to seal the silent vow he kissed her firmly on the lips. He dipped his tongue briefly into her and then drew away just far enough to mumble, "We definitely can't let that happen."

With regret, he got up and wrapped one of the extra blankets around himself. He shuffled over to the door and nudged it open a crack. "What the hell is it, Riley? Can't you see I'm busy!?"

Riley's grin stretched from ear to ear. "Sorry. I just thought you might like to know I made those arrangements. Her flight leaves at four o'clock tomorrow afternoon."

"That couldn't wait until the morning?"

Riley just shrugged and continued to boast that stupid smirk.

"Get lost, Riley."

Wolf closed the door and hastily rejoined Lubica between the covers, where he entwined his arms and legs around her for maximum heat distribution.

Her lips brushed against his chest. "You've got the heat output of a thousand-watt furnace, you know that?"

"Mmm. Too bad I'm not portable."

"What was that all about?"

"You're leaving the country tomorrow."

"What?" She tried to draw away but he held her firm.

"I asked Riley to find a plane that was heading to Western Europe as soon as possible. There's one leaving at four o'clock tomorrow afternoon. I'm not sure of its exact destination but it doesn't matter. At the other end we'll have made arrangements to get you to England. I have some distant relatives there who've agreed to put you and Anja up until I finish my tour in six months. I figured that was ideal since you went to school there."

"What are you talking about? I can't leave my home." She nipped at his chest hair.

He yelped and pulled away. "What are *you* talking about? You can't stay. You're in danger and you yourself said your main concern is Anja's safety. How can you consider staying when you're being hunted like a fox with a pack of hounds on its tail?"

"Yes…but…"

Wolf laughed. "Finally, you're the one at a loss for words."

"How can I leave my country? It may be in tatters but it's still my home."

"It's not forever, Lubica." He cupped her cheek in his palm. "You can come back when things are better, and your daughter is older.

Maybe then you can make a difference and help to rebuild and forge a better Bosnia. But for now you have other priorities."

"Like you?"

"Like your daughter."

"And you?" She was grinning broadly, those huge eyes sparkling.

"And me," he conceded. It felt good to be somebody's priority.

"All right. I know you're right. I guess I knew it was inevitable. I just wasn't expecting it so soon."

"The sooner the better."

"But how can I impose on you like that? We've only known each other a day and you're offering your family to me for room and board? We're not exactly engaged. How can we plan for that kind of future?"

"Don't worry about that. I know we've still got a long way to go but these people have a huge house and they're glad to help out a refugee, especially one that I care about. For now, that's all we need to know, isn't it? That we care about each other and that we want to see if it will go somewhere? I just want to be assured that you're safe so we at least have the opportunity to find that out."

She stared at him, blinked once. "Okay. You're very persuasive. And I suppose I could also write some letters and maybe do some lobbying from England. Actually, I might be able to make *more* of a difference from there."

He narrowed his eyes. "When you set your sights on something there's no stopping you, is there?"

She brushed warm fingertips across his lips. "No… I guess there isn't."

"Are you saying you had me in your sights all along?"

"You'll never know, will you?" She was teasing him but her face was serene and her eyes lingered as they connected with his. "But before we go, will you do something for me?"

He dipped his head and nibbled her neck. "Well, it's a dirty job…but if you insist."

She giggled. It was a spontaneous, happy sound that made him think of lying on a sunny beach, soaking in the sun and the salt air. Maybe they'd get there. Someday.

"No, silly. I'd like to go back to my father's house before I leave tomorrow. It's still standing and I'd like to retrieve a few mementos of my family. I'm hoping it hasn't been completely ransacked."

He considered the request. "I don't know. It could be dangerous. What if we're spotted?"

Lubica's eyes grew wide with emotion. "Please, Wolf. It won't take long and you'll be with me. I have to have something to remember them by."

He sighed. There was no point in even trying to deny her anything. She had lost so much and she asked so little. "All right, on one condition."

"Mmm?"

His answer was to slide a hand between her thighs and knead her sex between his fingers. She caught her breath and wove her fingers through his hair. She planted her mouth on his and stole his breath.

He took that as compliance. Despite the lack of sand and sun, he could swear he could hear the waves crashing in the background, and feel the warmth of a tropical sun on his soul.

Chapter Sixteen

"This must have been beautiful once," observed Wolf.

Lubica glanced around the expansive living room. Hunks of plaster littered the floor and blue sky peeked through numerous holes in the outside wall. The furniture was in disarray and much of the upholstery had been ripped or the legs shattered. But even through the dust and rubble and chaos, the rich colors, classic lines and elegant tastes of the owner shone through.

"Yes, it was," she said wistfully. "It wasn't this bad the last time I saw it. Looters must have gotten to it."

Her eyes were shimmering, so he kissed her head and wrapped an arm around her and Anja, nestled safely in her arms.

Wolf had suggested leaving the baby at the base. Surely three or four armed guards could keep one small baby safe and entertained. It would have served Riley right for interrupting them last night. Besides, he needed the practice. He was eventually coming home to a new baby of his own. He had found out less than a month ago that his wife was expecting their second child. Obviously his last leave had been well spent.

But Lubica had been adamant. They had been separated too long. She couldn't bear to let Anja out of her sight, even for a moment.

"You must have a lot of wonderful memories. It must be hard to say goodbye to the house you grew up in." He released her and strolled over to a family portrait that had survived and still hung, somewhat askew, on an interior wall. He ran a finger along the gilded frame as he took in the faces of the people Lubica had loved.

"Do your parents still live in the same house?" she asked.

"Yes. Actually they're the third generation to live there." He wondered if someday he would carry on the tradition. Or whether that honor would fall to his sister. He had come so far from his roots. Sometimes you just couldn't go home again.

"My family has lived in this city for fifteen generations. Not in this specific house, but in this area of town."

"Wow! That's what I call roots."

She set Anja down on a section of floor that was free of debris, and knelt beside her. "Yes, we have roots that extend almost to the center of the earth. And she's the last."

Wolf knelt beside her. "Well, hopefully getting you two to England will ensure that she isn't."

Lubica leaned against him. "I hope you're right."

The two of them were so intent on nuzzling each other that neither of them took notice when Anja leaned forward on her hands and, with wobbly legs, managed to push herself upright until she was standing, completely unsupported.

Wolf was the first to take note of the event. "How long has she been walking?"

"What?" When Lubica saw her she sucked in her breath and held deathly still, afraid to startle her daughter and cause her to lose her balance. She whispered, "She wasn't, up until now." Lubica extended a hand. "Come on, sweetie. Come to Mommy."

A grin spread across the chubby little face and she managed to take two wobbly steps before falling forward into her mother's arms.

Lubica laughed. "You put on quite a show for the Captain."

Wolf bowed his head meekly. "I'm honored to have witnessed the first tottering steps of the last of the Saric line."

Lubica kissed his cheek. "Don't fool me with that humble act. It won't wash. You're one arrogant S.O.B."

Wolf's mouth dropped open in mock indignation but then his lips curved into a grin. "You almost say that as if it were a compliment."

"It is. In my experience you have to have some degree of arrogance to take on a command, and do it well."

"You truly have insight."

"In that way you remind me a bit of my father. He ran that paper like a military operation. He delegated but his was always the final word. He had the vision and the will to achieve it."

"You obviously loved him very much," said Wolf quietly. "What happened to your mother?"

She hugged her daughter. "She died a few weeks after my youngest sister was born. It was a brain aneurysm, a freak thing. I think part of my father died with her. But he resolved to be both mother and father to us." She gazed up at Wolf and her eyes were full. "I think he did a pretty good job." Wolf nodded affirmation as she stood, still holding Anja's chubby fingers in her own. "Would you mind carrying her while I find what I'm looking for?"

Wolf, deeply honored by the request, stood and swept up his tiny charge. He perched her on his shoulders to Anja's giggling delight. "It would be my pleasure. And, you're right, we should get a move on."

Wolf followed Lubica through the house, entertaining Anja as they went. He tickled her feet and played horsy, kissed her cheeks and made funny faces, all to both her and her mother's delight.

He had always known he would someday want a family, but had been hesitant to make such a commitment while he was still so dedicated to his career. He didn't want to be a military husband and father who was always shipping out for long stints away from hearth and home. He had grown up in a house where both mother and father were home every night for supper and where family outings were common. He wanted no less for his children.

But now, perhaps the time was right. In six months he would be free to commit to the kind of life he had dreamed of. And, perhaps, he had finally found the one to commit it to.

Lubica eventually managed to scavenge a few family photos and special mementos from the drawers and cupboards that had been left intact. They exited the front door and she turned around to place her hand on the carved oak in a silent farewell. Who knew what might be left of the structure by the time she returned.

They got into the jeep and headed back toward base. The traffic was light. They were almost at the halfway mark when Wolf turned a corner to find a barricade of jeeps and two tanks blocking the way.

"Shit!" he muttered. "What the hell is this?" He scanned for an alternate route but the only alternative was to turn around and go back the way they had come. He put the jeep in gear and had just managed to turn it around when all hell broke loose.

A grenade exploded and bullets whizzed about like deadly mosquitoes. He felt one of the tires on the jeep blow out and a troop of men appeared in their path. They weren't focused on Wolf and Lubica but they were a formidable obstacle. He made a quick decision. "Out!

There's a narrow alley between those buildings. Let's take cover until this blows over."

They hopped out of the jeep and dashed for cover. As he feared, the alley was a dead end, but at least it afforded them cover. They headed to the far end, which wasn't far enough to suit Wolf. Lubica clutched a wailing Anja to her chest as they ran. When they reached the end, Wolf pressed Lubica and Anja into the bricked-in corner and stood in front of them, shielding them with his own body. If not for the background noise of gunfire and explosions the setting could have almost been described as cozy.

He gazed down at her and smiled. "Hopefully this is the last time you have to deal with something like this." He touched Anja's cheek. She had stopped crying and was snuggled tightly between them.

"I'm glad she won't have to grow up learning that this kind of thing is normal," said Lubica softly.

Wolf kissed the top of her head and they waited there in silence until the activities in the street seemed to either die down or move away.

Lubica looked up at him as he pulled away slightly. "Think it's safe?"

Wolf was about to speak when they heard the very close report of a machine gun.

He felt like the wind had been knocked out of him and Lubica's eyes registered surprise as Anja began to scream.

"Lubica?" he yelled but she didn't respond and he felt her knees buckle. Only his body pressing her against the wall kept her upright and kept Anja from falling to the ground. Lubica still said nothing but she was blinking furiously.

He pulled away and saw the blood on Lubica's coat. Panic rose up within him and clawed at his insides like a caged beast. "Oh God!" he groaned. How had they managed it?

Blood drenched Anja's clothing as well but he wasn't sure if it was Lubica's or her own.

He scooped them both up and stumbled back toward the jeep, cursing obscenities all the way. Someone must have seen them in there and specifically targeted them. How else would bullets make it all the way to the end of the alley? He could take a pretty educated guess as to the identity of the culprit but at that moment, Lubica was his only concern.

When he burst out of the alley he saw that most of the activity had moved on. It should be all right to drive back to base. To the hospital. To safety.

The world spun about him but he managed to lay them in the back of the jeep. "I'll get you back," he whispered. "You're going to be fine." God, he hoped she was going to be fine. She *had* to be fine. He vacillated between denial and panic. This couldn't be happening! Not after all this. Not now.

There was so much blood he couldn't see where the wound was. And Anja had stopped crying. That worried him. He was about to head to the driver's seat when Lubica's hand snaked out and snagged his jacket.

"We've got to get back to base," he rasped. But she held on. Her huge brown eyes seemed unnaturally dull, despite the tears that glistened there. She mouthed something but her voice was so faint he couldn't hear her. He nodded impatiently. "I know," he responded, even though he wasn't sure what she had said. He had to get moving.

He stumbled around and slid in behind the wheel. He was having trouble breathing and had begun to sweat but he chalked it up to anxiety. He revved the engine and peeled away at full speed, heading toward the base. It couldn't have been more than three or four minutes but the time slowed to a torturous pace. It reminded him of the dreams where you try to run but feel like you're slugging through molasses, every movement a test of stamina, every breath requiring a supreme effort of will, every thought an exercise in concentration.

At last he drove through the gate.

He leaned on the horn as he passed the sentry, and pulled to a stop outside the barracks where there were sure to be men at this time of day. The hospital was on the far side of the compound and he was beginning to have difficulty focusing on the road.

A half a dozen men spilled outside to see what the ruckus was about. He recognized Brooks and Neilsen and felt a welcome wash of relief. They were young and they were screwups but they were *his* screwups. He slouched forward across the steering wheel.

"In the back," he wheezed when they reached him. "Lubica..." Why the hell couldn't he breathe? His body was betraying him. A dark curtain seemed determined to settle over his eyes.

The next moment rough hands were pulling him out of the jeep. "No, no, you idiots." He made a weak attempt to fend them off. They had probably seen Lubica's blood on his clothes. "Not me. In the back." But then he was on the ground looking up at concerned faces. He tried to sit up but his body refused to follow orders.

Then Riley's face came into view. "Wolf?" Riley's eyes raked over Wolf's body. "Jesus Christ! What the hell happened? How did you drive back here?"

Riley's questions confused him. Wolf licked his lips but moisture seemed to elude him. "Lu…" His tongue felt thick and sluggish, making speech impossible. But surely they had found her.

Riley confirmed his thoughts when he called out. "Where the hell is the medic? And where are the fucking ambulances?" *Good. They were going to get her to the base hospital.*

Just then the pressure in Wolf's chest became intolerable. He coughed reflexively and heard Riley again. "Jesus! Sweet Jesus." Then, "Thank God." Riley said something else but it seemed distant…muffled. He couldn't make it out.

Then a man that Wolf knew as a field medic appeared in his field of view. He tried to shake his head. What were they doing? They should see to Lubica and her baby.

He heard Riley again. "Is that morphine?"

The medic said something incoherent and Riley responded with, "No? Then what the hell is it? God, I…" The voices, the light, the sense of reality—everything began to dissolve like a sugar cube in water.

Wolf was confused. *Morphine?* Through the haze, he caught sight of a syringe. But he was in no pain. In fact, come to think of it, he couldn't feel much of anything. Was he injured? Lubica must be all right. She must already be on her way to the hospital if they were fussing over him like this. Maybe she was being looked after and he could finally relax.

"Wolf!" Riley yelled directly into his ear. "Stay with me, here!"

Wolf focused on him again. He realized he had been fading, the curtain getting heavier, but now he looked up at Riley. He could swear there were tears in his friend's eyes but he was past questioning why. At that moment he was just tired. God, he was tired. If he could just close his eyes, just for a minute. But Riley kept nagging at him, keeping him awake. "*Shut up, Riley!*" formed in his mind but wouldn't make it to his lips.

He felt himself being lifted onto a stretcher. Always Riley's voice was in his ear, goading him, nagging him, annoying him. He wanted to swat him away like an irritating fly. But his hands didn't seem to want to move. His fingers felt numb.

Finally his eyes closed. Nothing would keep them open any longer. The black velvet curtain settled. The darkness was deep, seductive.

As if from very far away, as if he were in the bottom of a deep, empty well, the distant echo of Riley's familiar taunts reached him. "Don't you dare die on me, dammit. Don't you fucking *dare!* Wolves have nine lives, remember?"

Deep in the well, Wolf laughed at Riley's mixed-up metaphor. He never could keep that stuff straight.

Wolf allowed himself to drift in the void. *At least Lubica and Anja are going to be okay.* He had gotten them back. He couldn't live with himself if something happened to them. They had come so far and they were the last. They just had to make it.

Then, finally, Riley shut up and he settled into a profound, blissful silence.

Part Three: Wounded Souls

Perth County, May 1999

Chapter Seventeen

So much blood.

Leah Lichty ran until her lungs burned. The tall grass whipped at her bare legs as they pumped like slender pistons. Through a cloud of tears she dodged groundhog holes and cow pies. At last she scaled the fence. Her skirt caught and tore on the wire but she pressed on. She ducked under tree limbs and found some solace amidst the dappled shadows of the trees that rimmed their farm. But she knew she wasn't safe. Not here. Not yet.

There had been so much blood.

Blood wasn't strange to her. Blood was as much a part of her existence as oxygen or sunshine. Blood meant life.

She had often peered through the barn doors and watched in fascination as hogs were slaughtered, the meat hacked from the bones and eventually hung in the smoke house to add flavour and tenderness. She had watched headless chickens cavort and flap about the barn until finally resting in a lifeless heap. She had watched as beef cattle were killed and bled, gutted and skinned.

Even at the tender age of eleven, Leah was well acquainted with blood and death. It was a necessity, an essential part of life. But this time it was different. The images flooded back as she crashed through underbrush and slipped on the soft mulch.

She was sure he hadn't seen her. She had hidden in the haymow until she was sure he was gone. Then she had quietly climbed down the stairs, holding her breath as her heart pounded against her chest like a carpenter's hammer. She had edged past the limp figure on the barn floor. Her eyes had been drawn to his face but all she could see was the blood and the pale mask of death. She knew without a doubt that her father was gone and there was nothing she could do for him. So once she cleared the battered old walls of the barn that had once meant happiness and security, she ran. She ran like she had a hell hound on her tail. And still she ran.

Their words echoed in her head…

"I won't let you do this. You have no right."

"No right?! How dare you speak of rights! You're a hypocrite. I'm sick of your preaching and your self-righteousness. You don't deserve my trust or my respect."

"How did you figure it out?"

"It's so obvious. I was a fool not to have seen it sooner. But, God help me, I was blinded by my trust."

"Well, it's a little late now, wouldn't you say?"

"It's not too late to see you exposed and maybe seek forgiveness."

"You're crazy if you think that will ever happen."

"It has to. You can't be allowed to continue with your lies. Too many have suffered already."

"And just how do you propose to stop me?"

And then the shovel had come flying through the air. The blood had poured from the gash on the side of his head and he hadn't moved again.

Tears streamed down Leah's face as she fled. But where was she running to? She couldn't go home. What if *he* came back? She couldn't possibly face him, with those images so fresh in her mind. She couldn't tell anyone. Who would believe her? She didn't believe it herself.

She continued to run, without direction, her auburn braids bouncing about her shoulders. She silently cursed the full skirt on her old-fashioned, flowered dress. She wondered, for the millionth time, what it would feel like to wear pants like the men did, or shorts and running shoes.

Sometimes she hated her clothes, hated being different. Sometimes she longed to be like the people she saw in town, the people who looked at her and her family oddly, whose children stared and pointed fingers and laughed at their strangely painted cars.

Leah breached the far side of the bush. She stepped out into blinding sunshine and stopped. She suddenly remembered a conversation she had overheard several months earlier. Her parents had thought she was asleep but she had heard every word. She had been riveted by the information that pertained so directly to her, but which she had never had any hint of before.

There *was* someone she could go to. There was someone to whom she had a connection, someone beyond the community. There was someone in the outside world, someone who would protect her, and maybe even love her.

Now she just had to find her.

Chapter Eighteen

"Why do you do this to yourself?" moaned Heidi as she picked at a cuticle.

"What do you mean?" Ronni's eyes swept to the left and right as she checked the endless ribbon of highway for non-existent traffic. Satisfied, she pulled away from the stop sign and settled into her seat for what promised to be a tedious journey.

"You know perfectly well what I mean. It's been…what? Eleven years now? Let go, already. You're obsessed." Heidi picked up her purse and fished around until she found a nailclipper. Her purse was enormous and Ronni didn't know how she ever found anything in that pit.

"I'm not obsessed," said Ronni.

"What would you call it?"

Ronni remained silent, keeping her eyes focused on the road in front of her. She tried not to see the rolling farmland that spread out around her. The corn had just started to sprout and a fine green haze coated the landscape. The air that wafted in the open windows was fresh with the spring scents of damp earth and apple blossoms. But she tried not to think about that. Those things reminded her of her life on the farm and those memories were far too painful.

"Is it really so terrible to make one lousy trip out here every year? I hardly call that an obsession," said Ronni in exasperation.

"That's not all there is to it and you know it." Heidi had already discarded the clipper and traded it in for an emery board. She glanced out the window as she stroked expertly at her nails. "God, how do you stand it? The drive alone is boring me to tears." Heidi was a city girl through and through. A drive into the suburbs tested her patience.

"Look, you didn't have to come. I tried to talk you out of it. I don't understand why you insisted." Ronni really wished Heidi hadn't come. She preferred to do this alone. It was the one time of year that she felt close to him and she didn't like sharing it with anyone. But Heidi had been adamant.

"I just had to see where you grew up, and see the marker for this Greek god of yours."

Ronni gritted her teeth against the rage that instantly bubbled up inside her. "I never said he was a god."

"You never said it but you sure act like it. Who else but a god would be worth pining over for eleven goddamn years?"

"That's it!" Ronni pulled over and screamed to a stop, churning up dust from the shoulder of the road. She twisted in her seat to face her friend. "I like you, Heidi. God knows you're the best friend I've ever had. But if you don't shut the fuck up and let me drive in peace you can get out right here. I'll pick you up on my way back. Why do you have to be like this?"

"Because I care about you, Ronni!" Heidi's eyes flashed their own fire. "Dammit, somebody's got to wake you up to what you're doing to yourself."

"I don't need psychoanalysis; I need a friend. Now, what's the decision? Stay here and shut up, or get out and wait under that tree?"

Heidi's blue eyes blazed as she tossed her blonde curls back out of her eyes. She grunted in frustration. "Oh, all right. I'll shut up. I just wanted you to know how I feel."

"God, I know already. You've been chanting the same mantra for years."

"It obviously hasn't done any good."

"Right. So why don't you shut up about it, already?"

Before Heidi could say anything further, Ronni popped in a tape and cranked up the stereo. The familiar saga of 'Jack and Diane' pounded through the interior of the car and leaked out the open windows, the words grieving the loss of innocence and urging the listener to savor their youth, to hang onto it as long as possible. Today of all days, the lyrics struck a sensitive chord in her soul. She turned it up another notch and let herself share in John Mellencamp's lament.

Cruising down the highway, Ronni chose not to look at her friend who no doubt had donned a fresh frown. Heidi didn't like her music that loud and preferred the more recent hits but this was Ronni's show. Heidi could like it or lump it. Ronni floored the accelerator and the speedometer topped a hundred and twenty clicks. The music blared and the hot wind whipped her hair up through the sunroof of her red, 1994 Firebird.

Twenty minutes later they pulled to the side of the road near a grove of ash and willow trees. Ronni turned off the ignition and stared out over the two-acre plot dotted with pink and gray polished headstones. It was a peaceful scene. Idyllic. So, why did it evoke such turmoil in her? She bit her lower lip to ward off tears. Somehow, Heidi's presence was making her more vulnerable. She didn't usually cry this soon.

Finally, Heidi offered a scrap of sensitivity. "I'll wait here," she said softly. "I'll come over when you wave to me that you're ready."

Ronni nodded and, in grateful silence, got out of the car. She walked with purpose toward the far side of the cemetery to the familiar gray stone. It was nestled under a willow tree whose branches hung low enough to give her the illusion of privacy. She touched the rough upper edge of the marker, then sat cross-legged, facing the polished face. With a copper-painted fingernail she traced the letters of his name.

"Hi, Jesse," she whispered.

Maybe Heidi was right. Maybe this was crazy. She was going to sit here, probably for the next twenty minutes, talking to a hunk of rock. She knew full well that he wasn't here. Not even his spirit was here. That was the one belief from her childhood that she still clung to. She had to believe he was in a better place. She couldn't live with the idea that he had just—poof—ceased to exist but this was where she felt closest to him. Not just because his body was beneath her, but because she was in the middle of the country where they had spent all their time together. She felt like his spirit touched her here. Even after eleven years, she still needed to feel his spirit.

"Things are going well, Jesse. The band signed a contract for another year, and even got a raise to boot. I'm still working at that insurance company part-time. I hate the job but I really can't complain. Mr. Endecott is really supportive. He lets me take time off if we have to go out of town and he's even come to see us for himself a couple of times." She smiled to herself. "He has a daughter about my age. I think maybe that's why he's so nice to me." She silently cursed her own father. She still hadn't forgiven him. She never intended to. "I think he would have liked you."

She combed her fingers through her hair. It wasn't as long as it used to be but it still hung below her shoulders in thick waves. The curl was natural. She had just never realized she had wavy hair before because the weight of all that length had pulled it straight.

Heidi often complained that Ronni had no right to have such gorgeous hair, and not have to work at it at all. Heidi got her hair color out of a bottle. Come to think of it, that's where her curls came from too. But Heidi made no apologies for her affectations. Heidi made no apologies for anything.

"Heidi came today," she continued. "She's a good friend but she doesn't understand. She wants me to let go of you, to forget about you." She shook her head. "But that's impossible. Everything I am, I am because of you." A tear trickled down her cheek. "God, I still miss you. You jerk! Why'd you have to go and crash your damn car?" She often vacillated between anger at Jesse, despair over his absence and fury at her family. These visits tended to culminate all those emotions into one heart-wrenching ritual.

"Ronni?" The man's voice startled her. She roughly wiped at her eyes and stood up but, when she turned around, she didn't hesitate to embrace the man behind her. She fell gratefully into his arms and tried to soak up a little of his strength.

"I wondered if I'd see you here today," said Jesse's brother as he rubbed her back.

She sniffled and pulled away. "You know I wouldn't miss it." Sam was the one person in the world who seemed to fully understand her anguish. He shared her sorrow over the loss and her outrage at the people whom they saw as the cause of Jesse's death. Unfortunately he was gone for much of the year, as his work as a photographer took him abroad for months at a time. But he always managed to make it back for a visit to the cemetery on the anniversary of the accident.

In a strange way, Ronni was grateful that Sam looked nothing like his brother. He was about the same height but there the similarity ended. Where Jesse's hair had been dark and straight, Sam's waves gleamed a ruddy blond. Like Jesse, his eyes glinted with mischief but they sparkled hazel rather than blue. His features were softer than Jesse's and he had one distinctive dimple in his left cheek. Where Jesse had looked the rogue, Sam embodied the boy next door.

He had come to see Ronni a few weeks after she talked to his father. He had gone on a drinking binge that had lasted a week, and then had taken a week to recover before going to see her. He and Jesse had been close and Jesse had confided much to him in letters and over the phone, so he knew, even better than their father, how much Ronni had meant to him. Ronni had to admit that he probably felt the void even more keenly than she did. He had lost a brother he had known for twenty years. But he never belittled her grief. They shared it as equals.

He brushed a tear from her cheek, the gesture intimate but brotherly. Their relationship had never been anything other than friends. "How are you doing?"

She shrugged. "All right. I always cry when I come here. But otherwise things are good." She fished a tissue out of her pocket and dabbed at her eyes. "Are you going to come hear us while you're in town?"

"I'd like to. When's your next gig?"

"Tomorrow night."

He smiled warmly. "It's a date. I can never get enough of your voice. Jesse never exaggerated about that."

Like his brother, Sam never feigned his admiration for Ronni's talent. His compliments were sincere and meant more than even the most glowing newspaper reviews. "Thanks, Sam. I need all the fans I can get."

"I can't understand that you've never landed a recording contract."

"I've never really pushed that hard for one. I'm not sure I want to get into that scene. I do it for fun and a little money is nice. People enjoy it and I get to sing. That's enough for me."

Sam chuckled. "You're way more mature than me. I'm always looking for public adoration for my work. And the money sure is nice too."

"Hey! You forget about me, or what?" Heidi picked her way through the anklehigh grass.

"Oh shoot," muttered Ronni. When Heidi reached them she apologized, "I'm sorry, Heidi. Sam sort of distracted me." She made the necessary introductions.

Heidi extended her hand. "Okay, Ronni. If Jesse was half as cute as his brother I can understand why he's so unforgettable."

Sam snorted softly. "Don't underestimate my brother. He was ten times more handsome."

Ronni grinned. "Don't sell yourself short, Sam. He was only five times more handsome."

Sam smiled but it was half-hearted at best. He took a step forward and touched the stone. It was a fleeting gesture but it made Ronni's throat go tight again. He turned back to her and something indefinable flitted across his features. "I gotta get going. I promised Dad I'd take him out to supper. But there's something I need to tell you."

"Yes?"

He took a deep breath. "Your father's dead, Ronni."

She just looked at him, blinking stupidly as the words sank in. *Her father? Dead?* She wasn't sure what she was feeling. Or was she feeling nothing at all? It was difficult to sift through the layers of protective armor she had built up with regards to her family. "Dead?"

"Yes, he died less than a week ago. My dad read about it in the paper. He would have called you but he thought for sure your family would have notified you." He sighed. "I wasn't so sure."

"No, they didn't call me. Not that I'm surprised." She glanced at Heidi, who was obviously dumbfounded by the news. Ronni had told her she was not on speaking terms with her family but she obviously wasn't aware of the extremes to which the feud had gone. How ironic that Sam and his father had become her surrogate family. Her parents' quest to keep her apart from the questionable influence of *The Wards* had not met with much success. In fact, that was probably what had pushed them together. She didn't see them that often but, when she thought of family, it was their faces that sprang to mind. "How did it happen? He was awfully young for a heart attack."

Sam scratched his head. "That's the funny part. The paper didn't give a cause of death and the word around is that the cops were crawling all over the Lichty place for days."

"Cops?"

"You think somebody killed him?" asked Heidi, a wicked sparkle in her eye. No doubt the hint of scandal intrigued her. Heidi was always looking for adventure, was always looking to the horizon and what lay beyond, or latching onto the most unlikely cohorts. Ronni was sure that was part of the reason for her initial attraction to Heidi as a friend. Heidi had the courage and the audacity to go her own way and speak her mind no matter what anyone thought. Especially in the beginning, Ronni had drawn strength from that.

"I don't know. It was more likely a farm accident," responded Sam.

Ronni nodded agreement. Such accidents occurred all too frequently around here. Anything from silo gas to grain augers to a tractor rolling down a hillside could claim the life of a farmer or a member of his family. All too often they claimed the lives of romping, careless children as well.

Sam continued, "But it's just weird that nobody's saying anything."

Ronni knelt down in front of the stone again and stared at it as she sorted through the tangle of emotions his news had woven in her heart. "Thanks, Sam. It's good to know."

"Yeah, well, I just thought you should know. I didn't exactly figure you'd fall apart." He shifted his feet awkwardly. "I gotta go. I'll see you tomorrow night. Nine o'clock?"

Ronni nodded. "Say hi to your dad, okay? Give him a kiss for me." She allowed a smile to flit across her lips.

Sam shook his head and his eyes twinkled in that way that reminded her of his brother. "That's one message you'll have to deliver yourself. 'Til tomorrow." He bent low and pecked her on the cheek before nodding to Heidi and heading back to his car.

Heidi knelt beside her. "You okay?"

"Yeah. I always get a little misty on these visits."

Heidi frowned. "No, I meant about your father."

"What about him?"

"Come on, Ronni! You don't have to keep up the act for me. Your father died a few days ago. You have to feel something."

Ronni turned to look at her. "Do I?"

"Jesus! What did he do to you?"

"You know the answer to that, Heidi. He stole Jesse from me." She touched the stone once more before standing and heading back the way she had come.

Heidi ran to catch up. "It's not like he deliberately killed Jesse."

"Isn't it?"

Heidi grabbed her arm. "Stop and talk to me!"

Ronni whirled around and glared at her friend. "Okay, here it is. You've heard it all before but I guess I have to spell it out for you. I had given up everything. I had given up my baby, my family, my friends, my home. Everything that had ever been important to me was gone because they didn't approve of Jesse's lifestyle and my feelings for him. He was the only friend I had left. My parents knew full well how strongly I still felt about him, and yet, going against explicit instructions from me, they deliberately tried to keep him from me." She looked into the distance, trying to regain control of her emotions. The blue of the sky seared her retinas with its purity.

Purity. Trust. Faith. Those words used to mean something to her. Now they were just vivid reminders of the hypocrisy she had witnessed…and escaped. "Well, they succeeded, didn't they?"

Heidi floundered, trying to think of something to say.

Ronni continued relentlessly, "Maybe they didn't intend for him to die but even when he was dead, they didn't allow me the God-given right to mourn for him properly. They turned away his father's attempts to find me so that I could attend the funeral and say goodbye along with the other people who loved him." She turned back to meet Heidi's eyes. "Now, you tell me, Heidi, what did they have to gain from that? Nothing. They did it out of spite, pure and simple. Does my father deserve my grief?" She plodded back toward the car. "I don't think he does."

Chapter Nineteen

Silence.

That was the thing Wolf loved the most about being out here—the absolute silence. It was too early in the season for crickets and the birds had settled down for the night. All that could be heard was the wind in the oak and pine trees, and the crackling of the fire. No gunfire or explosions echoed in the distance. The horizon didn't flicker perpetually like a macabre Christmas tree. There were no shouts or screams of people running for their lives or loudly wailing as they mourned loved ones who had been slain and left to rot at the side of the road.

Wolf sat up and poked at the fire. He scolded himself silently. The whole point of this trip was to dispel those images, not dwell on them. Sparks flew up, crackling and sputtering like tiny fireworks as he continued to prod the dry kindling. He finally put down the stick he had been using as a poker and lay back down on his sleeping bag. It was a clear night and legions of glittering stars marched across the heavens. But no night sky could compare with those of his childhood.

The summer skies in the Yukon boasted more stars than anywhere in the world and when the northern lights made an appearance, those bands of iridescent color outshone the most elaborate fireworks displays man could devise. Wolf's father used to refer to them as The Watercolors of God. It was as though the Lord himself had brushed the hues across the dark horizon.

Since leaving Bosnia, Wolf had often found his thoughts turning to the quiet faith that his parents had lived. They had never gone to church—there weren't many to choose from in their little corner of the world—but organized religion wouldn't have been Neil and Diane's style anyway. There had been Bibles in the house but Wolf had rarely seen his parents poring over scripture or spouting platitudes. Rather, their faith manifested itself as more of an all-pervasive attitude, a way of looking at the world.

Thanks were always given before a meal and in the event of good fortune befalling one of them. Bedtime prayers were non-negotiable until they were old enough to put themselves to bed. But even then it was understood that it was a household policy. Occasionally Wolf would come in from a hard day of playing or schoolwork to see his mother sitting silently in the living room. He asked her once what she was doing and her response was, "Just getting God's advice on how to keep you guys out of trouble."

Somehow his parents had a two-way relationship with the Almighty. Wolf hadn't quite managed that yet but his months spent in a hospital bed had given him plenty of time for reflection and he had decided that his parents had at least been on the right track. If there was no God what was the point? After all he had seen and been through, he knew that much. There had to be a point. There had to be a reason, a plan. If there wasn't he may as well have put a gun in his mouth.

His injuries and the other events that surrounded them had joined forces to throw him into a deep and prolonged depression. He had spent a month considering doing just that. If he could have lifted a revolver he might actually have gone through with it. In that respect his brush with death had served him well. In an odd twist of fate it had saved his life. It had forced him to take the time to consider the decision and it had given Riley a chance to snap him out of it.

Riley had shown up at Wolf's bedside with his new son. As usual, Wolf had refused to speak to him. He had looked the other way, away from his friend and the gurgling baby. Riley had ignored his reticence and had laid little Trevor on his lap and left the room. Incensed, Wolf had shouted and cursed and threatened to no avail. But regardless of his bluffs and bluster, he was utterly helpless to move himself or the baby from that damn bed. Riley refused to return until Wolf picked up the child.

The gurgles had eventually turned to complaints and then full-fledged screams. Wolf had finally given in to instincts and despite shaky hands had picked up the squalling baby. His hands may have been unsteady but they were strong enough to snuggle the ten-pound infant to his chest. They were strong enough to stroke and soothe. And they were sensitive enough to absorb the soft, sweet-smelling, undeniable evidence of *life* that they held.

The baby had responded to Wolf's gentle caresses and the screams had eventually quieted.

Riley had returned about ten minutes later. "See, old buddy?' he had said, his voice thick with emotion. "Despite what you've been telling yourself, *life does go on.*"

Riley had scooped up his son and Wolf had broken down and shed the tears he had been holding onto for months. Tears of grief for Lubica and her child and the future he had lost. Tears of guilt for letting them down and managing to survive himself. And tears of rage for the bastards and the mentality of hatred that had done this to them and so many others.

His time with Lubica may have been brief but it had touched him deeply. She had embodied everything he had hoped for in a partner and the timing had been right. In those few short hours his hopes and his spirits had soared. The crash and burn had been a hell like he never imagined.

After the catharsis with Riley, he had finally allowed himself to grieve and had eventually decided that hating back would bring him nothing but bitterness. He struggled through bouts of rage and regret. He cherished the moments of peace, and fought to hold onto them as long as possible. The battle continued but he thought, maybe, he was winning.

Visiting with his family back home had felt like an oasis amidst his turmoil. Their joy at his safe return had rubbed off on him like a balm. He had felt happy and loved—for a time. Too soon he had become restless and he acknowledged with some sadness that he didn't belong there anymore. He had to find a new place. A new home. Whether it existed on a prairie, atop a mountain, beside a lake or merely as some elusive zone within himself, he couldn't rest until he found it. Perhaps when he found it, there too he would find healing.

The search for that zone had been a major factor in his decision to undertake this extended hiking trip. He was taking the time alone, with no one depending on him and no one to distract him, to refocus and decide where he was going from here.

He needed a trail that was long enough to sustain a month or two of rigorous hiking, and remote enough to allow him the solitude he so desperately needed. The Bruce Trail that ran along the limestone cliffs and outcroppings of the Niagara Escarpment for seven hundred kilometers from Niagara to Tobermory, had fit the bill. The trail ran along expansive cliff-top vistas that overlooked the crystal clear waters of Georgian Bay. It ribboned over rocky climbs, rolling farmland, and even ran through the occasional small town. Wolf chose it because it was isolated but yet within easy reach of civilization for supplies and emergencies if necessary. This wasn't survival training; it was therapy. He already knew how to survive.

He pulled a light blanket over himself and closed his eyes. Then he heard it.

He sat up like a bolt of lightning had struck him. He could have sworn he heard whimpering. He scrubbed his face with his hands. He must be losing it. He was reliving the night he had first found Lubica in that gutted building. He lay back down but the instant his head hit the pillow he heard it again. It wasn't his imagination. There was someone just outside the circle of firelight and they were crying.

He got up and tried to focus on the sound. He stepped out of the light into a small grove of birches. The whimpers continued. "Hello?" he said softly. "Who's there?"

The whimpers stopped, but then resumed again, more loudly. It was a child; he was almost certain. "It's okay. I'm here to help. Did you lose your mom?"

"Yes," was the tiny response.

The word startled him. He was almost on top of her. She was huddled just a few feet ahead of him at the base of a tree. In two strides he reached her. He knelt beside her but refrained from touching her. "Are you lost?" *Stupid question, idiot!*

But she seemed oblivious to the obviousness of the answer. She nodded vigorously, "I'm looking for my mother, but…" She shrugged.

He tried to smile reassuringly. "Well, you've found the right guy to help you. I'm great at finding moms." *Yeah, and you're great at losing them again too.* He banished that thought before it could take hold. "How long have you been out here?"

She swiped at the moisture that shimmered on her upper lip. "I dunno. A few days."

Wolf's eyebrows shot up. *A few days?* The child couldn't have been much more than ten and yet she had survived, on her own, without food or a blanket to sleep on, for *several days!* True, the nights had been warm and there had been no rain, but still…

Not wanting to alarm her with an exaggerated reaction to her news, he glossed over his amazement. He kept his expression calm and non-threatening as he held out his hand. "Well then you must be half-starved. You wanna come over to my fire? I've got some Chef Boy-R-Dee ravioli. I bet you love that stuff."

She studied him only briefly before taking his hand and following him. "I don't know. What is it?'

He stopped dead in his tracks. "You've never heard of Chef Boy-R-Dee?"

She shook her head. "No. Is it food?"

He laughed as a tiny bit of tension seeped out of him. "Sort of. You eat some and let me know what you think."

He led her back to the fire, amazed at how easily she seemed to trust him. Maybe her parents hadn't drilled into her to be wary of sexual perverts lurking in the woods. For once, maybe that was a good thing.

He told her to sit on his sleeping bag while he stoked up the fire. Once the flames were licking voraciously at a fresh chunk of birch, he grabbed his backpack and rooted through it until he withdrew a familiar red and white can. He opened it, dumped the entire contents into a tin saucepan and set it on the small grate over the fire.

"So, how old are you?" he said as he stirred the concoction that had been such a rare treat in his childhood. These days it seemed that North American children ate such prepared foods with frightening regularity. Even their children had been swept up in the proverbial rat race. He wondered how it was that this child had been left behind.

"I just turned eleven."

"Wow, you're almost all grown up."

"Nope, I got a ways to go yet."

He chuckled. Obviously wise beyond her years. He continued stirring. "Were you camping or something when you got lost?" He actually found it hard to believe that that was the case. She was hardly dressed for camping, in that simple little flowered dress and leather shoes. The clothing was surprisingly clean and intact considering how long she had been out here. But even so, he would have to find something else for her to wear as soon as possible.

"Nope, I ran away."

His spoon froze in mid-stir. "I thought you said you were *looking* for your mom."

"I am."

Okay, where do we go from here? "Who did you run away from?"

"Well, I thought she was my mom but she wasn't."

So much for escaping the stress of civilization. He had obviously imported his own private soap opera. Maybe he should leave this conversation for the morning, maybe with a good night's sleep and a full stomach she'd make more sense. The ravioli was steaming, so he spooned some out into a bowl and handed it to her. "Watch out, it's hot."

She took the bowl and leaned over it, blowing on the little meat-filled squares. He couldn't help but notice her hair, which hung in loose waves below her shoulders. Even several days without a bath couldn't hide the brilliant auburn highlights that glowed in the firelight. She was fine-featured, a beautiful child. What was she running from? What was she running to?

She took a bite.

He allowed her to chew for a moment before he asked, "So? What do you think?"

She smiled and nodded. "I like it."

"Go figure."

"What?"

"Nothing. Eat as much as you like. You can sleep in my bag tonight, and in the morning we'll see what the police know about you."

The bowl dropped and the spoon clattered against the tin. "No, please don't do that. They'll take me back. I know it. I can't go back there. You said you'd help me find my mom." Tears shimmered in her eyes. "You promised."

"But I'm sure the police will know where your mother is."

"No, you don't understand. I know where she is, I just got lost trying to find her."

He blew out a long, slow breath. "Okay, okay. Where is she?"

The child chewed on her lower lip. "She lives in this place called Kitchener. I don't know the address but it can't be that big. I lived near Wallenstein. I didn't think it was that far. I thought I could walk it in a couple of days but I think I got turned around. If you could just take me there I know we could find her. Maybe in the phone book. Just…please don't tell the police. I just know they'll want to take me home."

Wolf studied her. She certainly had gotten turned around. She had gone in quite the opposite direction, from what he knew of the region, and she had come a long way. Amazing. She was obviously a very resourceful eleven-year-old. And not typical, considering his limited experience with children. The children in Bosnia didn't really count. Their childhood was ripped from them before they really had a chance to experience it.

He drew himself back to the problem at hand. He didn't understand all the nuances of this yet but maybe he could go along with it for a while, at least until the picture got a little clearer.

"You know your mother's name?"

"Yes. It's Veronica Lichty. Unless she got married. I don't know about that."

"You've never met this woman who is supposedly your mother?"

"No, it's just…well…I think she couldn't keep me."

What if she just didn't want you? What if she still doesn't? But he couldn't very well verbalize that. He hoped he was wrong; it was obvious that the child desperately needed her mother. At least, she needed *someone*. "How about you? What's your name?"

She seemed to relax, sensing that maybe he was going to do as she asked. "Leah."

"That's a pretty name." And he meant it. A pretty name for a charming girl.

"Thank you. Does that mean you'll help me?"

"I take it if you go home you'll just run away again?"

She nodded.

Honest, too.

He shook his head woefully. "Well then, you don't leave me much choice. You can tell me more tomorrow. I was supposed to get picked up next month, so I don't have a vehicle. We'll have to find one somewhere but I'll worry about that." He realized he was rambling as he considered what would be involved in this little journey. "You just eat up and don't worry about anything." He smiled gently. "Okay, Leah?"

She nodded and picked up her bowl. "What's *your* name?" she asked.

"Wolf."

She perked up. "Really? I didn't know that was a name."

"I kinda like breaking new ground."

"Oh," she said and returned her attention to the ravioli.

He smiled at the simple response and her easy acceptance of the explanation.

He watched her eat. Somebody was worried about her, but who? He hoped this wasn't a mistake but his gut said otherwise. She struck him as an intelligent girl, not hysterical or unreasonable. So, for now, he'd do as she asked. He just hoped he wouldn't get nabbed for kidnapping. He could just see the headline, *Retired Army Captain Kidnaps Child in Psychotic Episode Related to Critical Injury.* Well, they might condense it a bit more than that but essentially that would be the gist of it. So, he'd just have to be sure to not get caught.

He crossed an arm over his abdomen and rubbed at his floating rib. Right now it was aching with a vengeance.

Then he smiled to himself. Compared to previous exploits, this little adventure should be a breeze.

Chapter Twenty

Verna stirred some sugar into her tea. The spoon clinked against the sides of the antique china cup. "Thank you for coming. I know you aren't responsible for visitations any more."

"Don't be ridiculous. We're friends and I know how difficult this must be for you," he said as he sipped from his own steaming brew.

As if his words alone had drawn them out, a fresh wave of tears spilled out of her eyes. She dabbed at them with a fresh tissue from the box beside her.

He continued, "Losing a husband and a granddaughter in the same day is beyond imagining. I think you've held up remarkably well considering the circumstances."

"Anna and the boys have been wonderful."

"You're very lucky to have such a supportive family."

Her smile was wan. "And everyone from church has been wonderful too. I have more casseroles and cakes than I know what to do with. And, of course Stephen has taken over the farm. Roy and Cliff are helping until he gets settled with everything."

He smiled warmly. "The Lord hasn't forgotten you either. You know he's there for your needs."

She nodded. "Yes, I know. I just don't understand why someone would come onto our property and steal her away like that." She stifled a sob. "And why hurt Glenn?"

"You know the police's theories on that, Verna. I'm loath to repeat the words out loud."

"I know." Her voice wavered. "It's too horrible to consider."

He reached across the table and covered her hand with his. She had aged in the last few days, he thought. Her loss had taken its toll on her, and on him as well. Helping a friend through the loss of a loved one tended to be a draining experience even at the best of times. But this time was worse. Infinitely so. "The police are doing everything they can and the prayer chain is working overtime. I'm sure we'll get her back safe and sound. You have to leave things in His hands."

"Yes. Of course, you're right."

"Now, I really should go and let you grieve in peace." He stood to leave, feeling the weight of his burden keenly.

She moved as if to rise. "Thank you again."

He motioned for her to stay seated. "You sit and rest. I know the way out. Is someone staying with you tonight?"

"Yes, Anna is bringing the baby and staying the night."

"Good. I'm sure that little bundle will do wonders for your spirit." He reached the door to the kitchen. "Don't hesitate to call again if you need anything." Then he walked out and slipped through the back door.

He slid in behind the wheel of his car and took a moment to rest his forehead against the steering wheel before turning the key and driving out the long lane.

He shrugged off the malaise and mentally congratulated himself. What an incredible stroke of luck! Leah's disappearance on the very day that Glenn was killed had been an answer to prayer. That was one loose end that he no longer had to worry about. Naturally the police had assumed that Glenn had stumbled upon the abduction and had been killed in the struggle. Family and friends had been questioned routinely but the bulk of the suspicion lay with an outside party. Likely someone had had their eyes on Leah for some time, they thought. How unfortunate that Glenn had almost spoiled their near perfect plan.

He chuckled to himself. Verna had mentioned that Leah had been somewhat distracted the last few months. They had hardly expected her to run away but, if she had to do it, she couldn't have picked a better time. Yes, it was an extremely happy coincidence that she had picked that particular day.

He slammed on the brakes, churning up dust and stones on the gravel road. Coincidence? *Was* it a coincidence? He had been so focused over the last week on keeping up the charade of the calm, cool family supporter that this possibility hadn't even occurred to him. Why *had* she run away just then? Then it was crystal clear. How could he have been so blind? His palms began to sweat and he had to concentrate on keeping his breathing slow and steady.

What if she knew? Or worse yet, what if she had seen something? *Oh God, oh God!* He cursed silently then berated himself for his weakness. But where was she? If she had fled in panic maybe she had gotten lost, or fallen and hurt herself. With a little luck she had already died of exposure. God forgive him for hoping such a thing but this was for a greater good.

If she wasn't dead… If she was found alive and well, what would she tell everyone? And with police poking around, what if they revealed her connection to his other indiscretions. He took a deep breath and mopped his forehead with his sleeve. That simply couldn't be allowed to happen. If she were found and brought back here she must never have the opportunity to talk. The encounter with Glenn had left him shaken, but not as badly as the first time. Each time it got a little bit easier. Leah would be no different.

He would find the strength somehow. It was the Lord's will. It had to be done. There was no other way.

* * * * *

Wolf smiled in his sleep. He felt the soft, tentative brush strokes as an animal nuzzled his cheek. *An animal*? Suddenly his reflexes kicked in. His eyes flew open and in the same instant his hand darted up to fend away whatever beast was invading his space. His hand latched around something small and fragile.

"Leah," he said on a sigh of relief. He let go of her wrist and sat up.

Her lower lip was trembling but she hadn't cried out.

"I'm sorry, I didn't mean to frighten you." He picked up her hand and let it rest in his palm as he examined those gossamer-like bones for damage. "Did I hurt your wrist?'

She shook her head and tugged her hand away. She rubbed her eyes. "No, I'm okay."

Okay, I'm a shit. Scare little girls who are just trying to be affectionate. Nice going you big macho GI jerk.

In as soft and non-threatening a voice as possible he asked, "What were you doing?"

"I've never seen a beard before."

"What?" he laughed. "How can that be?"

"All the men in our church shave. I know the Amish grow beards but I've never met one and I think theirs are different anyway. They don't have mustaches with it."

Amish? Church? Slowly understanding began to dawn. That explained the dress and the shoes. But despite his fascination, he didn't want to make too big of a deal out of the new information. He stroked his beard and pulled down the corners of his mouth in a mock frown. "I guess I have gotten kind of scruffy. I've been out here for three weeks. I decided there was no way I was shaving on the trail." He exaggerated the frown until his eyebrows almost met in the middle. "I must look pretty scary," he growled. He winked at her to make sure she knew he was teasing.

She giggled. "No, not at all."

The child was truly amazing. Despite the jest, he had expected her to show at least a pinch of discomfort. He knew two-hundred-pound men, and one arrogant Colonel in particular, who thought he looked scary and that was without the beard. But she seemed completely sincere and at ease. Maybe she had a gift for seeing beyond the surface.

His face smoothed into a smile. "Well, I'm glad you don't think so. I certainly don't feel scary. Now, how about breakfast? I'm afraid it won't be fancy, just cereal bars and juice boxes." He cocked an eyebrow at her. "I don't suppose you drink coffee?"

She giggled again. "No, my dad says it would stunt my growth."

The next moment her face fell. All signs of the smile disappeared.

Wolf frowned with concern. "You okay?"

She stared at the fire pit, now black and dead. It bore no hint of the gay flames that had danced there such a few short hours ago. "I guess I'm just hungry."

Wolf wasn't so sure but decided not to push it. He wondered if this father she had mentioned was her natural father. Or did she even know?

He rummaged through his supplies and found a couple of granola bars and some orange juice. He pulled out his portable propane burner and put water on for coffee. He drank instant on the trail because he couldn't be bothered with the fuss of a percolator.

As they munched he asked casually, "You mentioned a church. What kind of church would that be?"

"Mennonite."

"Mmm. I've heard of that but I'm afraid I don't know a whole lot. What can you tell me?"

She took a sip of her juice then gave him a brief outline of Maple Grove's theology and what was expected of its members. Wolf listened with genuine fascination. She seemed very knowledgeable for an eleven-year-old but he guessed that should hardly be a surprise considering she and her family lived their faith on a daily basis. Their church *was* their life. He could see definite advantages, and drawbacks, to such a philosophy.

He sipped from his steaming mug of coffee as she finished her narrative. "So, were you happy there?"

She shrugged. "I guess so."

Not a terribly enthusiastic response but she was only eleven. She was just coming to the age where the world seemed to open before you like a blooming rose. Early puberty came with the dawning of raw maturity and understanding. It was a time for new discoveries and endless questions. And with those questions often came dissatisfaction.

"This mother you're trying to find, does she live like that?"

"I don't think so. She lives in the city, so I really doubt that she goes to a church like ours. I think she left after I was born."

"You said last night that you thought you were living with your mother but then you found out she wasn't. What made you say that? When did you find out that the woman you were living with wasn't your mother?"

She chewed on her lower lip and fidgeted with her empty granola bar wrapper.

"It's okay, Leah. I won't get angry. But if you don't want to tell me, that's okay too."

She looked up at him with a trust that tugged at his heart. "I overheard them talking one night."

"Who?"

"My mother and father. They were talking about her. I had come down late at night because I had to go pee. I stopped on the stairs when I heard them talking because my dad sounded so angry."

"Angry?"

She nodded. "I think there was an article or something in the newspaper about her, because he kept whacking at the paper while he talked."

"What sorts of things was he saying?"

"He said it was a blessing that she gave me up because I'd probably be on drugs already if I had stayed with her. He was angry that she had turned away from everything she had ever been taught. He said something about how she looked like a prostitute in the picture in the paper. And then he said something about how he wished she had moved farther away. He said that Kitchener was too close for comfort and what if she decided she wanted to come see me some day? That's how I know where she lives."

Wolf's brows furrowed in concentration. "Did you ever see that article?"

"No. I think he burned it that night. He could hardly stand the sight of it." She gazed up at him from behind timid eyes, hooded with guilt. She shifted her position on the sleeping bag. "I looked through the garbage the next morning and couldn't find it."

Wolf suppressed the smile that threatened his lips. She had just confessed to him. Little things like eavesdropping and picking through the garbage were wearing on her soul. If she only knew the darkness that stained the soul of her confessor.

He resumed the questions. "Did your mother—I mean, the one you lived with—did she say anything through all this?"

"No, not much. She's always very quiet around him. She just agreed with everything he said. But later I heard her crying. I kinda wondered if she missed her."

Wolf was impressed with her insight. "It sounds like maybe this Veronica is their daughter. Is that what you were thinking?"

"Mm hmm. They didn't say that exactly but I'm pretty sure that's the way it sounded."

Wolf considered the story. *Drugs? Looked like a prostitute? She had her picture in the paper?* What exactly had this woman gotten into? He had to remind himself, however, that considering what he knew of Leah's 'parents', those statements could be meaningless. A woman in tight jeans and a cropped T-shirt might look like a prostitute to them. He had better reserve judgment until he actually met this Veronica.

He drained the last of his coffee. "Okay, that's enough jabbering. We've got a lot to do. Can you help me pack all this stuff up?" She immediately stood and started gathering garbage. Wolf watched her quick, efficient movements. "Then we've got a bit of a hike to the closest town. Are you up for it?"

"Sure. I feel a lot better after a nice sleep and some food. I was getting kinda hungry. I found some berries and stuff while I walked but there wasn't much."

"It sounds to me like you did very well. You kept your head and didn't panic."

She beamed at the compliment.

"But when we get to town we're going to have to get you some new clothes. Does it have to be dresses or would you mind pants or shorts?"

Her eyes sparkled with excitement. "Really? Could I try some jeans and some shorts? I'm sure my mom could pay you back."

Ah, a dissident, he thought. "Don't worry about that. I think I can spare a few bucks. Then we have to find a car and then comes the hard part—finding your mom."

"Don't worry," she said as she began folding a blanket. "We'll find her. I just know it."

Wolf wished he could share her naïve optimism. He figured the odds were against them but he had given her his word and he had every intention of following through on it. He would only give up the quest after all other options had been exhausted.

For now they faced the more immediate problem of getting back to civilization. And they had to avoid the cops while they were at it. If Riley were here he'd say Wolf was certifiable for going through with this. He missed Riley.

Riley was back home in B.C. now with his family. In a way Wolf's experience had changed his life as well. He had decided he'd had enough of the military life. He wanted to see his kids grow up and grow old right alongside his wife. These things were too tenuous to take for granted. They had started up their own sporting goods store, something that had been his dream for years.

Right now Wolf didn't have a dream, didn't want one. Dreams meant hopes and hopes were so easily shattered. For now he was living one day at a time, searching merely for direction and purpose.

But he did want to visit his friend soon. As soon as he knew what the hell he was doing with his life he'd pop in on old Riley. Considering what Riley had done for him, that was the least Wolf owed him.

* * * * *

"Wow!" squealed Heidi. "They're beautiful. Who're they from?" She sniffed deeply from the colorful bouquet of daisies, carnations and freesia that sprouted out of Ronni's desk.

"Who do you think?"

Heidi screwed her face into a frown as she studied her friend. "Well, you're not smiling so they can't be from Sam or Jason." Jason was the lead guitarist in Ronni's band and another good friend. They occasionally sang duets together.

Heidi continued, "I doubt they're from Mr. Endecott so that leaves only one possibility. Wayne."

"Your powers of deduction are truly amazing, Heidi."

"You're going to break up with him, aren't you?"

Ronni turned back to her computer. "I've got a lot of work to do."

"Why?" she huffed out in exasperation. "He seems perfectly nice to me. He sends you flowers. He's got a sense of humor and a good job. Maybe he's a tad skinny but he even likes your music." Heidi knew better than anyone how important that trait was to Ronni. If they didn't like Ronni's music they were out the door in a drum beat.

"I don't know," Ronni hedged. "We just don't click. He must have sensed I was a little cool on the weekend. I think that's why he sent the flowers."

Heidi sighed. "You know why you don't click."

Ronni scrolled down her computer screen, feigning boredom. "No, I don't. But apparently *you* do."

Heidi plucked a carnation from the bouquet and sniffed. "You don't click because you don't want to. You're being faithful to a ghost."

"This is a tired subject, Heidi."

"You're telling me. Have you ever slept with anyone else?"

Now Ronni swung around to glare at her friend. She poured every ounce of indignation she possessed into that stare for fear Heidi could see past it to the truth. "First of all, that's none of your business and second of all, I really do have some work to do. Endecott is letting me off early so I can rehearse before we open tonight and I don't want to disappoint him by slacking off while I'm here. Now, get lost!"

"Is that a hint?" Heidi tucked the carnation behind her ear and batted her thick eyelashes. The picture of innocence. *Huh!*

Ronni growled.

"Okay, okay. I'm going already. Just answer me one more thing."

"What?!"

"Sam's going to be there tonight?"

"You got the hots for him?" Ronni relaxed and let herself smile again.

"Why not? You yourself said he was cute."

"True, but tread carefully. He's away a lot and his career is very important to him. I'm afraid any woman would come in second to that."

Heidi shrugged. "It's not like I'm giving up the love of my life. I'll give it a shot. If he's game, I am."

"Okay, I'll wish you luck. He might actually go for you." The sentiment was sincere. Ronni thought Sam spent far too much time alone. Their friendship filled a void for both of them but it wasn't enough. Sam wasn't bound by his ghosts in the same way that Ronni was. Perhaps he had a shot at happiness.

"You sure you're not interested in him for yourself? He *is* Jesse's brother. They must have a lot in common."

Ronni shook her head. "No, we're just friends. It would feel too strange."

"Okay, your loss."

"Now, will you take off?"

Heidi waved a finger at her friend. "If you're not careful I might start to think you don't want me around." But then she grinned and tossed her curls back as she strutted down the hall toward her desk. "See you tonight," she called.

With a smile, Ronni turned back to her computer screen and refocused on the report for Mr. Endecott. She wanted to do it quickly and well. He placed a lot of faith in her and she didn't like disappointing him.

He had given her a job when her skills were questionable and her experience non-existent. After waitressing for almost a year she'd realized she needed to expand her skills if she wanted to get anywhere. A night school course had provided her with basic clerical skills but her lack of experience had seemed like an insurmountable handicap and resulted in numerous rejections.

Mr. Endecott had been able to see past the résumé. He had said she seemed responsible and like a hard worker, so he had given her a chance. She had tried very hard to live up to his expectations and her efforts had been rewarded. She had gotten several raises and a couple of promotions. But, best of all, he had been open to reducing her hours when the band's schedule had become too hectic. All he asked was free admittance to the club on occasion. Ronni obliged happily.

She put the finishing touches on the report and printed it off. She grabbed up the small stack of paper and headed toward the corner office.

"Can I go in?" she flashed a smile at the matronly woman who served as Mr. Endecott's executive secretary.

Mrs. Strewn peered at her over half-glasses balanced precariously on the end of her laser straight nose. Her mouth remained a grim line as she considered Ronni's request. "Yes," she replied at last. "I suppose so."

Ronni smiled brightly just to spite her. "Thank you and have a lovely day."

Mrs. Strewn scowled as Ronni passed.

Ronni swept into the office. "Mr. Endecott?"

"Ronni, come on in." The pleasure in his voice was genuine. "Did you finish up that quality assurance report?"

She handed it across the desk. "Here it is. If you'd like to glance over it quickly, you can make sure it's up to snuff. I still have time to make changes before I leave."

"I'm sure it's fine." He accepted the report and dropped it on his blotter without even glancing at it. "You're singing tonight?"

"Yes. Did you want to come?"

"I'd love to but we have a birthday dinner for my wife's mother tonight."

Ronni grimaced. "I'm so sorry to hear that, sir." Endecott's mother-in-law seemed to take pride in living up to every stereotype ever conceived for the position. He leaned back in his leather executive's chair and laughed. "Thanks for the sentiment, Ronni. I'll survive and I'll try and make it on Saturday."

"You should bring your wife sometime. Didn't you tell me once she likes to dance?" Ronni had never met his wife but her picture had decorated his desk for years. She was slender with short red hair and dazzling blue eyes. Ronni thought the two of them made a striking couple.

Karl Endecott had held on to his physique very well considering his proximity to the fifty-year mark. His full head of salt-and-pepper gray had just begun to thin around the edges and a neatly trimmed mustache set off his intense gray eyes. A pair of small silver-framed glasses were his only concession to his age. In every aspect of his life, Mr. Endecott radiated refinement and subtle sophistication. For Ronni that package often included fatherly concern.

"I'm afraid your music is a bit of a departure from her usual taste but thank you for asking. My daughter would be a better prospect but she comes home so rarely."

"Well, I think it's wonderful that you and your wife have separate interests. I've heard that makes for a healthy relationship."

"Spoken with the wisdom of someone who has never married," he said lightly as he stood and rounded the desk.

"Are you sure the report's satisfactory?" she asked, unfazed.

"Yes, of course. You always do excellent work." He leaned back against the edge of the desk and crossed his arms as he studied her. "Why haven't you ever married, Ronni? You're intelligent and attractive and talented. Any man would be lucky to have you."

She smiled weakly. "But I'm not happy with *any man*, Mr. Endecott."

"You're right," he conceded. "You deserve someone very special."

Ronni was astounded at herself but she suddenly found herself fighting tears. Maybe it was her visit to the cemetery the day before, or maybe it was Mr. Endecott's genuine concern, or maybe a combination of both. Not that it mattered. All she knew was that at that moment she felt vulnerable and raw. She could feel the protective layers sloughing off right before his eyes. She couldn't withstand his penetrating gaze another moment.

"If that's all, sir…" She took a step back but to her astonishment he reached out and grabbed her hand.

He held her firm. "What is it, Ronni? Did I upset you?"

She shook her head and bit her lip to keep it from quivering.

"Yes I did. You cared for someone and they hurt you, didn't they?"

"No, he didn't..." But she couldn't continue because she was mortified to realize that a tear had squeezed out of her eye. An apology and a suitable excuse for her behavior had just formed in her mind but she never got the chance to verbalize them. In fact they were driven completely from her mind when she found Mr. Endecott's arms around her and her cheek resting against his shoulder.

"Well, someone hurt you and you're still suffering for it. You deserve better." He ran his hand up and down her back. "I'm glad you trust me enough to let me see you cry. Maybe someday you can tell me about it."

Ronni had shed a few tears into the fine wool-silk blend of his suit coat but the supply quickly diminished when the strangeness of the situation began to sink in. He had never touched her like this before—never hugged her, never even held her hand. It seemed like a fatherly gesture, and yet...

Unsettled and uncertain, she dragged herself away from his grasp and wiped her eyes. "Thank you, sir. I appreciate your concern but I'll be fine. Really."

Worry still shadowed his face but he didn't touch her again. "Will you tell me about it someday, Ronni? I have a feeling you have a long story to share."

"You're right, I do. But maybe another time." She regretted the lie. She had never been anything but honest and forthright with him but, no matter how sincere his interest, there was no way in hell she was sharing such a painful and personal story with her boss. Ever.

"All right." He cocked a finger at her and the mood instantly shifted. "You get out of here and break a leg tonight." He tapped a finger on the desktop. "Is that right? Or is that just for actors?"

She smiled, at ease once more. "I'm not sure but thanks for the sentiment. Maybe I'll see you on Saturday."

He waved as she closed the door behind her.

She walked back to her desk and logged off her computer. She grabbed her purse and headed for the elevators.

That had definitely been strange. She had never gotten anything other than platonic or fatherly vibes from him before but today had been subtly different. Had she been imagining it, or had she just been naïve for the last nine years and was just now picking up on the sexual undercurrents? No, she didn't think she could have been that stupid. Today had been different. His hug and caresses had felt less fatherly and more suggestive. Maybe he was just depressed about the prospect of an evening with his mother-in-law. She grimaced at the absurdity of that reasoning. But there had to be a logical explanation for his behavior. He was a happily married man, and a responsible business executive. How dare she think such things of him.

She stepped out into the parking lot. The sun shone brightly and the air held the promise of the summer's heat but a fresh spring breeze caressed her cheeks and kept the humidity at bay.

She slid in behind the wheel and pulled into the early Friday rush hour traffic. As she drove she occasionally glanced up through the sunroof at the lacy clouds that skittered across the sky. She chuckled at the thought of Heidi's reaction if she ever realized the significance of that particular accessory on Ronni's car. Heidi would blow a gasket if she knew of yet another connection to Jesse that Ronni held onto.

She put thoughts of Mr. Endecott behind her. She would deal with that on Monday if she had to. If he came to hear the band on Saturday night she would very likely only have a moment to say "hi." Not too much could happen in that short span of time with several hundred people hovering nearby. There was no point in dwelling on it. So instead, she focused on the afternoon and evening before her.

She would go to the club and rehearse with the band until six o'clock. Then she would head home, grab a light supper and shower and change before heading back to take her place on stage.

She was always happiest there, on that stage, in the glare of the spotlight. In an odd way she felt more at home there than anywhere else in the world. The music blocked out everything else and filled up all the empty spaces. It made her feel alive, and surrounded her with its energy.

When she sang she touched paradise and a little piece of it touched her back.

Chapter Twenty-One

"What's a 'fast food place'?" asked Leah.

Wolf frowned, shifted his hands on the steering wheel. "It's a restaurant where they make the food before you order it. You walk in, tell them what you want and, *voila*, you've got your chicken fingers within seconds."

Leah's brows furrowed in concentration. "I don't get it."

"You know. They serve burgers and burritos and—"

"But chickens don't have fingers." She turned to face him. "Do they?"

He had to work at suppressing his laughter. She was so serious and he didn't want to embarrass her. "No, Leah. They don't. It's just a word for pieces of chicken that are breaded and fried."

"Oh." She seemed to accept that. "So if they make the food before you get there, how do they know what you want?"

Wolf shook his head in wonder. "It's complicated. But I'm sure you'll understand when you see it. Maybe we can have supper at a place like that when we get to Kitchener."

"Okay." Leah sat with her hands folded in her lap and turned her attention to the passing scenery. "I am kind of hungry already."

Wolf had found a used car at a lot in the little town of Creemore for nine hundred dollars. He barely fit behind the wheel of the old, rusted-out beast but with a little luck it would last a month or so. He hoped he wouldn't need it any longer than that. By the time he had hashed it out with the salesman, sorted out the ownership and finagled some insurance it had been time for lunch. However, he had felt quite self-conscious with the unkempt beard and a little girl in an extremely rumpled and grimy dress.

So, they had quickly found a discount store and purchased her some clothes and gotten a razor for him. Next they found a gas station and he had waited outside the washroom while she changed and brushed her hair. Of course a bath would have been ideal but, unfortunately, it was impossible. So, she had scrubbed her face and pulled her hair back in a ponytail and managed to look quite presentable.

Her face beamed as she stepped out of the cramped little room. The jeans fit well, just tight enough to hug her slender hips but loose enough to allow the freedom of movement that was so essential to the activities of childhood. She rubbed her palms against the stiff, blue denim and watched with interest as Wolf rolled up the cuffs. "So?" Wolf had asked as he took a step back and evaluated his creation.

A vigorous nod was her only response.

Wolf had to agree. The smart little button up T-shirt and brand new, white running shoes made her look like any other eleven-year-old on the street. Then Wolf had corrected himself—she looked much better. With her scrubbed face, clean clothes and polite mannerisms she put half of her peers to shame. Not to mention that she was one of the prettiest little girls he had ever laid eyes on. But then again, his opinion was hardly objective anymore.

He was going to have to watch himself. He was already developing an attachment to her. But he couldn't seem to stop himself despite the knowledge that it might well lead him directly into a gaping emotional chasm. He obviously hadn't learned that lesson very well.

Once she was finished he had stepped into the washroom and gazed into the cracked mirror over the sink while he shaved off the mangy crop of hair that had sprouted on his chin over the past three weeks. He had left the door open, not wanting to leave her alone or out of earshot for any length of time. When he finished he had stepped out into the bright afternoon sunshine and struck a pose. "So? What do you think?"

She had tugged on his shirt to bring him down to her level and then had run her delicate little fingers across his cheek. "Better. The beard was nice but I like smooth cheeks better." Then she had cocked her head to the side in a way that melted his heart. "You're kind of handsome, you know?"

He'd never received a simpler or more sincere compliment. He bowed politely. "Why, thank you, Madame. But I pale in the shadow of your ravishing beauty." Then he had extended his elbow. "Shall we dine?"

Giggling, she had accepted his arm and he had escorted her across the street to Sherry's Diner. It was typical of small town restaurants with Formica tables and red vinyl chairs and booths that lined the walls. It was clean and reeked of back country charm. The scents of fresh baking and roasting meat hung in the air and promised a down-home culinary experience.

The waitress had smiled congenially as she led them to the booth near the back. Wolf had specifically requested it in light of their semi-fugitive status. He was wary of Leah being recognized. It was unlikely considering how far from home she had wandered but he saw no point in taking unnecessary chances.

They each had beef barley soup and a sandwich and, as expected, the food was fresh and tasted homemade.

Leah ate ravenously and after paying the bill they had headed out to the burgundy Plymouth Sundance with the rusted out trunk. It had been an uneventful three-hour drive to Kitchener. Leah dozed occasionally and they stopped for snacks and sodas. But as they approached the city limits he heard her stomach growling again even though it was barely five o'clock. Likely, her body was trying to make up for the days spent without nourishment. So, he followed the smell of hot grease and pulled into the parking lot of the first burger franchise they encountered.

As they passed through the big glass doors he asked her, "So what'll it be? There's burgers, or chicken fingers," he grinned, "or pizza. At least I think they have pizza."

She clung tightly to his hand, and remained glued to his side. He guessed the crowded facility was a little beyond her experience.

"Um…I've never had pizza."

Wolf shook his head in amazement. "Pizza it is. Why don't I get a couple of burgers and you can try one of those too, just to see what they're like. One is never enough for me anyway."

"Okay," she said, and settled down to wait.

They stood in line behind a woman with two rambunctious toddlers and Wolf found his attention riveted to them. One of the children was just learning to walk and gripped his mother's pants with chubby fists as he walked incessantly around her legs. At one point he took a chance and took a few tottering steps before reaching the support of the order counter.

Wolf felt a tug on his hand. "Wolf?"

Feeling a little dazed, he drew himself out of his reverie and looked down at Leah. "Hmm?"

"What's wrong?"

He frowned in confusion. "Wrong?"

She nodded. "All of a sudden you seemed really sad."

Damn perceptive kid. He kneeled down to her level, and brushed a knuckle across her cheek. She just continued looking at him, a deep, very grown-up frown of concern creasing her brow.

"I was just thinking about somebody I used to know," he said softly.

"Do you miss her?"

How did she know it was a woman? "Every day."

* * * * *

"How was that, Jason?" said Ronni into the mike.

He gave her the thumbs up.

A voice echoed from the back of the hall. "Could we do the chorus one more time, guys? I'm having some trouble with feedback."

Ronni rolled their eyes. Eddy, their sound man, was one of the best but he was so damn picky. He heard nuances and problems in the music that the Bionic Woman would have had trouble picking out, even with her electronically enhanced hearing. But Ronni didn't complain since he probably shared a pretty good chunk of the credit for the band's success.

Three years earlier they had landed the job as the house band for Ruby's, one of the largest bars and night clubs in Canada. The club also booked big name bands like April Wine and Kim Mitchell but Celica played regularly, and opened for the bigger acts. They had changed the name to Celica after Ronni joined the group, and in honor of Jesse who had brought them together. It had taken eight long years of hard work and dedication to get to this point but everyone in the band pulled their weight and enjoyed what they did. It had been a joy as well as a grind. For Ronni in particular, it was a labor of love.

"Oh, all right, Eddy," she whined sweetly. "But could we do the first few bars of *Life after Love?* I'd like to open with that one tonight."

Celica's repertoire consisted mostly of current and classic rock hits. Ronni tended to favor the rougher edges of Cher, Madonna and

Amanda Marshall. But she could also paraphrase the sweet tones of Celine Dion and she wasn't restricted to female artists. She and Jason had even written a few original tunes.

And of course, Jason's original work, *With You I'm Free,* had become her signature piece. Shortly after she joined the band Jason had confided in her just how big a role Jesse had played in creating the song. He had given Jason free rein with the musical score, but had written several lines of the lyrics himself, insisting that it had to be just right. There were things he wanted to say and he wanted to say them right.

It had taken almost a year before she was able to sing it through without dissolving helplessly into tears.

Yet another little piece of Jesse trivia that she had kept from Heidi.

"One sec, Ron," said Jason as he tweaked his guitar. Jason looked like he had popped directly out of some seventies rock star mold. His lanky torso was perched atop long matchstick legs. Disheveled blond hair fringed his head like a dirty halo and four earrings glittered in his left ear. He had thin lips, a weak chin and no cheekbones, but to Ronni he outshone The Boss himself.

Jason had quickly become a dear friend and his voice and musical talent had endeared him to her in a way that no one else ever could. Their shared memories of Jesse had initially drawn them together but their friendship had quickly grown and taken on a life of its own.

On stage he rivaled Eddie Van Halen with his wild antics and boisterous musical style. But, in stark contrast to his onstage persona, offstage he was quiet and unassuming with a ready wit and a generosity of spirit that emanated from him like a visible aura. Ronni suspected he played from that part of his soul when he needed to coax those touching, mellifluous tones out of his guitar when Ronni demanded it for her ballads and silvery love songs. Ronni loved and appreciated both sides of the Jason coin.

In fact, she loved them all. *Celica* was almost as much of a family to her as Sam and his dad.

Jason played a couple of riffs and peered up at the sound booth. "Ready, Eddy?" he shouted. He winked at Ronni.

Ronni smiled. She knew Eddy hated that rhyme but there was just no other way to say it. Eddy ignored the teasing and gave them the go-ahead.

Twenty minutes later Ronni climbed in behind the wheel of her Firebird. They had finished a little early and she had just enough time to stop in on Wayne and break the bad news to him before heading home and getting ready for the show. He had asked if he could attend that night but she had put him off with some flimsy excuse and then said she'd stop by before the show to say hi. His chilly response had told her that he had some idea as to the real reason for her visit.

She really hated to hurt him. They had been together for two months and he had given her no good reason to not keep seeing him. But if she kept it up she'd just end up hurting him more by letting him think it could possibly go somewhere.

Maybe Heidi was right. Maybe she was being faithful to a ghost but she didn't quite know what to do about it. Was it possible to just make a conscious decision and leave behind all the love and the pain and the guilt? She had tried for years without success. Maybe she needed therapy. But other than her aversion to letting herself fall in love with someone, she was happy with her life. Her job and her music and her friends kept her occupied and involved and fulfilled. What more was there?

* * * * *

Wolf crammed himself into the tiny phone booth. Over his shoulder he said, "Okay, how do you spell Lichty?"

Leah patiently recited it for him.

He flipped through the pages until he hit the L's. "Okay, I've found it," He scanned the page. "Jesus. I mean…uh…there's an awful lot of them in here." He found the end of the listing and felt a nudge of hope. "Oh…but there's only two 'V's."

"Good. She must be one of them."

"Yeah," he said soberly. "Let's hope so." He dropped in a quarter and dialed the first number.

A surly man's voice greeted him from the other end. "Hello?"

"Hello," said Wolf as politely as possible. "I'm looking for a Veronica Lichty. Does she live there?'

"What? Veronica? Are you nuts? This is Verlus Lichty. You selling something?"

"No, sir. I'm sorry to have bothered you."

"Yeah, right. I bet you are."

"Well, thanks anyway. " Wolf hung up and glanced at Leah.

"The next one," she said hopefully.

And if not, then what? Then we go to the cops. I can't keep her indefinitely and I can't try every damn Lichty in the book.

He dropped in another coin.

"Hello?" said a woman's voice.

Wolf momentarily perked up. Leah was watching him and she noticed.

"Hello. Is this Veronica Lichty?"

The other end hesitated uncertainly. "Veronica? Oh, good gracious no. My name's Robena." She chuckled to herself. "My husband was Vernon. You probably wonder why I didn't change the listing, but, well, you know how it is. Since he died I chust haven't seemed to be able to find the time."

Wolf's face fell and, consequently, so did Leah's. "Oh, well..." But he couldn't continue because dear Robena was just getting started.

"Land sakes, alive, I haven't heard the name Veronica for years. My husband had an aunt named Veronica but she passed on years ago. I guess the name chust isn't as popular as it used to be." The Pennsylvania Dutch accent was as thick as syrup on her tongue.

Wolf rolled his eyes and was just considering hanging up when his ears perked up again.

"But now, come to think of it, there was another Veronica. My husband's cousin's brother-in-law— Ach, but you certainly don't care about all the *freund-schaft*. I should let you go."

"No, that's all right, ma'am. You said you knew another Veronica Lichty?"

Spurred on by a spark of interest she continued on, "Well, yes, I do believe there was. Something of a story, I gather. That's why I remember. From what I heard she ran off though. I don't know where she ended up. There was a big to-do because she got involved with this boy that everyone thought was trouble. And then, well I hate to spread rumors," her voice dropped an octave at the hint of gossip. "But the word was that she got pregnant, and ended up leaving her family. Her poor parents must have been beside themselves. I'm not sure what happened to the baby or the boy but there was something else... Oh dear." Wolf could hear the wheels turning as she sorted through years of scandals and stories. "My memory chust isn't what it used to be, dontcha know?"

Wolf was patient. "Anything you can—"

"Oh, now I remember! There was something about her name. She changed it. Yes, that's right. Can you imagine? Her parents took a lot of trouble to pick out such a beautiful name and then she goes and insults them by changing it. Terrible…terrible."

Wolf took a deep breath and said calmly, barely daring to hope… "Do you know what she changed it to?"

"Hmm. I'm not sure. I believe it was a man's name, actually. Not proper for a young girl at all. Now what was it again? Chust let me think for a minute." Then there was silence.

Wolf held his breath, not wanting to interrupt her thought processes.

The moment stretched and he was just about to give up hope when she exclaimed, "Ronni! That's it!" She laughed. "Maybe I'm not as old as I thought I was. Yes, I'm quite sure. She wanted everybody to start calling her Ronni. Ronni Lichty."

Wolf smiled down at Leah. Perhaps a child's faith was all it took. "Thank you, ma'am. You've been a great help."

"Oh, well, don't mention it. If you see her parents you must say hi to them for me. Heavens, I haven't seen them since Lovina Gerber's funeral. Oh, that was such a tragedy…"

Wolf very gently hung up the receiver. With a little luck she wouldn't notice the dial tone for a while. He turned to Leah. "If that lady was right, your mom calls herself Ronni."

"Is there one in the phone book?"

Wolf was already scanning the names. There were several 'R's and he was loath to try them one by one but, lo and behold, there was a Ronni listed. Many women on their own didn't feel safe listing their first names like that but she probably figured she would be mistaken for a man with that name. Another quarter clinked into the slot.

The phone rang a half dozen times, then a sultry voice reverberated inside his head. "Hi. You've reached Ronni. Sorry to burst your bubble but I'm not in. Leave a message at the tone and if you sound interesting I might call you back."

He hung up. *Cute.* He hated cute. "She's not there but why don't we drive on over anyway and see what we find."

Leah could barely contain her excitement. She almost floated off the sidewalk. "Do you really think it's her?"

They headed back to the car and Wolf opened the car door for her but didn't answer right away. Instead, he waited until he got in the other side. Then, feeling the weight of reality bearing down on him, he turned to face her. "Listen, Leah, I think you should be prepared."

"What do you mean?"

"I don't want to upset you but I think you should know what might happen. It sounds like she might be the one but you've got to remember she gave you up for adoption a very long time ago." Leah was watching him without expression, her eyes placid and trusting. It was somewhat unnerving. He swallowed dryly. "We don't know why she did that. So without knowing her reasons, who knows what her reaction might be to seeing you."

"You mean she might not want to see me?"

"I just thought you should know that's a possibility."

She chewed on her lower lip as she considered this new development. "Okay." She looked out the window. "What if she doesn't want to? What do I do then? I can't go home." She looked back at Wolf and her eyes were shimmering.

Shit! Shit! Shit! I should have kept my big mouth shut. Dear Ronni will probably be ecstatic and I'll have tortured this poor child for nothing.

Leah continued, "I can't go home. Really. I just can't." She was doing a remarkable job of keeping at bay the tears that hovered just below the surface.

Wolf sighed. "Let's just wait and see, okay? If that happens we'll figure something out. I won't let you down." *Right! I never let anybody down, do I? Big hero Captain Wolf Mercredi. You can count on him. You can count on him to get you killed.*

He slammed the door on those thoughts and revved the engine. He briefly consulted the city map he had purchased then pulled out of the parking lot.

Leah seemed to recover quickly. They had driven in silence for barely ten minutes when she piped up again with her usual vitality, "What do you do, Wolf? Do you have a farm?"

He laughed at the image of himself astride a tractor or mucking out stalls. "Hardly. Never pulled a weed in my life. Nope, I just finished a career in the army."

"Really? Did you shoot people? We're not allowed to have guns."

"No, I was lucky. I never had to do that. And that's a very wise thing."

"Did anybody ever shoot at you?'

"Look! We're here already." He certainly didn't want to tell his story to an eleven-year old. It might give the poor thing nightmares and he'd definitely had enough for both of them.

They pulled into the small housing complex. Rows of townhouse condominiums marched along the sidewalk like phalanxes of tight-lipped marines. He supposed a woman living alone would like the security but he would go stir-crazy in an environment like this. He needed wide open spaces, soft breezes and lush greenery. He chuckled. Maybe he had a bit of farmer blood in him after all.

At least the complex was clean and well kept. They pulled up to number forty-seven. There was no car in the drive but the garage door was closed and he thought he saw a glimmer of light through the front window.

He turned to the anxious figure beside him. "Why don't you wait in the car? Let me talk to her for a few minutes and see what she says, okay? We don't want to shock her too badly with everything all at once, right?"

She nodded weakly. "Okay. I'll wait here."

He reached out and stroked her cheek with the backs of his knuckles. "Don't worry, okay? It'll be fine."

She nodded again and he got out of the car. He plodded up the front steps. A few freshly planted petunias bloomed in a small bed beside the front door. The front stoop was decorated with a wicker rocking chair and a terra cotta pot that had yet to boast greenery. It was still early in the season, so that was hardly a surprise. A large *Welcome* wreath adorned the front door. He hoped she wasn't kidding.

He rang the bell.

A few moments later the door swung open and the woman beyond the threshold stared up at him with complete bafflement. "Yes?"

What the hell was this? She was an apparition. Auburn hair the exact same shade as Leah's cascaded to her shoulders in thick full waves but that wasn't what drew his attention. It sparkled with a thousand tiny flecks of gold. The effect was obviously artificial because her face sported similar decoration. She wore heavy makeup in bright, striking colors and her cheeks shimmered with the same iridescent gold flecks. His eyes traveled down.

Her blouse hugged her torso and exposed an enticing wedge of pale flesh. The lustrous emerald silk matched the green of her eyes but the fabric also sparkled with a hundred other colors that flickered away too quickly for the eye to identify. Tight, black leather pants sheathed long, slender legs. High-heeled leather boots completed the ensemble. Her fingernails carried the continuation of the gold theme.

Prostitute? He had never seen one dressed like this. But from what Leah had said, her mother had certainly come a long way from her roots.

She sighed, obviously frustrated by his mysterious silence. "Have you got the right house, mister? I'm in kind of a rush."

He swallowed and dragged his eyes back to hers. "Uh…are you Veronica Lichty?" This apparition hardly approached his usual taste in women but he was hard pressed to ignore the sudden tightening in his groin. She definitely made an impression.

She frowned. "Veronica? I haven't gone by that name for years. Who wants to know?"

"My name's Wolf Mercredi."

"No kidding? Are you a friend of Jason's? He said he had some buddies in the States and I figured some of them might have some weird stage names."

Stage names? That would explain a lot. "No, I don't know Jason. Look, can I come in for a minute? This is kind of hard to explain."

Her eyes grew wide. "You've got to be kidding."

Of course, how could he even think to ask such a thing? "Okay, I'll try and make this brief." He took a deep breath and plunged in. "I was out hiking yesterday on the Bruce Trail up near Creemore and I came across this little girl. She had run away from home and was looking for her birth mother." There it was. She was starting to react. Her features had gone slack and it was hard to tell beneath the makeup, but he thought the color had begun to drain from her face. "I don't really know why she ran away but she's adamant that she can't go back…terrified, actually. We did a little digging and we're pretty sure you're her mother."

Silence.

More silence.

She just stood there staring at him. She chewed on a copper-colored lip before asking, "What's her name?"

"Leah. Leah Lichty."

More silence. Then he felt the whoosh of air as the door slammed shut in his face. There was a pause before he heard from the other side, "I don't have a daughter. Leave me alone!"

"Shit!" *Now what?* Luckily, from Leah's vantage point in the driveway she couldn't see the front door. It was hidden by the garage, which jutted out past the front stoop. He leaned out so she could see him and held up one finger. He smiled and mouthed, "One minute," then turned back to the door and pounded. "Please! She's out here in the car. Just let her meet you, for God's sake."

"I told you," yelled Ronni from the other side. "I don't have a daughter." Her voice caught in her throat at the end of the phrase. Part of his heart went out to her. This was no way to stage a reunion. He couldn't blame her for reacting irrationally but his first concern was Leah.

He leaned up against the door and spoke more quietly and, he hoped, less threateningly, "I don't blame you for being upset but don't lie to me. It's painfully obvious that she's yours." He waited. There was only silence from the other side. "She's got your hair," he added as an afterthought.

A few agonizing moments later the latch clicked open.

Chapter Twenty-Two

Ronni was leaning heavily against the oak panels of her front door. She rested her forehead against the cool wood and remembered to breathe. This couldn't be happening! Not today.

She had just returned from an emotionally draining session with Wayne. He had not taken the news well and Ronni had felt like the supreme heel slash bitch. Add to that the confusing episode with Mr. Endecott, and the fact that she was still recovering from her trip to the cemetery the day before, and now *this?* The end result was a woman on the verge of emotional meltdown.

She had been so looking forward to performing tonight, to losing herself in the music and the atmosphere, to letting her spirit soar and harvesting her own private piece of paradise.

Then this man shows up. When she first laid eyes on him she thought she must be hallucinating. He was like some character out of a spy novel—tall and athletic, bronzed and striking. An imposing figure in ratty jeans and a well-worn T-shirt. She wouldn't say he was handsome, exactly, but he was definitely someone you noticed. Those black eyes could drill holes into your skull.

And then he informs her that her daughter is here to see her. *Ran into her on the trail, you know. What a coincidence. So I brought her here. Nothing to it! She's just here to say hi. Oh and by the way she ran away from home and is terrified to go back.*

Then he accused her of lying. Well, of course she was lying. She knew it was obvious but she hadn't known what else to do. Then he had made the comment about the hair.

Her throat was aching from the strain of battling her emotions, and then he had said that and she lost it. Of course she had to see her. The last time Ronni laid eyes on her baby she had been bald as a billiard ball, with blotchy skin and had been wailing like a miniature banshee. Ronni hadn't touched her, had barely glimpsed her as they had wrapped her in a blanket and taken her out the door to give over to the open arms of Verna and Glenn Lichty. Then had come the torrent of tears. Were they never going to stop?

She wiped at her eyes. So much for the make-up job. She cracked open the door and peered up at him.

He smiled at her. "Feeling better?"

"Actually I feel like shit. Thanks for asking."

He shrugged. "I do tend to have that effect on people."

She smiled in spite of herself, and opened the door further. "I'm sorry about that. You sort of caught me off guard."

"Understandable. This whole situation is a little unusual, to put it mildly."

She licked dry lips. But the effect was nominal since her saliva, much like her composure, had completely abandoned her. "What did you say your name was?"

"Wolf Mercredi."

"Hmm. Fitting. You're definitely a predator."

He sighed and something indefinable glinted in his eyes. "I hate to push this but Leah is waiting. Can I bring her in?"

"Oh…uh…yeah. Sure, bring her in." Ronni's palms started to sweat and her heart thudded against her chest like it was trying to break free. She gripped the doorknob for support as she watched him turn away and head down the stairs. She stood there, immobile, afraid that if she took a step she might fall over. Voices drifted to her from around the corner of the house—his and a little girl's.

She still hadn't moved when she first glimpsed them come around the corner, and then climb the stairs. She was still as stone when the canny canine and his sidekick stopped and stood just a couple of feet in front of her. She barely heard Wolf make the introduction.

"Leah, this is your mother."

The creature with the auburn hair and the brand new jeans and runners extended a hand in greeting. "Hello."

For just a moment the world went black and then Ronni felt strong arms around her waist. "Are you okay?" It was the Wolf. No sheep's clothing here. He attacked without warning, slicing to the heart and leaving his prey raw and bleeding.

She gazed up at him. "What?"

"I thought you were about to faint. You got very pale and started to sway. You looked like you saw a ghost."

She found her feet and pushed his arms away. "I-I'm fine." She purposefully turned away and headed back into the house. "Come on inside." Her legs wobbled like rubber truncheons but somehow she stayed erect as she traversed the long hall, past the bathroom and the stairs to the second floor. She reached her living room and kitchen area. The living area was small, but open concept in bright vibrant colors with big bright windows and deep, plush furniture. She liked her house. She liked her life. But she had a feeling it was all about to be turned upside down and rearranged like a crazy patchwork quilt.

She heard them walking behind her.

She couldn't look at that face again. Leah was the spitting image of *him*. Other than the hair, every other feature belonged to him. Facing her was facing every painful memory of that nightmare of eleven years ago. Maybe if she sat down…

She made it to the burgundy armchair across from the couch and gripped the arm rests in a desperate attempt to keep her bearings. Wolf and Leah sat across from her. Wolf's disapproving glare wasn't lost on her. She had shunned her daughter's extended hand. How could she explain that to him? She also noticed how the girl clung to him. She seemed to trust him, count on him. How long had they been together, anyway?

Leah's face was fearful, anxious. Ronni longed to put her at ease but she couldn't begin to focus on anyone else until she found a piece of solid footing for herself.

Ronni blinked and focused on the Wolf. "You said you found her while you were out hiking?"

He put an arm around Leah, the gesture protective. He was protecting her from her mother? That was ridiculous. Ronni was the one who was quaking in her boots.

"Yes," began Wolf. "She had run away five days ago. She managed on her own all that time." He smiled down at his charge. "She's quite the little trooper."

Leah's eyes remained glued to Ronni. She spoke next, a hint of awe in her voice. "You're very pretty."

Ronni laughed nervously. "Thanks. You caught me in full gear. I'm due on stage in a little over an hour." She had managed to meet Leah's gaze. That was an accomplishment. Was this really the same child as the one she had given birth to eleven years ago? The notion exceeded the limits of her comprehension. The world continued to waver as if she were observing it through a gauzy curtain.

"Stage?" It was Wolf's voice but now she couldn't take her eyes off Leah.

"Yes. I sing in a band at Ruby's."

"Is that a bar?"

Ronni swept her gaze up to meet his. "You're not from around here, are you?"

He shook his head, his eyes still unforgiving.

"Yes, it's a bar. One of the largest in Canada. We're the house band." Talking about the band grounded her, gave her a sense of reality and substance.

"That must be very fulfilling work," said Wolf. The words were agreeable but the tone caustic.

His hostile demeanor confused her. She frowned. "Yes, as a matter of fact, it is. I enjoy it very much."

"A productive, contributing member of society. Where would the world be without people like you?"

Where a moment before her blood pressure had been precariously low, now, suddenly it shot through the roof and she could feel the color rise in her cheeks. "I suppose it would be a lot quieter, and a lot more dull." She would have loved to say more and wipe that superior look off his face but she didn't want to upset the child. He was judging her. He wouldn't get away with that. She just didn't put up with that shit. Not anymore.

"Certainly quieter," was his only response.

Leah wasn't immune to the tension in the room. "I'd like to hear you sing."

Ronni tried to ignore Wolf's incessant stare. "I'd like that too but they don't allow children in there." She glanced at her watch. "Speaking of which, I should get going." There was too much to talk about, too many questions, too many emotions. She needed time to sort through it all.

Wolf growled at her. No kidding; he actually growled out the words. "I thought you said you had an hour before you were due on stage."

"An hour before the show starts, but I have to fix up my make-up, and we have to warm up and set the levels. I really don't have that much time." *And I can't face all this at once. I need a little time. Please. Just a little more time.*

Wolf set his jaw. "Can I talk to you privately for a minute?"

No. I'd really rather not. You scare the hell out of me, Wolf-man. "Certainly," she said. Then to Leah, "There's sodas and milk in the fridge if you'd like to help yourself. The glasses are in the cupboard beside the sink." She added a hesitant smile in the hope that it would help put the child at ease.

Leah glanced at Wolf for tacit permission before heading to the kitchen. Then he got up and moved over closer to Ronni. He seated himself on the coffee table that had been between them. Only a hair's breadth separated their knees.

"What do you think you're doing?" he hissed.

"Doing?"

"This is the first time you've seen your daughter in eleven years. You've hardly spoken to her. She's in trouble, anxious to talk to you, and you're going to blow her off for a goddamn stupid side show?"

"For starters, it's not a *stupid side show*. It's a very high-class place and we're a good band. Secondly, I didn't invite you here. You appoint yourself as some sort of macho guardian angel over my daughter, come in here, drop a bomb in my lap and expect me to cut open my chest and let you chew away at my heart. I'd like to preserve the little bit of one that I have left, thank you, and I wouldn't mind a little time to digest this. I know this is hard for her and I appreciate that, but it's no picnic for me, either. I'm only human, you know. I have feelings, too. Let me adjust."

She ignored his intense gaze and steadied herself by smoothing back her hair. She took a deep breath before continuing but the Wolf seemed to be sucking all the oxygen out of the room. "Also, there are a hell of a lot of people who paid good money to see us tonight, not to mention the members of the band and the club owners who are counting on me to be there and I'm even expecting some special friends. I can't just blow them off either." She shifted on the soft, familiar cushion. "I'm sorry it worked out this way, but you're welcome to stay here and wait until I get home." She supposed she had no choice but to trust this man. Turning him away meant turning away her daughter and she wasn't willing to do that. Not again. "I warn you, though, it's usually after two until I get back."

He shook his head. "I appreciate the generous offer. " His tone left little doubt as to his true opinion of her excuses. "But it's no deal. I'd like to let her get cleaned up. She's in desperate need of a bath but then I think we should come along."

Ronni rolled her eyes heavenward. "I told you, they don't allow children."

"Make arrangements," he said through clenched teeth. "After all, she's your daughter and you *are* the *star*."

Ronni lowered her voice to a whisper but her words were anything but demure. "Look, Mr. Wolf-man with a fucking attitude, I don't appreciate being patronized. And I appreciate your obvious distaste for my profession even less. But I honestly don't give a shit what you think of me. However, for her sake, I'll see what I can do. Maybe you can sit in the back, out of sight. But if you think I'm going to tell everyone she's my daughter you're nuts."

"You're ashamed of her?"

Ronni flopped back against the cushions and threw her hands up in exasperation. "God! Who the hell are you? Of course not. But none of these people know about her and I don't want to spend the whole night making awkward explanations. So, for tonight she's my niece. Can you handle being my brother-in-law? Just for one night?"

Leah reentered the room.

"All right," he muttered.

Leah stood there sipping her milk and staring at the two conspirators as they huddled together and plotted her fate.

Ronni turned to her. "There's been a change of plans. I'll take you upstairs and you can take a quick shower. And then, how would you like to come to the club to hear me sing?"

Leah looked to her mentor. "Will Wolf be there?"

"Yes, of course," he said warmly. The tone was completely different when he addressed the girl.

Leah brightened. "Okay. That sounds great!"

"Good." Ronni stood. She turned to Wolf and said under her breath, "When we get back I've got a few pointed questions for you, as well." She graced him with an accusing stare of her own before making the effort of will that was necessary to extend a hand to her daughter.

Leah slipped her hand into Ronni's and followed her mother up the stairs.

It wasn't much but it was a beginning.

* * * * *

Wolf sipped his scotch on the rocks. The liquor seared his throat and settled warmly in his gut.

During his recovery he had approached liquor like he might approach an armed nuclear warhead—carefully and with tremendous respect. It had the potential to numb him against the pain he had experienced, and therein also lay the potential for destruction. But gradually, as he felt himself heal, he allowed himself to indulge a little more frequently. Tonight, in particular, he welcomed the mild anaesthetic effects of the alcohol.

Leah sat beside him in the booth. She was snuggled between him and the wall, as far back out of sight as possible, but she was taking everything in with wide-eyed wonder.

Ronni hadn't exaggerated. The place was huge, with four separate bar areas, seating for a potential two thousand patrons, a large dance floor and raised stage. The lights flashed and the recorded music blared. The crowd was gradually building as show time approached.

So far, no rowdy drunks had staggered past their table but Wolf knew it was inevitable. Maybe forcing Ronni to allow Leah to come had been a mistake but then he looked at Leah, sitting there, sipping her soda and he reconsidered. This was her mother's world and, if they were going to get to know each other, this would have to be a part of that journey—no matter how Wolf felt about it.

A bouncer stalked by and eyed the odd couple, but said nothing.

Ronni had spoken to the manager and he had been agreeable to Leah's presence as long as they stayed out of sight. The bouncers had been informed as to Leah's and Wolf's identities but they kept a sharp eye on the duo. Leah, oblivious to the questionable attention, was far too busy soaking in the atmosphere and watching the medley of diverse and unique characters who paraded past their table.

The women strutted their stuff in jeans and mini-skirts, with tube tops and cropped shirts, almost all with extravagant makeup and jewelry. The men were just as varied—some with short, spiked hair, some with hair below their shoulders or pulled back in a ponytail.

Several men with earrings walked by and she took it all in stride. But when a man with a particularly colorful tattoo of a dragon on his forearm strode by their table, it was too much for Leah to absorb without explanation.

Her eyes were wide when she turned to Wolf. "What was that?"

Wolf chuckled softly. It was hard to imagine how all this looked through her eyes. "That was a tattoo. It's like a drawing on the skin that you have forever. It never washes off."

"Do you have one?"

"God no! You'd never get one of those needles near me."

Leah looked like she had another question on her mind and Wolf's attention was focused exclusively on her. So the arrival of the boisterous blonde with the bobbing curls startled him and irritated him beyond reason. The wide grin that pulled at her full lips grated on his already tenuous good humor.

She slid into the booth as if she had been invited and extended a hand in greeting. "Hi, I'm Heidi."

Wolf glared his silent disapproval, hoping this unwelcome intruder would take the hint. It had been a long time since Wolf had to put off female advances but he knew his stare could instill fear in the heart of the most jaded military personnel. Surely it could discourage a sloshed blonde with an overactive libido.

But her hand just continued hovering over the center of the table.

Wolf ignored it. "Look, I'm just here for the show, I—" He was interrupted when Heidi caught sight of Leah.

"Oh, my God!" she squealed.

Wolf grimaced as her voice lanced directly to the center of his brain.

"So you're Ronni's daughter." She redirected her hand toward Leah who accepted it gingerly. "I never thought I'd get to lay eyes on you."

Wolf was confused. "Excuse me…Heidi?"

She redirected her beaming face toward Wolf. "Yep. That's me."

"I take it you're a friend of Ronni's?"

She nodded, the curls dancing an irritating jig about her face. "Yup, been best friends for almost nine years now."

"I thought Ronni said nobody knew that she had a daughter."

Heidi lowered her voice, as if their screaming could be heard over the boisterous crowd and loud music. "Well, I think I'm the only one. And the only reason I know is because she got so drunk one night after a trip to the cemetery that she let it slip. But I was sworn to secrecy on pain of having her rip off my acrylic nails one by one."

"Cemetery?"

Heidi slurped from her strawberry daiquiri. "Mm-hmm. She had been visiting Jesse. She's always on a downer for a while after that. I don't know why she puts herself through it. I bug her about it all the time. But God knows, she won't listen to *me*."

Wolf's irritation with this whole situation began to get the better of him. His control slipped and his voice right along with it. "Who the hell is Jesse?" he yelled. He immediately turned to Leah. "Sorry, honey."

"I assumed you knew," said Heidi, ignoring his outburst. "He was Leah's father."

Of course. He couldn't believe he hadn't even considered that question. But this man was dead? Obviously another key piece to the Ronni puzzle. He was about to pursue it further, but he didn't get a chance because just then the lights dimmed and the crowd quieted.

Heidi whispered, "Here they come."

There was no formal introduction but apparently none was needed because when the curtains lifted and the lights came up, a spontaneous cheer erupted from the audience. Then, over the rowdy applause, as the sounds from the stage gathered intensity, an enthusiastic announcer said simply, *"CELICA!"*

The spotlight flashed on, revealing Ronni in all her gold and leather-clad glory. An electric guitar opened with an elaborate riff and then she launched into a raunchy rendition of some piece of modern pop that Wolf had no interest in identifying.

The beat picked up and Wolf watched it seep into Ronni's body. It was obvious by the subtle flexes of her muscles, by the way she held the microphone, by the way she communicated silently with the Bryan Adams wanna-be beside her, that she was at home up there. She loved the beat and the rhythm as it pumped through her veins like a thousand-proof liquor. She literally lit up. From head to toe, every movement of her body blatantly advertised that she loved the music and was one with it. The crowd picked up on that and her passion seeped out across the stage, infusing them with energy. Soon the dance floor filled to capacity and those who weren't dancing were riveted to the group of performers on the stage. Feet tapped and heads bobbed. It seemed that no one was immune to her magic.

Heidi leaned over and yelled above the pounding beat. "So, what do you think?"

Leah answered. "I like it! She sings great!" Not even Leah could ignore the all-pervasive beat. Her tapping fingers and the subtle flexes of her shoulders revealed the extent of its effect on her virgin senses.

Heidi turned to Wolf. "What about you?"

"It doesn't matter what I think."

Heidi smiled knowingly. "You like it."

"Oh, really?" A note of irritated sarcasm edged his voice. "How can you be so sure?"

Her response was to look down at his hands, which had been resting on the table in front of him. He had to clasp his fingers together to stop them from drumming in sync with the music.

Perhaps his intense negativity toward Ronni's chosen career was somewhat irrational. After all, she wasn't hurting anyone and she was providing harmless entertainment and distraction for a good chunk of the local population. It wasn't like she was taking advantage of anyone, or exploiting her fans for purely selfish and greedy purposes. She obviously did what she did out of a sincere love of music and performing. So why was Wolf gritting his teeth and reminding himself continuously that he wanted—no *needed*—to disapprove of her? He sipped from his drink and contemplated the ice cubes. If he looked closely enough the answer was painfully obvious. But somehow, knowing the reason why, and knowing that it was completely unfair to the woman on that stage, didn't change a thing.

A delicate set of fingers settled over his. Surprised and pleased by the spontaneous show of affection, he interrupted his thoughts to smile down at Leah.

"I'd like to be able to sing like that some day." She grinned up at him.

Unsure how to respond to that, he just nodded.

Leah looked back at the stage. "And she's so pretty. Don't you think so?"

"Yes, she's almost as pretty as her daughter."

The little exchange wasn't lost on Heidi, who was smiling warmly at them when a finger tapped her shoulder. Startled, she looked up at a cockeyed grin.

"You gonna introduce me to your friends?"

Impossibly, Heidi's smile widened. "Hi, Sam. Actually, these are Ronni's friends. This is …" she turned to Wolf. "Sorry, I don't think I actually caught your name."

He extended a hand to Sam. "Wolf Mercredi."

The grip that met his was solid and the shake decisive.

Heidi laughed. "That's right, she did tell me. How could I forget a name like that? He's some distant cousin of Ronni's. You know those Mennonites, they're related to everybody. And this is his daughter, Leah."

Sam cordially extended his hand to Leah, then bent low and kissed her knuckles when she granted him her hand. "Charmed," he said to her delighted giggles.

Wolf's teeth clenched in response to the introduction. Now suddenly he was a distant cousin. Obviously brother-in-law would involve too many questions.

Heidi continued, "This is Sam Ward. He's a good friend of Ronni's."

"Hell," chortled Sam. "I'm the closest she's got to family, on this side of the tracks anyway."

The muscles in Heidi's face tensed. "Yeah," she chuckled nervously, "He's Jesse's big brother." She launched from her seat and grasped Sam's hand. "You owe me a dance, remember?"

Sam slapped his forehead with his open palm. "Right, how could I forget?" He turned to Wolf. "Nice to meet you. Maybe we can sit together at the break and Ronni can fill me in on you and Leah. She has so little contact with family. It'd be good for her to connect with some of them again." He saluted—not very convincingly to Wolf's trained eye—and dragged Heidi toward the dance floor.

Wolf watched them go.

Jesse's brother? And he obviously had no idea that Leah existed, or surely Ronni would have made an effort to let him know the situation through Heidi. But maybe Wolf was jumping to conclusions. Maybe she was waiting to tell Sam in person. How could she keep this from him? Leah was his own flesh and blood, his niece and possibly his only connection to a dead brother. Wolf was becoming more and more anxious for a moment alone with Ronni to get the full story. But that likely wouldn't happen for hours.

He'd have to take a lesson from his namesake and practice patience.

* * * * *

Detective Sergeant Gerry Pierce of the Waterloo Regional Police sleepily reached for the phone that trilled on the desk beside him. Sometimes he missed the old style phones with the ring that could stir an Egyptian mummy from its eternal repose. Tonight that was how he felt, like a mummy wrapped in a shroud of exhaustion, and that pathetic little warbling noise the new phones made just didn't cut it as far as slicing through the haze of fatigue at ten o'clock in the evening.

In slow motion he placed the receiver to his ear. "Pierce."

The receptionist spoke to him briefly and then forwarded an outside call.

"Yes, this is Sergeant Pierce. Can I help you?"

"Hello. Yes…well…I was kind of hoping I could help *you.*"

"Who is speaking please, ma'am?" He yawned broadly, making no effort to move the receiver away from his mouth. He stroked the mat of hair on his chin. The neatly trimmed beard and mustache had been his trademark since college. But in the last few years a touch of gray had crept into the ensemble. Thankfully it hadn't quite managed to reach his head yet. He may feel as ancient as a mummy but at least he didn't have to look it.

"Oh, sorry. My name is Lorna Reynolds. I work at a little coffee shop in Creemore and I just stopped in here on my way home. I was out visiting my mother-in-law, you see, and anyway I wanted to stop in to pick up my paycheck. I don't know why our boss can't get that automatic deposit thing…"

Pierce sighed and rubbed at his gray-green eyes. They were tired and dry and, as usual, more red than gray at this time of night. He pushed his wire-framed glasses up his nose before interrupting her. "Mrs. Reynolds, is there a point here? I'm afraid it's late and I'm off duty in less than an hour." As if to illustrate his point he leaned back in his chair and stretched his lanky frame. It didn't seem to matter how much he worked out; he could never seem to build up any decent muscle tone. So, after ten years of fighting a losing battle he had given up and, just as he had suspected, nobody had noticed the difference.

"Oh, I'm sorry. Anyway, when I got in I saw this picture you guys had posted of that little girl that was kidnapped down near Wallenstein."

Pierce dropped his feet to the floor and sat up straight. "Yes?"

"Well, I worked over lunch and I think maybe I saw her."

"Really? Was she with anyone?"

"Well, like I said I'm not a hundred percent certain it was her. She looked a little different from that picture, what with wearing jeans and runners and everything. But this girl sure resembled her and she *was* with this man."

"Could you describe him?" Pierce scribbled madly on the notepad beside the phone.

"Oh yes. That was the thing that made them stick out in my mind. He's not the type you forget easily. He was a real strong fellow, and honestly, kind of scary looking."

"Scary? How? Was he a biker with a lot of tattoos, or what?"

"No, no. Nothing like that. He was actually very clean cut. It was his eyes and the way he could look at you. Honestly, it sent shivers down my spine."

Pierce rolled his eyes. That wasn't exactly the sort of thing you could put on a police sketch. "Did the girl seem at all nervous or frightened?"

"No, actually quite the opposite. She seemed very at ease, even affectionate with him."

Pierce frowned. That, of course, could mean nothing. "Look, Mrs. Reynolds, I hate to impose, but do you think you could come into town and give us a statement, along with a description for a police artist? And maybe look at some mug shots? This little girl has been missing for almost a week and her mother is beside herself. It could make all the difference."

"Oh, I know. That poor woman. To lose a husband and a daughter in the same day." She paused momentarily. "Of course I'll come. When would you like me there?"

Chapter Twenty-Three

Ronni crushed a chunk of ice between her teeth and sucked on the frosty shards. "Are you having fun?"

Leah nodded vigorously. "You look like you are too," she said as she leaned across the table toward Ronni.

Ronni looked toward the stage. "You're very perceptive, Leah. That's my favorite place in the world, up there."

"Is it the adulation of the crowd?" asked Wolf over the rim of his tumbler.

She looked at him sharply. "No, I just love the sound of my own voice. Is that narcissistic enough for you?" She sipped from the ginger ale that a waitress had brought to the table for her. "Are you a priest, or a missionary, or something equally selfless and altruistic, Mr. Mercredi? You seem determined to label me a selfish bitch, therefore you must make a habit of picking up strays, donating blood, helping the homeless and generally being saintly." She continued to sip from her drink and allowed the fire in his eyes to attempt to bore through her armor. But the chain mail held. "Somehow though, my dear Wolf-man, you don't strike me as the saintly type. Honestly, you look like you could kill a man with your bare hands. In fact, I almost wonder if you have."

Heidi approached the table but wasn't given a chance to speak before Wolf erupted from the bench. "Would you like to dance, Ronni? I'm sure Heidi wouldn't mind staying with Leah."

Ronni almost choked on her ginger ale. "Dance?"

Wolf politely held out his hand. But Ronni wasn't fooled; his eyes were still shooting daggers at her. Besides that, the DJ was playing a Moody Blues tune that would require intimate contact. That possibility unnerved her for a number of reasons.

Wolf noticed the hesitation. "I promise I'll keep my claws retracted, if you will."

Ronni glanced at Heidi, who was barely suppressing a grin. "Go ahead," said Heidi. "I'll take Leah down to the ladies' room with me."

"All right," she said with a wary glance at Wolf. But then she turned to Leah. "Unless Leah wants me to stay."

"No, that's okay. I need to go to the bathroom anyway."

Great! Trapped like a rabbit in its hole. She gingerly took Wolf's hand and he led her out to the middle of the floor.

His arm snaked out and wrapped around her like a python. He drew her in so tightly that she had trouble breathing.

Then he was hissing in her ear. "What the hell do you think you're doing?"

She refused to let herself be intimidated by his tactics. So instead of making a futile attempt to push him away she ground against him and whispered back. Her high heels allowed her to almost reach his ear. "I thought you said you were going to keep your claws in."

"I lied. You had no business talking like that in front of Leah. She's insecure enough without hearing you rant and use that kind of language." His words were angry and menacing but his warm breath against her neck did things to her that she hesitated to acknowledge.

"Hey! Where do you get off judging me? That's what started it, you know. You're the one who seems determined to pick a fight. Every time I turn around you're criticizing something about me and you've only known me a few hours. Why are you so determined to hate me?"

"I'm not determined to hate you."

"You're a hell of a lousy liar, Wolf-man."

He gripped her tighter and his lips brushed across her ear when he whispered, "Stop calling me that."

Oh God. Please don't do that. Her knees had turned to gelatin but she managed to retain her aggressive posture. "Answer the question!" In retribution for the vise-like grip around her waist and his undesirable effect on her, she breathed those words into his ear and nibbled on his neck.

She knew he was responding to her. It was brutally obvious by the reaction she could feel straining against her belly and by the gooseflesh on his arm but he refused to acknowledge it. His back remained ramrod straight and she knew his expression hadn't changed. She secretly exulted in her modest success at retaliation.

He said nothing for a couple of minutes and when he finally spoke, Ronni was astonished to realize she had closed her eyes and laid her head on his shoulder. "I guess I can't understand how you could do it."

She jerked her head back to an upright position and scolded herself for succumbing to his physical charms under such ridiculous circumstances. "Do what?"

"Give her up. You must have done it at birth before you really knew her, but even so, I guess I just can't fathom how anyone could abandon a child like that."

"Abandon?" The word ripped from her lungs and tore her heart on the way out. She practically shouted it in his ear before pushing him roughly away. They were in the middle of the dance floor but the crowd faded into the background.

"You son of a bitch! You're right. You have absolutely no idea as to what I went through before and after that day. It was hell, pure and simple, and I'm still living it. In fact I'm beginning to wonder if you're one of Lucifer's minions sent to haunt me and draw me back down into it." She rammed a finger into his sturdy chest. "You have no right to judge me and I'm not obliged to justify myself or my decisions to a self-righteous bastard like you. I thought I got away from the likes of you but I should have known better. Obviously, you're everywhere."

Much of the crowd had stopped to gawk at her and she suddenly became aware of it. She whirled around and was about to stalk away when she ran right into a tall blond figure who had appeared behind her.

"Everything okay, Ronni?" asked Sam as he put an arm around her shoulder and fixed a hostile stare on Wolf. "Is he upsetting you? Family or not, I think I could teach him to play nice."

Ronni just shook her head and, without a word, led him back toward the stage. Despite her fiery response to Wolf's accusation, she felt drained and Sam's strong presence was a welcome comfort. "Thanks anyway, Sam, but don't bother. He's not worth it." She called to Wolf over her shoulder. "Wait for me in the booth after the show."

"You sure you're okay? What was that all about anyway?"

She forced a weak smile and squeezed his hand. "Just family stuff, Sam. Don't worry, I can handle him." They had reached the door that led back stage. "I should get ready. The second show starts in ten minutes." She embraced him and whispered against his shoulder. "But it really means a lot to have you looking out for me."

"It's my pleasure. Besides, it's my responsibility and I don't take it lightly."

She pulled away and studied him. "What do you mean, it's your responsibility?"

"Did Jesse ever tell you about Max?"

She frowned as she sorted through her memories. "No. I don't think so."

"Max was his dog. He was a mangy old mutt. Jesse had found him rooting through some garbage behind our house one night and they really took to each other. He had him for two years before he left for B.C. You probably never saw him because of the crazy hours you guys kept." He stroked Ronni's hair. "Before he left he made me promise to look after Max and all his stuff until he got back. I just figure you sort of fit into that category. He's just gone a lot longer than he anticipated."

Ronni had to bite her lower lip to keep it from trembling. "What happened to Max?"

"He died a few months after Jesse. He was old but I always kind of wondered if he died of a broken heart. He just wasn't himself after Jesse left."

Ronni embraced Sam again, drawing strength from him. Despite the fact that he and Jesse shared little physically, they shared a spontaneity and a vitality of spirit that she cherished. She and Sam shared one other thing that bound them together in a way few could understand. "You know, Sam, sometimes I think Max's way would have been easier."

Sam held her close until she pulled away and headed for the door. Before she opened it she stopped and tossed him a half smile. "Thanks Sam. That was a nice story. Was it true?"

"Cross my heart."

But his crooked smile left her wondering. She slipped through the door. She desperately needed to get herself back together before the second show started.

* * * * *

Wolf was waiting at the table when Heidi and Leah returned. Leah scooted in behind him and Heidi was about to sit down when she got a good look at the storm cloud across from her. That's what he felt like—a charged thundercloud with no outlet for the lightning crackling inside him.

"What's with you? You look like you could eat a kitten."

"What the hell is that supposed to mean?" He was so distracted he didn't even think to apologize to Leah for the language. His encounter with Ronni had affected him more strongly than he wanted to admit to himself. He had been distressed by his body's response to her and then that had been compounded by his reluctance to draw away even after he was sure she had become aware of it as well.

Despite the trepidation, Heidi sat down—as curious as that proverbial kitten, and just as close to disaster. "What happened out there?"

"Nothing. Not that it's any of your business. Ronni and I have some things to sort out."

A sly smile spread across Heidi's face. "Oh, I see. *Things*. In my experience there's only one thing that can get a guy like you so riled."

Wolf shot her a look that told her to leave that topic alone. She raised her hands in a placating gesture. "Okay, okay. I'll say no more. But I hope I'm right." The smile faded as she glanced at the stage where Celica was playing a few bars' lead into their first number. "Maybe somebody like you could snap her out of it."

"Out of what?"

"She hasn't—" Heidi's eyes darted to Leah. "She hasn't *been* with anyone for over eleven years."

"Huh! You're kidding."

"I wish I were."

"What about Sam? They seem pretty cozy."

Heidi laughed without humor. "No way! You kidding? Sam's his brother and that would be the cardinal sin. Worse than being unfaithful with a stranger."

"Unfaithful? What are you talking about? I thought you said this Jesse died."

She nodded. "He did. Eleven years ago. But that hasn't stopped her from dedicating her life to him." Heidi motioned to the stage. Ronni swayed slowly as she crooned a silvery love song. "See her up there? See the way her eyes are closed? She hardly ever opens them when she sings this one."

"I don't recognize this one. What is it?"

"Jason, the lead guitarist, wrote it a few years back." Heidi's eyes narrowed suspiciously. "I think it's about her and Jesse. She denies it but even if it's not, I'm sure she's singing it directly to him. I sometimes wonder if every song is for him."

Wolf watched Ronni for a few minutes and let the music seep into him and displace the anger.

"With you I'm free to live,

Free to love,

Free to see.

With you I'm free to be the one

I was always meant to be."

Heidi was right. At that moment Ronni wasn't on that stage, she was elsewhere, singing to some unseen figure. That was part of what made the song so moving. He had to admit, the words touched him. "Why would this guy have that kind of hold on her?"

"You're going to have to ask *her* that question. I've never gotten a satisfactory answer and I've known her for nine years."

She slid out of the booth and stood again. "Well, if you'll excuse me I have a tall blond photographer to corner. I need to persuade him that I'd be an ideal model…for his pictures, of course." She winked and walked away toward the last known location of Sam Ward.

Wolf felt a tug on his sleeve.

"Did you and my mom talk about my dad out there on the floor?"

"Not exactly, honey. It's kind of hard to explain."

Leah looked toward the stage. "It sounds like she must have really loved him if she's still so sad that he died."

"Mmm." Wolf didn't debate that point but he wondered if there was a little more to it than that. For a healthy, attractive thirty-year-old to deny herself male companionship for eleven years in order to be faithful to a lost love was a bit of a stretch. Was she really so dedicated to his memory or were there other reasons?

"I can hardly wait to ask her about him."

"I'm sure she'll be happy to fill you in." But Wolf wasn't really focusing on Leah's words—until he was jolted out of his reverie by her next contribution. "Did you kiss her?"

"What? Why would you ask me that?"

She shrugged. "I don't know. I just thought it seemed like you wanted to."

Damn. He'd have to watch himself around this kid. She was a little too perceptive for comfort. Or had it been that obvious? Heidi had even alluded to it. But it was ridiculous. It was purely physical. It had to be. He could never fall for someone like her. He had a list of qualities in mind for any potential love interest, and from what he had seen, Ronni fulfilled none of the required criteria.

And he had no interest in a casual roll in the hay. He wanted more. Hell, he wanted it all and he was determined that, next time, he was going to get it.

* * * * *

"This is the place," said Heidi as Sam pulled into the driveway of a small, neatly kept bungalow.

"You own this?" Sam surveyed the property through the car windows.

"Yep. I got a little bit of an inheritance from an aunt of mine and I had been saving for a while. The interest rates were good, so I thought, what the hell?" She grinned at him. She might act flip about a lot of things but secretly she was proud of her accomplishments and her home. And at that moment she was hoping for a chance to give Sam a more thorough tour of the property. Starting with the bedroom.

He nodded approval. "It sounds to me like that pretty much sums up your approach to life."

"Has Ronni been talking about me again?"

"No. I just got that impression."

"Well, you're right. I guess I figure life's too short to hold back. If you want to do something and it's not life-threatening and it doesn't hurt anybody, why not? I've rarely regretted anything that I've done."

Sam looked at her with new respect. "I wouldn't have had you pinned as a closet philosopher."

She shifted around in her seat in order to face him directly across the stick shift. "What about you, Sam? What's your philosophy of life?"

He shrugged and then stared into the darkness that hovered just beyond the hood of his car. "I never really thought about it but maybe it's similar to yours. I've certainly learned that you can't count on seeing another sunrise, so you better grab *what* you can, *while* you can."

"You mean because of Jesse?"

"Partly."

Heidi waited expectantly.

He sighed and returned his gaze to Heidi. "Didn't Ronni ever tell you about our mother?"

She tapped a bright red fingernail against her thigh. "No, I don't think so."

"She was killed in a car accident too, four years before Jesse. Drunk driver. The bastard forced her off the road over an embankment and took off."

Heidi's stomach plummeted at the pain in Sam's voice. "That's terrible! Did they ever catch him?"

"No. There was only one witness and all she knew was that the car was weaving around the road like crazy and that it was big and black. But up around us that describes half the cars in the county. It was hopeless."

She reached out and touched his hand which rested on the stick shift. "No wonder you have trouble letting go of Jesse."

She felt his fingers tense. "What does that mean?"

She withdrew her hand. "Oh come on, Sam. I know mourning can be a long process but you and Ronni have it down to a science. You feed off each other." As soon as she said it she regretted it. The whole point of asking him for a ride home was to get him into her house, and possibly into her bed, and criticizing his method of grieving was probably not the best way to go about it. But her mouth had a tendency to run away on her despite constant attempts to rein it in.

"What the hell do you know about it?"

Yep, definitely a mistake. "Forget I said it. You're right, Sam. That was out of line. I don't know what I'm talking about."

"Damn right. At least my mother died quickly. The coroner figured she died instantly, on impact." Sam's fingers wrapped around the steering wheel as if he were trying to choke it. "But not Jesse. No way. He was young and strong and vital, too strong to die quickly. He hung on for hours, in extreme pain, all alone in a ditch on some godforsaken back road. He bled to death slowly." He glared at her and Heidi didn't have a clue what to say. "Do you know what that's like?"

She shook her head.

"Well, afterwards I looked it up. If it's relatively quick, it can be like going to sleep. You just lose all your energy, gradually slip into unconsciousness and that's it. But if it takes long enough, like what probably happened with Jesse, it can be agonizing because you experience extreme difficulty breathing and then there's this intense, insatiable thirst." Sam's eyes returned to the darkness. His hands tightened on the steering wheel until the knuckles turned white. "Jesse was no saint. He would have been the first to tell you that but he was a good guy with strong ambitions, who worked hard and really cared about people and he didn't deserve that."

Heidi was smart enough to withhold her observation that his brother had lost his temper, was driving too fast on a gravel road with no seatbelt and had probably been just as much to blame as anyone. She had already made one mistake. She wasn't about to make another.

Then suddenly his grip relaxed. "But at least there's some justice in this world."

Heidi frowned. "What do you mean?"

"Ronni's father. I have to confess I was glad to hear that he died and he obviously didn't die peacefully in his bed. I can only hope he died bloody."

"Oh."

"I held him ultimately responsible for Jesse's death. If he hadn't lied to Jesse about Ronni, that never would have happened. He got what was coming to him."

Heidi whispered, "But will that give you peace?"

He laughed mirthlessly. "Of course not. I'm no fool. But I had a good, stiff drink in honor of Glenn Lichty's untimely demise and I thoroughly enjoyed every drop."

Heidi gazed out the window toward her house. The darkness had taken on sinister qualities and the windows in her house began to look like evil, empty eyes. This conversation was feeding that sense of gloom and isolation. She wasn't sure where to go from here. The silence in the car was oppressive.

She jumped when she felt Sam's hand on her shoulder. "I'm sorry about that. That must have sounded terrible—my celebrating someone's death." He squeezed her shoulder then dropped his hand as if afraid she would shrink from his touch. "I'm really a nice guy if you get to know me. I don't generally take pleasure in others' suffering."

"Don't worry. I didn't think that." She hesitated and decided to take the plunge. "Would you like to come in?"

"Actually I would, but..." He took a deep breath.

"But?" Heidi sensed impending disappointment.

"You're Ronni's friend so I feel like I need to be honest with you. I can't have her mad at me because I hurt her friend. Besides, I like you, Heidi. I can see why you and Ronni are friends, so I figure you deserve the truth. I'm leaving again soon and I might not be back for months. That's my life and I don't plan to change it. So if you're in the market for a *settling down* kind of guy, I think I should just drop you off and I should head back to my dad's."

Heidi couldn't hide the amusement that teased at her lips. "So, not all your women get this speech?"

"Nope. You get special consideration because of Ronni. Besides, despite what you seem to think, I don't exactly have women battering down my door."

Heidi tapped a finger on her chin as she knit her brows and stared at the ceiling of the car. "How long are you here for?"

"Well, I'm here for two weeks and I got in last Friday. So that gives me exactly one more week."

Heidi considered. "Okay. Coming?" she said as she opened the car door.

He cocked his head and his voice sounded skeptical. "That's okay with you?"

"I'll take *what* I can, *while* I can. Some guy with green eyes and a dimple said that to me once. I kinda thought it sounded like a good plan. So I'm game if you are." She grinned. "Besides, Ronni already warned me that you were a cad. I know full well what I'm getting into."

Sam's response was to get out and come around to Heidi's side of the car. After she closed her door he pulled her close and, much to her delight, planted a firm, wet kiss on her lips.

"You don't waste any time, do you?" she breathed after he had finally withdrawn his tongue from the remote recesses of her mouth.

"I guess not. It must run in the family." He bent to kiss her more lightly then whispered, "We're a lot alike; no wonder we hit it off. Ronni must be drawn to spontaneous, reckless people like us."

"You're right," said Heidi as she worked at catching her breath. "So, I wonder what she sees in Wolf."

Sam had taken her hand and begun leading her toward the front door. But when she said that he stopped. "What?"

Shit! Her mouth had run way ahead of her brain that time. She blamed it on her over-stimulated libido. She still didn't have the faculties to think clearly. She couldn't put together a rationalization.

"Isn't he her cousin?"

"Distant cousin. Mennonites, and all their inbreeding. You know the drill." She tried to sound flippant but he saw through the ruse.

"You don't lie very well. Why would she lie to me about that? Surely she knows I wouldn't care if she got involved with someone. I think it would be good for her."

Heidi did some quick thinking. "I wouldn't be too sure about that. Maybe she's afraid you'd feel like she was betraying Jesse. Maybe she doesn't even consciously realize it herself."

"I hope that's not it. But maybe I should talk to her about it." He resumed walking.

"Why don't you just wait and see how this thing goes with Wolf. It might not be worth bringing up." Ronni would kill her if she knew she had implied to Sam that she and Wolf were a *couple*. Even though it seemed obvious to Heidi and she couldn't believe Sam hadn't felt it, too.

"Well, okay. I'll leave it for now, just in case you're wrong. But if I ever see anything that makes me think that's the case, I'll have to set her straight. She can't make decisions based on my feelings. That's just crazy."

They reached the door. Heidi slipped in her key and a moment later they were standing in her living room. "Okay, that's enough of the serious stuff." She ran her palms up the front of his crisply pressed, cotton shirt. "That kiss got me real curious. Are you going to keep me in suspense all night?"

"Of course not. I'm no tease," he said as he traced the outline of her lips with a curious finger. As if he had marked the target area, he honed in on it with his mouth, sealing their lips together with a ferocity that startled and fascinated her. As his hand slipped beneath her short, cropped camisole Heidi considered that, if Sam and his brother had *this* in common, it was no wonder Ronni still pined for him.

No wonder at all.

* * * * *

"I hope you'll be able to sleep here," said Ronni as she tucked the covers around Leah. "It's a lot noisier here than it is at home." Ronni was amazed at herself for referring to the Lichty farm as home. She hadn't thought of it in those terms for years.

Leah yawned broadly. "I'm so tired, I don't think I'd hear a thresher going outside the window." A thresher was a large, noisy farm machine that separated the grain from the chaff.

Ronni smiled at the reference. She also hadn't thought about farm life in a very long time. She stroked Leah's hair. There was no doubt, Leah was hers. But believing it in her head and knowing it in her heart were two different matters.

"Why did you run away, Leah?" she asked quietly.

Ronni instantly sensed the tension in the girl's face. "I just wanted to meet you and I knew they'd never let me."

At that, Ronni decided she needed to say this without any prompting from Leah. "You know I didn't give you away because I didn't like you or because I didn't want you. Giving you up was the hardest thing I've ever done in my life but I knew you'd be better off with my parents. I had to leave and I knew you'd be happier with them than you could ever be with me, all by myself. You deserved a family and I couldn't give you that." She smoothed the light blanket and folded back the sheet. She looked up to see that Leah was studying her intently. "You were happy there, weren't you?"

Leah nodded but something in her face made the breath catch in Ronni's throat. Had she made a mistake? Hadn't they treated Leah well? Had they somehow taken out their anger at Ronni on her daughter? Surely her parents weren't that petty and vindictive. Despite their harsh treatment of her and Jesse, surely they wouldn't extend those feelings to their innocent grandchild. But then something dawned on her. "Were you upset by Glenn's death?" She couldn't bring herself to refer to him as Leah's father despite the fact that she had doubtless been calling him that since birth. "Is that why you ran away?"

Tears sprang to Leah's eyes and Ronni decided she had found the source of the problem. They should probably talk about this more but now wasn't the time. Leah was exhausted and they had the whole day tomorrow. She kissed Leah's forehead. "Okay, let's stop talking. We'll discuss it in the morning. You just get some sleep. I'm right across the hall and Wolf will be sleeping on the couch downstairs if you need anything."

She got up to leave but Leah's voice stopped her again. "What was my daddy like?'

Ronni turned around and forced the word past her constricted throat. "Daddy?"

"Yeah. Heidi said you really miss him." Leah chewed her lower lip in concentration. "She said his name was…Jesse. Is that right?"

Ronni hesitated briefly. "Yes, I miss Jesse every day and I'm sorry you never got to meet him."

"Is he why you had to go away?"

Ronni's jaw went slack. How had Leah figured that out? Or had Heidi been talking a blue streak about her past. If that was the case she'd get an earful. "Yes, he was a big part of the reason. But that's a long story. Right now you need to get some sleep. We'll have lots of time to talk tomorrow."

"Okay," said Leah as she rolled over. "Goodnight."

"Goodnight." Ronni flicked off the light and closed the door behind her. It was gradually getting easier to face Leah and to believe she was her daughter. If only she could face the rest of it.

She headed down the stairs and was astounded when the scent of freshly brewed coffee reached her nose. She walked into the kitchen to find Wolf sitting at the table already sipping from a huge mug. He had found a newspaper and was scanning the World section. His back was to her and he hadn't heard her come in.

Ronni stood in the doorway and watched him for a moment. His presence dominated the room although he wasn't a hulk by any means. He actually had more the build of a dancer rather than a fullback. But, of course, she would never verbalize that comparison—at least not to him. But despite that fact, he seemed larger than life. Even seated, silently drinking coffee, he emanated authority and strength. Again, she wondered who he was and what the hell he was doing in her house.

She headed to the liquor cabinet and pulled out the vodka. Then she got a carton of orange juice out of the fridge. Wolf finally noticed her as she mixed the screwdriver in a tall highball glass. "Do you drink a lot?"

Ronni clenched her teeth. "Yeah, I'm a real lush. I bathe in the stuff regularly." She picked up the glass and seated herself across from him at the table. "Not that it's any of your business, but I never drink when I'm performing, and rarely afterward. But somehow, tonight, I need something to calm my nerves." She raised her glass to him. "Go figure." She took a large sip and savored the tingle as the vodka slipped down her throat. "Besides, I'm not crazy enough to drink coffee at two in the morning."

"I just figured we might be up for a while. I think we have a lot to discuss."

Ronni nodded knowingly. "Right. You want to give me the third degree. You want an explanation as to why I gave her away. Because, after all, you're her self-appointed guardian angel. *You* know what's best for her. *You* are the supreme authority on Leah Lichty. *You* decided not to take her back home and let my mother probably worry herself to death over her lost child."

"I didn't take her back because she was terrified."

"Huh! She's just upset because my father died. Things probably felt a little strange at home or maybe my mother was short with her because of her grief. Leah must have heard about me somehow and decided I was a good prospect for a little vacation from reality. That's all." She slashed the air with her hand.

Wolf was shaking his head. "No, that's *not* all. It wasn't just a case of running away because somebody scolded her, or because she was feeling unsettled." Ronni had filled him in as to Glenn's death on the drive home. "She was *terrified*. You should have seen the look on her face when I suggested taking her to the police so they could take her home. She was close to panic and she pleaded with me to bring her to see you."

"Well, that's ridiculous. My parents would never hurt her."

"They hurt you, didn't they?"

Those words slammed into her like so many bullets. "Heidi has been talking far too much," she shot back.

"Nobody had to tell me that. It's obvious that your parents did something to make you leave your home. It must have been something pretty terrible to make you completely abandon your way of life." He looked her up and down. She could almost feel his eyes on her. "It's hard to imagine you taking up a lifestyle that was any *further* from your roots. I assume it has something to do with why you gave up Leah as well."

"I suppose you think you deserve the whole sordid story. I don't know why I should make the effort. I doubt that anything I could tell you would change your opinion of me, so why bother?" She took another sip of her drink but found no fortification there. "Not that I give a flying fuck what you think of me."

"Why do you talk like that? You don't *look* like you were born in a gutter."

Ronni froze, her drink poised at her lips, his words ringing in her ears—like echoes from the past. "What did you say?" she whispered.

Wolf's eyebrows drew together slightly. "You heard me." He sipped from his mug and Ronni tried to use that time to reestablish her bearings. "Why? What's wrong?"

"Nothing, just leave me alone." Still fighting for control, she stood and carried her drink into the living room. Her first encounter with Jesse had always been one of her most vivid memories. She had relived it numerous times in the past eleven years. Maybe it was because, in that short span of time, he had awoken feelings in her that she never knew she possessed. From that day on, as their relationship had progressed, he had cultivated them, made her feel special and strong and had helped her to break free of the constricting molds that had been placed upon her. He had, quite literally, given her wings.

Wolf seated himself on the couch across from her and watched her for a moment. "Something I said reminded you of him, didn't it?"

Ronni closed her eyes and groaned. "I'm going to kill Heidi." She sighed. "Okay, I give up. What made you ask me that just now? Obviously Heidi told you all about Jesse."

"Not a lot, just that you're hopelessly devoted to a dead man, even after eleven years. And that he was Leah's father." He sipped his coffee and propped his ankle on the opposite knee—completely at ease while Ronni slowly fell apart. "I figured you were thinking about him just now because you had the same look on your face as you did on stage tonight, when you were singing that one song."

"Oh." She didn't have to ask him which song he was referring to. She gazed down at her drink. "Yes, I was thinking about him."

I think about him every day. I try not to. I try to get through just one day without thinking about him but I can't. How can I let go of him when I can't say goodbye to him. I can't let go of the guilt. I'm to blame. I'm the real reason he's dead. God! How can I live with that?

She slammed the door on those thoughts. If she allowed herself to dwell there she'd dissolve. She couldn't let Wolf see that. "Okay," she said instead. "I'll tell you my story but first you have to tell me yours. I think you owe me that much since you've practically dismantled my world, and judged me to be an airhead and a lush all in the course of a few hours."

"All right, fair enough. What do you want to know?"

Ronni noticed that he didn't refute anything that she had said. "Well, for starters, what do you do for a living? You must be on vacation from something."

"I was in the armed forces. I recently returned from a tour in Bosnia. I retired and am currently between careers. I'll probably have to retrain for something. There's not a lot of call for experience with grenade launchers in the business world."

Ronni couldn't conceal her smile at that little tidbit. Somehow, it wasn't a surprise. "I must admit that's fascinating. What was your rank?"

"Captain. I commanded thirty men."

Again, not unexpected. "Did you see any action over there?"

His face darkened. "It's kind of hard *not* to see action in Bosnia. Next question." She noticed he crossed his arm over his abdomen and absently rubbed a finger across his lowest rib. She could swear she had seen him do that at least once before at the club.

But then she refocused on his face. There was obviously a bigger story here that he didn't want to pursue. She decided to leave it—for now. "Okay, where did you grow up?"

Wolf gave her a brief history of his childhood and family. "Okay, is that all?" he said when he had finished.

"Just one more thing. What makes you think you have any say at all in Leah's and my life? You're one arrogant S.O.B. and I don't appreciate the meddling from a stranger who seems to think he's God's own emissary." Then she laughed at herself.

Wolf was posed to make a cutting retort but her laughter confused him. "What's so funny?"

"As if there's a god. I can't believe I said that."

"You don't believe in God? Even after your upbringing?"

"Nope. No loving god would have allowed the things that happened to me and to Jesse. And I've found his staunchest advocates to be the biggest hypocrites." She regarded him critically. "Why? Do you?"

"Yes." The expression on his face left little doubt in Ronni's mind that he was telling the truth.

"Even after the horrors you must have witnessed over there? How can you say that?"

"I have my reasons. But that brings us to your story. This promises to be a doozy."

"First answer the question. What gives you the right to even be in my house?"

"I have the right because Leah asked me for my help. And despite the fact that she's only known me a short time, she's come to trust me and depend on me. I take that kind of responsibility seriously. I owe it to her to find out everything I can and to be her advocate. She obviously needs one."

"Against me, you mean," growled Ronni.

"Maybe."

Ronni stood and walked to the window. She had to admit his reasoning followed a certain twisted logic. He cared about Leah—of that she had no doubt—and ultimately that was all that mattered.

She drained her glass and turned back to face judge and jury. "Okay, Wolf. Here's my story, but rest assured, if you still disapprove of my reasons I'm not going to lose any sleep over it. I have a clear conscience." *Liar!*

"Okay. I'll keep an open mind."

She scoffed. "Yeah, right." She seated herself in the chair again and launched into her narrative. It was twenty minutes later when she finished with the story of Jesse's death and her parents' final betrayal.

Wolf had sat quietly, listening with rapt attention through the entire account. When she finished he said nothing, just sat there staring at her.

"Well?" she said irritably. "Am I exonerated or am I still beneath contempt?"

"I just don't understand why you never called him in all those months."

"I told you. I was afraid if I talked to him I'd spill the fact that I was pregnant and I knew he'd give up his education to come back. I couldn't allow that to happen."

"It was his child. Don't you think he had a right to know?"

Ronni stood and walked to the window again. She gazed out at the full moon that hovered over the trees in her backyard, and thought of another moonlit night beside a gurgling stream. "I did it for him. I had his best interests at heart."

"Were you ever going to tell him?"

"Yes. Once he came home, then I was going to tell him everything. I figured by then it would be too late. My parents had Leah and it would be harder, and pointless, to get her back. I figured I'd be able to convince him that his schooling was more important." She wiped impatiently at her eyes. She was so damn tired of tears. "But I never got the chance. I was never able to explain it to him, to tell him why I hadn't called. To tell him…" Her voice trailed off.

"Is that why you're so tied to him? Because you never got to say goodbye and to tell him that he had a child?"

"Yeah, something like that."

Wolf frowned at her tone. Even Ronni knew she didn't sound convincing but she was too tired for any more soul-searching. She stood and was about to speak when he interrupted her. "What about Sam?"

She stiffened. "What about him?"

"Don't you think he has a right to know that he has a niece?"

"I'm not ready to tell him."

"When do you think you will be?"

Wolf's eyes were frankly accusing but she just didn't have the energy to explain herself anymore. "Look, I'm tired. Sam is *my* friend and *my* business. I'll tell him when the time is right and I'd appreciate if you stay out of it. In the meantime can you understand my reasons? Can we get past this? I admit you're going to be a fixture for a while so it would be nice to get along for Leah's sake."

"Yeah, sure. I guess I can see your point of view."

Ronni just glared at him. He obviously still thought she was an irresponsible, selfish, sorry excuse for a mother. "You know what, Mercredi? Fuck you! You can make your own damn bed. There's blankets in the hall closet. Knock yourself out. If you get the urge to leave in the middle of the night don't let me stop you. Leah and I will make out just fine." She stalked out of the living room and stomped up the stairs, cursing wolves and foxes and every conceivable canine as she went.

Then, later as she lay in bed she cursed herself. What he thought *did* matter and she just couldn't figure out why. But she desperately wanted him to understand and empathize with her reasons. And that drove her to distraction.

Shades of dawn were chasing away the darkness when she finally fell asleep.

Wolf lay awake for a long time as well. She was right, of course. He was being overly hard on her. But how could he get past the image of Lubica? Much like Ronni, she had lost everything, only under much more tragic circumstances. And yet she had fought tooth and nail to keep her child with her. She had risked her life, and refused to give up regardless of the odds. She had obviously loved her daughter with a devotion and a dedication that was beyond reason. But wasn't that what a mother's love was supposed to be? Beyond reason?

He rolled over and closed his eyes. He allowed himself the luxury of reliving his one night with her. It was stupid and pathetic and ultimately self-destructive but he did it anyway.

And he enjoyed every minute.

Chapter Twenty-Four

Wolf cracked an egg on the side of a glass mixing bowl. The coffeemaker sputtered noisily nearby and a package of bacon lay open on the counter. A half a dozen slices of bread were stacked beside the mixing bowl. He cracked in another egg, poured in a splash of milk and then hesitated. "Vanilla," he muttered to himself. "Where would she keep—"

"What are you doing?" asked a familiar voice from behind him.

He didn't turn around. "Morning, Leah. Got any bright ideas on where Ronni might keep the vanilla?" He started opening cupboards.

A moment later he heard her announce, with a note of satisfaction, "Here it is." She had opened a corner cupboard and found a lazy Susan, bedecked with a variety of baking supplies.

"Thanks," said Wolf as he surveyed her outfit for the day. She had chosen a bright red T-shirt and deep purple shorts. At least her socks matched the T-shirt. He guessed she was reveling in her newly discovered world of color.

Her hair hung loosely about her shoulders and suddenly it struck him. The combination of the hairstyle, the modern clothing and Wolf's new, more detailed knowledge of Ronni brought out a resemblance that he hadn't noticed before. It wasn't the physical so much as the expressions and mannerisms. They shared those traits. He found himself wondering what else they shared.

She moved over beside him and gazed into the mysterious depths of the bowl. "What are you making?"

"French toast."

"With vanilla?"

"Yep. Secret ingredient. My mother always put some in, along with cinnamon and nutmeg."

"Strange," she whispered.

"Really," he said, whipping the eggs into a froth. "It's very good."

"No, I mean seeing you cook. My father—" She screwed up her face in concentration. "I guess I mean my grandfather, never did anything in the kitchen."

"Is that against the rules of the church or something?"

"Mmm… No, not really. But it's just sort of the way it is. The men work in the barn and the fields and the women work in the kitchen and the garden. Sometimes he might help her with planting or weeding but that wasn't very often."

Wolf laid down the whisk and looked at her. "Do you miss him? It hasn't been very long since he died. Is that why you ran away?"

She blinked a few times and looked away. "I guess so."

Wolf's heart ached for the turmoil that she seemed determined to face alone. He put a hand on her shoulder. "Okay. We don't have to talk about it. But do you like this world so far? I mean the clothes and the cars, and the music last night, and now a man cooking. That must all be pretty strange."

Her mood shifted instantly. "Yeah, I like it. It's really *cool*."

"Where'd you hear that word?" He chuckled as he turned back to the bowl. It was obviously a new addition to her vocabulary.

"I heard Heidi and my mom say it a few times last night." She dipped a finger in the sugar bowl and licked the sparkling crystals with obvious satisfaction. "Are you mad at her about something?"

Wolf stopped with a strip of bacon dangling from his fingers. "Who?"

"My mom."

"What makes you think that?"

"A bunch of stuff. Are you?"

Wolf figured she was too perceptive to even attempt lies so, after wiping his hands, he took Leah's hand and led her to the living room. He sat her down on the couch and took up his favorite position on the coffee table in front of her.

She watched him curiously, her hands clasped in her lap.

He took a deep breath. "I'm not really mad at her but I like you, Leah. I think you're a really *cool* kid." She smiled at the compliment. "I guess I just have a hard time understanding how your mother could give you away like that. I know she seems to have her reasons but I have to wonder if that's all there is to it. It's not that I think she didn't like you, or want you, but I wonder if she was just…well…too scared or too lazy to take on the responsibility of a baby. And I guess, maybe that makes me a little angry."

Leah chewed on her lower lip. "But…that wasn't it at all." She said it with a calm assurance. "She wanted me but she really thought I'd be happier with Grandma and Grandpa. It made her very sad, though." Leah focused intently on Wolf and her eyes shone with a very adult concern. "She's so sad, Wolf. I'd like her to be happy again."

Wolf fought the urge to scoop up the child, hug her and banish all the little worries from her world. The urge was strong but he knew it was pointless. As he had learned over and over, childhood was no shield against pain. Innocence couldn't banish grief or worry. He couldn't shelter her but perhaps he could hold her hand and help her deal with the sadness of the world. For a little while, at least.

"Like I said," said Wolf as he stood. "You're a pretty cool kid and if anybody can make her happy, it's you." He extended a hand. "So, you gonna help me with breakfast? I figure your mom's used to sleeping in after her performances but maybe the smell of French toast and bacon can light a fire under her."

She slipped her hand in his and followed him back into the kitchen. "Okay. I hope she has maple syrup."

They worked diligently for about ten minutes. The coffee was done and the bacon was sizzling happily when Leah said quietly, "Do you hear something?"

Wolf flipped a piece of bacon and cocked his head to listen. He frowned. "Yeah. Is Ronni calling us?"

Leah had already started toward the stairs.

Wolf quickly removed the bacon from the heat and followed. Halfway up the stairs they could just make out some disjointed phrases. "No…I'm coming…wait…can't see you…please don't…"

They had just hit the landing when an ear-piercing scream shattered the air. Wolf dashed for Ronni's room, with Leah hot on his heels. He flung open the door just as Ronni sat bolt upright in the bed. Tears were streaming down her face and her eyes were wild.

He sat beside her and touched her shoulder. "Ronni? Are you all right?"

She looked at him but her eyes were vacant, focused elsewhere. She was drawing in sharp breaths as the occasional sob escaped her throat. He wondered if she were still dreaming with her eyes open. He touched her cheek, hoping the physical contact might help her break through to wakefulness. "Ronni, are you awake?"

Then she saw him. "Oh God, not again," she said as she clamped her hands over her mouth and tears filled her eyes.

On impulse Wolf pulled her close. She looked so alone and distraught and, despite his questions about her motives, he couldn't ignore that. She responded immediately. She buried her face in the cradle of his shoulder, and wrapped her arms about his neck. Her fingers clutched at his collar as fresh sobs consumed her, soaking his shirt with her tears. And, between the sobs, he could just make out the muffled words that she repeated over and over against his shoulder. "I'm sorry. I'm so sorry."

He noticed Leah looking on helplessly. "Leah," he urged. "Why don't you go downstairs and get her a glass of cold water." As an afterthought he added, "Maybe a cool cloth too."

Relieved to have something to do, she nodded and briskly left the room.

Ronni's sobs were quieting but she hadn't loosened her hold. He stroked her back. The material of the T-shirt she wore was old and worn and velvety soft, obviously an old favorite.

She took a deep shuddering breath and hesitantly pulled away. He handed her a tissue, and noticed the T-shirt was from an old Eagles concert. He absently wondered if it had been one of *his*.

Ronni wiped her eyes. "Thank you," she whispered.

"Bad dream?" *Let's restate the obvious shall we?* He chided himself for the stupidity of the question, and then he chided himself for the fact that he was fighting the urge to hold her again. She still looked so forlorn. And sad.

Fortunately she was too focused on mopping up the moisture on her face to notice his slip. She nodded. "Yes. It's been a long time but I guess telling you my story last night must have sparked it again."

Of their own volition his fingers reached out and stroked her hair. "You've had it before?"

She closed her eyes at his touch. They both seemed to have momentarily forgotten their mutual distrust.

"Yes. I'm walking through this forest when I start to hear Jesse calling out to me." Her eyes remained closed as she recalled the images.

"His voice is faint and I have trouble figuring out where it's coming from but I know he's in trouble and needs my help. Finally I come out of the trees and I see the car. It's a wreck, a horrible mess. It's all smashed up against this tree. I run toward it but I'm too late. There are some men there and they're already pulling his body out of the wreckage." She opened her eyes and looked away—out the window where a cheerful blue sky taunted her. "He's covered in blood and I know he's dead." She was obviously struggling against more tears but she plunged on, seeming to take solace from relating the story. "I get to him just as they lay him on the ground. I'm crying and pleading with God not to let him die. And just as I reach out to touch him his eyes open. And I know…"

Wolf frowned, "You know what?"

"Here's the water."

Leah's voice startled them both.

Ronni accepted the glass from her daughter. "Thank you." She drank deeply and gradually her color returned and her breathing became more regular.

When she handed the glass back, Leah gave her the cloth. As she wiped her face and neck Wolf said, "You didn't finish. In the dream…what did you know?"

"Nothing. It's nothing. I'm sorry I burdened you with that story. But thank you for coming to my rescue." She tried to smile but it was a feeble attempt.

Nothing? It was quite obviously *not* nothing. What was she hiding? There was something more to this story that she was obviously not sharing. It had happened eleven years ago. What kind of secret could be worth keeping for that long? But he knew now was not the time to push her. She was very vulnerable and he feared the slightest criticism could set off a new wave of tears.

Instead he kept the mood light and played the hero. "I could hardly ignore a damsel in distress, could I? I have an image to protect." The little demon on his shoulder laughed heartily at that statement. "But I'm curious… "

She had smiled at his attempt to put her at ease. "Yes?"

"Why did you say you were sorry?"

"I said that?" She seemed genuinely surprised.

"Yes. While you were crying, you kept repeating it."

"I-I'm not sure. I don't remember that part." She was lying. Her eyes couldn't meet his. But why?

She continued, "Do I smell bacon and coffee?"

Leah brightened. "Yup. Wolf and I were making breakfast."

Wolf accepted the change in topic but made a mental note of all the evasions. He stood. "Why don't you get dressed and come down? I should get back to the bacon. It was only half done."

"Okay, I'll just be a minute. That sounds wonderful."

As Wolf was closing the door behind him he stopped when she said his name.

"Mmm?"

"Thanks again. It's been a very long time since someone took care of me like that."

He smiled, surprised at how much that knowledge pleased him. "Hurry up and get down while the bacon's hot."

She nodded weakly as he closed the door.

Leah grabbed Wolf's hand as they headed down the stairs. "Is she okay?"

"Yeah, she's fine. Just a scary dream." But Wolf wasn't so sure. He'd had some experience with nightmares but it seemed to take her an exceptionally long time to come out of that one.

He tried to shrug off the malaise. It was a beautiful spring day outside and the smells from the kitchen were enticing. He hesitated to admit it to himself but he was genuinely looking forward to sitting down with Ronni and her daughter for a cozy breakfast. The cooking and then the episode with Ronni had brought out domestic feelings that he hadn't experienced for a very long time.

This was what had eluded him three years ago. He had been cheated. He had been dealt a winning hand and the cards had burst into flames in his hands.

"What's wrong, Wolf?" asked Leah as she watched him flip the toast on the griddle.

"Huh?" He looked over at her and was reunited with reality. "Sorry," he chuckled. "My mind just wandered." He refocused on the French toast and bacon sizzling before him and absently rubbed a thumb along his lowest rib.

"Why do you do that?" asked Ronni as she entered the kitchen and made a beeline for the coffee pot.

Wolf looked up. "Do what?"

She approached him and touched the rib he had just been massaging. "Rub at this," she said. He was startled at the nosedive his stomach took when she touched him there. To make matters worse she actually kneaded the flesh slightly with her fingers. "I noticed you do it several times last night. Does it hurt?"

He suppressed the urge to grab her wrist with the force of a vise to make her stop. He was disturbed to realize he was also suppressing the urge to grab her wrist and pull her snugly against him. Not choosing either option, he merely stepped away, just out of reach of those exploring fingers. He cleared his throat and made an evasive maneuver of his own. "It aches sometimes. Old injury."

When he looked at her he realized with irritation that she was smiling at him. "Old war wound, eh? Or did you fall off your bike as a kid and you just like to play it up because you're an army captain?"

He knew she was just trying to be playful but he didn't share the mood. He turned back to the frying pan and flipped the golden brown creations and the bacon onto the plates beside the stove. "Breakfast's ready. Why don't you sit down?"

* * * * *

Ronni stepped away and sipped from her mug, suddenly regretting the teasing. The last thing she had wanted to do was to upset him. She had cherished those few moments upstairs. It had been two years since she had that dream but usually she awoke from it alone, in the dark, in an empty house. Sometimes it took her hours to shake the depression that usually accompanied it. But awakening to strong arms and tender caresses and a listening ear had been extremely therapeutic. She had already shaken most of the heartache and loneliness. Unfortunately, however, nothing could rid her of the guilt.

She sat at the table and graciously accepted the plate that he placed before her. "Mmm. That looks good. I can't remember the last time someone cooked for me."

Wolf laughed. She looked up at him as he seated himself kitty-corner to her, and across from Leah. She realized that was the first time she had heard him laugh. It was more of a low rumble, the kind of sound you might expect the earth to make if it had a sense of humor. The deep throaty sound set off odd flutters in her gut. She hesitated to admit how much she liked it, and how much she liked his smile.

"What's so funny?" she asked, smiling back.

"I was just thinking that it's been a very long time since I cooked for anybody. I used to cook for my family sometimes, when my parents were working late in the saloon in Dawson. I was no gourmet but I always enjoyed it."

"Saloon?" asked Leah.

Ronni took the plunge. "Up in the Yukon, in the summers, they run the towns for the tourists. Dawson is like an old gold rush town, right out of the old west." Leah wouldn't understand that reference so she elaborated a bit on that before continuing. "And a saloon is sort of like their version of Ruby's. A bar with entertainment and gambling, and guys in chaps and spurs." She glanced at Wolf. "How'm I doin'?"

"Pretty good. You've educated yourself a bit since leaving home."

"I try to read but I never went back to school. It was always way too expensive and then once the band really got going I figured there wasn't much point. I'm already doing what I love."

Wolf's eyes turned oddly wistful. He focused on the plate before him but seemed to have forgotten all about eating. "You're very lucky to have found your true calling." He speared a morsel of bread and mopped up some syrup but the bite never made it to his mouth. "I'm sorry I was so hard on you about it last night. You really are very good. I'm not normally a fan of that kind of music but I couldn't help but be touched by your singing." At the end of the phrase his eyes lifted to hers and she saw only sincerity in their dark depths.

She was so shocked by the unexpected show of support and affirmation that her own bite of breakfast froze halfway between the plate and her mouth. "Thank you. That…that means a lot." But she couldn't help wondering why he *had* been so judgmental the night before.

Leah had been watching them with silent fascination but now, picking up on the positive mood, she played her hand. "Can we do something together today? All three of us?"

Ronni sipped at her coffee. "Well, I was thinking we really should contact my mother. She must be beside herself with worry." She hazarded a glance at Wolf. "And likely the police are looking for her. They may be an isolated community but they do rely on police for this type of thing." She grasped Leah's hand. "And I hate to admit this but I have no legal right to have you here. I gave up my rights years ago."

Leah bit her lip to keep it from trembling. She shook her head vigorously. "Please don't. Not yet. Just a couple more days. I can't go back. I like it here. I want to get to know you better." Her words tumbled over each other. "I can't go back. Not yet. Please don't make me. I just can't—"

Ronni felt helpless in the face of such innocent desperation. Perhaps Wolf was right. There was more to this than restlessness and dissatisfaction. She squeezed Leah's hand, "What is it, Leah? Why did you run away? Are you afraid of something?"

The tears brimmed in her eyes, "I…I… No. I just want to stay a little longer." She threw a pleading glance at Wolf, who looked just as helpless as Ronni felt.

Ronni answered. "Okay, I'll tell you what. You can stay for today. If Wolf wants to stick around we'll all do something together. We can show you the town, maybe take in a movie, go mini-golfing and do the go-kart thing." She glanced at Wolf who nodded. Those were all things that would be new experiences for Leah. "I have to stick around because I have a show tonight and Saturday's a big crowd so I really can't play hooky. I don't think you should come again, though. I was walking on thin ice as it was last night." She stroked Leah's cheek and was pleased to see the relief wash over Leah's features. "But tomorrow is Sunday and I don't have anything planned, so I really think we should take you home and see what's what."

Leah had begun to smile but, at the mention of home, the tension started to creep back into her face.

"But I promise we won't leave until we have a talk with Verna and sort out whatever it is that's bothering you. Okay?"

Leah was obviously not thrilled at the prospect but she knew it was a battle she couldn't win. "Will Wolf come along too?" she said hopefully.

"Of course. I'll stay as long as you need me to."

Ronni tried to thank him with her eyes. The strange connection he seemed to feel with Leah still puzzled her but she was beyond questioning it.

"Okay then, it's settled. We'll have to do the fast food thing for lunch."

Leah scowled with distaste. "Do we have to?"

Wolf smiled as he chewed his last bite of syrup-soaked dough. "You mean you didn't like it?"

"It was okay but it wasn't really like food."

The two adults laughed. "Truly a child with discerning tastes," said Wolf. "How about some wood-oven pizza? On the way here I saw a sign for a place that looked authentic, and I think you deserve to taste the real thing."

"And maybe Chinese for supper," added Ronni. "I doubt you've ever tasted that."

Leah beamed. She was obviously enjoying the casual familiarity and banter that was swirling about her. "That sounds like fun."

Ronni squeezed her hand and could almost feel the tingle of excitement in Leah's fingers. "You're in for the time of your life, my dear. I'll show you wonders like you never imagined."

* * * * *

Watching the two of them, Wolf felt a surge of warmth that both comforted and disturbed him. He knew he was heading for disappointment but he just seemed bound and determined to set himself up for these huge falls. He kept telling himself to hold back, to not let himself feel so much. It couldn't last. His part in their lives was temporary and if he didn't face that fact he was going to end up back in the same black pit that he had fought his way out of three years ago. But the warnings were useless. He couldn't seem to stop himself. It seemed that crash and burn was becoming a way of life for him.

After the dishes were cleaned up the women headed upstairs to get ready for their outing, leaving Wolf to use the downstairs bathroom. He had just pulled out his razor when he heard a tap on the bathroom door. "Wolf?"

He hastily pulled on a T-shirt and opened the door. "Yeah?"

Ronni stuffed her hands in the pockets of her jeans and abruptly pulled them out again. She combed her fingers through her hair and Wolf found himself smiling at her uncharacteristic battle with stage fright. "I was just thinking…that maybe…" She sighed and blurted it out, "Would you like to come to the club again tonight? I thought I could ask Heidi to stay with Leah. They'd probably have a great time doing each other's hair and painting their fingernails. Heidi gets to hear me all the time and Leah would enjoy it. I even thought I could rent a video game set for her. Heidi's got the fastest fingers this side of the Arctic Circle and can teach Leah all her tricks. You said you enjoyed it…so…well… I just thought I'd ask."

At that moment Ronni looked so vulnerable he just couldn't bring himself to say no. "Sure. That sounds great. Maybe Leah needs a break from me anyway."

Ronni smiled broadly. "Great. I'll call Heidi right away."

Wolf closed the door and swished his razor through the water. As he ran the blades across his chin he was startled to realize he was humming. It was one of the tunes that Ronni had sung the night before. Then he was startled to realize he was looking forward to the evening. He even caught himself thinking about sharing another dance with her. *Shit!* They had nothing in common. She represented a lifestyle he despised and she was toting around a boxcar full of old relationship baggage. It was suicide to allow himself to continue on his present course. But he knew there was no way he was leaving. Leah needed him. And, oddly, he seemed to need her.

Crash and burn, here we come.

* * * * *

Sam reached for the phone, "Hello?"

Heidi, snuggled up to Sam's cheek, could just make out the voice at the other end of the line. "Uh…Sam?"

"Ronni! Uh…yeah, it's me."

They heard a muffled snicker. "I suppose Heidi is right handy?"

"You don't know the half of it."

Heidi ripped the phone from his hand. "What's up, Ron?"

"It sure didn't take you long, did it?"

"He's only here for another week. There was no time to waste."

"Was it everything you hoped?"

Heidi traced Sam's shoulder with a bright red fingernail. "Everything and more."

Sam grabbed her hand and kissed it before throwing back the covers and heading for the bathroom. Heidi watched his retreating form with undisguised lust.

"Well, you might hate me for this but I have a favor to ask of you."

"Shoot."

Ronni made her request. Heidi sighed, but when Ronni finished she covered the mouthpiece of the phone and shouted in to Sam who had just turned on the water for a shower. "Ronni asked me to watch Leah tonight so Wolf can come to the club. What should I tell her?"

Sam came to the door and leaned against the frame, completely oblivious to his glorious nudity. Heidi, however, was not. "Well, I'd kind of like to go again, at least for a bit. I get to see her so rarely. But I'd really like to let her get to know this Wolf guy. She needs to find somebody special. How about you take her up on it and I promise to make it up to you after the show. And, as additional incentive, I'll even spend the day with you tomorrow."

"Throw in a steamy shower for two and you've got a deal."

"You got it, babe."

Heidi spoke into the phone again as Sam padded back into the bathroom, "Okay, Ronni, I'll do it. I actually think I'm getting a pretty good deal." Heidi wasn't about to admit it to Sam but she probably would have done it regardless. She, too, was hoping something might develop with Wolf. God knew Ronni needed a distraction.

"Thanks, Heidi. You're a peach."

"Okay, enough small talk. I've got a hot date in a steamy shower."

"Take it easy. You could break your neck in there."

"Maybe. But what a way to go."

Heidi hung up and snuck into the bathroom. Sam was already lathering up when she slipped past the shower curtain to join him. "Hey! You started without me."

He turned to face her. "I promise to make it up to you."

She wrapped her arms around his neck and pulled him down for a deep kiss. Soap-slicked bodies molded together. "I have high expectations," she mumbled against his lips.

"I don't make a habit of disappointing."

It wasn't long before Heidi was convinced. She again wondered if Sam had given his little brother lessons. If their skills were on equal par, Ronni had been very lucky indeed.

Chapter Twenty-Five

Stephen Lichty strolled into the Martin Dairy barn. Eli's wife had said he could be found there tending to one of the new calves. Stephen threaded his way through the maze of stalls and cobwebs, heading toward the back of the barn and the pens where the newborn calves were segregated. As he approached he heard a crash and Eli's raised voice startled him. "God dammit!"

Stephen broke into a run. He found Eli standing off to the side, away from the pens, glaring down at a large notebook laying open on an old desk. Pieces of glass from a broken feeding bottle glittered amidst the straw against the opposite wall.

"Everything all right, Eli?" asked Stephen with concern.

Eli, obviously startled, glanced up from the notes. His face briefly registered panic before he resumed his usual calm, controlled demeanor. "Yes, I'm sorry about that, Stephen. I guess I'm just a little on edge ever since your father's death." Everyone in the congregation carefully avoided the word *murder*. That sort of thing just wasn't supposed to happen here. So they pretended that it hadn't.

Stephen walked over and joined him at the desk. "More problems with the herd?"

"Nothing I can't handle. How are things with you folks? Are you handling the business okay?"

Stephen had taken over the dairy operation after his father's death. It had been decided years earlier that he would be the one to follow in his father's footsteps but he hadn't planned on taking the reins for many years. He knew the business inside and out but the realities of taking on the full responsibility for it had been daunting. Besides the fact that he was grieving for his father, he was also coping with a new baby and a relatively new wife. He felt a little overwhelmed by it all. And then of course there was the disappearance of his little sister.

Stephen raked his fingers through his chestnut hair. "Yeah, it's okay. But I'm worried about Mom. She's so quiet. I don't know how she'll cope if they don't find Leah soon. I've been thinking of calling the police and trying to push them to do more."

Eli settled a hand on his shoulder. "I'm sure they're doing all they can. And, I hate to say this, Stephen, but you had better prepare yourself and your mother for the possibility that they may *not* find her. From what I hear, the more time elapses the poorer the chances of finding her. Needless to say I'm a believer in prayer but sometimes the Lord just has other plans."

Stephen hung his head and stared at his boots. "I know. I'm starting to think the same way." A calf lowed plaintively from its pen and Stephen raised his eyes to Eli again. "Do you think we should notify Ronni? I mean, after all, she is her mother. She has a right to know."

"Does she? She's made no effort to contact your family for eleven years now. I'd say she either doesn't care, or has made a very conscious decision to sever all ties. I think, either way, we should respect her wishes. I know, as far as Glenn was concerned, Frany had ceased to exist as a member of your family." He squeezed Stephen's shoulder. "Wouldn't you agree?"

Stephen's eyes returned to the floor as he set his jaw. What Eli had said was true, however, it had been a two-way street. His parents had never made any attempt to contact their daughter either. And Stephen also knew how much Jesse Ward's death had affected his father. It had been a shadow in his life that he had struggled with for years. And it had been a big part of the reason that Glenn and Verna had deliberately never contacted their daughter. Stephen suspected that they had been too apprehensive to face her and the accusations that she was sure to throw at them.

But Eli's word was gold. "Yes, I guess you're right."

To appease his young relative, Eli offered, "I'll come over this evening and see how Verna's doing." He checked his watch. "But right now I have an appointment to keep. I'm finding the new responsibilities of being a Bishop to be just as demanding as a pastorship. Maybe more so."

"All right. Thanks Eli." His heart no lighter than when he had entered, Stephen turned and strode out of the barn.

* * * * *

Relieved to be alone with his demons, Eli returned his attention to the book on the table. He skimmed the notations with a critical eye before snapping it closed. The muffled crack lacked any sense of satisfaction. The figures might be out of sight but, no matter how hard he tried, he couldn't erase them from his mind.

He was so close to the realization of everything he'd ever wanted. But he had been so close for years. His dreams always seemed to hover on the horizon, glowing with the light of the dawning sun, but always just out of reach. Lately the doubts that plagued him had begun to gnaw at his hopes. Should he give up? Should he abandon the path that had seemed so clear fifteen years ago?

But he had sunk so much money into his breeding experiments, how could he stop now? He couldn't let all that time and money go to waste. If he could just sort out the kinks with this new breed, he would be destined for incredible success and acclaim. A breed with almost double the milk production without the use of controversial drugs and steroids. It was a guaranteed gold mine. But digging for gold took money and he had, once again, expended his resources.

He slid in behind the wheel of his diesel truck and chugged out the driveway.

That was what this little meeting was about today. Investment capital. That was what he needed. He didn't only have his own interests at heart. It was for the good of the church—the whole community. His means were justified. The Lord himself had sanctioned it.

Fifteen minutes later he pulled in the lane of Will Zehr's hog farm.

He found Will in the driving shed fiddling with the engine of one of the huge tractors. The wheels topped Eli's stature by several inches and the engine packed more horsepower than an entire brigade of buggies. These beasts represented an enormous investment but were a key tool for a successful farm operation. If you could fix it yourself, so much the better, because repair bills could be exorbitant. Five thousand dollars was not an uncommon bill for a farmer to receive from a competent mechanic.

"Hello, Will!" called Eli as he sauntered through the shed.

Will, a short, stout man with a receding hairline and overactive sweat glands, tended to remind Eli of a hog himself. Small eyes set closely on either side of a round, bulbous nose exaggerated the effect.

Will mopped his towering forehead with a rag, and then wiped his grease-stained hands. He extended a hand to Eli. "Hello! How's our new Bishop doing?" Will pumped Eli's hand as if he expected water to spout from his mouth. "I can't tell you how glad I was that you drew the Lot this time. I can't think of anyone I'd rather see take on the job."

"Thanks for the vote of confidence, Will. I really appreciate the support." Eli reclaimed his hand and stuffed it deeply into the pocket of his work pants.

Will nodded congenially. "So, what brings you to this neck of the woods? You haven't dropped by here in ages."

Eli battled butterflies in his gut and could feel his pulse in his temples but this was necessary. He leaned against the huge tractor tire and assumed an air of brotherly concern. "Well, Will, it seems that the church is a little short of funds for this time of year. I was hoping maybe I could persuade you to up your tithe a little."

Will frowned as he considered this unusual development. Money and giving were rarely discussed with such candor. And pastors almost never directly approached members for contributions, relying instead on over-the-pulpit persuasion to the congregation in general if the coffers were running low.

"I thought the givings were right on budget this year," replied Will.

"Not exactly. Those numbers are deceiving."

Will mopped his forehead with the rag again, leaving a slight grease smudge that had been inadvertently transferred from his hands. Eli had a vague recollection of seeing a picture of some Russian official with a similar stain across his brow. But world issues didn't generally concern him and he couldn't remember the name even if he cared to.

He refocused on Will's worry-pinched features. "I don't know, Eli. I'm a little tight this month. Pork prices are down. And I've been tithing like clockwork, sometimes even beyond the ten percent."

Eli's anxiety gradually lessened as he settled into the familiar routine. He shook his head mournfully. "That's all well and good, Will, but sometimes sacrifices are needed." He pursed his lips and fixed Will with a steady stare. "I would think that business with your son a few months back would make you doubly grateful for your supportive church community."

Will swallowed and fresh beads of sweat popped out on his forehead. "How did you know about that?"

"Well, my position as Bishop requires that I be filled in on all such matters. That was very reckless of him. It's a good thing that girl decided not to press charges. Rape is a serious crime. It could have been disastrous and I believe the Church's assurance that he would be watched very closely was a key factor in the police's decision to overlook it this time."

"He didn't actually do it, Eli." Will wrung his hands and the sweat trickled along his jaw. "He just scared her a little."

Eli shook his head again. "But he wanted to, didn't he? It's a grievous sin and I'm sure you wouldn't want the whole church to know about his transgression. That could prove very awkward for you, and for your son. Surely the young women would think twice about going somewhere alone with someone like that if they knew his history."

The color had gradually drained from Will's face. In a close-knit community like this one, it would be impossible to escape such a stigma. The boy's social status would degenerate to that of a leper. It could take years to outlive such a label and he would likely end up leaving the church, much as Veronica Lichty had.

Eli knew that Will would do almost anything to prevent that from happening to his eldest son. In fact he was counting on it. He almost regretted his course of action but it was necessary. He didn't have a choice.

"What are you saying?" whispered Will.

The smile that hid behind Eli's face was sad and knowing. His poor parishioner knew perfectly well what Eli was implying. He just didn't want to face it.

"I'm sure the church would be more than happy to let this go, and keep it from becoming public knowledge if it were assured of your commitment. You've been an exemplary member. What's a few thousand dollars in comparison to keeping your and your son's good name intact?"

Understanding gradually dawned across Will's features. Understanding and disbelief. But Eli wore his earnestness and commitment to his duty like a mask. He continued to drive his point home. "I would think the difficulties that your nephew encountered after a similar incident would be enough to make you wary."

Will blinked. "Myron?"

"Yes, Will. Myron. He managed to overcome the stigma after he was accused of making lewd and, may I say, rather disturbing suggestions to that woman down at the Tavern but it took time. And that was just *words*, Will. He never laid a hand on her or anyone else." Eli only hesitated a moment before adding. "That the congregation knows of, that is."

Will's expression registered confusion, and then suspicion over what Eli was suggesting. Then he seemed to accept the truth of it—of all of it. He wiped his forehead with the back of his sleeve. The grease smudge spread like a disease.

"Yes, of course. I see your point. I suppose it's the least I can do. I'll be sure to put an extra large check in the offering on Sunday."

"Why don't you get it out of the way right now, Will? I'll be happy to accept the check today. We wouldn't want it to slip your mind on Sunday, would we?"

Now Will saw the whole truth. The glaring certainty of it was almost more than he could accept. But a moment later he hung his head in defeat and headed out the door. "Yes, of course. That would be best. I'll go get my checkbook right now."

Eli watched him shuffle toward the house and sucked in a deep breath. He always hated to do this to these people who looked up to him and trusted him. But they had appointed him to lead with good reason. He had the vision and the direction. They would eventually see that it was for their own good. In the end the benefits would be reaped by all. He knew best. God himself had affirmed Eli's gifts. The Lot was blatant proof of that.

The road stretched out before him as clear as the path the Lord cut for Moses through the Red Sea. It may be difficult—the way of the Lord was narrow and rocky—but it was very clear and he couldn't deviate from it now. He had come too far and made too many sacrifices.

* * * * *

Sergeant Pierce dragged his eyes away from the notes he had been poring over and glanced at the photo on his desk. His wife and two daughters gazed back at him, all smiles and dressed in their Sunday frills, their hair twisted into intricate curls and their hands and faces scrubbed and fresh. They had shed their usual jeans and grime and cleaned up rather nicely for the special birthday photo. *His* birthday. They thought it a crime that he had no pictures of them at work, so they had conspired to remedy the problem. Normally the photo brought a smile to his lips, but not today.

When he looked at his daughters all he could think about was how he would feel if one of them were in Leah Lichty's place. His daughter, Jackie, was just about Leah's age and it made his blood boil to think of her in the clutches of some pervert who was capable of killing a man in the process of abducting her. If he ever got his hands on this one, he didn't plan to let go easily. He only hoped that Leah was still alive to rescue.

"Hey, Pierce," called a tall portly cop with gelled-back hair.

"Yeah, Witmer?"

The younger officer plunked himself down at the desk across from Pierce's. "I think I got something *big*."

"Oh, for God's sake. I haven't got all day." Witmer's love of melodrama had a knack for turning even the most mundane conversation into a tedious trek through the land of *Hill Street Blues.*

"Still banging your head against the wall in the Lichty case?"

Pierce suppressed the urge to roll his eyes. Witmer knew exactly how the case was going. "Yes." He reached for a tepid cup of coffee that he vaguely remembered being there when he started his shift. "Those Mennonites are either so pure they never get angry about anything, or they're so damn closed-mouthed that you couldn't pry a motive out of them with a crowbar. And so far that sketch is leading us down the high road to nowhere."

"Well, I may have a new, juicy lead."

"Really? No shit! Do share, Witmer."

Witmer seemed unfazed. "Okay, I don't know much yet but there's a guy…" He flipped open a small note pad and scrutinized it momentarily. "Sam Ward's the name. I was up questioning some people at the local hangout up there—the Elmwood Tavern—and apparently this Ward fellow held quite a grudge against Lichty. Blames him for his brother's death a few years back. It has to do with his brother and this girl. I don't know that whole story but apparently Ward came back to town about a week ago—"

"Right around the time of the murder?" Pierce's juices were flowing despite his annoyance with his partner.

Witmer nodded grandly. "To the day. And anyway, a couple of days later he shows up at the Tavern. Claimed to have seen the write-up in the paper about the death. I guess he got good and sloshed, but not out of grief. He was toasting poor Lichty's demise until the wee hours. He was overjoyed at the news. Got downright rowdy."

"Is he the one that the waitress saw in the coffee shop?"

"It doesn't sound like it. This guy's blond with green eyes. Unless he's a master of disguises I doubt it's him."

Pierce stroked his scruffy chin. "That's definitely interesting but it still leaves a lot of questions. How does the girl figure into it?" He didn't have to verbalize the possibility that Leah had witnessed something and had thus become a liability. Abduction wasn't the only possible explanation for her disappearance. Although, thankfully, that possibility had dwindled considering the sighting in Creemore. "And what about the fellow in the sketch? I wonder if they could be in cahoots. Of course Ward's involvement is far from certain but we definitely have to talk to this guy. You know where he is?"

Witmer shook his head with exaggerated mournfulness. But there was a twinkle in his eye.

Pierce waited for the other shoe to drop.

"Nope. He's apparently staying with his father while he's in town but he hasn't been there for a couple of days. I stopped in and the old man told me this isn't uncommon. He's got this *friend* in Kitchener, that he often goes to see when he's here. He might be staying with her."

"Okay," said Pierce slowly, knowing Witmer was still holding out for the pièce de résistance. "Let's check her out and put out an APB on this guy. I want to find him as soon as possible." He paused as he stood and grabbed his jacket. "What's the woman's name?"

A slow, self-satisfied smile spread across Witmer's face. "Ronni. Ronni *Lichty*."

* * * * *

The trio tumbled in the front door.

Wolf slammed the door and leaned against it as he panted from exertion and the heat of the day.

"Oh my God!" exclaimed Ronni as she glanced at her watch. "Look at the time! I've got less than an hour to get ready." She pointed an accusing finger at Leah. "It's all your fault. We were having far too much fun. If it wasn't for you I'd already be dressed and ready to go, and sitting all by myself with a frozen dinner, watching the clock tick until it was time to go."

Wolf stood quietly and watched them, all the while fighting the subtle but insistent tug on his heartstrings.

Leah understood the teasing perfectly. She beamed. "Can I help? I wanna see that gold stuff you put in your hair."

Ronni smiled and cupped her chin. "Sure. I just have to have a really quick shower first. Why don't you flake out on your bed for a few minutes and I'll call you when I'm ready for you."

"Okay." Leah headed for the stairs but then she seemed to think better of it. She came back and wrapped her arms around Ronni. She said nothing, but squeezed tightly before letting go and tossing Wolf a sappy grin. Then she bounded up the stairs.

Ronni stood riveted to the spot and watched her go.

"She'll sleep tonight," said Wolf as he watched the emotions play across Ronni's features.

"Yeah, I think we really wore her out." She was still staring at the stairs. She turned back to Wolf, and registered surprise when Wolf's finger brushed across her cheek.

"You're crying." His finger came away damp.

She turned away. "Am I?"

He followed her to the kitchen where she opened the fridge and pulled out a pitcher of cold water.

"Do you ever regret it?" he asked as he leaned against the wall.

She filled a glass. "Yes and no. I regret it for me, but not for her. I regret that I never nursed her, or changed her diaper, or helped her with her first steps, or heard her first laugh. How could I not regret those things? I never even held her. They took her away the moment I gave birth. I wanted it that way. I was afraid if I held her I'd never be able to let go. And today has proven it to me."

"But?"

"But I still believe that, for her sake, I did the right thing. I had no skills. No education. I'd never even ridden a bus, for chrissake. I couldn't have given her a decent life. She would have been with baby-sitters constantly. Either that or we would have had to go on welfare."

"You could have stayed with your family."

Her eyes turned as icy as the cubes in her glass. "No, that was never an option. I would have been miserable and that would have made me a terrible mother."

"What if this Jesse character hadn't gotten himself killed?"

In the next instant Wolf was gasping for breath as he blinked rapidly and wiped ice cold water out of his eyes. "What the hell was that for?" he roared.

Her eyes burned. In stark contrast to the heightened mood of a few moments before the room was deathly quiet and Ronni's eyes blazed with a rage that almost frightened him.

"First of all, he was not a *character*. He was a wonderful man who changed my life and gave me more than you could ever imagine. Secondly, he didn't get himself killed. He was a victim of circumstances and he was angry because he loved me. We were both betrayed by people who were *supposed* to care about me. Thirdly, the question is moot because he *didn't* live. A fact that I am reminded of every day of my life and I don't need you to point it out for me." She slammed the empty glass on the counter. "Now, if you'll excuse me I have to get ready. If you still plan to go, be warned, the subject of Jesse Ward is strictly off-limits."

She brushed past him, breathing ice-cold fire out of her nostrils.

Wolf reached for a towel to dry his face. *Wow!* He would definitely heed the warning. She had a temper like a— He chuckled at the thought. Riley would get a kick out of that one.

She had a temper like a *she-wolf*. And he couldn't deny, it intrigued him.

Once he had recovered sufficiently he gathered a few things and headed to the main floor bathroom. He stepped into a steamy shower and allowed the spray to massage well-used muscles. He might be fit, but nothing could prepare him for keeping up with an excited eleven-year-old.

They had done everything they set out to and more. Leah had taken it all in with the eyes of a newborn. In a sense that was exactly what she was. So much of this world had been denied her—her first movie, her first time on a Ferris wheel, her first taste of sweet and sour chicken balls. And there was no hiding her delight at being with two people that she had quickly come to care about.

Wolf couldn't deny how much the day had meant to him as well. Sitting in that bucket, sweeping an arc thirty feet above the earth, listening to Leah's squeals of delight and seeing Ronni smile, with his arm around them both, as they nestled in snugly against him…

Nope, he definitely had not learned his lesson.

He let the water sluice down his face. He closed his eyes and tried not to let those feelings seep in too deeply but soon conceded defeat because, within moments, his thoughts turned back to Ronni. Maybe she was right. Her life as a single mother with a child and no education would have been difficult—maybe impossible. She had a choice. She knew she would be leaving Leah in caring, capable hands, with a family that she had loved and trusted for years.

Lubica didn't have that choice. Where could she have taken Anja that would have been safe and secure? Lubica had no family left on whom to depend. The safety net in her community was in tatters, if it existed at all. In her world the safest place for Anja was with her mother. And even that had been a tenuous thing.

In the end, it hadn't been enough.

He stepped out of the shower and toweled himself off. He rubbed his hair vigorously and reached for his clothes. "Shit!"

He had neglected to bring in the clean socks and underwear he would need. They were still safely stashed in his backpack in the living room. So, he wrapped a towel about his middle and stepped cautiously into the hall. A quick survey of the area satisfied him that it was safe to venture out.

He hadn't counted on Ronni's exuberant progress down the stairs.

He had just passed the opening to the stairwell when he heard her rapid footsteps. He turned around with the intention of quickly heading for the cover of the bathroom but, in his haste, he almost bowled her over.

She laughed. "Sorry! Forget something?" Then her eyes traveled down his torso and she lost her smile. "Oh my God!"

Wolf would have loved to move the towel up to cover his chest and abdomen, but that would have left other, equally embarrassing areas exposed. So, instead, he just stood there and allowed her to gawk at him.

"Shall I turn around and give you the unedited version?" he said with irritation.

She didn't notice his caustic tone. She didn't draw back from his chilly demeanor and withering glare. Instead, she extended an inquisitive finger and touched one of the deep, ugly souvenirs that had accompanied him back from the edge of hell. His skin shivered at her touch.

"What happened?" she breathed.

"Machine gun."

She continued tracing her fingers along the deep welts lined with stiff colloidal tissue, heedless of the fact that she hadn't asked his permission. She was utterly captivated by his deformity.

"How do you survive something like this?"

"Not everyone does."

She looked up at him, alerted by the edge in his voice. "You lost someone over there."

No, I lost everything over there. "Look, I'd love to give you my life story but I'd rather do it with my clothes on."

"Right, sorry." But she didn't remove her hand. Instead she covered the lower part of his rib cage with her open palm. "Is this where it aches sometimes?"

At that moment he had every right to bat her hand away and make a hasty retreat. But he couldn't quite bring himself to move. "Yes."

She gently massaged the muscle and underlying bone. "Does that help?"

That shocked him into action. He grabbed her shoulders and railed at her, "What do you think you're doing?"

He was amazed that, despite his harsh tone, he saw no fear or animosity in her eyes. "I'm not sure," she said simply. "You must have experienced a lot of pain. I just thought you needed to be touched."

He found that to be an odd thing for her to say but it was bang on. Maybe she and her daughter shared some weird ability to sense what others needed. The trouble was, at that moment, he needed more than a few brush strokes from probing fingers. At that moment he had visions of a hell of a lot more.

She just kept looking at him. He felt as if he could swim around indefinitely in those green eyes that were as deep and inviting as the Mediterranean on a summer afternoon. Her gaze was patient, and vaguely expectant. She was waiting for something—waiting for him.

And what exactly was he waiting for? Was *he* being faithful to a ghost? A ghost that he had known for little more than two days?

Ah hell! he thought. He decided he wasn't going to fall into that trap, especially after criticizing her for doing exactly that. He lowered his head and settled his lips firmly on hers. She was receptive and soft and pliant. Her hands skimmed up his torso, over his chest. They left a searing trail in their wake, until they finally came to rest on his shoulders.

He wrapped his arms around her waist and she wove her fingers through the hair at the nape of his neck. She smelled of soap and shampoo, and some spicy perfume that he couldn't identify. He felt her breasts grinding against his bare chest. Only the silk of her blouse separated them and that whisper of denial spurred his desire. He dipped his tongue into her mouth and tasted peppermint toothpaste. It made him crazy.

He plumbed her more deeply, and felt her wilt beneath his hands. He held her more tightly, supporting her, devouring her, until he became painfully aware of his reactions to her.

To continue was to flirt with disaster. Tonight she was wearing a leather mini-skirt and, considering his attire, it wouldn't take long for things to get out of hand. But, even knowing that, he felt powerless to stop the tidal wave of momentum that seemed to be carrying him forward.

Ronni was the one to latch onto a thread of sanity and break the kiss. "Leah fell asleep upstairs." Her breath ruffled the hairs of his chest.

He breathed deeply. Calmly. "Right. Leah."

"What just happened?"

"I don't know. I thought we were mad at each other."

"Me too. Must be a turn on."

"I should get dressed." But he didn't move. Instead, those soulful green eyes and delicate hands held him captive. She felt fragile beneath his hands but he had learned years ago how much of an illusion that could be.

She met his gaze and traced his jaw with her thumb. "Will you tell me about it later?"

"Yes. While we drive." At that instant it hit him with blinding clarity. How could he have been so blind to the experiences and losses that they shared? Small wonder they felt a connection that seemed to transcend their differences.

Hesitantly they separated, touching fingertips briefly before Wolf headed for his clothes. When he brushed past Ronni on the return trip to the bathroom he noticed that she hadn't moved. "Did you come down here for a reason?"

She frowned. "I was just standing here trying to remember."

He smiled and stroked her cheek. "I must have really had an effect on you."

She smiled coyly. "I *know* I had an effect on you."

He didn't debate the issue. He headed to the bathroom and five minutes later approved his image in the hallway mirror. He was thankful that he had thought to throw the belted khakis and white polo shirt into the bottom of his backpack. He hardly needed such attire on the trail but one just never knew what unexpected circumstances might crop up during several weeks of hiking through unknown terrain. This definitely fell into the realm of the unexpected.

He walked into the kitchen where Ronni was drinking the water she had been cheated out of earlier.

She surveyed him. "You look very handsome. But those pants look a little loose. Have you lost weight?'

"Some. I bought these several years ago and I've dropped about twenty pounds since. I just haven't gotten around to do the shopping I need to."

"Was the weight loss related to your injury?'

He nodded, but didn't get a chance to respond because the doorbell chimed cheerfully.

"Heidi," said Ronni. "I should probably wake Leah." She hesitated before heading to the door. "Or maybe you should go. You have to see her before she wakes up. She's curled up like a cat. She must have fallen asleep the minute she hit the mattress."

"I'll do that," smiled Wolf as Ronni headed to the front door. He took the stairs two at a time, his feet barely touching the Berber as he passed.

* * * * *

Ronni opened the door and Heidi immediately barreled through. She followed Heidi's subtle trail of Poison into the living room. "So, was Sam bitterly disappointed?"

"Yes." Heidi propped her hands on her skinny hips. "Bitterly. You owe me big time."

Ronni looked her friend up and down. She was glowing—just like she always did after a night of good sex and sinning. "You hardly look like you're suffering."

"I'm just a good actress." Her lips formed an exaggerated pout. "He's going to be there tonight. His undying devotion to you is scary. You sure you two never…?"

"Positive." Ronni grabbed her purse off the hook by the door. "Maybe he and Wolf can sit together. It would be nice if they could become friends."

"Really? What does that mean?"

"Nothing," replied Ronni, with an innocent bat of her eyelashes. "Here he comes with Leah."

Heidi wasted no time. "Hiya, kid. You ready for a complete makeover?"

"Makeover?" said Leah, rubbing sleep out of her eyes. Ronni's heart melted. What she wouldn't give to see that every morning.

"Boy, do you have a lot to learn." Heidi turned to Ronni and Wolf. She contorted her face into an exaggerated grimace. "What are you two waiting for? Get lost! Beat it! Vamoose! Me and the kid'll be fine."

"All right," sighed Ronni as she followed Wolf out the door. She wasn't worried that Heidi didn't know how to care for Leah but she wondered what kind of apparition would greet them when they returned from the club. Heidi never did anything half way.

"Should I drive?" asked Wolf when they reached the driveway.

"If you think we're taking that old heap, you're nuts."

"I meant your car."

"*Nobody* touches my car. Besides, you've got some talking to do."

Two minutes later they were whizzing down the highway. She broached the subject gently, even though the image of Wolf's ragged scars had scorched her retinas and spiked her curiosity. "Those scars look deadly, Wolf. What happened?"

"Five bullets from a machine gun. They practically cut me in half."

Ronni felt her stomach clench. "Holy shit!" she whispered.

"Yeah. Holy shit."

"Were you in some sort of—I don't know—battle?"

"Not exactly. I was being real heroic, hiding in an alley, trying not to get shot. It didn't work."

"Were you with someone?"

"Yes. A woman and her child. They didn't make it."

Ronni accepted that in silence. Obviously the pair he had just referred to so casually, were anything but casual acquaintances. She waited patiently, trusting that he would fill in the rest when he was ready.

Cars and trucks flashed by in a blur. Streetlights and billboards passed too quickly for the eye to focus on. The sun sank toward the horizon, casting the sky in varied shades of peach and gold. But Ronni doubted that Wolf saw any of it. He was far away—at the end of an alley, in the middle of a war, halfway around the world.

"I was standing in front of them," he began at last. "Thinking, naively, that I could shield them if any stray bullets made it down the alley. The fighting had moved on and we were just thinking about coming out when someone apparently noticed us down there and thought we looked like easy targets. 'Fish in a barrel', I think is the term," he added bitterly. But then he knit his brows as he recalled the rest. "It was so strange. I didn't even realize I had been shot, even though the bullets had all passed through me first. They ripped through my lungs, my liver, kidneys, you name it. But not bad enough to kill me, at least not immediately. But they hit Lubica's heart, and killed her daughter. Not right away though. When I picked them up and I carried them to the jeep, they were still alive. They were still breathing." He covered his lowest rib with his hand, as if the memories themselves caused it to ache. "The doctors are still dumbfounded as to how I managed it. I can't explain it either. But I did and then I drove back to base, still not realizing that I was injured, and thinking there was a chance to save them." He continued gazing out the windshield. "I guess it was sort of a miracle. At least for me."

She wondered if it was a miracle laced with guilt. "You never felt any pain?"

"Not until much later, when I regained consciousness in the hospital. Apparently, one of the bullets had come precariously close to my spinal cord. There was a lot of swelling and they weren't sure if I'd walk again. They figure that was part of the reason I didn't feel pain. The swelling must have already started but, the thing was, I shouldn't have been able to walk either."

"That sure sounds like a miracle."

"I guess."

"And later, when you did feel it?"

"At first it was welcome, because it meant I would probably walk again. But then the pain, together with the loss..." His voice slipped into oblivion. "It wasn't easy."

"I can't imagine."

"Don't even try. I'm trying to forget."

"How long were you laid up?"

"Six months. And then there was rehab. All together it was a year and a half. I'm still rebuilding muscle. That's why my clothes are loose."

Ronni concentrated on the road and considered what he had told her. Ruby's was in sight. There was no time to beat around the bush. "Did you love her?"

He took a moment before answering. "I'm not sure. We were trying to find that out. We hadn't been together long enough to know." He wrenched his gaze away from the distant horizon, which had shifted to searing shades of gold and purple. He met her eyes for the first time since beginning his narrative. "I feel I owe you this. She had lost her entire family to the war, all but her daughter, who had been kidnapped by Serbian forces. She risked her life to get her back." His jaw muscles clenched. "That's why I found it so hard to accept your decision about Leah."

"She sounds special."

"She was. She was a very driven woman. She wanted to facilitate change for her people. She was educated and committed to a cause. A noble one. She cared about something greater than herself."

The irony wasn't lost on Ronni. "Everything I'm not."

He didn't answer her and maybe she didn't expect him to. She could hardly blame him for drawing comparisons. Ghosts tended to be tough images to live up to—ethereal icons free from human weakness and frailty. Ronni didn't believe in haunted houses but she certainly believed in haunted hearts. She glanced at the somber figure beside her and took a chance. "Are you changing your mind about me?"

He studied her and there was a softness to his gaze that was new...and exciting. "I'm beginning to."

Ronni pulled into a parking spot and killed the engine. "Okay. I guess I can accept that." She flashed him a smile that spoke more than mere words. "Maybe I'm changing my mind about you too."

Chapter Twenty-Six

This time Wolf occupied a table close to the stage. He sipped his drink and waited patiently while he took in the surroundings and surveyed the crowd. The show was due to start in less than five minutes. He was quietly reliving the day with Ronni and Leah when a blond figure with a broad grin plopped himself down at the table.

"Hi."

"Sam, right?"

"Yup. I was just backstage and Ronni asked me to sit with you." Sam surveyed his companion. "Unless you'd rather be alone. I was just doing Ronni a favor."

"Suit yourself."

Sam shrugged and motioned to a waitress. "It's a good table."

"You and Ronni are pretty tight," observed Wolf.

"Don't worry, we've always been just friends. I wouldn't want to come between *cousins.*"

Wolf grinned. "So, you figured it out, eh?"

"Heidi let it slip. You two doin' the horizontal mambo yet?"

The slang caught him off guard. He laughed easily. "I thought we were living in the nineties. I haven't heard that term for years."

"I'm just an old fashioned guy," said Sam with a smirk.

"Right," grunted Wolf. Sam was about as old fashioned as a turbo jet engine. "Was your brother?"

Sam nodded knowingly. "So you're up against Jesse. Tough competing with an icon, eh?"

"Did you try?"

"Not with Ronni. But it's a tough road with my dad. Not that Jesse was perfect, but I think my dad expects me to make up for the son he lost, not to mention the wife. I'm never quite up to snuff, you know? That's part of the reason I travel so much."

Wolf nodded with sincere sympathy. No matter how old you got it was difficult to shed the need for parental approval and acceptance. For weeks after waking up from his surgery he had refused to see his parents for that very reason. He had held this strange notion that he had let them down somehow. But eventually he had come to realize that the disappointment he felt had nothing to do with them. It had come from within.

"Must be tough," he responded simply.

Sam shrugged. "I don't really blame him. He's been through a lot. I try to cut him some slack."

"Were you and Jesse close?"

"Yeah. You could say that. We were only a year apart in age, so we went through everything together. Even got arrested together."

Wolf raised his glass in a mock salute. "Now that's an accomplishment."

Sam clinked his tumbler against Wolf's. "Don't knock it 'til you've tried it." He downed the last of his beer.

"Small wonder Ronni's parents didn't approve."

Sam's tone turned chilly. "They didn't know him."

"Don't worry," said Wolf hastily. The last thing he wanted to do was alienate Ronni's friend. "I'm not condoning what they did." The lights were starting to dim. Wolf wanted to get this in before the music started. "Why does he have such a hold on her? She had a nightmare last night."

Sam considered his empty glass. "She told me once that she owes him everything. I think she meant that he gave her this." He swept an arm toward the stage. "He encouraged her to sing and hooked her up with the band. It's her whole life."

"Celica!" shouted the announcer.

The music started and Wolf considered what Sam had said. That was significant but it hardly explained the nightmare and the tears.

But then Ronni started to sing and he allowed himself to focus on the music. When he wasn't finding fault with her, he could actually enjoy her. But as the songs continued he gradually noticed something. It wasn't only her signature piece. Every once in a while, when she would close her eyes, especially during the ballads or the love songs, her face would take on this certain glow. There was little doubt as to what she saw when she closed her eyes. How could he presume to compete with that? And did he want to?

* * * * *

Heidi propped her hands on her hips. "What do you think?"

Leah scanned the image in the mirror and a smile bloomed on her lips. "I love it! Can I leave it on until my mom gets home?"

"Well, that's gonna be pretty late. You should really be sleeping by then and that would smudge it all up. We can do it again sometime." Heidi surveyed her handiwork. "But you're just as much a beauty as your mom." Heidi wondered if she looked like Jesse because, other than the hair, she really didn't see a resemblance to Ronni. It was too bad Ronni never had any photos of Jesse to put up. It would be nice to put a face to the ghost. Maybe if she asked real nice Sam would show her some. She could be very persuasive when she set her mind to it. She dragged her attention back to the picture of blossoming womanhood before her.

"Do I have to wash it off right away?" Leah pleaded with her eyes.

"Nah. You can leave it on for now. Let's go down and try those video games your mom got." Heidi led her out of the bedroom and headed down the stairs.

"How do they work?"

Heidi shook her head in amazement. "You've never even seen one?"

"No. Are they a lot of fun?"

"Most guys seem to think so. With girls it varies. I like 'em but I know your mom can't stand them."

"Do you think Wolf likes them?"

Heidi smiled as she flicked the switch on the video game unit. "You like him?"

Leah smiled, the answer written across her features. "Yes. He's very nice. Do you think he likes my mom?"

"I'd bet my last acrylic fingernail on it." The reference seemed to confuse her little neophyte, so Heidi elaborated. "Yes, I'm pretty sure he does. He just hasn't figured it out yet."

"Oh. I know what you mean. I think my mom's the same with him."

"You're a smart kid, Leah." Then she turned her attention to the screen, "Okay, you see that little guy with the hat and the mustache? That's Mario. That's you. And you gotta kill all those little chomper guys."

Heidi continued her tutorial and it was no surprise that Leah took to the logistics of it easily. She was soon jumping and shooting and bashing like a pro.

It was just shortly before nine-thirty when the doorbell rang.

Heidi unfolded her legs and stretched. She got to her feet and called over her shoulder. "You keep practicing, kid. I'll see who that is."

Heidi opened the door to face an odd pair in ill-fitting suits. She leaned against the doorjamb and said with a bored lilt to her voice, "Kinda late to be handing out the Watchtower, wouldn't you say, boys?"

His expression stony, the man with the beard flashed his identification. "Sergeant Pierce, ma'am. And this is Sergeant Witmer. Are you Veronica Lichty?"

She chuckled. "Hell, no! Why would the cops want to talk to her?"

"It's a private matter. Do you know where we might find her?"

"Yeah. She's down at Ruby's."

"Is she by any chance on a date with Sam Ward?"

Heidi's eyes popped open and then a laugh bubbled up from her chest. "Boy, are you guys in the wrong zone. He's there but they're not on any date. At least they better not be since he was bunking with me last night."

Witmer piped up. "It'll be hell to find her there. That place is a zoo. Maybe we should wait until they get back."

Heidi shook her head. "Don't you guys ever read a newspaper? There was a big article on Ronni a couple months back. You won't have any trouble finding her. Just look for the hot number belting out tunes from center stage. You find her, you'll find Sam."

"Oh, I see. Well, thank you very much." They turned to go.

"Hey, is Sam in some kind of trouble?" Heidi was suddenly having second thoughts about being so cooperative. Her big mouth was going to get her into big trouble one of these days but clamming up was about as achievable for her as scaling Mount Everest.

"We just need to ask him some questions."

Leah's voice reached them from down the hall. "Hey, Heidi! I did it! I killed that monster thing at the end!"

Heidi called back. "Good going! I'll be right in."

Pierce tried to peer around Heidi's wispy frame. "Who's that?"

This time Heidi took her time but saw no reason to not answer the question. "That's Ronni's kid. She's here for a little visit."

Pierce stared at her.

"What?" His gaze was making her strangely uncomfortable.

"When did she get here?"

"A couple of days ago." Now Heidi questioned her decision. Pierce's interest in Leah bordered on worrisome. But Ronni hadn't given her any impression that there was anything illicit going on.

"What's her name?"

"Leah."

The two officers glanced at each other before barreling past Heidi toward the living room.

"Hey!" she screamed. "What the hell are you doing? You can't just come in here!"

But they ignored her and then Heidi knew. It had finally happened. Her big mouth had really fucked her up this time. Ronni was going to kill her.

* * * * *

Time had flown and, forty-five minutes later, Jason announced the last song of the set. But then Ronni made some sort of covert signal to him and Wolf watched with interest as they conferred briefly and then spoke with the drummer and base player.

He stood in awe of anyone who could put themselves on public display like this. He could stare down irate colonels, and brave enemy crossfire but facing a critical audience, and doing so willingly, struck him as sheer insanity.

At last the beat picked up and Ronni began to sing. As he watched, it soon became apparent that she was singing *to* someone.

As she continued, belting out the words to the familiar Bonnie Raitt tune, it struck Wolf with terrifying certainty that she was singing, very specifically, to *him*.

"Let's give 'em something to talk about."

Then, to his horror she descended from the stage, microphone still in hand. By the time the chorus repeated she had reached him. He glanced imploringly at Sam to enlist his aid but his new acquaintance only grinned. Wolf was on his own.

She grabbed Wolf's hand and pulled him to a standing position. He couldn't believe this was happening.

"Let's give 'em something to talk about." She slid her hand up his arm, her voice rough, her expression sultry and suggestive.

She grabbed his shirt and pulled him further out onto the floor. He felt his face heat with embarrassment but refusing her would have only added to his disgrace.

She continued, belting out words of furtive lust and forbidden desire and then, to the crowd's delight, she nudged his hips with hers. There were hoots and catcalls and she was grinning like a Cheshire cat the entire time.

Then came the final humiliation. He realized he was enjoying it. *What the hell*? he thought as he wrapped an arm around her waist and pulled her tight. He forgot about the crowd and their penetrating eyes. He focused on Ronni and the music—on the beat and the heat. They did a little bump and grind together as the song concluded and Wolf couldn't suppress the smile that determinedly curled his mouth.

She laughed as the rowdy applause washed over them. She finally took a bow, insisted he do the same and then put off the crowd, promising them more surprises after the break.

When everything had settled down he pulled her over to the table. Sam was still grinning. "Is that how you dance with all your cousins?"

"Don't lay that crap on me, Sam. I know Heidi told you."

A waitress set down a tall glass of ginger ale. Sweat already trickled down its sides. She took a sip and turned to Wolf. "You were pretty hot up there. I might have to include you in all the shows. Think how great your name would look on a marquee."

He tried to be stern. "You should have warned me."

"And give you a chance to hide in the men's room? No way."

"Are you calling me a chicken?"

"Hostile bullets are one thing, a rowdy crowd is quite another."

"Hostile bullets?" That perked up Sam's ears.

"Long story, Sam. I'll tell you later." She took a long pull on her straw. "By the way, thanks for coming again. You know I love having you here."

"Stop the mushy stuff." Sam nudged Ronni in the ribs. "Are you two gonna dance for real? That little number was just enough to get me all hot."

"All right. Who am I to deny the request of a fan?" She grabbed Wolf's hand with both of hers, pulling until he relented and followed her out onto the floor.

"You're in an awfully playful mood," said Wolf as they began to sway.

"Singing always gives me a boost." She traced a finger around the curl of his ear and he thrilled to the little shivers that pranced down his arm.

"Is there anything else that gives you a boost?" he said as he nuzzled her neck. He was feeling rather playful himself. And he couldn't deny that he had found that little show to be intensely stimulating.

Ronni tilted her head against him. "Mmmaybe."

The rest of the room gradually fell away. All he was aware of was her, and how good every inch of her felt. Her arms were around his neck again and the nuzzling turned to nibbling. She uttered a soft moan that only he could hear and he could feel the pulse in her throat throb insistently against his lips.

She tilted her hips and nudged against him. He had completely tuned out the crowd around him when their mouths melded together again. This time her tongue was just as aggressive as his. She probed him, withdrew and probed him again. He moaned as the fire spread down from his mouth, flames licking him wherever they touched. He suddenly found it necessary to remind himself that they were in a room full of hundreds of people. He withdrew his lips and murmured against her cheek. He meant to say, *Shall we continue this later?* But instead he heard himself say, "Shall we continue this outside?" Was he insane? She would think he wanted to fuck her like a whore in an alley.

But she was smiling when he watched her lips for the words, "In a rush?"

He ran his hands up her back and laced his fingers through her hair, massaging her scalp. "Mm-hmm. This is killing me."

She stopped moving, abruptly, as if someone had flicked a switch. When he met her gaze he was shocked to see that the previous passion had been replaced by stark horror.

She whispered, "My God, what am I doing?" She wrenched herself away and stepped back. "I-I'm sorry. I just can't."

She whirled around and before he could assimilate what was happening, she was running toward the doors.

Paralyzed by confusion, Wolf watched her go. A moment later Sam joined him.

"What happened? You two looked like you were gonna do it right there on the floor and then she's running like she's got a hell hound on her tail. What did you say?"

Wolf shook his head in bewilderment. "Nothing. I just don't get it." Then his gaze rotated slowly to Sam as resentment and anger congealed in a dense ball in his gut. "Yes I do. It's that damn brother of yours. She suddenly remembered that she's not supposed to enjoy herself with anyone else. She didn't have a demon on her tail. It was a goddamn ghost!"

"What? You're crazy."

"Am I? What really happened between them? What did he do to her?"

Sam's eyes flared. "Hey! He cared about her. He didn't do anything to hurt her. You're out o' line."

"Well there's something else going on with her. It's more than your run o' the mill lost love syndrome. And I'm gonna find out what if it kills me." He headed for the door and was astonished to find Sam on his heels.

"Not without me, you're not."

Wolf didn't argue. He was too consumed by the task at hand.

* * * * *

Ronni ran until she rounded the corner of the building and slipped into the shadows. There she found the solitude that she craved and breathed deeply of the cool night air. The stars were out in full force, twinkling down at her, mocking her, just like they had that night in the clearing by the stream.

"Dammit!" She covered her face and sank to the ground.

Everything reminded her of him. How could she move on when she couldn't go a day without his face haunting her dreams or her thoughts? For a fleeting moment she focused her anger on Jesse. Then she turned it back on herself. It wasn't his fault. It was her own intense guilt and regrets that were holding her captive. Jesse would have wanted her to move on. She was sure of that. But there were too many strings attached to her past—strings that bound her and dragged her down as surely as lead weights tied to her ankles.

Wolf was wonderful. She saw potential there for a lot more. He cared about her and he cared about Leah. He emanated a quiet strength that she felt drawn to and fortified by. He shared the grief of a tragic loss with her. They shared a unique pain and both bore scars of past battles.

The hard lines of his body against hers were provocative and enticing. She recalled his smile and ached to feel that center-of-the-earth chuckle reverberating through him against her own chest. Out on the dance floor, she had wanted him like she hadn't wanted anyone since Jesse. Then when he had touched her hair that way, and said what he had said, the memories had come flooding back and she knew she couldn't betray Jesse like that. Not again.

She was startled by a presence very nearby. "Ronni?"

Her eyes flew open. "Mr. Endecott?" She stood and wiped at her eyes, sure that her mascara had smeared and run leaving her with raccoon eyes and black tear tracks.

"Are you okay? I saw you run out. Did that man do something to upset you?"

She shook her head, struggling to regain her composure and fighting the urge to run screaming from yet another intrusion on her grief. "No. Really. He was a perfect gentleman. It's sort of personal. Nothing for you to be concerned about." She pulled on her skirt, suddenly feeling exposed and vulnerable. "I'm glad you came to the show. Were you enjoying it?"

"Yes." He hesitated and it shocked Ronni to realize that Mr. Endecott was somewhat unsteady on his feet. He put out a hand to steady himself against the wall. "But I have to admit I was a little disturbed by your behavior with that man on the dance floor."

She smiled, suddenly uncomfortable and confused. "It was all part of the show, Mr. Endecott. I would never behave like that at the office."

He took a step closer. "Wouldn't you? Not even alone in my office, Ronni?"

With that her discomfort veered into outright panic. She took a step back in an attempt to keep a manageable distance between them. "Sir?"

"Please don't call me that. My name is Karl. You can say it." His words slurred and his eyes were dull. "Say it for me, Ronni."

Ronni darted a glance over his shoulder toward the parking lot, but saw no one. Her search for solitude had been a little too successful. She considered making a dash for it but then his hand clamped around her upper arm. "Don't run off. Don't you know how much I care about you, Ronni? I knew you were special from the first moment I laid eyes on you."

She writhed against his grip but he held firm. "Mr. Endecott, please. You're not yourself."

"Damn right. It's about time I woke up. Well, there's nothing to hold me back now. The wife left me yesterday. Found another man! Isn't that a kick in the head? I only kept my distance from you because of my wedding vows but they obviously mean nothing." He pulled her close. "There's nothing to stop us now, Ronni. I know you like me. You're always so pleasant and you work so hard for me." He stroked her cheek. "And you're so damn beautiful."

She could smell the liquor on his breath and see the lechery in his eyes. How could she have missed it before? She had looked up to him and respected him and all the while he was probably having fantasies about her. But surely he wasn't capable of this. Surely a man of his intelligence and stature could see that this was a mistake. "Please, Mr. Endecott. You don't want to do this. Please let me go."

His gray eyes registered anger. "You want *him*, don't you? That man from in there. Well, he can't give you a job, can he?" His grip tightened.

She could feel every bulge and lump of his body, and could almost taste the whiskey he had been drinking. Tears sprang to her eyes as she admitted to herself that even the man she had trusted and looked up to for the last nine years was capable of this betrayal. She admitted that he had always wanted something other than friendship. And she admitted that, once again, her trust had been woefully and tragically misplaced. With that realization she felt the fight drain out of her.

Endecott sneered. "If you want to keep getting that fat paycheck that I helped to arrange for you I'd say you better give something back to the company. Right here. Right now."

He forced her back up against the wall. She wanted to scream but the cry caught in her throat. All she managed was a pathetic whimper. "Please don't."

He ripped open her blouse and buttons clicked against the pavement. On a burst of resolve, she managed a little more volume. "You can't do this. This is wrong."

"No, Ronni," he hissed. "This is my due."

"No, asshole. *This* is."

Ronni watched in wonder as Endecott spun around. Wolf's hand had wrapped around his arm and wrenched him away like he was made of putty.

His eyes blazing like the God of War, Wolf held his target steady. His fist flew out like a piston and landed a blow squarely in the center of Endecott's bewildered face. Endecott's head snapped back and his body followed. He staggered back, lost his balance and fell.

Ronni gaped at her boss who lay sprawled on the ground, clutching at a bloody nose and moaning incoherent curses.

Wolf strode over and straddled him. His hand snaked out and grabbed Endecott's shirt. He lifted him clean off the pavement and snarled, "You son of a bitch. You picked the wrong woman to mess with. I've seen too much of this shit and I'm sick of it." His fist plowed into Endecott's jaw, sending him sprawling and scrambling for safety. But he didn't get far. Wolf stopped him with a foot on his back and ground in his heel until Endecott yelped in fear and pain.

Then Ronni became aware of an arm around her shoulders. "You okay?" asked Sam. "Did he hurt you?"

She nodded weakly and found refuge in Sam's familiar embrace.

"Hey, Wolf," called Sam. "Isn't this supposed to be your department? I could take over there for a bit."

"Deal," said Wolf as he bent down and grabbed Endecott by the shirt once again. He dragged him to his feet and had just rammed him up against the wall when they were all surprised to see a pair of uniformed police officers come around the corner.

They quickly took in the scene. "Back off," they called to Wolf.

Wolf dropped Endecott like he had suddenly developed the plague. He held his hands up as if in surrender. "Gladly. I was just holding him until you guys got here. Mind you, we hadn't called yet. That's what I call service."

Bleary-eyed and bleeding, Endecott slid slowly to the ground.

"What happened here?" asked the second officer as they approached the dismal scene.

In two strides Wolf reached Ronni. Sam surrendered her and she fell readily into Wolf's arms. She snuggled against him as if he could shut out the whole world but a moment later she felt him tugging at her blouse and remembered the sorry condition of her costume. She took a moment to tie the tails of silk together and felt some relief at that tiny morsel of control over her situation.

Sam began recounting the events for the officers but he had barely begun when another man in a beard and a cheap suit joined the little crowd. "What's going on here?" he demanded.

One of the officers replied. "We seem to have interrupted a sexual assault in progress, Sergeant Pierce."

He surveyed the group. "Well, isn't that lucky."

"Just hang on there a minute," challenged Sam. "Your guys came in after the fact. We had already pulled him off her."

Pierce turned to him. "And you are?"

"Sam Ward. I'm a good friend of Ronni's over there."

Pierce raised his eyebrows. "*You're* Sam Ward?"

"Yeah." He frowned, "Why?"

But Pierce didn't answer; instead he turned to Ronni. "And I take it you're Veronica Lichty?"

She turned her face away from the sanctuary of Wolf's chest. "Yes. Why?"

Then Pierce got a good look at Wolf. "Holy shit!"

Wolf laughed. "What's with you?" But he stopped laughing when he was faced with the nine-millimeter handgun that Pierce had pulled out from beneath his jacket. "What's going on?"

"Witmer!" yelled Pierce.

Another tall figure rounded the corner. "What's up?" Then he caught sight of Wolf. "Holy shit!"

"What the hell?" bellowed Wolf.

Ronni clung to him, her fingers clutching at the soft cotton of his shirt.

Witmer approached him, and said very deliberately, "Step away from the woman."

Wolf gritted his teeth. "I'm not going anywhere until you tell me what the *hell* is going on."

Pierce called to the uniformed officers. "Get that Ward character in the car. We've got to question him, too. This is a very cozy little gang we've stumbled upon."

Sam put up a token struggle but one of the officers was soon herding him around the corner of the building.

Ronni watched it all through a surreal haze. She suddenly realized she was shivering. Apparently Wolf noticed too because his arms tightened around her.

Witmer was just inches away. Wolf growled at him. "Look, I don't care if you're the goddamn cavalry. I'm not moving until you fill me in."

But Pierce was the one who spoke. "You're being detained under suspicion of kidnapping,"

Wolf's grip relaxed subtly. "Oh, shit."

But Pierce wasn't finished. "And the murder of Glenn Lichty."

"What?" The next moment Pierce snapped a set of handcuffs around his wrists.

"You can't be serious!" screeched Ronni. "He didn't even know my father." Ronni didn't have a chance to press them further because she was soon being herded toward the squad cars as well.

"We need to ask you some questions too, ma'am."

"But…this is crazy." This had to be a dream. A day out of a fairy-tale had turned into a night from hell. "If you'll just talk to my mother."

"All in good time, ma'am. Watch your head." Witmer said as he guided her into the back of the squad car.

She was waiting anxiously for Wolf to slide in beside her. She desperately wanted to be close to him again. The incident with Endecott had left her feeling shaken and vulnerable. But to her utter disappointment it appeared that they had put Wolf and Sam together, leaving her to fend for herself. Tears streamed down her face as she sank into the seat.

All she wanted was to feel safe and secure, to snuggle under the covers and shut out the images that were parading through her brain. She just wanted to go home.

And tonight, for the first time in years, she didn't want to be there alone.

* * * * *

Wolf yanked at his handcuffs as the car pulled away. "I don't fucking believe this!"

"What the hell are they talking about?" said Sam through gritting teeth. "Murder? And who got kidnapped?"

Wolf took a deep but negligibly calming breath. "Leah. She ran away from home but they obviously think I took her."

Sam screwed up his face in confusion. "Ran away? From who? I thought she was yours. And if that's the case, why bring her to see Ronni?"

"Ronni will kill me for this but I think you have to know. Leah is her and Jesse's child. Ronni gave her to her parents at birth."

Sam looked at him, and blinked as the information seeped into his befuddled brain. "Her and Jesse's child?"

"Yes."

Wolf was stunned when Sam began to laugh. "But that's impossible."

"Come on, Sam," said Wolf, not surprised by Sam's reaction. Of course he would have trouble accepting it. "You know how the birds and the bees work. It's obviously very possible."

The smile fell from Sam's face and his mouth settled into a grim line. "I know very well how the birds and the bees work and that's how I know it's *not* possible. Somebody's lying here because there's no way Leah is Jesse's kid."

"What? How can you say that?"

"Because he and Ronni never made love."

Now it was Wolf's turn to blink stupidly. "How can you be sure of that?"

"Jesse and I were close, remember? He told me things. He wasn't one to brag about conquests but his frustrations with Ronni were something he did share with me. He didn't blame her for putting him off—he tried real hard to understand where she was coming from—but it was making him crazy because he wanted her so bad."

"But…that last night."

Sam shook his head. "No. If they had done it he would have told me. We talked numerous times over the winter and all he could talk about was how much he was looking forward to the summer because Ronni had hinted that she might be willing by then."

Wolf was silent. Now that he thought about it, Ronni had never actually said that she and Jesse had consummated their relationship. She had said something to the effect that they had seen each other that night, had an intimate evening by a stream and three months later she found out she was pregnant. Wolf had made the obvious assumption. Apparently, he was meant to.

"But Leah is definitely hers?" asked Sam with rank disbelief.

"She claims to have given birth to her."

"How old is she?"

"She told me she just turned eleven a few weeks ago."

Sam did some mental calculations and some finger counting before turning back to Wolf. "Well then, somebody else screwed her and she hid it from Jesse, because that would put conception right around the time Jesse left." He clenched his fists. "She's been lying to me for years."

Wolf looked out the window. *Not exactly,* he mused to himself. She hadn't exactly lied, but had allowed everyone to come to the same logical conclusion. It was a lie of omission.

"You're not the only one, Sam." But then he turned to face him. "But if Jesse isn't the father, then the question is…who?"

Chapter Twenty-Seven

The old Mustang convertible crept down the Perth County Town Line.

"Hey, Rick! Damn. What's wrong with you? Put the pedal to the metal my friend! We'll miss all the action at Ian's place if you keep driving like an old woman."

"Gimme a break, Mike. This is my dad's car. It's like his *baby*. If anything happens to it he'll cream me good."

"Wuss," muttered Mike, taking a swig from the two-liter bottle of lime soda clutched between his knees.

"And don't spill that stuff. If the upholstery is sticky he'll have a hissy fit too."

"Jesus, Ricky. I'm never driving with you again." Mike took another swig, and then sputtered, "Hey! Watch out!"

Rick had seen it at exactly the same moment. He slammed on the brakes and inevitably the Mountain Dew splashed all over the console.

"Man! You gotta clean that up!"

"It's not my fault. You should be watching closer. Besides, what the hell is he doing?"

They both gazed out the windshield at the tail-lights that were weaving in an erratic pattern across the road. Rick pulled away again, following at a safe distance.

"He's drunk as a skunk."

"Nah! You think?" muttered Mike.

"Stop being a jerk. We gotta get past him or we'll never get there."

"Follow him close and when he's over to the side, just blast past him. He's not going fast enough to veer over and hit you."

"You hope."

"Well, it's up to you. It's your dad's car. But I know for a fact that Katie Slater is going to be there tonight and she's got it bad for you. But she's got a curfew. If we don't get there soon we'll miss her."

Rick hesitated—for about five seconds. "All right." They trailed the car for about a kilometer, until they were pretty sure he was holding a straight path on the right side of the road. Then Rick floored it and blew past him on the left.

The two boys laughed as they left the big black car eating their dust. "See? Nothing to it."

Rick checked the rear view mirror. "Yeah, but he's gonna kill somebody. Maybe we should call the cops when we get there. I got his license."

"You do whatever you want. I'm gonna be too busy sidling up to Wanda Riker. I bet her bra cups could hold the entire contents of this bottle." He grinned and held up his Mountain Dew.

Rick silently agreed as he pulled up to the stop sign, a T-intersection overlooking a steep embankment. He was dutifully checking to the right and left, and never saw the big black beast bearing down on them from behind.

* * * * *

"No, I don't have an alibi for that day," muttered Wolf impatiently. "I was on the trail alone. I'd love to give you the address of the chipmunks and squirrels that saw me out there but those little fellows can be so reticent. Even if you found them I doubt they'd cooperate."

"There's no need for sarcasm, Captain. I'm just trying to do my job." Pierce had quickly confirmed Wolf's identity, and was distinctly uncomfortable with the line of questions that he was obliged to follow. Considering what the girl had already told them, together with the Captain's story and his service record, Pierce was becoming increasingly certain that this was a wild goose chase. In fact the conversation with the military records personnel still resounded in his head.

"Who?" squeaked a reedy voice on the other end of the phone. The second the man had picked up, Pierce had envisioned Corporal Radar O'Reilly from *MASH*, complete with glasses and chewing gum.

"Captain Wolf Mercredi."

In the background he heard the tap of computer keys.

"Who'd you say you were?" asked the young man between snaps of his gum.

Pierce had reiterated his identity and the reason for the request.

"Oh. Well, technically you have to make a written request. We don't give out that kind of information over the phone. But…"

"But what?"

"Off the record… Let me save you some trouble, Mac."

"The name's Pierce."

"Whatever. What you got him on again?"

"Suspicion of murder and kidnapping. Trust me, he's a mean-looking son of a bitch." Wolf had already fixed Pierce with one of his steely stares and it had given Pierce a severe case of the heebie-jeebies.

"Yeah, I got his picture here and I think I know what you mean. But trust me, you had damn well better be sure you got the right guy."

"Why?"

The corporal had then given a brief account of Wolf's accomplishments and his injury, complete with commendation. "From what I've heard," he continued, "you piss this guy off without a damn good reason and you'll be pissing at the North Pole after a request has been made for your convenient relocation. Or maybe they'll ship you off to the Cap's old stomping grounds—Bosnia itself. Judging from his record, the big guys think he shits gold. They tried everything in the book to keep him from retiring. So you had better have an ironclad case before you so much as finger-print him, especially with those kinds of charges in mind."

Pierce's gut had twisted in on itself as he silently digested that.

In the brief silence that followed, the other end sniffed up a wad of phlegm before concluding his soliloquy. "So, like I said, you have to make a written request. *I can't tell you anything over the phone*. Got it?"

"Yeah, I got it."

So now, after confirming that the little girl thought the sun rose and set on Captain Wolf Mercredi, Pierce was just itching to get this unlikely and career-breaking suspect out of his hair. An alibi would have been a nice neat reason to let him go but, no matter how many times he asked the question, the answer that he hoped for continued to elude him. Besides that, he didn't particularly enjoy pissing off Armed Forces veterans who had been decorated by NATO after suffering critical injuries in the line of duty. Captain Mercredi had obviously seen enough anguish. Pierce had no desire to inflict more. He also had no desire to indirectly inflict anguish on himself, courtesy of Captain Mercredi's ball-busting NATO buddies.

But he had little choice. Protocols had to be followed.

Pierce's pen tapped a rapid tattoo on his notepad. "Are you sure you don't want a lawyer present?"

"No. I've told you this before," said Wolf heavily. He plodded through the words like he was slogging through thigh-deep mud. "I have nothing to hide and the last thing I want in here is another cheap suit."

Pierce ignored the gibe. He could hardly afford Armani on his salary, and refused to apologize for it.

He heard the grating of dental enamel emanate from Wolf's general direction. "Look, is there anything else? Or am I going to be spending the night behind bars?"

"I doubt that will be necessary, sir." Pierce cringed at his instinctive use of the respectful address. He rarely had reason to have anything but contempt for the people who usually sat in that chair. But tonight, he had the distinct feeling that he was outranked, and likely outclassed, by the man who sat across from him. It was somewhat unnerving, to say the least. The captain had stripped him of his security blanket—the protective insulation of self-righteousness and smug superiority that he usually wore when dealing with suspects. He felt naked and vulnerable without it.

He flipped a page in his notes.

"How's the girl?" asked Wolf quietly.

"Hmm?" Pierce looked up from the papers before him. The shift in Wolf's tone confused him.

"Leah. You said you had taken her into custody at Ronni's house. Is she okay? She's probably frightened. This is all very strange to her."

Pierce licked dry lips. Suddenly he felt like the one under the microscope—like the one with something to hide. "She was a little upset by it all." *Terror stricken,* actually. Instead of being relieved by the appearance of the authorities she had exhibited undisguised panic, and had pleaded to be allowed to stay with Heidi, who had barely restrained herself from throwing household appliances at them when their intentions became clear. Her language had left little to the imagination. But he certainly didn't want to share all that with his *suspect*. "But we managed to settle her down. Her mother…er…I guess it's her grandmother, is on her way. She just had to find a ride."

Wolf nodded with solemn understanding, and then raised his gaze to meet Pierce's. "You've talked to her grandmother and seen the family. Do you have any idea why she's so afraid to go back there?"

"I'm afraid not." Pierce shared Wolf's concern and bafflement in this area of the case. "She was very cryptic when it came to questions about that. However, when it came to questions about you and Ms. Lichty she was very clear…and very complimentary. She's been begging to see you."

His suspect fixed him with another unsettling stare. "Does that sound like a likely kidnapping scenario to you?"

"To be honest, it's not uncommon for victims to establish an irrational affection for their captors."

"Great," growled the captain.

"However, on the other hand," and with that he snapped his notebook shut, "the fact that your and Leah's stories jive to the letter, and the fact that you have no apparent motive, and you brought the girl to her mother, and the fact that the grandmother insists that no charges be laid against her, have led me to believe that you have absolutely no business being here."

A surprised smile flitted across the captain's face. "Well, that's a relief."

But Pierce still felt the weight of the situation. "I wish I could share your sentiment, Captain. That still leaves us with an unsolved murder."

"You don't seriously suspect Sam Ward."

"Do you know him well?"

"Actually, no. But he just doesn't strike me as being capable of that. And believe me, Sergeant, I've looked into the eyes of plenty of killers."

Pierce believed him. His pen tapped a new and uneven rhythm on the notepad. "I can appreciate that but I'm afraid I can't make my judgments based solely on gut instinct. Mr. Ward had motive and opportunity. He came back to town mere hours before the murder, and didn't arrive at his father's until that evening. And he has made no secret of his feelings for the victim."

Wolf shook his head. "I understand your position but I just won't believe it."

"That's certainly your prerogative."

Wolf assessed Pierce with a gaze that could cut through steel. "I trust that you won't be making hasty judgments based on convenience, Sergeant. I would hate to see an innocent man arrested for the sake of pushing through a dead-end investigation."

Pierce tugged at his tie. It had gradually been tightening throughout the interview and, at the moment, it felt like a tourniquet around his trachea. "Don't worry, Captain, I don't make a habit of such things. Now, if you'd like to get out of here?" He stood and motioned to the door. *Please…get out of here.*

* * * * *

The hard oak of the chair beneath Ronni's butt had become uncomfortable. She shifted in her seat but the relief was nominal and the movement caused the chair to grate across the worn tile floor. The sound echoed down the long bare hallway and her anxiety edged up another notch.

She tugged at the T-shirt that one of the officers had kindly found for her, then she clasped her hands on her lap again. What was taking them so long? She gazed at the door that she had seen close behind her mother and brother. Leah was in there too. What the hell were they talking about in there? And where were Sam and Wolf? *Wolf.*

She had been aching for him ever since they had put her in the back of the squad car. Despite the T-shirt she still felt exposed and vulnerable. She wanted his arms around her again, wanted him to take care of her again, like he had in the alley beside Ruby's. She had been taking care of herself long enough.

Finally, the door squeaked open and she saw her mother and brother exit the small room and step into the hall. Her mother grasped Leah's hand firmly in her own. At the sight of her family, Ronni felt the familiar stirrings of anger and disappointment. And guilt. Perhaps it was guilt that she felt clawing at her heart. Guilt or rage, it made little difference. Her reaction merely confirmed something she already knew. Those people had stopped being her family a very long time ago.

While she watched them, they had yet to see her. The trio had turned toward the *Exit* sign at the other end of the hall. She stood and was about to move toward them when a moment later she heard a feverish rendition of Wolf's name.

A strange and new sense of warmth and pride washed over her as she watched Wolf scoop Leah up in his arms. He had stepped out into the hall and been forced to move quickly, or endure a full body collision with the tiny projectile.

Sergeant Pierce looked on and shook his head in wonder.

Ronni saw her mother put a hand on Stephen's arm. She clutched at the black fabric of his jacket, apparently trying to draw strength from her son. God forbid Verna Lichty not have someone to look after *her.*

Poor Verna, she thought wryly. Wolf himself was an imposing sight all on his own. But the vision of him with Leah plastered to his chest must have set her heart aflutter.

She still hadn't moved, choosing to watch the events unfold without interference. As yet, no one had noticed her.

Stephen led his mother down the hall toward the unlikely pair. "We would appreciate if you would return Leah to her rightful guardian," he said. His voice was deliberately calm and even but, despite the years of separation, Ronni could detect the anxiety.

Part of Ronni sympathized with him. He was young, and out of his element. He was struggling to maintain his composure and be the pillar of strength that his mother obviously needed. Glenn's death had left several voids that needed filling.

Wolf, who had been stroking Leah's back and speaking in soft, comforting tones, merely opened his arms wide to reveal the extent of Leah's *attachment* to him. "Just give her a few minutes. I guess she's gotten used to running to me over the last few days." He hugged her tightly again and his eyes closed. He had obviously been worried about her and was relieved at her safe return. That knowledge endeared him to Ronni more than anything else that had transpired in the last twenty-four hours.

Verna Lichty spoke for the first time, her soft voice barely discernible above the echoes of footfalls and distant conversations. "You've obviously been very good to her, sir. We appreciate that."

Stephen's incredulous eyes riveted on his mother. "Mom! He's had her for days, knowing full well we didn't know where she was. I'd hardly call that being *good.*"

"I take responsibility for that." Ronni moved forward, stepping up behind her mother and brother. As she walked she had tried, unsuccessfully, to catch Wolf's eye. In fact, he seemed quite determined to *not* look at her. However, she didn't have time to question it because Pierce, obviously sensing an imminent, and possibly volcanic confrontation, decided to run interference.

"You all obviously need to sort some things out," he said to the group in general. "May I suggest you take it outside or, perhaps, to the coffee shop across the street? This hallway is rather crowded." He tossed an apprehensive gaze in Wolf's direction. "We'll be in touch as the investigation progresses. Obviously Leah's disappearance and Mr. Lichty's death were unrelated incidents."

Ronni continued watching Wolf. She saw his eyes rivet on Pierce as he said that but then she was jostled into movement as Stephen brushed past her. Wolf followed, still sporting his latest fashion accessory draped around his neck.

Ronni stopped him just before they exited the big glass doors at the front of the building. "What about Sam?"

"I think they're keeping him here for a while yet. I'm afraid he's a suspect in your father's murder."

"What?! That's ridiculous. Sam couldn't hurt a fly!"

"I tend to agree but I'm afraid our opinion doesn't count for much." He stroked Leah's back and drilled into Ronni with his eyes. "However, when he does get out I believe he will be wanting to talk to you. You two have some things to discuss."

She frowned. "What? What things?"

"Not now." He motioned with his head toward the door. "I think you have some things to discuss with your mother first." Then he abruptly turned away and strode out the large glass doors.

Ronni was paralyzed. His manner and tone left a heavy, ominous feeling in the pit of her stomach. She couldn't imagine why but she was sure he was angry about something. And at that moment she couldn't bear the thought of his wrath being focused on her. She needed his reassurance and support, not more accusation and judgment. She still felt shaken from her encounter with Endecott. She was also horrified at the prospect that someone had deliberately murdered her father, and even more stricken at the thought of Sam being subjected to accusations related to such heinous events. Sam was the closest thing to family that she had had for years and the thought of him behind bars chewed at her stomach like a hungry rat. And what else had Wolf said? That Sam would be wanting to talk to her?

Her confusion and anxiety continued to grow and that was the last thing she needed as she headed out to confront the family that had betrayed and abandoned her.

Ronni took a deep breath and tugged at her T-shirt and skirt, as if that could straighten out the rest of her as well. She may feel completely disheveled on the inside but there was no need to broadcast it to the world in general. This was going to be her first encounter with her mother in more than eleven years. She wanted to present herself as the mature, in-control adult that she usually presented to the rest of the world. The fact that most of the time she still felt like a frightened, confused teenager was not something she wanted to reveal to the family she had fought so hard to *not need* over the past eleven years. They had obviously *not needed* her either. She did not intend to be the one to toss the white towel into the ring.

She had just screwed up her courage when Wolf, finally relieved of his sidekick, peeked back in through the doors. "You coming?" he thundered. "I don't intend to face your family for you. I've gotten sucked into this thing far enough as it is." He glared at her, waiting for her to proceed.

She screwed up her courage and stepped forward. She exited into the cool night air beside him, now intentionally avoiding his penetrating gaze. She would deal with him later.

Wordlessly she descended the steps to the sidewalk. Leah now stood beside her grandmother, looking lost and forlorn despite her proximity to the only mother she had ever known. When Ronni reached the little trio she extended a hand, which Leah gratefully took as she went to stand beside her.

"I'm glad to see you're getting to know each other," said Verna. Ronni could never remember seeing her mother become excited or angry. She had hardly ever seen her laugh, and never seen her cry beyond a sedately dabbing Kleenex. "Ruffled" was almost too extreme a term to apply to her mother's incredibly tolerant and even-tempered disposition. Now, like never before, it irritated the hell out of Ronni.

"Yes, it was difficult at first, but," and she glanced at Wolf, "with help, we're both adjusting." Wolf's gaze was stony.

"We should go, Mom," said Stephen tightly. "Anna will be worrying. It's awfully late."

Verna nodded and extended her hand to Leah. "Come, Leah. This has been very unsettling for you. It's time to get you home to your own bed."

Leah didn't move. Her grip on Ronni's hand tightened and she cast a pleading glance at Wolf.

Ronni ignored the previous exchange and said what was on her mind. "Why didn't you notify me that my father had been killed?"

"We didn't think you'd care," shot Stephen.

"That should have been for me to decide." Ronni ignored his hostility and kept her own voice even. "I would think I at least deserved a card in the mail or a message on my answering machine."

"Why?" continued her brother. "Look at you! You've spat in the face of your family and everything we hold dear ever since the day you started running around with Jesse Ward. I can't imagine you losing one wink of sleep over our father's death."

"Stephen!" reprimanded his mother. "Think of the child."

"At least I'm not a hypocrite." Ronni's voice slipped up a notch. "With me, what you see is what you get. I don't preach one thing and then, behind closed doors, assume the identity of the rabble I publicly denounced five minutes earlier."

"What are you accusing us of…Ronni?" Her mother had never adjusted well to the name change.

"Forget it, Mom. You've had blinders on since the day you married Dad. You still think all the kids born at Maple Grove six months after their parents' wedding day were premature."

Verna didn't answer.

"That's enough, Ronni. We have to go." Stephen's face had gone beet red.

"Hang on a minute." Ronni squared her shoulders and faced her judges. "Leah is afraid to go home."

"What? That's ridiculous."

"A child's fears are never ridiculous." She spoke with an authority she didn't feel.

"You don't intend to try and keep her with *you*, do you?" Stephen had put an arm around his mother, as if to protect her from the devil's spawn that her daughter had somehow transformed into.

Ronni would have loved to simply say, "Yes. I'm taking her home with me," and be done with it. She now had the means and the emotional strength to raise her daughter. But she knew that would be flirting with disaster. She had given up her rights years ago. She couldn't simply change her mind at this late date. So instead she said, "No, that's not what I had in mind." She took a deep breath and loaded up on oxygen for the task that she now faced. She was about to humble herself and ask for an enormous concession on her mother's part but she had to do it. For Leah.

"I promised Leah that we wouldn't send her home alone, and that we wouldn't leave her there until we were assured that she had nothing to fear, or until we have sorted out the cause of her distress. So I'm asking you to allow us to come and stay at the house for a couple of days so that we have an opportunity to talk to her and maybe go over things to get to the root of the reason for her running away." She turned her eyes to Wolf. "I don't think I'll be wanting to go back to work right away, anyway."

"We?"

Ronni knit her eyebrows as she focused on Stephen's question. She had hardly realized that she had been using that pronoun. She licked her lips. "Yes. She has become very attached to Wolf as well and he's agreed to see this through."

A telltale vein ticked on Stephen's neck, indicating his level of annoyance and impatience. "Why don't you just ask her?"

"We have." This time it was Wolf's voice. "But she seems hesitant to talk about it or maybe she doesn't really understand it herself. We were hoping that going home might help her sort through it."

Stephen looked at his mother. "Well, Mom?"

She nodded. "Yes, of course." She looked at Ronni. "It will be good to have you home again."

Ronni didn't believe that for a minute but she chose not to express it openly. "Good." She dropped her eyes a fraction. "And…thank you."

Leah relaxed visibly. "Can I ride with you and Wolf?"

Ronni was poised to answer but Wolf beat her to the punch. "Leah." He knelt down in front of her. "I'd really like it if, just this once, you ride with your uncle and your grandma. Ronni and I need to go back to the house and pick up a few things and we have something that we need to talk about." The tension returned to Leah's shoulders but

Wolf reached out and took her hand. "I promise we'll only be an hour or so behind you. Nothing will happen. Okay?"

She nodded uncertainly.

"Good." He smiled encouragingly. "I can hardly wait to see your place. I've never been on a dairy farm before."

Leah brightened. "There are some baby calves and some kittens I could show you. And fresh milk really is the best."

"You can give me the full tour tomorrow."

Verna extended her hand again and Leah took it. She followed them toward their car, glancing back only once in a silent plea for a speedy reunion. They had gone a half a block when Verna stopped and spoke briefly to Stephen before returning to where Ronni and Wolf were standing. "I didn't want to ask in front of Leah, but..." She clasped her hands in front of her. "Will you two be occupying one room at the house?"

"Yes, Mother. I'm a sinner through and through. There've been dozens since Jesse." She took a step toward her mother, regretting what she was about to say even before it spilled from her lips, but feeling powerless to stop it. "Because, you see, Mom, no one could ever live up to him. I keep looking but I'll never be able to replace him. You and Daddy stole him from me." Her voice had built with a steady crescendo. She paused and made a conscious effort to dampen her temper. "You lied to him and you betrayed me on the grandest scale. Dead, or not, I will always hold Dad responsible for his death and you share the blame right along with him. Heaven forbid you question one of your husband's decisions. I know that Eli and Herb were in full agreement with that decision. The pillars of the church. What a joke! If Jesus loves the likes of you I want nothing to do with him."

Ronni experienced a smug satisfaction in the tears that were now brimming in her mother's eyes. Verna said nothing, merely backed away a step before turning and walking briskly toward the sanctuary of her son's car.

Once she was out of sight, Wolf grabbed Ronni's hand. "Come on, little miss *what you see is what you get*. We've got business."

The spike of anger had not yet waned. "What's your problem?" Ronni demanded as she tagged along behind him.

He stopped and turned to face her. "What was with the crack about us sharing a room? Did you just say that to hurt her? Or was it wishful thinking?"

"Maybe both. But I was under the distinct impression maybe it was your wish as well. You *did* practically drag me into an alley." She squared her shoulders and stood a little straighter. "And I hope you know I have *not* been with dozens of men since Jesse."

"Is that a fact?" The sarcasm stuck to those words like bloodthirsty leeches.

"Yes, that's a fact! Will you tell me what the hell is going on? Why wouldn't you look at me in there?" She was on the verge of tears but her encounter with her mother had renewed her strength. She wasn't going to expose her weakness to anyone now…not even Wolf.

Wolf turned away from her and started walking toward Ronni's car, which had kindly been transported there. "Later, back at your house."

"No, now!"

He stopped again and faced her, boring holes through her with the haunting black eyes of a predator. "No. Later."

The matter was obviously closed and Ronni was furious with him for treating her like his inferior. As if she were one of his men whom he had complete authority over and could order around on a whim. She would let it go for now but she had no intention of taking that kind of crap lying down. She had watched her mother defer to her husband's *better judgment* for years, based solely on the fact that he had external gonads and a few obscure Bible verses on his side. "Fine, Captain Mercredi," she muttered under her breath. "It's better for the shit to hit the fan in an enclosed space, anyway. It makes a hell of a lot less mess."

Chapter Twenty-Eight

"How do you account for your whereabouts between the arrival of your flight in Toronto at twelve-thirty, and the time you arrived at your father's home at," Witmer consulted his notes, "eight o'clock in the evening?"

Sam fidgeted with a wadded-up scrap of paper. He felt like the bare walls of the interrogation room were closing in on him, suffocating him. How could he focus on these inane questions when he was faced with another heart-wrenching loss? Ronni had lied to him, had lied to Jesse. He felt almost as alone as he had that day beside the gaping maw of Jesse's grave, as he had watched the casket being lowered into the cold, unforgiving ground.

Part of him had died that day as well. His friendship with Ronni had breathed new life into him, allowed him to share his memories as well as his grief. Had he lost her as well? Or had he never had her?

"Mr. Ward?" said Witmer.

Sam sighed, resigning himself to the inevitable. "I cruised around town and ran errands. I dropped off some films for developing, since I don't have a dark room set up here. I did the mall thing, you know, bought some new jeans and shit. Stopped somewhere for supper." He tossed the balled-up paper toward a wastebasket on the other side of the room. It bounced off the rim and joined a half dozen others on the floor. "I don't know, just a bunch of stuff. I was in no rush to get home and I had just gotten back from a month in the badlands of Alberta shooting film for some damn coffee table book. I wanted a taste of civilization before I headed up to boonie land."

"Do you have receipts for any of your purchases? Or a stub from the camera shop? Anything to confirm your whereabouts."

Sam just looked at him like he had suddenly sprouted horns. "You have *got* to be kidding. When was the last time you kept a receipt for a goddamn pair of jeans?"

"Did you use a credit card or Interac? We could check on the transaction records."

"Cash. I took out a wad at the bank when I arrived." The walls moved a few inches closer. "And as for the film developing, sure I've got that. I keep that stuff for income tax but that was the first stop. It must have been close to three o'clock. That won't help me one bit, will it?"

Witmer chewed on the end of his pen. "No, I'm afraid you're right. The murder occurred between five and six p.m. That would give you lots of time to get to the Lichty place."

"And whack him. Right?" Sam stood up and paced to the far side of the room. As if it wasn't bad enough that his mother and brother had died under tragic circumstances, now it looked like his father might have to deal with a son being tried for first-degree murder. Maybe he was being fatalistic but Ronni's betrayal, coupled with the possibility of a murder conviction, made him feel like his entire life was in tatters. He leaned heavily against the wall. What was the point in even trying anymore?

Just then Pierce sauntered in and seated himself beside his burly sidekick.

"What's the deal with Mercredi?" asked Witmer.

"I let him go. He didn't have an alibi but there was no way we'd make an indictment stick."

"So I'm your last chance, is that it?" growled Sam. "Gotta have somebody to lock up, right?" His rage slipped past his defenses. "But that didn't seem to bother you guys when my mother's killer walked away scot-free. There's some menace out there driving the highways. He may have already killed again but, when it comes to drunk drivers, I guess we all take our lives in our hands on the highways. They're just a hazard that goes with the territory, right? There's way too many of them to waste valuable police man hours on apprehending the likes of them." He stalked to the table and leaned on it, his weight on his knuckles as they whitened under the strain.

"Please, Mr. Ward. You're not under arrest. We just wanted to ask you a few questions. If you want a lawyer present you're more than welcome but, at this point, it's just a routine statement."

Sam sat down heavily. "Then why doesn't it feel that way?" He focused his attention on Pierce. "How did Lichty die exactly?"

Pierce glanced at Witmer but the other man merely shrugged. He turned back to Sam. "He was hit in the head with a shovel."

Sam let out a nervous chuckle. "You're kidding. If I had gone there with the intention of killing him, don't you think I'd have chosen a weapon with a little more finesse than that?"

Witmer cocked a finger at him. "Perhaps you only went to confront him. *Perhaps* you had been drinking and decided it was time to accuse Glenn Lichty face-to-face. *Perhaps* things just got out of hand and you grabbed whatever was handy."

"*Perhaps* I was never there at all!"

"Okay, okay," said Pierce in a placating tone. "We're getting way ahead of ourselves here. Could you just give us a more accurate picture as to the reasons behind your animosity toward Mr. Lichty?"

Sam was about to elaborate when a commotion out in the hall caught their attention.

Pierce crossed to the door and peeked outside. Sam could hear the raised voices clearly.

"I told you he'd kill somebody eventually."

"Jesus, Rick, will you shut up already? My head's got elephants running around inside it. Besides, we're not exactly dead."

"Not yet, you mean. When my dad sees that car…oh God. He'll kill me slow. I just know it."

"Will you just shut up?"

"There he is!"

Pierce had been joined by Witmer and Sam, who stepped into the hall to watch the retreating backs of the two teenage boys who were accompanied by a uniformed officer.

"You two go back in and finish the statement," said Pierce. "I'd like to see what this is about."

Witmer reluctantly led Sam back into the room and sat down at the table to complete Sam's account of the events. Sam managed to keep his temper under wraps, and was as cooperative as his dignity would allow. Five minutes later Pierce returned.

"What was that about?" asked Witmer, flipping through his notes.

"Those two kids got hit from behind by this drunk driver." He glanced at Sam, whose passive expression belied the turmoil those words had evoked. "Some old geezer from the black bumper crowd up near Elmwood. He was drunk out of his gourd. Still is, actually. He's still blowing twice the legal limit. Drives a big black Lincoln. The thing's as big as a tank. Small wonder those boys are alive to tell about it. They were just lucky to go over the embankment, not hit any trees, and not roll over."

Sam traced his index finger in a spiral on the surface of the table. With a disinterested air that suggested only mild curiosity he asked, "Where exactly did this happen? I wonder if I know the intersection you're talking about."

"It's a T intersection where the Town Line meets County Road 18."

"Oh," he sat up a bit straighter. "Are we about finished here? It's getting late and I'm beat. I believe I have an anxious little lady waiting for me in a cozy bed not too far from here." He spoke with a suggestive tone and a raise of his eyebrows. He had no intention of advertising the hammer-like thud of his heart or the moisture that now lined his palms.

* * * * *

Pierce scanned the notes that Witmer had taken in his absence. Even Witmer's longhand bespoke his love of melodrama. Flourishes and curlicues littered the page like so much flotsam. Pierce flipped the folder closed. "Yeah, I guess that's it for tonight. Just don't go anywhere for now."

Sam stood and stretched his back. "Wouldn't think of it. I intend to cooperate fully with the authorities in this. No point in making it any more difficult, right?"

Pierce narrowed his eyes. He didn't like Sam's new, buddy-buddy, citizen-of-the-year attitude. The change was too abrupt. Their guest was up to something but Pierce couldn't read behind the rigid set of Sam's jaw or the blankness of his eyes.

He accompanied Sam to the door.

Sam stepped into the hall and gazed around uncertainly. "You know, something's been bugging me. That one boy, you know the teen that got hit, there was something familiar about his voice. I could swear I know his folks. It's a small world up there, you know. Maybe I should check on him, or at least say hi. Where would they have taken them and that drunk, do you suppose?"

Witmer had stepped into the hall and hadn't picked up on Pierce's guarded demeanor with regards to Sam's new attitude. "They'd probably be down at the end of the hall, giving their statements. The drunk's probably next door getting booked."

"Thanks." And Sam stepped in that direction.

Irritated, Pierce glanced at Witmer. "Why did you do that? He can't go in there. He has to wait until they're finished." He turned toward Sam again. "Ward! You can't—"

But Sam broke into a run. Before Pierce and Witmer had a chance to get their bearings he had burst into the room where the perpetrator was babbling a blue streak of remorse and denials. The officer that was with him didn't have time to react. Sam crossed the room in a heartbeat and, just as Pierce and Witmer reached the doorway, Sam grabbed the suspect by his straight black coat and rammed him roughly against the wall.

"You lousy son of a bitch! You're the one, aren't you? Same place, same scenario, only this time they didn't die. They were luckier than she was. They could identify your slimy ass." Apparently, Sam was able to identify him as well. "Herb Brubacher," he sneered. "*Man of the fucking cloth.* We should have known. You live less than a kilometer from there. How many other poor slobs have you managed to exterminate over the past fifteen years?"

Herb shook his head and sputtered, "D—Didn't know… S-s-so sorry…didn't mean it… "

Sam pulled him away from the wall and slammed him against it again. Herb's head made an audible thud as it hit the plaster. Pierce and Witmer had reached Sam and were pulling on his arms, trying to force him to release his hold on his victim. But adrenaline had given Sam the grip of a python. "Admit it, you goddamn bastard! It was you, wasn't it? Tell them!!"

Herb nodded and tears streamed down his round, ruddy cheeks. "I didn't mean it! She was already dead; what could I do?" He drew a gasping breath as Sam's hands were finally wrenched from his clothes. He sank to the floor, sobbing. "He figured it out. He caught me that day—he saw the flask—I don't know how he knew." Herb lifted bloodshot eyes to the little group standing around him with puzzled faces. "How did he know?" He shook his head in besotted bewilderment. "He suspected. He said he wondered. And then he knew. He said he'd turn me in!" His face was stricken. The little group remained silent, digesting his words, allowing him to dig himself in even deeper. "How could I face everyone? My wife, my children. They'd hate me." He covered his face with his hands and wept openly.

"So you killed him." Pierce spoke very softly, his voice coaxing, seductive.

Herb spoke through his hands between hiccups and gasps for breath. "When he died I felt so terrible. It was all my fault. The terrible things I said. How can the Lord ever forgive what I've done?"

Pierce and Witmer locked eyes for a moment and then Pierce knelt down in front of the pathetic figure in the straight black coat and the mixing-bowl haircut. Pierce decided he'd have to take a more direct approach. In Herb's current condition any confession would be flimsy, at best. If it was coaxed out of him using underhanded tactics, any first year law student could cut it to shreds. A judge would be obliged to toss it out as worthless—barely good enough to fill a manure spreader.

"Mr. Brubacher." He spoke slowly and clearly so that Herb would be absolutely clear on the question. "Did you kill Glenn Lichty?"

Herb stopped sobbing as if someone had turned off a faucet. He removed his hands from his face, revealing red swollen eyes, and allowing his toxic breath to assault Pierce's nostrils. He sniffled loudly. "What?"

"Did you kill Glenn Lichty because he discovered your drinking and somehow deduced that you were responsible for Debra Ward's death?"

Herb gazed at Pierce and the drunken stupor seemed to lift marginally, revealing a trace of sentience. "Glenn? Did I kill Glenn?"

"Did you, Mr. Brubacher?"

He hesitated, the wheels of cognizance gradually grinding into action. He licked his lips. "No." He spoke slowly and deliberately. "Of course not. How could you think such a thing?" Another pause followed as he continued to collect his thoughts. "I-I just meant that I felt guilty after I heard of his death. I hated the things we had said to each other and that those were the last words he spoke to me."

"So you believe you were the last person to see him alive? His words to you were the last words he ever spoke?"

Herb blinked once. "No, no. That's not what I meant! I just meant…" Tears sprang to his eyes again. "I didn't kill Glenn. Not him. Really. I admit I've sinned. But he was my friend. Please…please…"

His speech deteriorated again until it was indistinguishable from the sobs and moans of remorse.

Pierce swore under his breath. Of course it couldn't be *that* easy. He stood and motioned to the young uniformed officer who had been watching with rank fascination. "Take him down to a cell to dry out. We'll have to talk to him again when he's sober and he'll need a lawyer. Better call up the public defender's office to send someone down."

Witmer scratched his head as Herb was led meekly from the room, trailing noxious fumes in his wake. "Did we investigate him initially?"

"We spoke to him briefly but I don't recall if we even took it to the point of establishing his whereabouts at the time. We had no reason to suspect him. There was no motive."

"That confession will never stand up in court. A defense attorney would make mincemeat of it."

"Maybe not, but at least now we've got somebody with a damn good motive. And he came awfully close to confessing. I suspect that if the right pressure is applied he'll crack. I can't see his type sitting through a lengthy trial." Maybe the confession had eluded them but it was a hell of a lot more than they'd had ten minutes ago.

"Can I go?" Sam's voice startled them. He had backed away from the group as Herb continued ranting and babbling.

Pierce frowned. "You okay?"

Sam was pale and drawn. He nodded weakly, stuffed shaky hands into his pockets. "It's just been so long. There was no one to blame, nobody to atone for her death." He slipped a hand out of his pocket, rubbed his forehead. "Now that I know…" His gaze was vague, as if he wasn't sure where to look, who to talk to. "I'll have to tell my dad and Jess—" He stopped and seemed to become aware of the two officers again. "I mean…" He seemed lost.

Pierce's heart twisted in spite of himself. "Would you like one of the officers to drive you somewhere? Maybe to your dad's place?"

Sam shook his head. "No, not yet. But maybe…could somebody drive me to Ron—" He hesitated. "I mean, Heidi's?"

"Of course. Witmer, can you see to that while I check on our new prisoner?"

Witmer motioned toward the door and Sam preceded him out into the hall.

"Damn drunks," muttered Pierce. He had to admit he was relieved that Ward appeared to be off the hook. The poor guy had lost two close family members already and the thought of throwing him in the hole for twenty years, and adding to his father's grief had rankled Pierce's sense of justice. But Brubacher was another story. They had him on a DUI charge, he had outright confessed to hitting Debra Ward and, if they could get him on the Lichty murder as well, that would make a very tidy little package indeed.

As Pierce headed down the hall toward the detention area he silently resolved to call his mother first thing in the morning. You just never knew.

* * * * *

Ronni slammed the door behind her. "Okay, Mr. I-Call-the-Shots, we're here. Now what the hell is this all about?"

Wolf stopped in the middle of the living room. He made a concerted effort to steady his pulse and calm his breathing before facing her. He noticed in passing that the room bore a striking resemblance to a battle zone. A lamp lay on the floor, its shade in tatters. Popcorn was strewn around the room like confetti and the coffee table had been pushed to the wrong end of the room. Heidi had apparently not taken the time to tidy up after the escapade with Leah's *rescuers*.

He gathered his thoughts, and feeling like he had himself under control, he slowly turned towards her.

He pointed an accusing finger. "You're a liar!" So much for remaining calm and detached. "You've been lying to everyone for years and then you have the gall to accuse your mother and your entire church of being hypocrites. That's the pot calling the kettle black if I ever heard it."

Ronni stood before him, a look of complete exasperation on her face. She threw her arms wide and pleaded with the heavens. "Save me, Lord, from the self-righteous S.O.B.s who obviously sit on your right hand and have the insights of the prophets." Then she propped her hands on her hips and focused on Wolf. "Okay, I give up. What have I lied about?"

"Jesse is *not* Leah's father."

She looked like she had been struck. Her face blanched and she took a step back, as if she didn't trust her knees to support her. "What—who told you that?"

Her reaction confirmed it and his blood edged up another notch toward a full rolling boil. "Sam. I made the mistake of thinking he had a right to know why we were all being hauled down to the police station. When I informed him that Leah was the fruit of Jesse's and your union he laughed in my face. While he acknowledged that Jesse loved you deeply, he swears up and down that you never slept together. If that had happened Jesse would have told him."

Fists clenched, he paused. His heart was pumping so hard he could almost hear the fragile tissue tearing under the strain. "That's the real reason you didn't want to tell him, isn't it? You figured he might know the truth and he'd expose you. How many men were you sleeping with back then? You profess to have loved one so profoundly that you gave up your whole world for him but I wonder if you were really just looking for an excuse so you could leave your church and your child and be free to go whoring around the countryside."

He ceased when the sting of Ronni's palm against his cheek put a stop to his verbal catharsis. He had begun to care about Ronni and he saw this lie as a betrayal of his ill-advised trust. His reaction was probably out of proportion to the levels their intimacy had reached but he didn't stop to question the logic of it. He was reacting on a gut level. That was not something that Captain Wolf Mercredi made a habit of and it was scaring the shit out of him.

He blinked and stepped away.

Ronni put a hand to her chest, pulled at the T-shirt as if it were constricting her lungs. "How *dare* you accuse me of leaving my child on a whim. Giving her up was the most difficult thing I've ever done in my life." Her voice vibrated with rage.

"But you don't deny the lie, do you? You slept with someone else."

She stared at him, her breathing still ragged but the crimson tinge of her face gradually paling to a dusty rose. "Yes," she said finally but it was so soft that Wolf could barely hear her.

"What?"

She took a couple of steps back as if she was having trouble keeping her balance in the face of such upheaval. She came up against the couch and sat down heavily.

"Yes," she said more loudly. "God help me, but I did. It was the biggest mistake of my life and I've been paying for it every minute of every day for the past eleven years."

Her face was so stricken Wolf almost regretted his harsh words of a few minutes earlier. But with determination he kept a razor sharp edge to his tone. "Who? Who did you deign worthy of your virginity, when you wouldn't give it to this Jesse whom you supposedly loved beyond reason? And who, apparently, made the mistake of loving you?"

She buried her face in her hands. "Please don't. You have to believe that I did. I loved him more than my life. He gave me so much, he made me feel special and beautiful and like I had something wonderful to offer the world."

She dropped her hands and gazed at the popcorn-littered carpet. "The next night after he left, and after the scene with my family, I missed him so much. I ached for him. I was feeling so alone, more alone than I had ever felt in my life. I was regretting the fact that we hadn't made love. I thought that maybe I could have held onto that, cherished it as a special memory until we could be together again." She lifted her gaze to Wolf. Through shimmering tears she added, "I never regretted it more than the moment I found out he had died and I realized I'd never know what it was like to share myself with him."

Wolf was melting and he knew it but he tried to keep up the exhibition. "Then who?"

She returned her gaze to some undefined point on the far wall. "Like I said, I was feeling so alone and I was questioning my decision. I went outside at midnight, hoping that he might come back to check on me. I walked out to the road but he wasn't there. I was disappointed even though I knew I had no right to be. All I could think about was how he had kissed me, and how he had touched me and how much I would miss him." She closed her eyes and a tear squeezed out of each to trickle, unchecked, down her cheeks.

"I kept walking and went into the barn. I was just wandering aimlessly. I was upset with my family for judging me so harshly and I knew I'd have to face that all alone for the next nine months until his return. I was searching for something, I guess. Something I knew I couldn't find." As if to illustrate her point she wrapped her hand around the arm of the couch. He could see her fingernails dig into the plush fabric. "He found me there. He was someone I had trusted and cared about for years. He was older and in a position of authority and he said it would be all right."

Wolf softened his voice. "Who was it?"

"My father's partner and cousin, Eli Martin."

Wolf silently digested that. "Wasn't he the one who caught the two of you and denounced you so severely?"

She nodded.

"Wasn't he married? And your pastor?"

"Yes." She still didn't meet his gaze.

"You went to him willingly?"

"Yes—I mean, no—I mean..." She expelled a long breath, and shook her head in frustration.

Wolf frowned. "Well, which is it?"

She wrung her hands and her voice barely rose above a whisper. "Yes. Of course I did. It was my decision."

Wolf wasn't so sure. He had the distinct feeling there was more to the story. Maybe something that Ronni herself was hesitant to acknowledge. He decided to push her. She had hung onto this for eleven years. Maybe it was time to purge all the demons and see what lay beneath. "What exactly happened, Ronni? Did he approach you and say something like, *How about a roll in the hay?* And you said, *Sure?* Was it that simple?"

She stood and paced to the other side of the room. She gazed out the window at the millions of stars that twinkled happily in the frigid cold of space. "I slept with him. What difference does it make *how* it happened? We had sex. We knew each other in the biblical sense. We screwed each other in the haymow!" She whirled around and her face contorted as if in pain. "What more is there to know?"

Wolf kept his voice calm and compelling. "Just answer me. Let me form my own opinion. If you had said no, would he have walked away without a word?"

"I did say no." Her eyes instantly lost their fire. Now they were distant, haunted, as far away as the stars. Perhaps she had crossed the expanse of time and was back in that barn amidst the fragrant hay and the chirping of the crickets.

"You did? Then it was rape, Ronni. It's as simple as that."

She shook her head in frustration. "No, you don't understand. I tried to put him off at first. But it didn't take long for me to change my mind. It didn't take long for me to—"

"How did he talk you into it?" pressed Wolf. He had a feeling that, unless he insisted she tell him everything, she would gloss over it, hide little pieces of the truth. Key pieces. Pieces that she had convinced herself were unimportant but were essential to her healing.

He kept his voice soft and compelling. "What did he say, Ronni? Maybe it would help if you told me exactly what happened. Tell me everything."

* * * * *

Ronni lifted her eyes to Wolf's and for just a moment lost herself in their comforting darkness. She fell into them, tumbling back through the years—to a summer night full of stars and disappointments and pain.

The scent of hay hung thick in the air, sweet and pungent. Crickets chirped and in the distance a dog barked. But Ronni was barely aware of any of it.

Eli's hands were on her, latched around her arms, the grip affectionate but unrelenting. He'd come to check on one of the new calves, he'd said. He'd seen her outside and had followed her here. He was concerned for her, worried.

He wanted to help. The man who'd berated and condemned her wanted to help.

"You're hurting, Ronni," he whispered, his voice laced with compassion. "I care too much for you to stand by and let you go through this alone."

Ronni found herself blinking away tears at the unexpected show of empathy. "Y-you mean you understand?"

He lifted a hand to stroke a cheek. "I understand that you've lost something important to you. You're grieving and you're feeling confused and alone. Very alone." He brushed his fingers over her hair. The gesture was familiar and it should have been comforting and yet… "Aren't you?"

She nodded at the truth of it. She'd never known loneliness like this, felt such desolation.

"You've lost the trust and respect of your family. You're feeling lost and you don't know where to turn."

Oh, she knew where to turn, or at least she knew where she wanted *to turn, but the one person who could offer her comfort was probably already hundreds of miles away. And it would be months before she could lay eyes on him again. Or feel the warmth of his touch.*

Suddenly, the certainty and completeness of her isolation hit her like a fist. She turned to Eli and allowed the man she had known and trusted since birth to hold her. "I didn't want to hurt them, Eli. But Mom and Dad hurt me, too. It's all just so…"

"Confusing? Overwhelming?"

She nodded.

"Isolating?"

She buried her face in his chest and let the tears come. Desperation and uncertainty twisted around her heart. Visions of Jesse's smile mingled with images of her father's rage and her mother's disappointment. Eli was warm and familiar and, despite his earlier judgment of her, she couldn't bring herself to question his apparent change of heart. If Eli could accept her choices – could accept her *– maybe she could make it through the next nine months after all. Maybe she could cope.*

"Believe it or not, Frany, I know what that's like."

She swiped at a tear. "You do?"

"Sometimes it's hard, hard to be the one that everyone looks to for advice or comfort or guidance. For the most part I feel blessed, honored that people see me that way but sometimes the pressure is so much. Sometimes it's a little overwhelming."

Then she felt his fingers on her cheek, the warmth of his words and his touch comforting.

"Sometimes it gets lonely, too." He separated from her slightly, just enough to tip her face up to his. "I seek my comfort in the Lord but I'm older and more experienced. It's harder for you and I understand that. But you don't have to be lonely, Frany. I'm here. You've got me."

And then he was kissing her. His lips joined with hers and immediately his tongue thrust into her mouth and she was so surprised she allowed it. Didn't quite know how to stop it.

She was shocked, paralyzed, completely overwhelmed by what was happening. She made no move to push him away but when his arms locked around her waist and he drew her in so tight that she could feel his erection through his trousers, she finally came to herself.

She braced her hands against his chest and shoved. "Eli!" she breathed. "What are you doing?"

His face was flushed, his breathing labored, but when he spoke his voice was still calm and measured. Soothing. "I want to help, Frany. I want to be here for you."

She nodded, blinking and trying to get her bearings. "I…I know you do. But not like this."

He stepped closer. "Yes, like this," he said, his voice firm. "It's the only way. It's exactly what you need."

"What I need *is Jesse!" The words came out harsher than she intended and, for just a moment, she saw anger flicker in his eyes. Unnerved, she lowered her gaze.*

"You see what he's done to you? When have you ever spoken to your elders this way? Is this how you show gratitude to your parents for all they've done for you? For how much they've loved you?" He stepped closer again. "For how much I love you? You must know that I care for you so much."

He cupped her cheek, his eyes seeking an answer. "Yes," she conceded although the word came hard. "Yes, of course I know that. You've always been wonderful to me."

"You've shared secrets with me before, honey." His thumb stroked her cheek. "And it helped you get through whatever you were struggling with. Isn't that right?"

She nodded at the truth of it. Up until that spring she'd always been able to share things with Eli, trust him with anything.

"Sharing with me is like a cleansing. You need to share this with me, too." His hand brushed down her arm, sneaked around her waist. "It will purge your heart, cleanse your soul. It's all part of the road to forgiveness, Frany. It's the only way."

He drew her in tight. His words and his imposing presence were confusing her. What he said made no sense, and yet… Everything inside her, every instinct, was screaming out that this was wrong and yet she felt the undeniable pull of his conviction, the subtle command of his authority. She'd looked up to him for years, trusted him, sought his guidance. How could she question him now?

"I don't know, Eli," she argued. "It doesn't feel right."

"Of course it does." His hand cupped a breast. "It feels perfect."

"B-but isn't it a sin?"

"No. I've prayed about this and I received my answer. It will be pure and holy, a gift from the Lord, and we do not take his gifts lightly. Lay with me, Frany, and I'll show you the full depth of the Lord's love and forgiveness."

He began to lower her to the soft bed of hay. "Please, Eli," she whimpered. "Please don't."

But he didn't hear her and she didn't have the strength to fight him. She didn't know if she should.

"I love you, Frany, and the Lord loves you." His hand had slipped beneath her dress and lay against the bare flesh of her breast. "Let me show you how much."

So she closed her eyes and let him. Because she thought she should. Because she thought she didn't have a choice.

But all the while she imagined another pair of hands, another pair of lips. And in that touch she did find some comfort – a comfort that eventually left her feeling hollow and even more alone.

She hooked some hair behind her ear and sighed. "What an idiot. At the time I thought there was no way I could possibly hurt more than I did that night. I had no idea how wrong I was."

* * * * *

Wolf watched her return to the couch and sit down. She moved as if she had a thousand-pound weight on her shoulders and was afraid she'd never be able to stand up again.

He had listened to her story, watched the emotions flicker across her face, the pain and confusion as fresh and powerful as they must have been eleven years ago. Perhaps more so. Years of guilt and self-doubt could deepen regrets, heighten torment.

She continued, saying words that had already been said, voicing regrets that ran so deep they must have etched themselves into her soul. "He said I needed it for healing. He said that he had loved me for years and it would be pure and holy. He said it would help me to get over my grief at losing the trust of my family…and Jesse." She scrubbed her face with her hands, as if she could scrub away the soil of betrayal. "He said it was God's will and, like a little idiot, I believed him."

Wolf's rage had returned but now it had a different focus. "That's rape, Ronni." He kept his voice placid for her sake but inside he fought his own private war.

She turned to really look at him for the first time. "What? No, that's crazy. He didn't hold me down and force himself on me. He just twisted around a few words and took advantage of my vulnerability. That's not rape. That's—" She struggled for the words. "That's stupidity. My stupidity. I believed him because I wanted to believe him and because I had this huge void that needed filling."

Wolf crossed the room and sat beside her. He took her hands in both of his own, and drew her eyes to his. "I know this is hard for you to accept after carrying around the responsibility for this for eleven years but what you've just described to me is as much a rape as if he had tied you to the bedposts and held you at knifepoint."

She frowned and made an attempt to speak but he continued without allowing her to interrupt. "He was in a position of authority over you. He was your elder, a friend of your father's, in a position of responsibility in the church. He was someone you had looked to for guidance on a regular basis. You were hurting and vulnerable and yes, looking for something to take away the pain, but that doesn't negate his responsibility. You were also eighteen, Ronni. That may technically be beyond the age of consent but that's still damn young. And even thirty-year-old women who are compromised by their priests or their psychiatrists can claim rape. There is something inherently vulnerable about that kind of relationship and the onus of responsibility lies on the authority figure. He has a sacred trust—the trust of his charge and it's up to him to uphold it."

Again she shook her head. "I don't know—"

Wolf felt a compelling need to convince her. She had carried her burden long enough. Too damn long. "He took advantage of your youth, and flagrantly misused the name of the Lord to further his interests." He squeezed her hands. "That's unforgivable."

She pulled her hands away. "But I said yes! How can I forget that? To blame Eli feels like I'm neglecting my responsibility in it. I had a responsibility—to myself, and to Jesse."

Wolf sighed deeply and decided to try another approach. "Did Eli ever acknowledge Leah as his own? Even to you?"

"No. When I announced I was pregnant I made sure he was present. I waited for him to speak up, to confess to the sin and take responsibility. He knew it was his. He knew I was a virgin when we were together. But he remained silent. He allowed me to bear the disappointment and rage all alone. They thought I had lied when I said I hadn't slept with Jesse. Who could blame them?" The words that had never been said aloud tumbled over one another in their haste to be heard. "I just allowed everyone to continue believing it had been him. So I do hold Eli responsible for that. He abandoned me, and his child.

And he abandoned his beliefs in favor of maintaining his image. We were never alone together after that, and never spoke of it."

"Why didn't you just tell them the truth yourself?"

She smiled indulgently. "Eli was then, and still is, an icon for that church. He was respected and revered. That spring he was chosen as pastor by Lot. That was like an affirmation that he had been handpicked by God himself. And here I was, right on the heels of an illicit relationship with the scum of society. Who do you think they would believe?" Wolf remained silent, thinking that she had just listed yet more reasons for Eli's culpability. "I was trapped. There was no way I could stay and feign a civil relationship with him, not to mention my family and church who had already judged me a liar and a fornicator.

"I had to leave. I couldn't face him on a daily basis and I couldn't look after Leah. Everything hinged on Jesse." She continued without prompting, the guilt and remorse spewing forth like pus from an infected wound. "That was the real reason I didn't talk to him that whole time. I was afraid if he heard my voice he'd *know*. He'd know that I had been unfaithful to him. And how could I possibly ask him to take on the responsibility of another man's child? I had to make sure Leah was safely in my parents' hands before I told him my story." She looked pleadingly at Wolf. "You have to believe I was going to tell him. I just had to do it after she was born and I had to do it face-to-face. I really believed he'd forgive me… But I never got the chance to find out."

Convincing her of his view of things was obviously going to take some time. He was asking her to see herself as a victim and he had the sense that she was too strong to accept that role willingly. He decided, for the moment, to indulge her and try to understand, more fully, the baggage that she had been carting around for the past eleven years.

He spoke softly. "You're judging yourself very harshly. Even if we go on the assumption that this wasn't *rape,* you weren't married or even engaged to Jesse. There was no concrete commitment or promise of fidelity that you were breaking."

She shook her head fiercely. "It didn't matter. In my eyes, and I was sure he felt the same way, we had made that commitment. He was supposed to come back that summer and I knew I would wait for him. No one ever made me feel the way he didand I risked that for a fleeting moment of physical comfort."

"So *that's* why you can't let go of him. *That's* what he knows in the dream."

She nodded. "He died believing in a lie. I've been living my life trying to live up to his expectations… Trying to live up to the lie."

He just couldn't let this go. "You were only eighteen, Ronni." He could hear a note of desperation creeping into his voice. "It was a mistake born out of grief, with a man who should have known better. You can't keep beating yourself up for it."

"Don't you think I know that? And I know he wouldn't have wanted me to deny myself happiness. But knowing it and living it are two different things."

He wiped away one of her tears, trying to silently communicate his understanding and, for what it was worth, his forgiveness.

But she continued, working through guilt that had festered for eleven years. "I would tell myself that and then I would see his body, covered in blood, being pulled from the wreckage and I would know he died because of *me*. I tried to blame my father and, to a certain extent, I still do. But in my heart, I know that if I hadn't betrayed him he wouldn't have been on that road, in that rage that day. I would have talked to him through the winter. He wouldn't have worried about me like Sam told me he did. And he would have come to our house and I would have been there waiting for him." She leaned against Wolf. She shivered and he wished that the warmth of his body could seep into the bitter cold of her soul. He raged silently at the man who had betrayed her trust, and condemned her to a decade of heartache.

She continued quietly, "Hardly a day goes by that I don't wonder what my life would have been like if that had been the case—if I had been stronger."

He whispered into her hair. "You've never been with anyone else, have you?"

She gazed at her hands clasped on her lap. "For a long time I told myself that it was my upbringing—that I couldn't get past the idea that I had to be married. But gradually I accepted that it was the guilt. I tried. A few times, I came very close, but when it came right down to it, I'd almost panic at the thought. I had this fear that it would just bring on more guilt and remorse and I couldn't possibly bear that."

Wolf took a chance and wrapped an arm around her shoulders. "Are you sure you just didn't find the right person yet? Someone who could help you get past the guilt?"

She pulled away and stood up. She crossed to the other side of the room before facing him. "I know what you're thinking but I'm not ready. Maybe if I go home and face Eli, maybe if I can hash it out with my family and come to terms with things, maybe then I can get past it."

"That's an awful lot of maybes, Ronni. Do you really think any of that will make a difference?"

"I don't know." She was wringing her hands, fighting with herself—a battle she couldn't win. "I like you, Wolf. I like you a lot and I love the fact that Leah sees something special in you and it felt so good when we spent the day together. I admit I feel an attraction to you like I haven't felt in a very long time." The words were unspoken but clear, *not since Jesse*. "But I just can't. Not now. The time just isn't right." She glanced at her watch. "You promised Leah we wouldn't be long. We should get going."

As he stood she added, "Does this mean you understand? I can't expect forgiveness for the lies and I don't look forward to the confrontation with Sam but maybe you could understand? Just a little?"

He shook his head in wonder. "No, Ronni. You're wrong. Despite what you seem to think, forgiveness *is* possible. I forgive you and I'm sure when Sam hears the whole story, he will too. I wish I could help you see that the blame isn't yours. But I know that will take time and it's always hardest to forgive yourself. I wish I could help you with that as well." She moved to walk past him toward the bedrooms but he grabbed her arm. "You, of all people, should understand about forgiveness. Isn't it one of Jesus' most basic teachings? There's a word for it, Ronni. Grace. I know you say you've stopped believing in a loving God but surely you must believe in that."

Her shoulders drooped with fatigue and her eyes were dull. "I'm just not sure what I believe anymore." She pulled away and plodded up the stairs.

Wolf watched her go, then reached for his duffel bag and thoughtfully stuffed the few remaining belongings inside.

Grace. Forgiveness without strings. There was no penance, no atonement, no guilt. Transgressions were forgotten and erased as if they had never been. There was no logic to it, and no limits. For the most part it was beyond human understanding. Maybe that was the one thing about his parents' beliefs that had sustained the little bit of faith he had managed to hang onto thus far. Perhaps what he had seen in Bosnia had forced him to cling to it more strongly than ever. How could you live with that kind of anger and hatred? You had to let go of it sooner or later or it would eventually consume you. The men who had perpetrated his loss were faceless. They were beyond the reach of justice and retribution. Maybe he hadn't forgiven them, exactly, but he *had* let go of it. And the familiar and comforting concept of grace had been a cornerstone for that cleansing.

But how could he help Ronni to see that? She had to forgive herself and that kind of grace was very hard to come by.

A few minutes later she reached the bottom of the stairs with a bag slung over her shoulder. She had traded in the slinky-wear for sweat pants and a T-shirt. Her hair, still flecked with gold, was pulled back into a tight ponytail. "Ready?"

They exited the house and, after she had locked the front door, she tapped his shoulder. "Would you mind driving? I'm just not feeling up to it tonight."

She tossed him the keys and he snatched them out of the air. "I'm honored."

"You should be. I've never let anyone else behind that wheel. But I figure if you can dodge traffic and bullets in a war zone like Bosnia, while bleeding from multiple gun shot wounds, maybe you can be trusted to drive the treacherous roads of Perth County."

She was smiling as she got in the passenger side but her lips were stiff and wooden.

As they drove, Wolf caught himself wondering what it would have been like to know her twelve years ago when she wasn't carrying the weight of the world on her shoulders. He cursed Eli for abusing his sacred trust and ruining a young life for a few sinful pleasures. And he caught himself silently cursing Jesse Ward for being such a hothead and getting himself killed.

But then Wolf had to acknowledge that at the age of twenty he had hardly been the patron saint of restraint. It had taken a few hard knocks to convince him that he had better learn to control his temper and think before he acted. He had just been lucky that none of *his* mistakes had been fatal. At least, not for him.

* * * * *

"Sam?" said Heidi as she opened the door.

"Can I come in?"

"Yeah, yeah. Sure."

Sam waved to the patrol car that waited, engine running, in Heidi's driveway. It pulled back out onto the street as Sam stepped inside the house.

"You look like shit," she said as she led him into the living room. She'd only known Sam a short time but he had struck her as someone who lived life to the fullest and made no apologies for it. He normally radiated vigor and energy and his eyes sparkled with roguish charm. But tonight he moved as if the life had been sucked right out of him and his eyes were as dull as thirty-year-old silver. "You want a drink?"

"Yeah. You got any whiskey?"

"Sorry, just rum or vodka."

"I'll take the vodka."

Heidi returned a moment later with a small tumbler. Sam downed it in one noisy gulp.

She sat beside him and rested a hand on his shoulder. "Okay, what's the scoop? Did Wolf kidnap her for Ronni, or what?"

"Nah, she ran away."

"Then how come they kept you down there so long? I called almost an hour ago and they said Wolf and Ronni had left but you were still in with the detectives."

"They thought maybe I killed Ronni's dad."

"What!" She vaulted from the couch. Her sympathy for whatever turmoil Sam was experiencing mutated instantly into righteous indignation at such an injustice. "This is just too much. First they come blasting into Ronni's place, practically rip that child out of my arms with her screaming bloody murder the whole time. Then they haul me down for a bunch of questions. As if I don't feel guilty enough after telling them where to find you guys, now they wanna lock you up?" She paced back and forth across the carpet, her fists clenched and her jaw working. "Shit, I need a drink." But Sam's hand on her arm stopped her before she could make it to the liquor cabinet in the kitchen. "What?"

"Heidi." His voice was soft, laden with emotion. "They're not pressing charges. They've found somebody else to investigate."

She turned to face him. "Well that's a relief." But her relief was nominal. Sam's demeanor wasn't exactly consistent with that of someone who had recently been exonerated of suspicion in a violent murder. Her eyebrows knitted. "Then, what's wrong?"

He shook his head. "I don't know. Tonight…I just need somebody." He drew a hand down his face. "God, I miss him. I know it's been a long time but tonight I'd really like to talk to Jesse. I can't talk to Ronni. Not yet. And my dad's getting old." He sat down on the couch, his head lolling against the high back, eyes focused on the ceiling. "Lately…I don't know. He just seems so old. I should probably stay around more, but…" He looked at her as if she had the answers. "He wants me to be what he needs. He wants his wife and his other son back and I just can't face the disappointment on his face when I'm not them."

Heidi sat beside him, and traced a finger around the curl of his ear. "What is it? Why can't you talk to Ronni?"

He looked away and she saw his Adam's apple bob slowly. "I don't want to talk about that right now. In fact, I don't think I want to talk at all." He met her eyes once more, and reached for her. He encircled her in his arms and drew her in tight. "Can we just be close tonight, and forget about everything else?"

She smiled coyly. "Are you suggesting wordless, mind-numbing, window-rattling, drive-everything-else-from-your-mind sex?"

His hands had already made their overture. "Yeah. Something like that."

"Okay."

True to her word, that was the last word that she spoke until the sun broke over the horizon the next morning.

Chapter Twenty-Nine

"Who was that, dear?" asked a sleepy voice from the bedroom.

Eli gently replaced the phone in its cradle. He stared at it for a moment before returning to the room at the end of the hall. "That was Verna. They have Leah back home, safe and sound."

Mary perked up and flicked on the lamp on her bedside table. "Really? That's wonderful! Did she say anything else? Where was she? Did someone take her?"

Eli methodically lifted the covers and slid in beside his wife. Her figure was not what it was when they got married but that was hardly a surprise after eight pregnancies. Even with a few extra matronly bulges, Mary was still very pretty. She was a good wife and mother. She was everything he could ever hope for. So why could he barely stand the sight of her? "She was with Veronica."

Mary was dumbfounded. "Veronica Lichty?"

Eli nodded. His mind was racing. He was having trouble retaining his focus on this inane conversation. "Yes. She and some friend, or *lover* of hers will be staying with Verna for a few days until Leah is settled again." Frany was coming back. The woman who could conceivably unravel his entire world was re-entering his life. Was that the real reason for her return? Was she finally seeking retribution for his dishonesty eleven years ago? Did she plan to reveal his indiscretions, ruin his marriage and his position in the church? That couldn't be allowed to happen.

Mary lay back on the pillows and rested her hands on the colorful quilt that had been a wedding gift to them almost eighteen years ago. "You know, sometimes I can't help but wonder what kind of life she ended up having. Did she regret what happened? Or was she happy with the way things turned out? It really was too bad about what happened to that boy, don't you think?"

"Yes. It was a tragedy. The Ward family has had more than its share."

Mary nodded agreement. "We've really been so fortunate. I thank God every day that our children are all safe and healthy. But I guess you never know what the future holds."

Despite the coolness of the room, Eli was perspiring. He discreetly wiped at his forehead. "Yes. We have to be vigilant that our children don't fall into a trap like that. We must pray daily for guidance." He recited the words. They rolled off the tongue so easily. They should have brought comfort and solace but they hardly even registered in his brain. His thoughts were far away.

She stroked his arm. "You've been such a good father to them, Eli. You always seem to know the right path. I hope when they're grown they'll appreciate that."

"It's late, Mary. Let's get some sleep. We can stop in and check on Verna and Leah tomorrow after church."

"You don't think they'll go to services, do you?"

That thought made him lightheaded. His stomach alternately clenched and rolled and only a fierce effort of will and faith kept him from heaving his supper all over that beautiful blue and yellow quilt.

He hadn't even considered that possibility. What if that was the plan? Go to church, and then, during sharing time, go forward and spew her venom for all to hear. He couldn't possibly do anything before nine o'clock tomorrow morning. He briefly considered sneaking into her room during the night and confronting her. But that was obviously impossible considering she was going to be sharing her bed with someone.

That thought disturbed him. Even after all these years the thought of Ronni's body could elicit the most lustful thoughts. That night with her had been incredible, intensely erotic, like nothing he had ever imagined before. Her youthful exuberance and newly awakened sexuality had aroused shameful thoughts that he still had trouble suppressing. He blamed her for souring his taste for his own wife.

He shook his head, trying to focus again on the problem at hand.

He would have to trust that that wasn't her plan. He was doubtful anyway. He couldn't imagine her setting foot inside that building again and facing all those people. Mind you, she faced a thousand or so people every weekend when she stood up on that stage and cavorted about, dancing and singing to that all-pervasive beat. He swallowed against the bile that rose in his throat.

No, it would be late when they got in, surely they would want to sleep. Speaking to the entire church just wasn't her style. She would want to confront him first. Privately. "I sincerely doubt it, Mary. I doubt she's set foot in a church of any kind in the last eleven years."

"Yes, I'm sure you're right." Mary silently turned on her side and flicked off the light. "Good night, Eli."

He didn't respond. His eyes remained riveted, unseeing, on the blackness directly in front of him—a blackness that grew heavier and more oppressive with every heartbeat. A thick blackness that threatened to crush him.

Mary was right. He had people counting on him. He had children who needed him, and a church that depended on his judgment. If Ronni came forth with her accusations that would all be jeopardized. His current position as Bishop was essential to his plans. In that capacity he was privy to the private turmoil of the members of four local congregations. He had to preserve it.

And then there was Leah. Something had to be done.

He would talk to Ronni tomorrow. But what if she wouldn't listen to reason? Perhaps more drastic measures would be needed.

He closed his eyes and prayed.

Perhaps.

* * * * *

Wolf stopped the car in front of the large, white farmhouse.

The simple, box-like design, with a quaint wrap-around porch, was nestled amidst small clusters of pine and oak trees. Ronni stared at it and something stirred inside her but to put words to those feelings would have been like describing a Van Gogh to the blind.

"Has it changed?" he asked.

She shook her head. "No, not a bit. Let's go. Staring at it won't make this any easier."

He followed her to the side door. Ronni had pulled open the screen and was about to reach for the inner door when it swung in of its own accord. Ronni gazed into the face of her sister. Neither spoke.

Anna took a step back to allow them to enter, and closed the door behind them. They entered the family room. It was just as Ronni remembered it. The same woodstove, the same furniture, the same wallpaper…the same pain.

"Hello, Ronni," Anna said finally.

"Anna." She turned to Wolf. "Wolf, this is my younger sister, Anna." Then to Anna, "This is Wolf. He's been a good friend to Leah and me over the last few days."

Anna didn't extend a hand. She merely nodded. "I sent Mom to bed. She was exhausted. When she told me you were coming I decided to wait." She glanced at Wolf, her hazel eyes appraising him as she spoke. "Mother asked me to make up a bed for the two of you in the spare room."

Ronni demanded her attention. "There's been a change of plans. We're not sharing a room after all."

"Lover's spat?" said Anna with open disdain.

"Something like that," growled Wolf.

Anna actually took a step back at the hostility in his tone.

Ronni put a hand on his arm, drawing strength from his presence. She didn't know if she could have faced this alone. "Contrary to what I told Mom, we are not lovers, Anna. I was just trying to hurt her."

"Well, it worked. You haven't lost your touch."

Ronni took a measured breath. "Did you wait to pick a fight with me, Anna? Because I'm up for it. I could easily come up with a list of things this family and others have done to hurt me."

Anna swallowed her obvious uncertainty about Wolf and addressed him directly. "Mr. Wolf…"

"Just Wolf."

"Oh. Would you mind if I spoke to my sister alone?"

Wolf queried Ronni with a glance. She nodded. "You take the bag upstairs and get to bed. You can take the double bed that she made up and I'll make up my own bed next door."

"All right," he said softly. And before she could object he leaned in and lavished a lingering kiss on her lips. She allowed herself that moment out of place and out of time before he drew away and touched her cheek. "Think about what I said."

She didn't acknowledge the words, but looked instead to her sister. "Last door on the left, Anna?"

Anna nodded and Wolf reluctantly withdrew from the battle zone.

Anna headed for the kitchen and Ronni followed. Anna reached for the kettle that always sat on the stove. "Would you like some tea?"

"Actually, I'd love a glass of milk."

Anna acknowledged the request silently, and pulled a couple of glasses out of the cupboard. She spoke as she poured. "He certainly acted like you two have been intimate."

"Only on a dance floor."

That managed to raise Anna's eyebrows.

Ronni suppressed a smile. "Don't worry; we didn't actually have sex in the middle of a dance floor. It just sort of felt like it." She briefly allowed herself to recall what it had felt like to fit against him so snugly, moving suggestively to a sexy beat. The memory elicited a response deep within her that she hesitated to acknowledge.

Anna frowned and shook her head. "Whatever." She set down the glasses and sat across from her sister.

"Was there something you wanted to talk about?" Her sister had aged. The last time Ronni had seen her she had still been a girl, brimming with youth and promise, eager for a marriage that was planned for less than a month after Ronni's departure. Now Anna was a woman. She had a home and children and all the responsibilities and drudgery that went along with it. Ronni wondered if she had also reaped the joys.

Anna lifted her eyes from the glass in front of her, and met Ronni's gaze. "Are you happy?"

"Ecstatic. Next question."

"Come on, Ronni. Really? Are you glad you left?"

"You mean am I glad I was driven away."

Anna bristled. "Leaving was your decision. You made the choice to sleep with him."

Ronni choked on her response. Not now. Not yet. Let her continue to believe in the lie. For the purposes of this conversation it didn't really matter anyway. "I loved him, Anna. At least I got to experience what that felt like, even if it was brief. Can you honestly say that you love Mark? Do you have a clue what that feels like? To want someone so bad that it hurts? To know that he feels the same? To know that his desire for your happiness almost outweighs his own needs? To know that he respects you and sees you as his equal?" She took a small sip of the icy freshness and savored the rich texture as it slipped down her throat. "To know that you're a better person because of him?"

"I'm happy, Ronni. I have a place and a life. I know what my future holds. Can you say the same?"

"I don't know for sure but I think maybe my future looks pretty damn good. And you didn't answer the question."

Anna traced a finger around the rim of her glass. "I went to see you once, you know."

"What?" The fact that Anna still hadn't managed to answer her question wasn't lost on Ronni. But perhaps that was an answer in itself.

"A few weeks after that article in the paper, I just had to see what it was all about."

Ronni's jaw almost hit the table. "You came to Ruby's?"

Anna nodded. "Yes. I got some clothes, and snuck out late one night. I didn't want Mark to know. I didn't stay long, just a couple of songs."

"And?" Her disbelief grew.

"I kind of liked it. You do have a beautiful voice, Ronni. And I could tell you loved it. Maybe I envy you that. Just a little."

Ronni took a large swig of her milk, like it was straight bourbon and could help her deal with this little trip into wonderland. "Thanks. That took a lot of guts."

Anna nodded and pushed her chair back from the table. "I guess that was all I wanted to say."

Ronni's voice stopped her. "Anna, wait. I need to ask you something."

Anna stopped with her hands resting on the back of the old press-back chair. "Yes?"

"Does Leah have a good life here? Is she happy? Please be honest."

"It's complicated, Ronni." She sighed. "They love her and have treated her like one of their own, but…"

"But what?"

"They held her so tight. Even the little bit of freedom they allowed us was denied her. I think they took her into town once since she was born. They always watched her like a hawk, hardly letting her out of their sight. They wanted to protect her, but…" She struggled for the words. "I'm afraid they smothered her. I can't help but wonder if they were afraid that she carried *his* genes…and your tendency toward disobedience. They were afraid that if they weren't careful she'd fall into the same traps."

Ronni could have laughed out loud at the irony of that. Leah carried the genes of the most respected man in the church. But of course she couldn't share that.

"I guess I'm not surprised. Do you think it will get better now that Dad's gone?" Glenn had always held to his rules and ideals as tightly as a miser held his money. He ran his family like he ran his farm—by the book. Verna hadn't been quite so rigid. If you could catch her alone, Mom was the one to run to if you needed permission for some dubious activity. Ronni wondered if, in his absence, her mother might relax her hold on Leah.

Anna shook her head. "I don't know, Ronni. Honestly, I don't know how Mom's going to handle it alone. Leah still needs a lot of guidance and, since Dad's death, she has suddenly gotten so old."

"What if I took her?" The words were out of her mouth before she realized it. She instantly regretted it, afraid Anna would panic and order her out of the house on their mother's behalf. But the response surprised her.

"I know you won't believe this—I'm having trouble believing it myself—but I actually think that would be best. Mom will fight it but maybe with some persuasion and some time…maybe then she'd agree. There's someone else who would be the real stumbling block."

Ronni frowned. "Who?"

"Eli. And Mom listens to him."

Then she nodded knowingly. "Of course. Who else?" She slugged back the last of her milk. "Don't worry, Anna. I think I can handle him. I might just have some arguments that he won't be able to refute."

"I hope you're right." She checked the clock. "Good Lord, look at the time. I have to get going. I just had to come and be here when Mom brought Leah home." She stood and grabbed a jacket from the hooks by the door. "Maybe I'll see you again."

"Maybe."

Anna pulled open the door and was about to step out into the fresh night air but she hesitated on the stoop and spoke into the cool darkness. "I've always wanted to tell you how sorry I was about what happened. I cried for you, you know…when he died. It was all so senseless, and so tragic." She swallowed and Ronni was touched by the level of emotion that Anna seemed to be feeling. "Over that winter I came to see how much he meant to you. It was hard to accept but, I guess, on some level I did understand it." Now she turned to look at the woman who had once been a best friend and confidante. In another lifetime. In another universe. "Maybe I do envy you that as well. Just a little."

Ronni took the plunge. She reached for her sister and they united in a strong embrace. As it lingered, Ronni murmured, "I miss having a sister."

Anna nodded mutely as they pulled apart. She turned and stepped outside, walked briskly to her car.

Ronni closed the door and methodically went through the house turning out lights before ascending the old, familiar staircase. She headed to the room next to Wolf's, the room that had once belonged to Anna. Wolf was in her old room. She briefly considered going in but that seemed so complicated.

Instead she grabbed a blanket that was folded on the end of the bed and moved to the old rocking chair that her mother was storing in there. Other than that, the room was bare. The bed needed sheets and pillowcases and she just didn't have the energy. Instead she wrapped herself in the blanket, pulled the chair close to the open window and sat silently rocking, allowing the breeze, rich with the musty smell of hay and lilacs, to rustle her hair and fill her lungs.

She thought of happier times with her brothers and Anna. She thought of the last two days with Leah. She thought of her impending confrontation with Eli. She thought of Jesse. And she thought of Wolf.

His voice washed over her like the breeze. It settled over her senses, wrapping her in warmth like the thick, fuzzy blanket wrapped about her shoulders. "What are you doing?" he asked.

"Thinking."

"You should be sleeping."

"So should you."

"Are you glad to be home?"

"Maybe a little."

He was behind the chair now. He placed his hands on the back of it, slowing the rocking motion until it finally stopped. He lowered his hands to her shoulders.

Involuntarily she tilted her cheek to rest on the backs of his knuckles. "Is Leah asleep?"

"Yes. She managed to stay awake until I came in, but she drifted off as I sat with her. She was exhausted."

"Mmm." She nuzzled his hand. It was warm and just a little rough. "Lucky girl, to fall asleep while you watched over her."

He removed his hands and stepped around to the front of the chair. He knelt in front of her and clasped her hands in his own. "Come to bed with me, Ronni."

"To sleep?" she asked drowsily.

"Eventually."

His implication should have made her uncomfortable but instead it merely made her curious. "But I told you…I'm not ready."

"Maybe you'll never be ready but I think you want to. You just have to let yourself." He brought her hands to his lips and pressed a kiss to her knuckles. "Let yourself trust, Ronni. Let yourself trust *me*."

The events of the evening had thrown her into a whirl. She felt out of time, oddly displaced, sleepy and a little muzzy, and yet acutely aware of his touch and the heat it generated. "I don't know."

He tugged on her hands as he stood. She allowed him to pull her upright, and hold her against him. Then he lowered his head and kissed her. She was hardly aware of when it began but gradually that was *all* she was aware of. His lips were coaxing and persuasive, insistent and aggressive. His tongue slid between her lips as his arms encircled her waist.

His body was lean and firm and every inch of her cried out for more. She tilted her hips as he nestled himself against her. His lips broke from hers briefly. She silently despaired at the rude departure. When he rejoined, stroking her lips with his, teasing her with his tongue, she thought she could want nothing more.

That was when she gently pushed him back. Her lips drew away, as she fought the magnetic attraction they seemed to have developed over the last few hours. She held him at arm's length. "No. I just can't." At that moment the memories were thick. They clung to her like a wool blanket, heavy and suffocating. She wanted to cast them off but the implications of that were disturbing.

"Ronni," he whispered, "I'm not trying to talk you into something you're not ready for, or don't want. But I need you to think about this, to be certain. I think you want to but you just think you shouldn't. You think you shouldn't be enjoying it, that you shouldn't be happy. And you deserve to be. I just want you to be happy. That's all I want."

He tipped up her chin and drew her eyes to his. "Stop focusing on the guilt and the past, and start focusing on me and what you need. You don't have to forget him, Ronni. Loving someone else doesn't diminish your love for him. You're not being unfaithful. You're being a woman with needs and desires that deserve fulfillment. But you need to stop focusing on the past, and start focusing on what you're feeling here and now." He stroked her cheek with the pad of his thumb. "So tell me. What are you feeling? What do you want more than anything else at this moment?"

She felt the sting of tears but they weren't tears of grief or regret or even sadness. She wasn't sure what they meant. Maybe they were tears of release. "I want you. I want to be close to you and know what it's like to have your arms around me and have you inside me. But I just don't know if I can. I've fought those feelings for so long."

He scooped her up with an arm behind her back and one beneath her knees. He carried her like a doll toward her old room. "You can. Like I said, just focus on me. I want you, too, Ronni, and I think I can be what you need if you'll just give me the chance."

She nodded, her forehead against his cheek. A moment later he closed the door to the room and lay her on the freshly made bed. He hadn't even pulled back the covers yet. He must have spent the last half hour pacing the length of the room, waiting for her to ascend the stairs.

He took a moment and removed his shirt before lying beside her on top of the faded quilt. She ran her hands across his chest, and then down to touch his scars. "I can't imagine that kind of pain," she whispered.

"Oh, I think you can." He placed his mouth next to her ear, and kissed her neck. He drew in his breath when her hand continued its descent. It had slipped beneath his waistband but there she stopped, her slender fingers kneading the flesh gently.

He moaned as his lips found hers and he reached for the hem of her T-shirt. He didn't waste time, but slipped it over her head without ceremony. The thrill of his skin against hers intoxicated her. She felt almost drunk with pleasure and, to her amazement, desire.

He reached for the clasp of her bra and fumbled. He whispered a playful curse and she smiled. At that moment she knew he was right.

She was having no trouble focusing on him and letting go of her inhibitions. His words of encouragement and reassurance had struck the right chord. She had trusted him with a secret that she had never shared with another soul and he hadn't disappointed her. He cared for her deeply and they had already shared an intimacy beyond the physical. Perhaps she could trust him with this as well. Perhaps, for the first time in eleven years, she *wanted* to.

She undid the torturous clasp herself, reveling in the warm tones that reverberated in his chest as he cupped her breast and kneaded it beneath his lithe fingers.

He took her breast into his mouth and laved her with his tongue as his hand slipped covertly beneath her track pants and panties. Again she astounded herself when she reached down and tugged at the drawstring. "I don't want to wait, Wolf. I've waited long enough."

He quickly released her breast and kissed her hard before sitting up and removing the last remaining barriers, both hers and his own.

Their nakedness excited her. It was the first time she had known someone so completely. Never with Jesse, and even when she had lain with Eli they had remained partially clothed. And, of course, there had been no one since.

She savored every sensation—his chest and the fine spattering of hairs grinding against her breasts, his belly against hers as her arms wrapped around his waist. The warmth of his breath. The scent of his skin.

Her fingers detected the scars on his back and she explored them curiously as his erection nudged her thigh. She was aware of his thighs against her own and then of his teeth against her throat.

She felt a jolt of electricity when his hand reached between her thighs and sampled her, caressing and massaging and finally dipping inside her. He merely had to hint at what he wanted with the barest nudge of his knee against hers and she parted her legs to accommodate him.

His mouth moved down across her stomach, his tongue tasting and exploring until his breath ruffled the fine curly hairs at the apex of her thighs. She thrilled to the touches that she had denied herself for so long. No longer did they feel dirty or forbidden or laced with guilt. Now, with Wolf, they felt special and intimate. And, perhaps, even sacred.

She giggled when his tongue flicked across the sensitive skin just below her hipbone. She gasped when he nipped at her inner thigh. But the shock of what he did next knocked the breath out of her. His mouth joined with her in the most intimate way imaginable and she lost herself in the movements of his lips and tongue over her center. She struggled for breath as he caressed and tasted every fold and recess, his mouth hot and hungry.

A sudden, unexpected climax hit and she arched against him as it poured through her. It pounded her with wave after wave of pleasure that left her panting, yet not quite sated. She knew what she was lacking.

When he released her and moved back up to focus on her eyes, his face registered pleased surprise at the delicate touch of her hands on his arousal. She had only touched Jesse like that once, so briefly, but now, knowing the conclusion, it was different. She found it to be intensely erotic, and even caught herself wondering what he would taste like. But she didn't get the chance to find out. Not yet.

She stroked and explored his smooth rigid length. To her delight his breathing became ragged, matching her own and heightening her desire.

"Are you sure about this, Ronni?" His lips brushed her ear. "There's more at stake here than just trust. There are…consequences to consider."

It took her a moment to understand what he was asking. But somehow she found the presence of mind to shake her head, realizing to her own surprise that subconsciously she'd already considered this. "It's okay. It's late in my cycle."

He lifted his head and gazed down at her, brushed a wisp of hair from her eyes. "You know that's not the only reason. But if you'll trust me…" His words trailed off, leaving the question hanging, unspoken, in the air.

She smiled at the irony of it. "If I didn't trust you, I wouldn't be here." She brushed her thumb across the tip of his erection. "Would I?"

With a low growl and a soft passion his mouth joined with hers again. His lips caressed hers and his hands held her firm and, as his tongue eased into her, so did his sex. He entered her slowly, allowing her to savor every inch in that first sweet moment of intimacy.

He slid his hands beneath her hips to tilt her up to meet him but she needed little coaxing. Her desire was already building again as the new sensations tempted and teased and excited her. Wolf's gentle caresses and the attentions his mouth lavished on her exceeded her wildest dreams.

He uttered a rich curse as she accepted him completely. But she muffled any further articulations when she wove her fingers through his hair and sealed his mouth against hers again. He moved slowly, forcing her to endure sensations that threatened her self-control and her sanity. She released his mouth, closed her eyes and experienced the first ripples of pleasures to come. It was all so new and unexpected, she felt a little lost, a little out of control, a little afraid.

Sensing her hesitation, Wolf breathed in her ear, "Just let go, Ronni. Trust me."

He kissed her throat and she acknowledged his plea with the merest whisper of his name.

His movements accelerated and she met him eagerly. Her fingers held him tight, as if she were afraid he was an apparition that might slip away. So many things she loved had slipped away. She couldn't bear to lose this too.

But he was flesh and blood and heat and sweat, and as solid as a maple. He had no intention of going anywhere. Ronni allowed herself to believe it—and enjoy it.

When she climaxed, she could hardly breathe through the waves of ecstasy that cascaded over, around and through her. This time the throbbing continued endlessly. She would think it was over and he would move within her, sending a new wave of sensations washing over her. Finally he allowed himself to climax, his mouth against her throat, as the shattering conclusion released him.

He melted over her, for one exquisite moment crushing the air from her lungs, before he lifted himself up and met her gaze.

At that moment she thought his eyes the most beautiful things on earth. They were deep and dark but no longer threatening or predatory. They were a sea of midnight, a home for countless stars and she could swear she could feel the heat of a thousand suns radiating from them.

She stroked his hair that was as dark as his eyes, taking note of the hint of silver at the temples. "I did it."

He smiled. "Give me a little credit here. *We* did it."

"All I could feel was you."

"Was it enough?"

She chuckled. "Do I really have to answer that?"

He sobered then rested his forehead on hers as he closed his eyes. "Stay safe, Ronni. I couldn't face losing this again."

She wrapped arms and legs around him as tightly as she could. She took an odd pleasure in being the one to *give* comfort for a change. He needed her, perhaps as much as she needed him. And therein lay their strength. "I'm not going anywhere. You think I could bear to leave *this?"*

He didn't answer, just rolled off her and drew her tightly against him. They tugged at the colorful quilt until it covered them. The well-worn fabric encased them in a snug, warm cocoon. She absently ran her fingers over his scar, kneading the spot on his rib that she knew bothered him, and enjoying the sense of intimacy.

"I've been curious about your name. Is it short for Wolfgang?"

He kissed the tip of her nose. "No." He gave her his little account and told her about Riley. She smiled at Wolf's description of his friend and the fact that poor Riley still hadn't heard the story of Wolf's name despite repeated requests. Even after he claimed to have saved Wolf's life, Wolf refused to divulge his secret. "I don't know why but, for some reason, I just love holding that over him. He knows there's a story and it makes him crazy."

"Will you ever tell him?"

"Yeah. Actually, next time I see him I think I'll give in. It doesn't seem so important anymore."

She smiled.

"Should I stick around, Ronni? Would you like me to stay?"

She clutched him tightly. "You're here to stay, Wolf. I don't know if I'd survive if you left now." She hesitated. "But…maybe there's something you should know."

"Uh-oh. More secrets?"

"I'm considering trying to get Leah back. Anna even thinks it's a good idea. If we're together that will affect you. I know you care about her but having her as a permanent fixture in my life is a little different than picking her up on the trail and helping her find her mother."

"I was hoping that was what you were thinking."

She mumbled against his chest. "Thank you for bringing her back into my life."

"Don't thank me. It was all her idea. She amazes me, you know? She adjusted to you as if you two had been together for years. She never showed any resentment or reservations. She just seems to be able to accept people so easily, without question."

"She's been so sheltered. Maybe she hasn't learned to distrust yet. Or maybe she's just so eager for new experiences and new people. She's like a blank page that needs filling up."

He lay back and drew her in tight, pulling the quilt up snug under their chins. The breeze from the open window was cool and fresh. It carried the occasional low moo from the barn to their ears. It was so peaceful, so comforting. She had always found it ironic that this had been the site of her most intense turmoil.

He whispered into the silence. "Someday I want to take you to see my home."

"I'd like that," she replied softly. Her eyelids drooped.

He stroked her back and they both fell asleep basking in the warmth of success and renewal, secure in the promises the future held.

Chapter Thirty

Ronni felt a tug on the quilt.

"Mommy?"

She smiled at the word. It sounded so nice. Leah had never quite managed to call her that before. Another tug.

"Wolf?"

Leah? Her eyes snapped open. Sunlight streamed in the window and fell across the bed. She glanced down to confirm that the quilt was covering all the essential areas but Wolf's regular breathing indicated that he was still dead to the world. So much for her resident commando. He'd been ambushed by an eleven-year-old.

"Leah," she said, her voice cracking with the first words of morning. "What is it?" She clutched at the quilt, needing security against the possibility of it slipping down and revealing the sordid truth beneath.

Leah cocked her head quizzically. "Did you and Wolf commit adultery?"

That must have woken him up because Ronni heard that distinctive, center-of-the-earth chuckle from his side of the bed.

"Uh…well…" Ronni fumbled.

"Yes, Leah, we did."

Ronni shot him a fierce look but it bounced right off that irritating grin. "You gonna lie to her?"

Technically, adultery was inaccurate. Fornication was the proper term for this particular carnal sin. But Ronni elected not to go into the semantic details at that moment. She turned back to Leah, still not sure what to say, but that childish innocence saved her from further brain strain.

"Isn't that a sin?"

Ronni grimaced as if in pain. "Well, yes. You could say that."

"You're supposed to be married."

"Yes." She caught a glimpse of Wolf. He lay there, hands stacked behind his head, cocky half-smile plastered to his face, offering no assistance as she squirmed under the absolute scrutiny of childish honesty. He was enjoying her discomfort just a little too much. She'd have to find a way to make him pay for that.

But Leah saved her from elaborating. She was obviously sorting through it all herself, in her own way. "But you love each other?"

Now Ronni glanced at Wolf. If he was so smug *he* could field that one. She wasn't disappointed.

He took a moment before answering her, turning his gaze on Ronni and holding it. In those dark depths she saw desire and heat, understanding and compassion. They'd known each other only a short time but already they'd trusted each other with their deepest secrets, shared her worst fears. Maybe that didn't mean they were destined to spend their lives together but it meant there was something special between them—something worth exploring.

At last he answered, speaking slowly, his eyes still trained on Ronni. "We're not sure about that yet, Leah. Maybe. Love is a complicated thing. But for us, sex is part of figuring it all out."

"Oh." Leah's eyebrows drew together. "But if you do then that's sort of the same thing, right? I mean if you love somebody does that make it okay?"

Ronni sat up, holding the quilt tightly against herself. She just couldn't answer that one lying down. "For Wolf and me it does. But you need to understand that a lot of people don't feel that way—like your grandma and Anna. They think that you have to be married or it's *not* okay. In fact it's very wrong. You need to make up your own mind. You have to decide for yourself which way is right. But not now. You don't have to think about that for a long time."

She brightened. "Well I think you guys being together is cool. And you loved my dad, right? Will you tell me more about him soon?"

Ronni stared silently at her daughter.

"Mom?"

"Yes. I'll tell you more about Jesse soon. He was very special to me."

That seemed to satisfy Leah. Ronni didn't want to look at Wolf and see the disapproval that she knew would be in his eyes.

Leah plopped herself down on the edge of the bed. "Do I have to go to church? I don't wanna go unless you guys do."

Ronni closed her eyes and flopped back on the pillows. "The fact that the poor child didn't get to sleep until two a.m. isn't sufficient reason to miss services for once in her life. When we were kids we'd practically have to be afflicted with the plague before we'd be allowed to miss a Sunday."

Leah just watched them, waiting for an answer. Wolf sidled up beside Ronni beneath the covers, an early morning erection nudging the outside of her thigh, a vivid reminder of the night's activities. "I wouldn't mind going. I'd like to see what your old stomping grounds are like."

"Trust me," groaned Ronni. "You *don't* want to go. It's three hours of droning sermons and torturous singing. And afterwards everyone would just gawk at us like we were zombies resurrected from the dead."

"Oh," Wolf grunted. "Okay, I'm convinced."

She glanced at Leah again. "Okay, I'll talk to your grandma and get her to let you stay home but you have to go right back to bed and sleep for a few more hours, okay?"

Leah's eyes darted from Ronni to Wolf and her lips pursed slightly—as if Ronni hadn't quite hit the mark.

"Then, after dinner, I promise we'll go for a nice long walk together. That's one thing that I miss about living here—the long walks through the bush."

Leah's lips relaxed into a smile. "Okay. I'll go back to bed right now. You guys should sleep too."

Ronni smiled. "Thanks. Maybe we will."

Leah bounded out of the room and Ronni noted with relief that she thought to close the door behind her.

Ronni snuggled up to Wolf again. She ran her hands over his chest, savoring the sweet liberties she now had license to take with his body.

"You're not going to tell her are you?"

His tone was gentle—not accusing or judgmental. She was grateful for that. "What good would it do?"

"It would be the truth."

"I think the truth is overrated."

His silence told her she wouldn't get away with that. "Is it better for her to know that she was conceived out of my grief and his lust and that her father has been a part of her life for years but refused to acknowledge his responsibility? Or should she keep believing that she was conceived out of love by a special man who died before he could know her?" She rested her cheek on his chest and listened to the faint yet comforting rhythm of his heartbeat. "The truth would only hurt her. She's been through enough lately. I don't want to lay this on her too. Maybe when she's older, and she can handle it better. Maybe then I'll explain it all."

"I don't think you give her enough credit. She's stronger than you think."

"You just think I'm afraid."

Again, he was silent.

"Okay then, allow me my fears. I have a right to them." She threw back the covers and headed for her clothes. "Anyway, it's my decision."

He stacked his hands behind his head again and watched her slip her T-shirt over her head. "Okay. I won't interfere." She felt his eyes sweep over her body. "I thought we were going to *sleep* some more."

She fought a grin. "I have to talk to my mother, remember?"

"Then you'll come back?"

Feeling strangely playful, she turned a sultry smile on her new lover. With her jeans hanging open she crawled across the bed to him. "I promise," she breathed in his ear.

Despite inexperience, her attempt at seduction had the desired effect. He slid his hand in the opening at the front of her jeans. "I'll hold you to that," he whispered as she groaned and allowed some intimate explorations.

She fought a sudden urge to strip again and straddle him, and tore herself away.

"But you better do those up or your mother might suspect you've been a naughty girl," he teased.

She zipped her fly and saluted him. "Yes, sir!"

He rolled his eyes. "Can I come on your walk? Or is it just for the womenfolk?"

She stopped with her hand on the doorknob. "I guess you can come. I haven't been on a walk-a-mile for years."

"Huh?"

"That was one of the more exciting activities of my youth. A group of twenty or so young people would go out in the evening and pair off for a walk. You hold hands, but two people, a boy and a girl, are designated as runners. They split up and each pick somebody and sort of *cut in*. Then they say *You go back four,* or however many they choose. The displaced person has to cut in to the designated couple, and so on."

"Sounds kinda like a singles bar on wheels."

She laughed. "Yeah, kinda. More than a few matches are made that way. Now can I go please? I want to get back before you fall asleep for real."

"Nag," he said as he rolled over and pulled up the quilt.

She muttered as she left the room, "No respect. No respect at all."

She entered the kitchen with a distinct bounce to her step. She did have vague memories of skipping through this kitchen in search of a cookie after a long day at school. She remembered giggling with Anna as they washed dishes and plotted revenge on their nasty older brothers. She could recall countless hours spent at that kitchen table, inhaling good home cooking and enjoying the warmth of family. For eleven years she had purposefully forgotten all that. Perhaps she had cheated herself.

As expected, she found her mother seated at the kitchen table, dressed in her Sunday best, sipping from a cup of coffee and spooning brown sugar over a steaming bowl of oatmeal. No doubt she was expecting Stephen or Anna to pick her up for church in another half hour or so. "Mom?" she said as she approached.

Verna looked up and smiled. She looked very tired to Ronni. Anna was right. Now, in the light of day, Ronni could see lines and wrinkles in her face that seemed premature, and far too deep. Maybe Ronni bore responsibility for some of them.

"Good morning. I hope you and your friend slept well." Verna poured a dollop of fresh cream over her porridge.

"Yes, thanks, Mom. We slept fine." She cleared her throat, suddenly nervous about taking on this new role on her daughter's behalf. But she had promised Leah. "I wanted to talk to you about Leah—"

She was startled by a voice behind her. "Did you really sleep, Ronni? Verna told me you were sharing a room with him. You've become a real woman of the world, haven't you?" Eli had been just out of sight, in the corner, beside the refrigerator.

She whirled to face him. He too had aged. Or maybe it was exhaustion. His eyes were puffy and dull with fatigue. His shoulders sagged forward, almost as if he were folding in on himself. He looked like he hadn't slept in a week. "Actually, Eli, you're absolutely right. But after all, I learned to fuck from the best, didn't I?"

"Veronica!" screeched her mother.

"Sorry, Mom," said Ronni, but she kept drilling her eyes into Eli whose pallor now mimicked a hunk of raw beef.

Through clenched teeth he said, "May I speak to you privately?"

She cocked her head, trying to decide how far to draw this out. How thoroughly could she manage to torture him in front of her mother without actually revealing her secret? But then she decided she'd rather get this over with so she could return to the warm, toasty hunk of flesh up in her old bedroom. "All right," she said amicably. "Shall we go outside?"

He didn't answer, merely stalked out the door, assuming that Ronni would follow.

Verna watched them go with puzzlement as she sipped her coffee.

The spring morning was bursting with the scents of honeysuckle and apple blossoms, along with the lilac scent that had drifted into her room the night before. Ronni's bare feet shuffled through the lush grass, the sweet dew clinging to her toes.

She and the unmasked Eli took up positions beneath mottled shade of the one lone birch tree in the backyard. But neither of them bothered with their charming surroundings.

"What are you doing here?" he hissed.

"I'm visiting with my family and I brought my daughter home. You got a problem with that, your royal Bishopness?"

"Not if you plan to keep your mouth shut."

"Am I a threat to your perfect little Utopia, Eli? Did you really think you'd make it to the grave without ever laying eyes on me again?"

"You didn't answer the question. Are you planning on dishing up your dirty little secret for the whole church? No one will believe you, you know. You'd just look like a fool and a lying slut."

Ronni was genuinely shocked. "Eli! Such language. If I didn't know better I'd swear you were panicking. But if I'm destined for such humiliation why the worry? You obviously have the flock in the palm of your hand. My accusations would fall on deaf ears. I'd be laughed out of town." She crossed her arms, and narrowed her eyes. "Or maybe I wouldn't. Is there something I don't know?"

"Just answer the question."

His demeanor intrigued her. She hadn't really planned on divulging her secret, mainly because it would only hurt Leah. But the possibility was obviously torturing Eli and that was delicious. She decided to draw it out to its full potential. Surely a few moments of reciprocal suffering weren't too much to ask.

She dropped her hands and stuffed them deeply into the pockets of her jeans. She took a few casual steps away. "I don't know, Eli. I'll have to think about that one. I hold you partly responsible for Jesse's death as well, you know. I'm quite sure you advised my father to try and keep us apart. After all Jesse was the one other person who would have figured out our dirty little secret. And the police told Sam that you were here that day. Maybe you said some things to make him angry as well. Things he didn't deserve to hear." She turned to face him, drilling into him with a stare that she hoped mimicked Wolf's darkest glare. "Can you give me one good reason not to rip you apart and leave you torn and bloody, just like you left Jesse?"

He blanched. "What?"

"Jesse died a slow, torturous death, Eli. Didn't you know that? Maybe you deserve some suffering all your own."

His shoulders drooped and the color gradually crept back into his cheeks.

His demeanor confused her. She remembered Eli as being so calm and in control—the picture of pastoral leadership. But perhaps she shouldn't be so surprised. She represented a potential threat to everything he held dear—his leadership in the church, his family, his reputation. Perhaps a touch of irrational panic was to be expected.

Eventually he regained his composure and his resolve and stepped toward her. He grabbed her shoulders. "Be warned, Ronni, if you come forth with this you'll be very sorry."

"I've been sorry for eleven years, Eli. Sorry that I ever laid eyes on you. Sorry that I ever trusted and respected you. You're a Pharisee and a hypocrite on the grandest scale and I would love nothing better than to see you exposed."

His fingers dug into her shoulders like talons, his expression a study in anguish.

"Let go!" she cried, as she tried to pull away. He didn't loosen his grip. "You're hurting me."

His eyes burned and he was about to speak when another voice reached them. "You heard her, Martin. Let go before I rip your goddamn arms out of their sockets."

Eli let go and stepped back, reeling, as if he had been physically struck.

Wolf reached her with two long strides. "You happened to pick a spot right below our window. I heard every word." He touched her cheek with a possessiveness that she found oddly comforting. "Are you all right?"

"Yes. But I'm not so sure about him." She shot a glance at Eli.

But he had regained his usual self-assured air. She marveled at what he was capable of. In front of her he could let loose his venom, become Mr. Hyde, but for Wolf, Dr. Jekyll resurfaced. Almost every trace of the panic and torment of a few moments before was banished to some dark place that no one ever saw. His mask restored, Eli Martin approached Wolf with outstretched hand, and exceptional civility. "I'm Eli Martin, an old friend of the family. You must be Ronni's..." He taunted her with a deep frown. "What exactly is he, Ronni?"

"Lover." She said it with strength and pride. And to emphasize her point she slipped a hand into the back pocket of Wolf's jeans and squeezed visibly.

"Ah yes. The euphemism for fornication. Still, it's nice to meet you Mr..."

Wolf kept his arm around Ronni, obviously not taken in by the charade. "Captain Wolf Mercredi." He paused only briefly "And don't bother with the show. I know who you are and *what* you are. I suggest you leave before Leah catches wind of this."

"Spreading your lies to the general public, Ronni? And a military man, no less. The antithesis to everything you were raised with. Sex and lies weren't enough. You had to expand into guns and killing. You must be desperate for attention."

"Get out!" growled Wolf. "This may not be my property but I'll bodily carry you away if you don't leave her alone this minute."

Eli wasn't fazed. He ignored the threat. "Verna invited us for dinner but perhaps we should do it another time. I don't suppose you'll be attending church this morning?" He raised his eyebrows in a mocking salute. "I didn't think so. Maybe it's best that your father died before he could see how completely you turned your back on him. You may have spread your legs for me the first time but they obviously never quite managed to close again, did they?"

In a heartbeat Eli found himself splayed on the grass, holding a palm to a bloody lip.

Wolf stood over him, sending out waves of palpable hostility and rage. "I told you to leave. Believe me, I can do a lot worse and I don't even have my M16 with me." He seemed to consider that image for a moment. "Damn shame."

Eli dragged himself to his feet and stood, somewhat unsteadily. He glared silent retribution at Wolf before shuffling back to his car.

"Asshole," muttered Wolf.

Ronni approached him from behind and slid her hand into his. "I'd never heard him talk like that before. I didn't know he was capable of that."

"He's obviously feeling cornered. That can turn even the most placid pet into a vicious, dangerous animal."

"Well," said Ronni as she tugged on his hand, "I don't want to waste my day worrying about him—pet or pit viper, he's not worth it. Let's get back to bed and catch up on our *sleep*." She bobbed her eyebrows and slid an arm around his waist.

"Are you going to be an insatiable nymphomaniac?"

"Maybe. If you're lucky."

"I'm definitely feeling lucky."

* * * * *

Eli pulled over to the side of the road. He couldn't see straight. He couldn't think straight. His hands were shaking and his jaw was throbbing.

She planned to expose him. She had as much as said it. But when? And to whom? She had told that man of hers but he was no threat. He was an outsider; his accusations would be meaningless. It was Ronni who was the threat. Leah obviously didn't know but she was still part of the problem.

He raked all ten fingers through his hair, stopping midway to clutch at the blond strands. He fought the sudden urge to tear the hair out of his own scalp. *Ronni*. Seeing her again, being close to her—it had been hell. He hated her for what she could do to him but, God help him, he still wanted her. She had clearly been with *him*. She had admitted it, and the way they looked at each other…it was obvious. He had even smelled it on them—the recent evidence of a carnal union. It had made him sick. And it had made him crazy.

She was to blame. *She* was doing this to him, just like she had done it to him twelve years ago.

That Ward boy had changed her—possessed her somehow. Eli hadn't realized it at the time but, when the truth of Veronica's illicit activities came out, he had realized that it was only after she had started seeing *him* that Eli had begun to have lustful thoughts about her. He had always loved Ronni, seen something special in her, but not before that summer had he ever had anything but pure thoughts about her. Somehow Jesse Ward had awoken her, made her into a sexual being. And now, twelve years later, she had truly blossomed. It was worse than ever. She was possessing him, controlling him. She had to be stopped before she made him sin again, and before she could ruin everything he had built. There was no doubt in his mind anymore. He had prayed about it and his path was clear. Yes. No matter what the cost, she had to be stopped.

And she had to be stopped soon.

* * * * *

Wolf smacked his lips. "That was absolutely delicious, Mrs. Lichty. I haven't had a meal like that since… Well, I don't think I've ever had a meal like that."

"Didn't your mother cook…Wolf?" Wolf smiled inwardly at the hesitation. It had taken a lot of persuasion but Ronni's mother had finally agreed to call him by his first name. He hated *Mr. Mercredi* so she had tried *Captain* for a while but that had sounded ludicrous rolling off her tongue.

"Well, yes. But nothing like this. I have never been to a meal with two meats, three vegetables, three salads, pickled beets and homemade bread." He slapped his full belly. "And I don't even want to talk about dessert. Just thinking about it packs on the calories."

Ronni leaned over and kissed his cheek. "If you want to get in my mother's good books you're on the right track. Her cooking is her pride and joy."

"Do you still cook, Ronni?" asked Anna as she stood to clear the table. She and her family and Stephen's family had joined them for dinner. Stephen, however, had remained sullen and quiet throughout the meal, his eyes riveted to Wolf as if he were, quite literally, the wolf among the sheep.

Wolf wasn't exactly clear as to the nature of the brother's animosity. Did it stem from Wolf's military background? Or did he mistrust someone who would dare defile his mother's home with inappropriate acts of intimacy?

After another session beneath the quilt, Ronni and Wolf had taken advantage of the empty house and had showered together while Leah slept. So the physical evidence of their activities had been washed away. But their demeanor and the energy crackling about them had changed dramatically. It was quite obvious to even the most casual observer that they were recent additions to the ranks of passionate bedmates.

But no matter what Stephen or the rest of his family thought—whether their union was condoned by the laws of Moses or Christ or Mohammed—what had transpired the night before had not felt the least bit inappropriate or sinful. It had felt good and right and, dammit, Wolf intended to enjoy that feeling. He had found those moments in life to be too few and far between to be taken for granted.

He snuck a hand under the table and squeezed Ronni's thigh.

He delighted in the smile that twitched at her lips. She deserved to be happy and he had every intention of ensuring that she stayed that way. That both of them did.

Ronni was responding to Anna's question. "I cook a little but I admit that I use a lot of the convenience foods and take-out. I just have better things to do with my time."

"Are you implying that good, wholesome food is a waste of time?" Stephen had ventured into the conversation.

Ronni sighed and answered patiently, "Not at all, Stephen. But for me, I'd just rather be doing other things."

"Yeah, I'll bet." He sipped his coffee then turned a dark glare on Wolf. "So you served in the military, is that right?"

"Yes," said Wolf guardedly. He knew this was bound to be a sensitive topic in this house. "I retired after finishing a tour with NATO's Stabilization Forces in Bosnia."

"Doing what exactly?"

"Trying to keep the natives from killing each other."

"By shooting at them?"

Ronni broke in. "Stephen! We've had a nice meal; please don't ruin it."

But Wolf grasped her hand. "No, that's okay. They need to know who I am—where I'm coming from." He returned his gaze to Stephen and kept his voice even as he answered. "Sometimes. Sometimes with cannons, or bombs or guns. Whatever it took."

Stephen shook his head ruefully. "How can you justify that? They're human beings and you just cut them down like wheat."

Wolf took his time. He had no wish to further antagonize these people whom Ronni so desperately needed to reconcile with. But he had no intention of lying to them either.

"I know what you believe and I respect it. Peace and passive resistance are noble ideals and often they are the best option. But these people are zealots. They believe their cause to be righteous and some of them believe they have God on their side. There's no reasoning with them. We tried peaceful methods and they didn't work."

Stephen began to speak but Wolf stayed him with his hand.

"Let me finish. Maybe the right leader with the right resources and the right vision could turn them around but so far he hasn't made an appearance. There's no Gandhi or Christ figure on the horizon, ready to lead these people into a new age of peace and prosperity. So the options are to either let them kill each other, women and children included, or step in, hold them at gun point, bowl a few over as necessary and do whatever it takes to seize their weapons and keep them under control.

"One fanatic with God on his side can be restrained and controlled without bloodshed but a whole country is another story."

He waited for Stephen's response but none was forthcoming. "Unless you have any suggestions?"

Stephen remained silent, maybe conceding the point, but Wolf wasn't sure. He didn't get the chance to find out because Verna piped up. "Stephen, why don't you and Mark and Wolf take your coffee into the living room while we clean up."

Without meeting Wolf's gaze, Stephen and his brother-in-law dutifully picked up their mugs and headed for the comfort of the upholstered furniture.

Not anxious to face Stephen and his judgmental gaze alone and not eager to leave Ronni, Wolf remained glued to his chair. "I think I'll stay and give the ladies a hand. I'm no stranger to washing dishes."

The room fell silent and Wolf immediately sensed that he had made a blunder. He shifted uncomfortably in his seat and shifted his eyes to Ronni hoping she might rescue him from a dubious fate.

* * * * *

Ronni chuckled to herself at the uncharacteristic confusion and helplessness that stole across Wolf's features. The invincible commander brought to his knees by a group of flabbergasted females.

Verna, Anna and Sarah, Stephen's wife, stared at Wolf as if he had started speaking in tongues. They would be completely lost with a man puttering around the kitchen. They wouldn't be able to chat freely, and would be deathly afraid that he would drop the good china. It was just too much to ask of her mother. But she didn't want to relegate him to the hostile territory of the living room either.

"I have a better idea." She stood and grabbed Wolf's hand. "Why don't you come with me. I want to call Heidi, and check in. Maybe Sam is there. I need to make sure they let him go last night."

Wolf seemed to understand that she was trying to rescue him from a dubious fate. He acceded to her suggestion and allowed her to drag him to his feet. He followed her meekly into the parlor. Leah stayed behind to help with her usual duties.

The phone only rang twice before Ronni heard Heidi's sleepy voice at the other end. "Are you *still* in bed?" teased Ronni with an exaggerated groan. It wasn't really a surprise. Heidi rarely got out of bed before one on a Sunday, usually owing to Saturday evening's illicit activities. She doubted the previous evening had been an exception.

Heidi didn't answer immediately and Ronni could just see her squinting at the clock. "Okay, so I overslept a bit. But sleeping until two is hardly reason to call out the Marines."

"We don't have Marines in Canada."

"Whatever."

"Are you alone, Heidi?"

"Of course not."

"Is it Sam?"

"Of course it is."

Ronni sighed with relief. "Can I talk to him?"

"Um." There was an exceptionally long pause, during which Ronni heard muffled voices. Heidi had no doubt covered the mouthpiece while she conferred with Sam. "Is Wolf with you?" Heidi sounded upset.

"Yes. Why?"

"He won't talk to you but he'll talk to Wolf. What's going on, Ronni? Sam won't tell me a goddamn thing."

"It's a long story, Heidi. If he won't tell you, I'll fill you in later." Ronni instantly lost the buoyant mood that had persisted after her shower with Wolf. Dealing with Sam was obviously going to be more difficult than she'd anticipated. If he wouldn't even speak to her, how were they ever going to resolve this? She wasn't willing to give him up so easily. He had become far too important to her. But all that would have to wait until she could face him in person. "I'll put Wolf on." Her voice sounded dead.

Wolf took the phone with a sympathetic glance in her direction. "Sam?"

He listened in silence for a long time, his expression changing intermittently. He smiled briefly. He shook his head. He frowned. At one point he glanced at Ronni again, his eyes wide with disbelief. Ronni's frustration had just about reached its limit when Sam finally seemed to run out of steam and he allowed Wolf to respond to whatever news Sam had offered. "So, is it official? Are you off the hook?"

Wolf gazed off into near space as he listened.

"Okay, but listen for a second. I've talked to her about it and I really think you need to hear her out."

Ronni began to wring her hands anxiously, hoping Wolf could pave the way for her toward a reconciliation.

After another brief pause he added, "Yes, and I think, when you know the whole story, you will too." He shook his head. "Give me a little credit, Sam. I'm not swayed simply by a few tears on a pretty face." He awarded Ronni a half smile.

"All right, I'll tell her." He dropped the phone back in its cradle.

"Well? What did he say?"

Wolf settled down on the overstuffed love seat. "Quite a bit. First though, he said he'll call you later when he's a little less rattled. He said he'll meet with you to discuss your…differences."

"How very diplomatic." To be more accurate Sam was *pissed*. But she let it pass and urged Wolf on. "What else? Is he just rattled because of me and the cops last night?"

"No, that was the other thing. To condense it a little, Herb Brubacher—you know that name?"

Herb Brubacher? The name sent a tiny shiver of disdain down her spine. Did she know it? How could she forget it? How could she forget the name of yet another man whom she had once trusted and respected but who had turned his back on her and played an active role in turning her family against her? She had tried to forget the name and the betrayal but the rage and the pain had clung to her like the persistent odor of smoke that lingers on your clothes after you've watched your house burn to the ground and everything you love go up in flames.

Her thoughts ran on but all she said was, "Yes. He was our pastor for years. He retired several years ago but I think he stayed on as elder and helps Eli out every once in a while."

"Did you know he was a heavy drinker?"

She considered that. Oddly, it didn't shock her. She frowned and shook her head uncertainly. "No. I had no idea. Why?"

"I guess he was DUI last night and hit a car with a couple of teenagers in it."

"Oh my God! Are they okay?"

"Yeah, they're fine. But I guess Sam overheard some of this when they brought him in and apparently it happened at the exact same spot where his mother was killed." He paused to see how she would digest that.

She looked at him dumbly. She blinked. Her hand flew to her mouth. "Are you saying…?"

He nodded. "I guess when confronted with Sam's accusation Herb pretty much admitted to killing Sam's mother."

Ronni stared at Wolf for a moment, trying to let the implications of that sink in. Her pastor had killed Jesse's mother. It was the answer to a question that had haunted Jesse long before she had known him, and had continued to haunt his brother. Hence it haunted her because it affected those she cared for. Now Sam had his answer and so did she. She should feel relief, closure, release. And yet she felt none of those things.

She couldn't sit still. She stood and paced to the window. She drew back the white eyelet curtain and looked out toward the gravel road. A car flew past and churned up a cloud of dust. For a fleeting moment she imagined it was Jesse screaming past in his fiery chariot.

For a moment he seemed so close—close enough that she caught a breath of his cologne. For a moment she could feel his body next to hers, his face in her hands, his arms around her, as he grieved the loss of his mother and raged at the hypocrisy of a killer who preached of honor and faith and integrity. For a moment she felt his spirit so clearly…but then it dissipated like smoke in the wind and she wanted to cry.

Wolf quietly broke into her reverie. "That's what's got Sam so unnerved. I guess it's an adjustment after having no one to blame all these years."

He stopped but she sensed a tension in his silence. She turned to look at him.

"But there's more."

Still feeling somewhat numb, she whispered, "What else could there possibly be?"

"Herb was drunk and he rambled on a bit. Apparently your father figured out that he had a problem, and even that he was responsible for Jesse's mom's death. I guess he said some other incriminating things as well, so now he's the prime suspect in your father's murder. They wonder if Herb killed your father to keep him from revealing the secret."

"Holy shit!" Ronni dropped down beside Wolf again. The wheels continued turning as she struggled to remember events that she had long tried to forget. "This could explain so much. If Herb was responsible for that accident, he was probably scared spitless of Jesse. Jesse often talked of finding their mother's killer. Maybe Herb knew that and was afraid that if Jesse hung around too much he'd figure something out."

Wolf shook his head. "I don't get it."

"I heard Herb advise my parents very strongly that they should just let me go and that they should do everything in their power to keep Jesse away from me and the church. At the time I just figured he was trying to protect the church's fragile reputation. But maybe there was more to it."

"Maybe. Self-preservation is a powerful motivator. Should we tell the others?"

"Yes, definitely. It will be hard for them to hear but they have to know." She raked her fingers through her hair and was startled to realize they were shaking. "Herb Brubacher killed a woman and ran away. And he possibly murdered his good friend. It'll shake them to the core." She shuddered as she considered further implications. "No doubt they'll want to call Eli as well. He'll have to know." She pressed her fingertips to her temples. The very thought planted the seed of a migraine. "Oh God, he'll probably want to come over and talk to everyone—you know, offer support and condolences…all his usual bullshit. We'll just have to be sure to be out on our walk when he gets here."

She took a deep breath and dragged herself to her feet. She grabbed Wolf's hand and laced her fingers with his. "Come on, Captain. I'll need you to back me up in there."

He squeezed her hand and kissed her cheek and, in his touch, she found the little bit of strength that she lacked.

She led him out of the parlor.

They gathered everyone together in the kitchen and told the incredulous group of Herb's admitted and suspected transgressions. There were some murmurs of disbelief but Wolf assured them of its veracity.

Once the exclamations had died down and the tears of disappointment had dried, as expected, Verna insisted on calling Eli. The rest of the group moved into the living room to rest and rejuvenate, all but Stephen, who headed out to the barn to check on one of the cattle that was due to deliver any day.

In search of a moment alone, Ronni headed upstairs to fetch her running shoes for the walk she had promised Leah.

* * * * *

Wolf leaned against the wall in the kitchen and listened to the echo of Ronni's bare feet on the stairs. She stepped lightly but he wondered if a new heaviness had settled over her heart. He had seen the shock and the grief pass across her features as she had learned of yet another breach of her trust and faith—of yet another reason to cling to her regrets over Jesse. Herb Brubacher had been her elder, her pastor, someone she respected, a representative of her church and her faith. Now he represented a connection—however indirect—to Jesse's grief over his mother.

Ronni had banished the hurt quickly and had tossed him a smile before bounding for the stairs. But where had she stored it? Had she merely added another layer of scar tissue to a poorly healed wound?

Their union the night before had been cathartic—for them both. He had experienced a joy and a feeling of completeness like he hadn't felt since Lubica. Perhaps not even then. He felt a connection to Ronni that surpassed even his time with the tiny, driven Croatian woman with the big eyes and the huge dreams. And for the first time since, he had allowed himself to hope.

She had found healing as well. He was sure of it. But Ronni's wounds ran deeper.

She had opened herself to him and been freed of the regrets and guilt that had bound her. But how deeply had it penetrated? How long would it last? Could one night of sharing and passion banish eleven years of pain? Probably not. It would likely take much longer. His task didn't promise to be easy. There would be setbacks and disappointments. She would give a little and then balk and fight him once again. But Wolf had never been one to give up easily. He loved a challenge, enjoyed a quest. Especially if the prize at the end was Ronni Lichty. He'd do whatever was necessary to win her for his own. He had no intention of sharing her with anyone. Not even a ghost.

Wolf felt a tug on his sleeve. He knelt down to Leah's level.

"Yes, honey?" He fingered the tight auburn braid that fell over her shoulder. At that moment he saw it. No wonder Ronni had blanched when she had caught sight of Leah for the first time. Leah was, indeed, the spitting image of her father.

Leah's blue eyes flicked to the living room and then back to Wolf. She whispered as if she were leading a covert conspiracy. "Herb didn't do it."

"What? What do you mean?"

She shook her head and chewed on her lower lip. "He just didn't. Is he going to get into trouble? I don't want him to get into trouble when he didn't do it."

"Leah, what's this about?" Wolf's puzzlement began to shift towards concern. "He confessed to hitting that woman. And as far as Glenn is concerned they're not sure about that. Is that what you mean? He didn't kill Glenn?"

Once again, she glanced toward the living room before nodding.

"But how can you know that?"

She licked her lips and chewed on a small, pink fingernail. "I just do. Please make sure he doesn't get into trouble."

Verna walked into the kitchen and distracted Wolf from Leah's distress. "Eli will be here in about half an hour. He was terribly upset by the news but he wants to make sure everyone here knows they have his support."

"Yeah," muttered Wolf. "He's a real peach."

Verna didn't hear him.

A few moments later Ronni joined them. She immediately grasped Wolf's and Leah's hands and towed them toward the door. As they slipped into their shoes she regaled Wolf with tales of the sun-dappled trail that wound through the hardwood bush that ringed the farm. She told of the thick carpet of rotting leaves dotted with trilliums and ferns and jack-in-the-pulpit. She boasted of the mighty maples that yielded some of the finest, purest sap in the country. And she described the rough-hewn lean-to and the ancient evaporator pan where the pale, thin, vaguely sweet sap was boiled and transformed into a thick, luscious confection.

Of course, at this time of year the sap was no longer running but it was still a lovely walk and the sugar shack would still be fascinating for someone who had never seen maple syrup in the making.

Ronni glowed as she told her tales and described a favorite sanctuary from her childhood and youth—and Wolf forgot everything but the gleam of happiness in her eyes.

* * * * *

They had just stepped out the door when they heard Stephen's excited cry from the door to the milking parlor. "Lila's calving! Get Mark to come and give me a hand." Then he dashed back into the barn.

Ronni smiled to herself at the familiar notes of excitement and anxiety that were inherent in those two short words.

"Calving?" asked Wolf.

But Ronni turned to Leah first. "You go in and get your uncle for Stephen, then we'll get going." Then to Wolf, "Yes. One of the cows is having a baby."

"Really?" And he looked toward the barn.

Ronni noticed the obvious interest on Wolf's face. "Would you like to see it?"

"Well..."

She laughed. "Why don't you go ahead? Leah and I have seen it dozens of times."

"But the walk?"

"After she calves just ask Stephen to point you toward the sugar shack. We'll wait for you there." She paused and gazed at the distant tree line. "Actually, maybe this is best. I think we need a little time alone."

He wrapped his arms around her waist and drew her close. "Okay. Who knows? After I see this I might realize I should become a vet. I'm still looking for a new career, you know."

"You don't want to be a farmer?" she asked innocently.

"Nah. Too violent."

She laughed and pushed him away. "Get going and don't let Stephen give you any of his bullshit. I used to be able to beat him up when we used to wrestle in the haymow. I bet I still can."

Wolf started walking toward the barn. "I'll bet you can too. Maybe you can give me a demonstration later."

She chuckled as Leah came back outside on Mark's heels. Ronni grabbed her hand. "Wolf wants to watch the calf being born. So it's just you and me for a little bit. Is that okay?"

Leah beamed up at her. "Yup. Do we get to talk about him?"

Ronni smiled. "You're growing up too fast, Leah." And they set off through the fields toward the bush. "We'll talk about Wolf and maybe I can tell you about Jesse too. Two of my favorite topics."

Chapter Thirty-One

"Where is everyone?" asked Eli as he shrugged off his straight coat.

"I'm sorry, Eli," said Anna, as she closed the door behind him. "I should have called and told you to come by later. Lila's calving, so the men are out in the barn. And Ronni and Leah went for a walk." She chuckled. "You can't even talk to Mom. She fell asleep on the couch. She's exhausted from all the excitement last night. And today."

"Yes, there's been no lack of excitement around here lately."

Anna tugged at her bun, which had suddenly grown too tight. She had never been entirely comfortable around Eli. She couldn't put her finger on it but something about him set her on edge. Especially lately. "Horrible news about Herb," she offered.

"Yes, shocking." Eli glanced out the window. "You said the men were in the barn. Is Ronni's friend with them?"

"Yes. He's never seen a calf born. He was very interested."

Eli nodded and pursed his lips in thought. "And Ronni and Leah went for a walk?"

Anna nodded.

"Do you know where?"

"I think they were going back to the bush. Wolf is going back later to see the sugar shack."

"How nice."

Anna thought that he seemed a little distracted. Usually Eli spoke with much more certainty and eloquence. "Is something wrong, Eli?"

"Hmm? No, no. I guess I'll come by later, when Verna's awake. Be sure and tell her I was here though, will you?"

"Of course."

Eli slipped out the door and Anna watched him drive down the lane. As she turned around she realized he had left his jacket. She glanced out the window and saw his car turn onto the road. Too late.

But it was of no concern. He was returning later. She retrieved the jacket and hung it on a hook in the kitchen where it was sure to be seen.

She shuddered imperceptibly. She wished she could identify what it was about him that irked her. Obviously she was alone in her opinions. *Everyone* loved Eli. She was definitely bucking the system by finding fault with him. But what was the fault? Maybe that was just it. He was too perfect, and too well liked. There had to be *something* wrong with him. He was just too good to be true.

* * * * *

"Do I look like him?" asked Leah.

Ronni shuffled through the carpet of leaves that coated the floor of the bush. The mulch beneath was rich and dark and moist, the perfect medium for the snowy trilliums that sprouted all about them. The three-petaled flowers amazed her. They bloomed only once every seven years and yet they were so abundant. Obviously the majority of the roots were hidden, sleeping beneath the warm carpet of leaves and compost, waiting for their turn to bloom and dazzle the world with their brilliance.

That was a little bit like how Ronni felt. She felt like she had been half asleep for the last eleven years, hibernating until it was her turn to awaken and really experience the life that she had been drifting through.

Suddenly everything seemed fresh and new. She had purged so much of the guilt that had been holding her back from experiencing an intimate relationship and really opening herself up to someone. And Wolf had proven himself more than worthy of the honor. She chuckled at herself. Who was she kidding? He was the reason for her rebirth.

He deserved all the credit, and all her appreciation and she intended to lavish her undying gratitude on him until he begged for mercy.

"Mom?" Leah squeezed her hand. "You didn't answer me."

"What?" Ronni stumbled over a root as she was drawn back to the present.

"Do I look like my dad? You said he was very handsome."

Dammit. Despite what she had said to Wolf, she hated lying to Leah more and more with every fresh deception. Maybe he was right and she was underestimating her daughter.

Ronni sighed and sat down on a stump. She could just make out the weathered barn-board and tin roof of the sugar shack a few meters away beneath a dense canopy of maple leaves. In early spring, thick wood smoke and sweet steam perpetually wreathed the tiny structure. That ramshackle building brought back such happy memories.

The hours spent collecting the buckets of sap, dumping them into the evaporator, stoking the fire and finally draining off the thick, rich, amber-colored liquid were lighthearted times spent with caring family members.

Like fresh milk, their house was never without a jug of the sweet staple in the refrigerator and no one would think of putting anything other than the real thing on homemade pancakes and waffles.

She smiled at the thoughts of sitting around the kitchen table with her brothers and Anna, sharing gooey grins as they poured syrup over stacks of pancakes and sopped up the excess with slices of homemade bread.

Then she looked at Leah sitting among the leaves so patiently. She deserved happy memories too. She deserved honest ones.

This was a good spot to stop and wait for Wolf. Maybe it was a good spot for a good long talk, as well. "Yes, Leah. You look very much like your father. But there's something I need to tell you about him."

"What do you think you're doing, Frany?"

Ronni practically fell off the stump at the sound of Eli's voice. She vaulted off her makeshift stool and whirled around to face him. He wore no coat but his forehead glistened with perspiration and he was out of breath as if he'd been running.

Ronni's heart beat double time. "Is something wrong, Eli? Is everything all right at home?" But why wouldn't *Wolf* have come looking for her? "Oh my God! Is Wolf okay?"

Eli scowled. "Your concern for your new lover is heartwrenching."

She returned the scowl in kind. "Well then, what the hell is it? Why are you here?"

"You were just about to tell her, weren't you?"

Ronni glanced at Leah and the terror in her daughter's eyes startled her. "Leah, sweetheart? What's wrong?"

But Leah just backed away.

"You stay right where you are, child." Eli's harsh tone froze her in her tracks.

Ronni rounded on him once more. "You have no right to talk to her like that. Now, why are you here? We were having a *private* conversation."

"I need to talk to you too, Frany. It's important."

"We have nothing to talk about."

"Oh, I think we do. But not here. If you'll come with me." He reached out and touched her hand.

She recoiled as if the serpent from the Garden of Eden had bitten her. "Don't you ever touch me again! And I'm not going anywhere with you."

He shook his head. "You really don't understand, do you?" It was then that she noticed the heavy chunk of maple he clutched in his left hand.

"Mommy?" Leah's voice was almost a whimper.

Ronni turned toward her daughter and Leah was the last thing she saw before the pain blasted through her head.

* * * * *

Wolf wiped his hands with an old rag as Stephen slapped him on the back, "So? What did you think?"

"It was a rush," grinned Wolf.

"Yup, nothing like it." Stephen leaned against the gleaming steel of the cooler. "Nothing like bringing a new life into the world, even if it is only a cow."

Wolf looked down at his hands, which had so recently been streaked with fluids from the womb. "Yeah, beats the hell out of watching people kill each other."

Stephen didn't respond and, when Wolf looked up again, he realized Stephen was studying him.

"I'm sorry I was so hard on you," said Stephen softly.

Wolf had gradually noticed the change in Ronni's brother. Somehow sharing an experience like that brought people together and allowed them to see beyond their differences. He shrugged off the apology. "Don't worry about it. Ronni has a lot of stuff to work out with you guys. I'm just along for the ride."

"Did you ever actually shoot anyone?"

Wolf was getting really tired of that question. But he was still glad of the answer. "No. Thank God."

Stephen checked the temperature on the cooler. "*Do* you believe in God?"

"Yes, in my own way. I wish I could say the same for Ronni." He noticed Stephen's watch. "Oh shoot! What time is it?"

"Actually it's milking time."

"Where's the sugar shack?"

Stephen laughed. "You're not going now, are you? They must be back by now. We'll be having supper right after milking. Ronni's probably in the kitchen helping Mom right now."

"Darn!" He was trying to modify his language for this crowd. "I wanted to see that shack."

"Don't worry, it'll be there tomorrow. She won't mind another walk. She always loved walks. She didn't think anybody knew but she would always sing while she walked." He led Wolf out the door toward the house. "I'll come with you. I should change my clothes."

"I'll be sure and ask her for a demonstration tomorrow."

"Leah sings too. Did you know?"

"No. I guess that makes sense." As they walked, he tucked his shirt back into the waist of his jeans. He wasn't sure why he felt the need to bring this up but something about it was nagging at him. "She doesn't look much like her mother though, does she?"

"No. The last year or so she really started to look like Eli. Funny how the family tree works, him only being a distant cousin and all."

"Just in the last year?"

"Yeah, I guess she always sort of did but, the last while, as she started to lose that *little girl* look, it just sort of struck everyone. People started commenting on it. I think it started to bother Dad. The week before he died he blew up at somebody for saying something in front of her. I think it bothered him because, for all intents and purposes, she was his daughter. It was tough enough taking that on considering everything."

Something about that didn't sit right with Wolf. He stopped walking and Stephen followed suit. "Wouldn't you think he'd be glad she looked like his cousin, rather than Jesse?"

Stephen shrugged. "I don't know. I guess that would make sense too." A cloud of anger passed over his face. "But we can't ask him, can we?"

But Wolf didn't respond. He was standing stock-still, his eyes unfocused. *But Herb didn't do it.* Leah had sounded so certain. *Glenn was disturbed by the resemblance to Eli.* That just didn't make sense. Eli was Glenn's friend and partner. Why would the resemblance bother him? Then he recalled the image of Eli gripping Ronni's shoulders, a look of fierce rage on his face. A disturbing thought wormed its way into Wolf's mind, weaving a complex pattern through the maze of information and ideas.

"Wolf?"

"I have to talk to Ronni." He dashed into the house.

Verna, as predicted, was puttering about the kitchen as she worked at putting together platters of cold meats, cheeses, raw vegetables and condiments.

"Where's Ronni?" he demanded.

Verna's hands froze over a stack of summer sausage. "She's still on her walk." Then she checked the clock. "Oh my, they *are* gone a long time, aren't they?"

Wolf rubbed at his rib, which had begun to throb. He heard the back door swing closed and Anna walked in, her four-year-old in tow.

"Hi, Mom. I forgot my purse." She rummaged around the kitchen pulling out chairs and checking in cupboards. "Gary, did you hide Mommy's purse?" She continued her search and said absently, "Mom, did Eli ever come back? He came while you were sleeping and he said he'd come back later. He forgot his jacket. I was hoping he'd pick it up."

"No, dear. I'm afraid I never saw him. But he's so busy—Wolf, where are you going?"

He called back as the door slammed shut. "I'm going to find Ronni and Leah." It was pointless to share his suspicions. They would think him a lunatic. He checked the sky. He had several hours of daylight left. With a little luck he was being paranoid and he would find them waiting impatiently at the sugar shack.

Rats! He saw Stephen step out of the house behind him. "Stephen. Which way to the sugar shack?"

Stephen gave him brief directions. The trail was easy to follow and he shouldn't have a problem. Stephen tried to allay his fears. Ronni knew those woods like the back of her hand. Nothing could happen to her in there. No dangers lurked in the tame environs of maple trees, squirrels and deer.

Wolf thanked him and sprinted away from the house. Stephen called something to him as his strides devoured the meters across the back pasture but Wolf paid no attention. He was too focused on the deceptively peaceful bank of trees ahead of him. No dangers? There were dangers everywhere. Just when you thought you were safe—just when you thought the fighting had moved past you, and it was safe to venture out again—that was when they got you. That was when you heard the rapid report of machine gun fire, and felt the bullets rip through your body, destroying life and hope and everything you had come to hold dear. Maybe there was no machine gun this time but the scenario was all too familiar.

He hoped he was wrong.

He prayed he was wrong.

But in his gut, he knew he wasn't.

Chapter Thirty-Two

Hay.

Ronni smelled hay, sweet and musty, felt its scratchiness against her cheek. Then she became aware of the pain behind her eyes. It throbbed inside her skull like the deep bass beat emanating from a thousand-watt speaker. She shifted and the beat picked up speed.

"Finally awake? I was beginning to worry."

Ronni worked herself up to a sitting position and touched the huge goose egg at the back of her head. "Y-you hit me." She heard herself say it, but still didn't quite believe it.

"I had to, Frany. You gave me no choice."

She squinted and blinked and finally brought him into focus. He sat, perched on an old, moldy bale of hay. His hair and shirt were rumpled and plastered to his scalp and body with sweat. His shoe tapped a nervous rhythm against the battered barn board floor.

"Why?" she demanded. "I don't understand. Why did you have to?"

Then he looked at her—met her eyes for the first time—and she didn't know him. His eyes were those of a man possessed, maybe not by demons, but by something she couldn't comprehend.

"You were going to tell them." He said it with sincere regret. "I couldn't let that happen. There's too much to lose. I had to protect the flock. They need me. They wouldn't have understood."

The world still spun around her. She couldn't orient herself, couldn't focus or make sense of what he was saying. "I wasn't going to tell them, Eli. I just said that to scare you. I wanted to hurt you like you hurt me."

He stood and shook his head viciously as he continued to fight with himself. His body screamed out in protest of the battle. She could see the tension in the rigid set of his shoulders and the white-knuckled balls of his fists.

"I don't believe you. You're just trying to distract me. You're trying to save yourself."

She swallowed, her mouth suddenly dry, as she began to grasp Eli's state of mind and the potential peril of her situation. "Save myself? What's going on, Eli? Why did you bring me here?"

She had recognized it instantly. It was an old relic, a partially collapsed barn, abandoned years ago, situated in a hollow in the woods. It had to be close to a hundred and fifty years old. Kids used to come here to play, bringing along bales of hay or straw to make beds with. They used to play house, or jump from the rickety rafters into the soft fluffy mounds of old hay. Then someone had gotten hurt and they were all banned from ever returning. Ronni had ignored the warning. She used to come here on her walks, sitting for hours soaking in the ambiance of the ancient wood and stone. It seemed to know so much. She had found it warm and inviting despite the dangers. But not today. Today it embodied evil and menace.

"I can't allow you to do it, Frany. You're so much like your father. He wouldn't listen to reason either. He guessed, you know. I denied it but he knew."

"My father? He guessed that Leah was yours?"

"Yes. She looks so much like me. He gradually put it all together. He was going to come forward. He was going to ruin everything I had built. I couldn't let him go through with it." His cold eyes burrowed into her. "Can't you see that? I just couldn't." He was trying to convince himself as much as her.

Ronni was incredulous. She hated Eli. He was a hypocrite and a liar, but a murderer? There had to be a mistake. She must have misunderstood. "You argued with him?"

He nodded and wiped the sweat from his forehead with his sleeve. "Yes. We screamed at each other. We were both furious. The shovel was right there. It was so easy. It was so much easier than the first time. I thanked the Lord for that."

Ronni couldn't breathe. An intolerable tightness clutched her chest. Tears stung her eyes but she held them at bay. She had to stay clear and focused. What had he said? He had admitted to killing her father. He was insane. She had to get out of there. She had to tell someone. Who knew what he was planning? Her eyes darted about in search of a weapon, an escape—anything. Then she stopped—*first time?*

Slowly, she drew her eyes back to the man who had stolen her virginity and her peace of mind. "What was the first time, Eli? Did you hurt someone else?" She tried to keep her voice even despite the tidal wave of emotion that flooded through her.

He smiled sadly, indulgently. "So naïve, Frany. Of course. There was someone else who could reveal our secret. You said it yourself. I thought it would be easy with him. He was so rude and unclean. And it was so necessary. And besides, he had ruined you. It was because of him that I began having evil thoughts about you. I didn't realize it until later but it was just after you started seeing him that I began seeing you…like *that*."

He lifted his eyes to the heavens as if silently asking for guidance. "But it was harder than I thought. When it came right down to it, I had to ask for strength. But I did it. That's why I was so relieved when it was easier with Glenn."

Ronni clamped a hand over her mouth. Her heart raced and her vision blurred. "Jesse?" The earth heaved beneath her. "Oh my God! You killed Jesse?"

He frowned at her, as if she were a child struggling with a concept as simple as one plus one. "I cut the brake lines on his car. I had hoped that would be enough."

"But…it wasn't?" The hand over her mouth trembled.

He paced as the sweat continued to bead on his forehead and stain his shirt. His fists rhythmically clenched and relaxed. "No. I was angry with the Lord for that. He should have been dead. But when I got to the car he was injured and in pain but I knew he'd survive if someone found him." He laughed. It was a strained, disturbed sound and it grated across her nerves like fingernails on a chalkboard. "He thought I was going to help him. He thought I was going to go for help."

"What did you do, Eli?" Ronni's whole body was shaking now but she kept her voice soft and compelling. Her revulsion and hatred for Eli was building but she suppressed the urge to lunge at him and claw at his eyes with her fingernails. She knew it would be useless and she wanted to hear the rest. She needed to hear the rest.

"There was this sharp piece of metal on the ground." Eli looked down at the floor in front of him, as if he could see the shard there among the rough boards and straw. "It had been ripped from the body of the car. I picked it up." He raised his hand in front of his face, holding an imaginary object between his fingers. He turned it slowly, examining it from every angle, then dropped his hand to his side and looked at Ronni, his eyes slightly vacant, as if part of him were back there, standing beside the crumpled car, gazing at the helpless victim inside. "I reached in—he was trapped, he could barely move—and...*zip*." He slashed the air with his hand. "He started to bleed. I couldn't watch anymore. I left."

Ronni had closed her eyes, the images too vivid for her to bear. She quelled the screams that welled up, the epithets that she longed to utter at the monster that had once been her friend. She stifled the moans of anguish for the tortures Jesse had endured—had endured because of her. "Did he say anything?"

"He stayed true to character. He yelled obscenities at me, right up until I was walking away." Eli's features pinched with disdain. "But then he yelled at me...something else."

"What? Oh Jesus! What did he say?"

"He asked me not to hurt you. Just after I did it I told him why. As the blood pumped slowly out of his neck, he asked me. So I told him. And then he asked me not to hurt you." He paced, his feet thudding softly on the rotten wood of the barn floor. "I tried to honor his request, Frany. They were his dying words. He was one of God's children, after all. But then you came back. What choice did I have?"

So Jesse had known. In the end he had known the truth. The last words he had heard had informed him that the woman he had loved and waited for had lied and been unfaithful to him. He had known of her betrayal, and had still thought of her safety. Had he forgiven her as well? She laughed silently at such a ludicrous idea.

After Eli left, as he lay there with his life seeping out of him, he must have cursed her. Surely, in the hours before he died, as he prayed for rescue, he must have also prayed that she experience the same torment that she had inflicted on him. It was only human nature. She deserved no less and perhaps it was self-inflicted but that was exactly what she had gotten. She didn't begrudge him that.

As vivid images of Jesse's last confrontation with a madman flitted through her tormented mind another thought struck Ronni with the force of a hammer. *Leah!* Why hadn't she thought of it sooner? Eli was obviously capable of even that atrocity.

"Where's Leah?" she croaked through muffled sobs. "Eli, please tell me you haven't hurt her! You can't. She's only a child."

"She saw me, Frany, with Glenn. Why do you think she ran away? She's my own…but I have other children to protect."

"No, no, no…" Ronni repeated it over and over as she rocked back and forth—a mantra of despair. "What have you done to her?"

"She's safe, Frany. I wouldn't do it if I didn't think she'd be better off. She'll be happier there." He stood perfectly still. He rested his eyes on her, his gaze almost possessive. "You will be too. I am sorry for what I've put you through. But it's almost over."

She felt so impotent, paralyzed. Her mind flooded with images of Jesse, helpless as his life was leeched from him by a demented fanatic who thought he was doing the Lord's bidding. And Leah…

They had only just found each other again. Obviously God had a twisted sense of humor, and was having a hearty chuckle at her expense. She covered her face with her hands and felt the tears leak through her fingers.

Then she sensed his presence near her. He stood over her. A tangible evil radiated out from him. It crept towards her like a dark, icy mist. She dropped her hands to the floor and crawled away—scurrying like a mouse caught in the sights of a prowling tabby. "You're insane, Eli," she screamed as she increased the space between them.

He stood still, watching her. So calm. Too calm.

"The God I loved would never have expected you to do those things. What you did was out of hatred and fear and malice." She reached the far wall. She was trapped. She clutched at the boards for support as she stood to face him. Her head protested the change in elevation but the throbbing faded in the face of her rage and fear. "Jesus preached salvation through love. I don't think you know how to love."

"Oh but I do." His expression sagged with profound sadness. "I loved you, Frany. But I couldn't have you. Why would God have placed such a love in my heart, a love that I couldn't ignore? That night in the barn, it was almost more than I could bear."

She shook her head. "That wasn't love. That was lust. It was evil and you know it. You just can't admit what you've become. All you can see is yourself and your own sick needs."

"You're wrong." He walked purposefully toward her. "It wasn't lust. It was love. It still is." He stood directly in front of her. They were separated by mere inches—two thin layers of cotton and a gaping chasm of contempt. "Do you have any idea how beautiful you are?"

She sobbed. "Eli, please don't."

He ignored her and stroked her hair. "I have to admit, I like the way you dress now. I tire of those plain old dresses. I know they have their purpose, but still…" His hand descended to her breast.

"Eli!" she screamed. "Are you going to add rape to your list of crimes? Because that's what this is. Stop and think about what you're doing!"

He stepped back, his expression stricken. "My God! What have you done to me?"

"What? You're blaming *me* for your sins?"

His hand lashed out and manacled her wrist. He dragged her after him. "This must be stopped. The evil in you is growing daily. It started the first day that heathen touched you and it won't stop until I do what I must."

She fought him but his grip was like iron and his strides just as strong. She silently called out to Wolf and she silently grieved for what would follow for him. If she died he would have lost again—lost someone he cared about. She couldn't bear to put him through that again.

* * * * *

Wolf reached the sugar shack. He searched the little shanty, banging on walls and peering in blank, dark windows. It was empty. Nothing. He screamed Ronni's name. Then Leah's. His heart pounded against his chest like rapid machine gun fire. Sweat soaked his shirt and stung his eyes.

Eli had found them. There was no other explanation. But where would he take them? They could be anywhere. Surely not his house; that would be too obvious. Were they already dead? That thought made him want to sink to the ground and give in to despair. It couldn't happen again. A woman and a child that he cared about were going to die again. And he seemed powerless to stop it.

Where? Think, man. What had Stephen yelled as he had run off? Something about an abandoned barn. Ronni liked it there, he had said. Maybe they got tired of waiting for him and Ronni took Leah to see it. But where was it? It couldn't be that far, this bush wasn't that big. He hadn't seen anything on his way in. He should keep going. Maybe the path led right to it. He *had* to keep going.

He turned as if to go and then, abruptly, he stopped. Had he heard something? A voice calling to him from down the path? No, that wasn't right. It hadn't been a call or a scream. It had been more of a…whisper. But that was ridiculous.

He shook his head to clear it, sure his fear was playing tricks on him. But when he set off at a dead run, his direction was certain and he didn't think to question it. He had the sense that he knew exactly where he was going. And exactly what he would do when he got there.

For the first time since leaving the hospital he longed for his M16. With little effort and no regret Wolf could picture Eli's body jerk violently as Wolf pumped him with round after round of cold, biting steel. If Eli had hurt those two, Wolf swore on Lubica's grave, he would kill him with his bare hands. Ronni had been right after all.

It wouldn't be the first time.

* * * * *

She stumbled after Eli as he dragged her up the stairs. One of the steps cracked and gave beneath her weight. If Eli hadn't been holding onto her wrist she might have fallen the ten feet to the barn floor. When they reached the top he pulled her after him. He didn't stop until they reached the edge of what had once been the haymow.

A twenty-foot drop stretched below them, down to what had once been a row of stalls for cattle or horses or some other such large domestic animal. The stalls had once been enclosed, built up with blocks of stone and concrete. But the blocks had long since succumbed to the elements. Years ago the roof above them had been ripped away by high winds, exposing the interior. Battered by the elements, jagged, sharp edges and irregular hunks of stone and cement were all that remained of the walls that had once been a home for the valued beasts.

Then Ronni screamed. Down below, nestled amidst the rubble lay a new white running shoe.

She couldn't see any more than that but she was sure it was Leah's. Strengthened by rage and grief, she turned on Eli. She grabbed his clothes, tore at his face and screamed for his gruesome return to his maker. She managed to inflict an ugly gash across his cheek with her fingernail before he restrained her. She twisted and writhed against his arms but he held her firm.

"You see, Frany," he said, his voice calm and eerie as he spoke above her sobs. "You fell to your death during your foolish exploration of this old relic. You should thank me. If the Lord is forgiving, perhaps you'll be with Jesse again."

"You bastard!" she screamed as she drooped, spent and hopeless, in his arms. "You're going to hell! Damn you to hell!"

"No, Ronni, he's already there."

She froze at the sound of the familiar growl. "Wolf?"

"Let go of her, Martin." He stood at the top of the stairs—proud and fierce, his face a mask of rage and revulsion. He was flushed and sweaty and the most beautiful thing Ronni had ever seen in her life. "It's pointless now. Prison is inevitable, but if you hurt her, I swear to God, I'll kill you."

"You just don't understand, do you?" mourned Eli. "It's far too late." And with that he gave Ronni a mighty shove, which sent her flying into space.

She screamed for Wolf as she fell, the note as high and clear as the shattering of a piece of fine crystal.

* * * * *

Wolf uttered a feral cry as he lunged for Eli. He smashed into the madman with the force of a tank. They landed on the floor of the haymow, precariously close to the overhanging edge.

Despite years of manual labor and the strength of the possessed, Eli was no match for him. Wolf had experience on his side—experience and the presence of mind that Eli lacked. They struggled briefly but, within moments, Wolf had Eli pinned by the wrists as he straddled Eli's heaving chest. Sweat, mixed with tears, dripped from Wolf's nose and splashed into Eli's eyes. "You son of a bitch!" he screamed. "You goddamn son of a bitch!" Then he directed his voice over the edge. "Ronni!"

But all he heard was the whistle of the wind through the skeletal rafters above him.

Fresh, hot tears sprang to his eyes. Suddenly there was no God. *Grace* be damned. He wanted revenge. The urgent need for it wrapped around his soul and squeezed, cutting into him like a swathe of razor wire.

Eli looked up at him, his eyes now haunted and fearful. The eyes of the prey instead of the predator.

"I had to do it," he whined. "Don't you see? She's evil."

"Shut up!" Wolf shook his head and took rasping breaths as he faced his own demons. But he barely had to think about it. The decision had been made for him.

He rolled his victim over, grasping both of Eli's wrists in one hand as he rammed a knee into Eli's back.

He leaned down very close to Eli's ear and hissed, "People often ask me if I've ever shot anyone and I tell them 'no.' But that's not the right question, is it? They should ask if I've ever killed anyone and then the answer would be different." His breathing grew rapid and ragged. He felt almost giddy with lust for the death of this man. But not too quickly. Eli needed to suffer first—to feel the anguish. Like his other victims. Like Glenn had suffered. And like Ronni. Eli needed to look over the brink of death and dread what awaited him.

"I was alone one night," continued Wolf as Eli struggled impotently, "just a few weeks after I got to Bosnia. I found this girl. She couldn't have been more than thirteen. She was dead, her body torn and bloody from a brutal rape. The Muslim scum that had done it was snoozing not twenty feet away, cuddled all snug and cozy under the cape that he had stolen from her body. This is what I did to him." Wolf gripped Eli's chin, his fingers a vice of righteous rage. "One little tug in the right direction and it's all over. The neck snaps. No pain, just blissful silence. No one ever knew. I left him there, beside his victim." Wolf flexed his fingers on Eli's jaw, testing the tension, relishing the fear.

Eli yelped in pain.

"That was why I retired. They wanted to promote me. I had done such a damn fine job, you see. But they didn't know the truth. They didn't know what I was capable of. I had to get out before I killed again. Before I became what I despised. And look at me now."

"Please," Eli whimpered.

"Shut up. At least meet your end with dignity." He regarded the pathetic form beneath him—a wretched life, a moment away from oblivion. "As if you have any."

Wolf closed his eyes, tightened his grip and—

"Wolf!"

His eyes snapped open. "Sam?" Sam stood frozen at the top of the stairs, Stephen a heartbeat behind him.

Sam licked his lips and said again, "Wolf." He spoke slowly and evenly, very much like someone trying to soothe a wild dog and coax it away from its prey. "What are you doing?"

Wolf didn't release his grip. His fingers refused to let go. "He pushed her, Sam. Ronni. She's down there." He motioned with his head as a tear drilled its way down his cheek. "He killed her."

Stephen rushed to the edge and looked down while, with shaky steps and beseeching eyes, Sam moved closer. "You can't kill him."

Wolf closed his eyes to shut out the concern on Sam's face. "He deserves it, Sam."

"But you don't. Think of the consequences. Let him go. He'll get his due." Sam's voice cracked. "There's been enough pain. Dammit, there's been enough death."

"She's moving!" yelled Stephen.

Wolf dropped Eli like he was a rotting piece of carrion. He rushed to Stephen's side and gazed down into the pit of rock and rubble.

Ronni was clearly visible below them. She had landed on a relatively flat hunk of concrete. Her leg was twisted at an odd angle and was probably broken. She had a gash on the side of her head and her eyes were closed but she was definitely moving…and moaning.

Relief flooded through Wolf and he dropped to his knees. "Ronni!" he called so that she would know he was with her. "Thank God. Stephen, run back and call for help. Ambulance and police. I'm going down there but we probably shouldn't move her." Stephen didn't move. "Now!"

Wolf stood and sprinted for the stairs as Stephen rushed from the barn.

As he passed, Wolf noticed that Sam had found an old piece of bailer twine and was wrapping it around Eli's wrists. Eli continued to mutter incoherently.

"Sam?" said Wolf, his voice thick and his emotions raw and confused.

Sam's eyes met his. "I know. Now get going."

Wolf bounded down the stairs and reached Ronni's side. He touched her hair, her face, her hands. He whispered in her ear, "You're going to be okay." He rested his forehead against hers and closed his eyes. "You have to be okay."

She whispered, "Leah. She's over there. Maybe..."

Leah. He hadn't yet had a moment to consider what had happened to her. He stood and scanned the area. His eyes finally rested on the little white running shoe.

And the world slipped out from beneath him.

Part Four: Healing

Chapter Thirty-three

May 1999

"Ronni?"

She felt a squeeze on her hand. She smelled antiseptic mixed with a familiar spicy cologne. Her eyelids felt heavy but the voice compelled her. She cracked them open to dazzling sunlight. She was in a hospital room.

"Good." The voice sighed with relief.

"Sam?" She felt disoriented and woozy from pain and drugs. But with some effort she focused and turned her head toward him. When she saw him, tears instantly sprang to her eyes. "Sam! I'm s-so sorry. I know I should have told you. About Eli. And—and Leah. But it was so hard. I was hurting so much. And now…Eli…he told me…Jesse…" The words tumbled over each other, as muddled as her thoughts. She couldn't seem to focus on anything. Everything was mashed together in a hazy jumble of images and ideas. Eli in the barn. Wolf looking deadly. Flying through space…

Sam took her hand and squeezed. "Shh. Don't worry about all that. That's why I'm here." He looked down at her hand as it lay in his. "Wolf filled me in on everything. I didn't like it but…I understand it. It's okay. I'm not angry anymore and I want my friend back. I want my *family* back. You don't need to bear any more guilt, especially because of me."

She shook her head and felt thankful when the world didn't spin. "You don't know about Eli. What he did to Jesse."

"Yes I do."

"What?"

"When the police got there he babbled on like a maniac. He told them everything. Gave them every grisly detail. He confessed to anyone who would listen. He murdered your father and he murdered Jesse and he's going to be put away for a long time."

"What will happen to him?"

"He's going through a psych evaluation. He snapped. It must have been coming for a long time. He confessed to other things. He was extorting money from the congregation, holding secrets over their heads to get money for his breeding experiments. Even Herb was one of his victims."

Ronni stared, unseeing, at the ceiling. "I don't understand how it could happen. He was always so solid, so committed. I really thought he had it together. Sure he made a mistake with me but his faith seemed so strong."

"It sounds like that night with you was his undoing. The guilt of that ate away at him. He hadn't lived up to his own expectations, and the expectations of everyone he cared about. He couldn't face it. He started looking for excuses and he started to hear the Lord telling him to do things that he couldn't take responsibility for himself."

"If I had been stronger," whispered Ronni. "If I hadn't been so selfish that night and given in, none of this would have happened. Jesse would be alive." She felt a tear burn down her cheek. "And he knew the truth before he died. Eli told him what I had done, and about Leah." She gripped the sheet in her clenched fingers. "He must have hated me."

"Ronni, you have to stop this!" Sam's vehemence startled her. "You can't take the blame for Eli's decisions. Your only mistake was being too young and vulnerable. Eli is responsible for Jesse's death. And Jesse didn't hate you. That's just ridiculous. His last words were on your behalf, for God's sake." Sam paced to the window. He gazed out through the glass for only a moment before turning back to her. "Now just let it go and concentrate on getting out of here."

She nodded but couldn't meet his gaze.

"Dammit!" he muttered. "I'm getting Wolf in here. Maybe he can scare you into being reasonable. If anybody can, it's him."

Sam moved to go but her voice stopped him. "Sam, why were you there yesterday?"

He stopped at the foot of her bed and faced her, his hands resting on the steel rails. "I had brought Heidi up to see my dad, and to tell him about—" He looked away and his eyes were full. "To tell him about Mom. I called to see about getting together with you and they told me that Wolf had run off looking for you. I just got this feeling, like something was wrong. I could almost swear I heard a voice telling me that you were in trouble." He shrugged and returned his gaze to hers. "I drove out right away."

"Thank you."

He pointed a finger at her. "You just get better and get back on that stage. Your fans will miss you, me included."

She smiled as he walked to the door and it closed behind him.

Her eyes had just begun to droop when the door swung open again, and an ominous figure sauntered in, eyes the color of gunpowder, and just as explosive. "What's this I hear? You're on a new guilt trip?" He stopped beside the bed and glowered down at her—an iron mask hiding a velvet heart. "You just found happiness and now you're going to try and throw it away again, aren't you? Well, I won't hear of it. I'm not going to let you wallow in that pit again. You're going to be happy if it kills me."

She laughed in spite of herself. And then regretted it as pain shot across her ribs. "Don't worry, I won't do anything stupid. I wouldn't dream of turning you away. That would be suicide."

"Damn right."

"I just need a little time," she hedged. "Jesse's death was bad enough, but now to find out he was murdered… That's a big pill to swallow."

He pulled up a chair and straddled it. "Okay. I'll give you time. You'll be in here for a while anyway."

She touched a tender spot on her abdomen. "What did they do?"

"You had some internal injuries. They operated to repair some damage to your liver and spleen. They almost took the spleen but managed to save it." His eyes softened. "It was touch-and-go there for a while. I never want to go through that again."

Ronni studied him and then something struck her. "How did you find us, anyway?"

"Stephen had mentioned the abandoned barn as I took off."

"But…but you had no idea where it was. It's hidden. In a hollow. How—"

Wolf shrugged as if it was of no consequence. But the look in his eyes hinted at uncertainty and…embarrassment? There was something—

"I don't know. I just did. I followed the path and I saw this rise and it looked—I don't know—suspicious. I just had a…" He shrugged again. "A feeling that I should check on the other side."

Something about his answer niggled at the back of her mind but her brain was far too muddled to explore it further. She accepted it at face value. "How's Leah?"

"A little battered, but she'll be fine. We'll bring her by tomorrow."

"Why do you think he spared her?"

Wolf let out a heavy sigh. "I'm not sure he was going to. Leah said he had her up on the ledge and was getting ready to toss her over when her shoe fell off in the struggle. Then he just stopped. He couldn't seem to go through with it. He locked her in the barn cellar after that. He says he was going to take her away somewhere but who knows what he might have been capable of if he'd succeeded in killing you."

Ronni shuddered. "He's a monster, Wolf. I may have my criticisms of our church but I hope you won't judge them all on the basis of him and Herb. There are a lot of good people."

He touched her cheek and the warmth of his fingers penetrated through the protective layers. "Don't worry. I've seen the good too. Stephen and Anna have been wonderful. Your mother's a little worse for wear, though. This has been tough on her."

"I'll have to talk to her. I think we can work it out. I hope we can work something out with regards to Leah, as well."

"That's my little surprise."

She brightened at the prospect of some *good* news. "Surprise?"

"Leah was so worried while you were in surgery. She clung to me like a little leech. Your mother noticed and asked me about us." He grinned mischievously. "She wanted to know my *intentions*."

"Oh God, leave it to a mother. What did you say?"

"Well, I didn't want to speak for you but I told her I was going to be sticking around until we could make some decisions about our future."

"And?"

"She seemed satisfied with that. She told me privately, that if we decided to get married, she would consider letting Leah come with us without a fuss."

Ronni held her face rigid as she sorted through her feelings.

"I'm not pressuring you, Ronni, but I thought you should know what the deal was."

She nodded absently. "I know. I want Leah and I think I want to be with you but—"

"But you're not ready to let go of him yet, are you?"

She shook her head. "It's not that."

"Don't lie to me, Ronni. This murder thing has stirred it all up again for you."

The tension in his voice cut her but she felt powerless to assuage his concerns. If she was honest with herself she had to admit that she wasn't yet ready to give herself completely to anyone. Not even Wolf.

She had come so far, but perhaps not far enough. It was as if an invisible, and indefinable tendril of doubt had snagged her and refused to let go. To marry him under such circumstances would be dishonest and unfair to him.

"I don't get it. This should absolve you. All the blame lies on Eli's shoulders. But I guess guilt isn't logical. I don't understand it but I'll wait. We need more time together anyway and I'll give it to you. You can come to terms with it as you see fit, in your own time."

"I hear a but," she said warily.

"But I won't wait forever. I won't play second fiddle to a ghost for the rest of my life."

"I wouldn't expect you to. I know I'll get past it. Just let me work on it."

He nodded and leaned over to kiss her. His lips lingered on hers, as he mumbled, "I thought I lost you. Please don't make me face that again."

She reached up with her right hand; the left was bandaged for her sprained wrist. She cupped the back of his head, her fingers laced through the dark hair at the nape of his neck. "I won't. I promise."

They heard the door swing open. "Neckin' in a hospital bed, eh? You two got no class at all." Heidi sauntered over as Wolf straightened and stood up. "You look like hell, girl."

"Thanks," grinned Ronni.

Wolf moved to leave.

"Don't you go anywhere, Wolf-man. I'm not staying long. Sam and I are heading out in a minute. He's shipping out in a couple of days so we're doing the town."

"Thanks for taking care of him for me, Heidi."

She waved away the gratitude. "Believe me, it's been my pleasure." She bobbed her eyebrows. "Believe me." Then she propped her hands on her hips and spoke with conviction. "You're damn lucky, you know that? He was so angry at you, and then when he thought there was something wrong, he was a man possessed. I think if he had lost you too, he would have imploded. I would have been left with a shell of a man." She pointed a fiery red fingernail at Ronni. "So it's a good thing you're okay or I would have been royally pissed."

Ronni laughed. "Get lost, Heidi. You're stinking up the room with your bullshit."

Heidi smiled warmly. "Glad you're okay. By the way, Endecott resigned. He was grateful you weren't pressing charges but I don't think he could face you back at work."

"I guess I'm glad. If he hadn't left I think I would have. It's such a shame, though. He really was good to me. If his wife hadn't fooled around, who knows..."

Heidi nudged Wolf with a bony elbow. "I have to wonder if he was scared shitless of your new boyfriend. Can't say as I blame him."

"Me either," said Wolf with a straight face.

Heidi sized him up with a languorous sweep of her eyes. "You ever kill anybody? Sam said you came damn close to doing in old Eli."

Wolf set his jaw and the muscles worked around the words, "Weren't you leaving?"

She shrugged off his irritation. "Touchy." Then to Ronni, "Take it easy, you lucky bitch. I'll see you in a couple of days." Then she turned and left the room, her curls swinging cheerfully.

"I think she and Sam are a good match," observed Wolf.

"Maybe he'll actually stick around a little more. I'd like that." She reached for his hand. "You didn't like her question."

He sighed and examined her hand at length. "I have a story for you, but not now. Ask me again when you're better. Right now I should probably go and let you rest." He combed his fingers through her hair. "You look tired."

"Please stay. I'd like to fall asleep with you watching over me." A sleepy smile stole across her lips.

"Well, if you insist on twisting my arm." His eyes were full. "I'll stay until you fall asleep, if that's possible. I can't believe the nurses left you alone *this* long."

She nodded and closed her eyes. His hand covered hers like a protective shell. She listened to him breathing beside her. She struggled with her regrets, and with her feelings for him. She knew one thing for certain—she didn't want to lose him. She'd get past this.

She had to.

Chapter Thirty-Four

July 1999

Ronni strolled through the tall weeds and grasses. The wild oats brushed her calves. Purple loosestrife, Queen Anne's lace and goldenrod dotted the clearing by the brook. She plucked a milkweed pod from its stem and broke open the dried husk. A soft, white cloud scattered and billowed on the breeze—tiny, feathery seeds destined for unknown adventures. They would find fertile new soil in which to grow. They were going to strike out fresh, leave the past behind and make a new home as they sprouted and flourished.

That was why she was here. Things were going well with Wolf and her body had healed. Tonight she was going back on stage for the first time since their adventure. And Eli had been hospitalized indefinitely.

If he ever became sane enough to stand trial, he would surely go to prison for a long time. That was comforting but part of her ached for his family. Mary and the children didn't deserve to be sucked into his web of madness but it was inevitable. Mary visited him religiously, only to be met with either tears of remorse, or insults and threats. Ronni was thankful that Mary and her children had a large extended family and a compassionate community to rely on. Not everyone had that kind of support.

Ronni trampled down the weeds and spread her blanket beside the stream. The early afternoon sun sparkled on the gurgling water. She probably should have waited for nightfall but she was anxious. The doctor had removed her cast a week earlier and this was her first chance to come out here. Wolf was being very patient. She suspected he would be willing to wait months or even years for her to adjust, and agree to marry him. But she wasn't so tireless. She knew she needed to confront her regrets and her memories in order to get past them. And this was the best place to do it. This was the site of her last happy memory with Jesse. Maybe here she could sort through things, and clear her conscience.

She needed to know in her heart that she was forgiven—that he would have forgiven her if he'd had the chance.

"I already have, Ronni."

The voice startled her. She craned her neck and squinted against the blinding sun. The tall figure seated himself beside her on the blanket. Sheathed in faded denim, his long legs stretched out before him. A hole had worn through the toe of his red Converse high tops but his white T-shirt looked clean and fresh. He leaned back on his hands and studied her intently.

She blinked in disbelief. She was hallucinating. Maybe she was still on those painkillers in the hospital and they were wreaking havoc with her mind.

He quirked a smile. "Don't worry, you're not going insane."

"Jesse?" Her lower lip trembled. He was just as she remembered—dark hair and mischievous blue eyes, the contours of his face lean and familiar. She wanted to reach out to him, but held back, afraid she'd be disappointed and her fingers would meet empty air.

"It's me, Ronni. Please don't cry." As if in answer to her fears he touched a finger to her trembling lip. It was warm and firm.

Then she believed. She no longer questioned it. She accepted what her senses were telling her. Perhaps this was the first time she could see him but perhaps it wasn't the first time he had come to her. Maybe he had been with her all along. Maybe he had visited Sam as well.

He continued, "I can't stay long but I had to talk to you."

She swallowed against the lump in her throat and struggled to stay the tears. "I'm sorry, Jesse."

He frowned, the concern in his eyes deep and sincere. "That's why I'm here. You have to let me go. I love you too much to watch you do this to yourself."

"But I need…"

He covered her hand with his. "No buts. I forgave you before I died. You're human, Ronni. I was hardly perfect and I never expected you to be." She felt his thumb stroke across the back of her hand. "You're the only one who expects that."

She accepted his words, made them a part of her. Suddenly it was so easy.

She laced her fingers through his, longing for more and knowing it was too much to ask. "I missed you so much. I still do."

"I know. But you have someone who wants to be there for you now. He's a good man, Ronni, and he loves you. Please let yourself be happy. I won't love you any less because you love him."

She remained silent, trying to immerse herself in these few moments they had been granted, memorizing his face and his touch all over again. His eyes were still playful but they held something new. When she had known him he had still been a boy, had barely reached the age of responsibility, and was still testing the waters of independence. His eyes had shone with the fires of youth and recklessness. But he had matured. Now he was a man and she knew with certainty that he was at peace.

"I've heard you sing," he said softly. "I'm glad I was a part of that."

"You gave me a lot more than that."

He looked at her hard. "Will you do as I ask? Can you let it go?"

She nodded. "Yes, I think so. I just needed you to know that, no matter what I did, I loved you."

"I never doubted it. Be happy, Ronni. You deserve it."

"What's it like, Jesse?"

He smiled. It was a smile beyond her understanding. It was the smile a parent might grant a four-year-old who had just asked how deep is the ocean, or how long is forever. She wasn't ready for the answer. "That's not why I came. You have to find that answer for yourself."

She felt his lips brush against hers, warm and delicate. The touch was brief but replete with meaning. She closed her eyes and, when she opened them, he was gone. But in her mind she heard, *Tell Sam for me,* and she understood.

She lay down on the blanket and closed her eyes, allowing the sun's rays to warm her as she listened to the voice of the stream, and heeded the voices in her heart.

* * * * *

"Ronni?"

She didn't open her eyes right away. Instead she relished the feel of his body lying next to her, his hips nestled against hers, his heart beating strong against her shoulder.

He kissed her cheek, and then moved on to nibble her earlobe. She smiled and opened her eyes. "Is it time already?"

"You said to come back in a couple of hours. I take my orders literally. It's two hours to the minute since I dropped you off here."

"Leah?"

"She's at your mom's. They were baking cookies when I left." For the summer, Leah was spending the weekends with Ronni and Wolf. "I asked if she could stay for a while, 'cause I suspected this might be an intolerably romantic setting." He raised his head and smiled down at her. And at that moment she knew. She finally allowed herself to accept something she'd been denying for months.

She loved him—wholly, completely, without reservation or regret. She touched his cheek, allowing the truth of it to sink in, to seep into her touch.

She looked into his eyes and smiled. "Is your offer still open, Wolf?"

"Which offer is that?" he asked as he dipped his head and nuzzled her throat. His hand slipped beneath her T-shirt and traced her ribs.

She suddenly realized she was wearing a tight little T-shirt and jeans. Leave it to Jesse to be sure he saw her like that, at least once. "The offer of marriage."

Wolf's lips and hands froze in their respective positions. He drew away and propped himself up on an elbow as he gazed down at her. "Yes," he said slowly. "Why?"

"Because I'm ready to set a date. If you are."

"Okay, what happened? One little trip to lay beside a stream and gaze up at the sky and suddenly you're a new woman, ready to take on the world and leave the past behind?"

"I talked to him."

Wolf frowned. "Talked to whom?"

"Jesse."

Wolf chuckled. "A dream has set you free?"

She sat up to face him and shook her head. "No. He was here. Really. I touched him."

Wolf's expression advertised his skepticism.

She laughed. "Don't worry. I'm not losing my marbles."

"You're telling me you just talked, face-to-face, with a man who's been dead for over eleven years. You touched him...and you're not losing touch with reality? I don't know. That sounds damn scary to me."

She took both of his hands in her own. "You told me you believe in God, right?"

He nodded.

"Believing in God implies belief in spirits and the afterlife, right?"

He nodded again, more slowly this time.

"So why is it so outrageous to believe that God might choose to let the two worlds mesh occasionally if he sees the need? Jesse saw the need. He came to tell me that he forgave me, that he loves me and that he wants me to be happy. Does that sound like the ravings of a person on the edge of insanity?"

"Well, no..."

"You carried a woman and child to safety when you should have been paralyzed and close to death. You had your miracle, Wolf. This was mine."

He frowned, apparently still unconvinced. And then she remembered...

"Let me ask you something."

He slid her a look, apparently picking up on the undertones in her voice. "Yes?"

"That night, when you came looking for me. When you were in the bush looking for the abandoned barn, and had no idea where it was..."

She saw something flicker in his eyes, and pressed on.

"How did you find it, Wolf? You said you just, sort of...knew. But how? How did you know?"

He swallowed, looked away and then shrugged. "All right, you've got me. I heard something."

"Heard something?"

He nodded, met her gaze and smiled. "I told myself I heard you calling for me but in my heart I knew that wasn't right. It was a man's voice and it was like he was whispering in my ear, telling me exactly which direction to go."

She blew out a long, slow breath. "Jesse."

"Yeah," he conceded. "I've gone over it a thousand times in my mind in the weeks since and…" He sighed. "Yeah. Jesse."

"Wow," was all she could think to say. He *had* been with her. Maybe more than she would ever know or suspect.

Wolf squeezed her hand. "Okay. So you've got your own private guardian angel."

She shook her head slowly. "No. Just someone who cares about me. And I think his job is done now. He's officially handed it over to you."

A smile trickled across his face. "I'm honored."

She smiled back. "You should be."

"So, what did he say that changed your mind?"

She considered that question. Perhaps the answer wasn't quite as obvious as she thought. "It wasn't so much what he said, as what I felt."

He waited patiently while she collected her thoughts.

"It wasn't just his forgiveness I was seeking and it wasn't just a chance to say goodbye. It was more." She struggled, her brows knitted in concentration. Finally they relaxed, her brow smooth and serene. "Even though I never actually saw it, my last image of him was of them dragging his body out of that car. You know, like in my dream."

Wolf continued for her, "You needed to know he was no longer in pain." He said it in a hushed tone, his words and expression a testimony to his understanding of what she was feeling.

"Yes, and I needed to know he was happy and at peace. I think it was even more important once I knew that he had been murdered. That knowledge rekindled my fears that he had died in turmoil." She glanced at the stream. The sun was lower now and it danced playfully across the bubbling surface of the water. "But the moment I looked at him I knew I needn't worry. He's where he's supposed to be." She looked back at Wolf. "Did you have this kind of struggle after she died?"

He dropped his gaze and plucked a few blades of grass. He rolled them between his fingers and tossed them into the breeze. A mourning dove cooed its lament from a tree not far away. It was a long time before he answered.

"When I carried her back to the jeep and laid her down, she grabbed my clothes and said something. At the time I didn't understand because her words were so quiet and I couldn't take the time to ask. But as the months passed in the hospital I had time to think about it and I finally realized I hadn't *wanted* to hear her." He lifted his eyes to Ronni's. "She had said 'thank you.' That may not sound like much but I had trouble accepting it, because I thought I had let her down. How could I accept her thanks, when I allowed that to happen?"

"What was she thanking you for?"

"I think she was thanking me for reuniting her with her daughter, and giving them those hours together, giving her the time in her family's home, and for the time we had spent together." He paused and the wind ruffled his hair. "Maybe just for giving her a taste of humanity again before she died."

"And once you accepted that, you could let go of her…and the guilt and anger of letting her down."

"Pretty much. Or, at least, it was a start."

She touched his cheek again. "You didn't really let her down, you know. You're the only one who thinks that."

He shrugged and she saw the doubt that lingered in his eyes.

She persisted. "You tried to convince me once that I had no reason to feel guilty for what happened to me, that the…rape," despite how far she'd come, that word still came hard, "was his responsibility and no one else's." She dropped her hand from his face and laced her fingers with his. "I finally believe it, Wolf, and you need to, too. What happened to them wasn't your fault and you have no reason to feel guilty."

"I guess I believe it." He leaned in and touched his forehead to hers. "Or at least I'm starting to."

"There's something else I need you to believe, too."

He drew away, waiting expectantly. "Oh? And what's that?"

She met his gaze, losing herself in the familiar dark depth of his eyes. "That I love you, Wolf. I love you so much—so much that sometimes I feel so full I think I'll burst. I'm sorry I haven't told you that before. I've known it for weeks now but I think it scared me. I couldn't let myself accept it because…because I wasn't sure about so much."

He touched her hair and his eyes were full. "But now you know. Now you're sure."

"Yes. I've never been more sure of anything in my life."

"Well, I'm glad to hear it because I'm pretty sure, too." He kissed her then, his lips a whisper of warmth and intimacy across her own. "Sure that I love you, and sure that I want to spend the next fifty years proving it to you."

She closed her eyes and embraced him, relishing the ripple of muscle and sinew, and the assurance of a strong, beating heart. She held him tight, certain she could feel the difference. It was as if there had been a thin sheet of tissue paper between them. They had been together but still separated by an invisible barrier. And now it had dissolved. She felt closer to him than ever. She wanted to be closer still. She pulled away and tugged his shirt out of his waistband.

"I figured this setting would be too romantic to pass up," he whispered in her ear.

As his hand slipped beneath her bra, however, a thought struck her and she said abruptly. "You have to come tonight."

He looked at her, somewhat dazed by the interruption. "What? Leah and I were going to play a round of Scrabble." His face lit up. "I can hardly wait to tell her about us."

She shook her head. "There's lots of time for that. This is special. I'll get Heidi to come again. I have a surprise for you."

"If I say yes can we continue what you started?" he said hopefully.

"Yup."

"Deal. Now shut up and help me celebrate our engagement."

She complied happily, lying back on the worn, soft warmth of the blanket. His mouth on hers sparked desires previously kept hidden. There was an urgency and a fire to their lovemaking that she found new and exciting. She realized that, despite their passion, she had still been holding something back. She had been unwilling to give herself completely, keeping part of herself closed off, as if saving it for the ghost she couldn't release. But now she was free to love without guilt and without boundaries. Her skin tingled with every touch and she uttered Wolf's name to the skies in blatant affirmation of her newfound liberty.

Later, as they rested, watching the clouds skid across the sky, their bodies molded together and their limbs entwined, she eagerly anticipated the look on his face when she unveiled her surprise that night. She could already picture the sparks in those soulful, black eyes.

* * * * *

Seated alone at the table closest to the stage, Wolf sipped his drink. The show had progressed without event and his curiosity as to Ronni's surprise continued to grow. The first set was drawing to a close and there was no hint of anything unusual.

The crowd had welcomed her back with boisterous cheers and applause. Her celebrity had grown with the media stories surrounding Eli Martin's arrest and confessions. And she had settled back into her onstage role as if she'd never left. He loved watching her up there. She sparkled when she sang and it had nothing to do with the sequins or the glitter.

Ronni was giving the eager crowd her own unique rendition of *Proud Mary* when Wolf heard the scrape of a chair. A man joined him at the table.

"So what the hell is this about, anyway?" asked the grinning figure with the tousled hair and the cigarette dangling from his mouth.

"Riley!"

They clasped hands.

Wolf felt a rush of pleasure at the long overdue reunion with his old friend. He laughed. "You must be the surprise. How'd she manage it?"

"She called me this afternoon, introduced herself as your fiancée and begged and pleaded for me to come and be here tonight. She paid for the plane ticket herself. I'll tell you, it was some rush to get to the airport on time."

Wolf shook his head. "She's something else."

"She'd have to be to snare you," said Riley as he glanced at the stage. Ronni winked at him and awarded him a special smile.

"So how's the store doing?"

"Great. We may actually make it into the black in the next few months. And the kids are great. Your nemesis, Trevor, could probably bowl you over now, he's so big."

"That's sounds great. I'm glad your life is in order. Really glad. "

Without looking at Wolf, Riley asked, "So, how about you, Wolf? You all straightened out?"

"Yeah, Riley. Don't worry about me. Physically I'm strong as a horse and I've got a future again, with Ronni and her daughter."

"Good. I was still worried about you, you know. Even after you got out of rehab you weren't yourself. You were still scary as hell, but in a depressing kinda way."

"Shut up, Riley." *Damn,* it felt good to say that again.

Riley flashed him his special *shit-disturber* grin. "How about the career? You know what you wanna do?"

"Actually, I'm going to try and get into the local fire department. Ronni needs to stay here. This band is important to her. I couldn't ask her to leave it. And, maybe then, we'd be able to afford for her to quit her day job." He smiled wryly. "And as a firefighter I get to rescue damsels in distress on a regular basis."

"Yeah. I hear you're finally getting the hang of it."

They both laughed but their chuckles were interrupted by a demand for attention from the stage.

"Ladies and gentlemen," Ronni began, "for my last number in this set I'd like to do something a little different. As most of you know I've had some rather difficult obstacles to overcome in recent weeks and this song is dedicated to the two men who helped me overcome them. One of them is seated here tonight and the other is here in spirit." She glanced at Wolf and he felt an odd flood of warmth at the shared secret. "It's not my usual style but I think if you'll bear with me you won't be disappointed."

She glanced at Jason, who gave her a single note from the acoustic guitar he had pulled out from behind the drums.

The crowd had continued to mumble and murmur through her little introduction but, from the first note, a hush fell over the room. People froze, their drinks halfway to their mouths, as their attention was riveted to the glittering figure on the stage. It was her voice alone, no guitar, no drums, no distractions. The clear, sweet tones wafted through the room, each note hanging in the air, delicate and strong as crystal forged with gold…

Amazing grace, how sweet the sound. Her eyes closed as the music swelled from her soul and burst from her lungs.

That saved a wretch like me.

I once was lost, but now am found. She opened her eyes and riveted them on Wolf.

Was blind but now I see.

A smile slowly spread across his face as she continued. In the second verse Jason picked up the accompaniment on the acoustic guitar.

By the last verse,

When we've been there ten thousand years,

Bright shining as the sun, there was hardly a dry eye in the house.

We've no less days to sing God's praise,

Than when we first begun.

And Wolf was no exception.

When she finished, the room remained still and silent. Applause somehow seemed unnecessary, out of place, even sacrilegious. But in the end convention won out and one hesitant pair of hands began the cascade of affirmation. Ronni took no bow but silently descended the stage and approached Wolf and Riley.

Wolf stood and greeted her with a warm hug. He slid an arm around her waist and kissed her cheek. He turned to Riley. "I think I really do believe in miracles. After all, I'm marrying an angel."

Also by Nikki Soarde

Duplicity

Legacy of Sin

Phobia

Redeeming Alec

About the Author

Nikki lives in a small town in Ontario, Canada. In the midst of the chaos that comes with raising three small boys, working part-time as a lab tech in a hospital blood bank, and caring for her ever-adoring husband, she dreams up her stories. Nikki's work is an eclectic combination of romance, mystery, suspense and humor with characters that have plenty of room to grow.

Nikki welcomes mail from readers. You can write to her c/o Ellora's Cave Publishing at 1056 Home Avenue, Akron OH 44310-3502.

Enjoy An Excerpt From: LEGACY OF SIN

Craig crinkled up his nose and sniffed. "What's that smell?"

"It's called fresh air, Craig." He rolled down the limousine window and let the wind flirt with his hair. He breathed deeply the scents of his youth. "It's called air without smog and pollution. We're almost to the lake, and I can smell the water and..." Unexpectedly his stomach clenched. He closed his eyes and leaned back against the buttery calfskin upholstery.

"And what?"

This was ridiculous. It had been years. It shouldn't still have such a stranglehold on him. He had to take control, and not allow his memories to consume him, and ruin his trip home. He pressed a hand to his gut. "And hay. Somebody's done a cutting of hay already. That's what that sweet, fresh-cut grass smell is from."

"Hey, man, you're pale as a ghost. You car-sick or something?"

"I think it was that trout I had on the plane." He wasn't about to tell Craig that the scent of hay had hung thick and heavy in the fall air the day he found his father's body. In fact, he hoped to keep reminiscing to a minimum for the duration of the trip.

"So, are we close to your old house?" asked Craig eagerly.

So much for idle wishes. "No. We won't be going by it. It's on the other side of Bay's Haven."

"Well, you'll have to take me out there later." Craig stuck his hand out the window and played with the breeze. "They *did* say they'd have a rental car available for our use, right? I like a limo ride as well as the next guy, but they're buggers to park at the mini-mall."

A smile tugged at Sloan's lips in spite of himself. "Yeah. This Mrs. Middleton I've been e-mailing assured me she'd try and have something nice and sporty available."

"Like a Porsche or a Beemer?" Craig sounded like a toddler asking for a lollipop.

"Hardly. I think we'll be lucky to get a Neon or Geo."

"Ugh. You sure know how to spoil a guy's fantasies."

"Hey man, I resent that. I make my living off of fantasies."

"True. But we're not in Tinsel Town anymore, Toto. In fact I've never *seen* so much empty space. Hard to believe this is one of the *most* populated regions of Canada."

"Yeah." Sloan gazed out across the endless fields dotted with quaint farmhouses, lone maple trees and strands of birches. He could just make out a hint of blue beyond the dense line of evergreens to the north. "It feels kind of empty after the sardine-land of LA and Burbank."

"I don't know. I think I could get used to it. At least for a while." Craig riveted an intense stare on his friend. "What the hell did you do for *fun* around here, anyway? Catch frogs, put them on rocks and watch them dry out in the sun?"

Sloan laughed for the first time since they'd disembarked the plane in Toronto. "You'd be surprised how much fun that can be. But we did manage to get a little more…innovative when the need arose."

"Oh? Care to elaborate?"

"Not particularly."

"Okay." And Craig left it at that. For now.

Fifteen minutes later the stretch turned down Killdeer Drive and rolled to a stop in front of Bay's Haven's finest guest house—The Wee Inn.

* * * * *

Across the street at the Eventide Café, a lone figure sat and sipped from a glass of imported beer. His eyes remained riveted on the long, black car as it vomited its passengers onto the street. The half-eaten club sandwich on his plate was suddenly forgotten.

He had requested a sidewalk table, and lingered over his lunch for the sole purpose of catching a first glimpse of the return of Bay's Haven's prodigal son.

The sight of Sloan hit him like a fist to the gut. When Bree had informed him of her plans he had sighed and smiled, and bent over backwards to play his role as the congenial family friend. He had honored her requests, but all the time he had secretly hoped it would all fall through. Sloan's exodus had been a dream, his return a nightmare.

"What does he *know*?" he whispered into the breeze.

He gripped his glass a little harder for fear it would slip through his sweaty fingers. He hated this—the waiting and the wondering. The not knowing was the worst. He liked to know all the variables, calculate all the angles. And he liked to make a decision and act on it swiftly. But Sloan was a wild card in an otherwise, well-ordered deck.

Sloan *might* be completely ignorant of the secrets that haunted Bay's Haven like restless ghosts in a ruined castle. He might be. And then again, he might not.

Had Sloan's mother followed through on her threats to tell him everything? Perhaps she had only hinted at things that could damage her as much as any of them. Perhaps she had only shared enough to ease her own tortured conscience.

But if that was the case, *how much*, exactly, had she revealed? Or had it all been a grand bluff? The Carvers always were adept at lying. All of them.

But if he didn't know, then why had he left? And why had he come back?

The questions were so thick that they clogged the airways and restricted the lungs. Questions and uncertainty could paralyze as surely as exposure. Something had to be done.

He picked up his sandwich and tore off an enormous chunk. He chewed methodically.

Sloan was still standing there, taking in the sights of his old hometown, his black-clad silhouette as trim and lithe as when he was eighteen. Resentment mingled with the uncertainty, coiling inside his stomach like a pair of hissing snakes. He pressed a hand to his gut, as if to still the writhing reptiles. But they would not be appeased.

But what to do? How to proceed without undue risk to himself or the business?

He drained the last of his beer and considered…

For now, uncertainty was the enemy. He had to establish the extent of the threat. There had to be a way to discern exactly how much Sloan Carver knew, and from there the course would become clear.

He would wait and watch. He would bide his time until an opportunity presented itself. And then he would decide. And then, if necessary, he would act.

If all went well, perhaps Sloan wouldn't have to die.

Why an electronic book?

We live in the Information Age—an exciting time in the history of human civilization, in which technology rules supreme and continues to progress in leaps and bounds every minute of every day. For a multitude of reasons, more and more avid literary fans are opting to purchase e-books instead of paper books. The question from those not yet initiated into the world of electronic reading is simply: *Why?*

1. ***Price.*** An electronic title at Ellora's Cave Publishing and Cerridwen Press runs anywhere from 40% to 75% less than the cover price of the exact same title in paperback format. Why? Basic mathematics and cost. It is less expensive to publish an e-book (no paper and printing, no warehousing and shipping) than it is to publish a paperback, so the savings are passed along to the consumer.
2. ***Space.*** Running out of room in your house for your books? That is one worry you will never have with electronic books. For a low one-time c ost, you can purchase a handheld device specifically designed for e-reading. Many e-readers have large, convenient screens for viewing. Better yet, hundreds of titles can be stored within your new library—on a single microchip. There are a variety of e-readers from different manufacturers. You can also read e-books on your PC or laptop computer. (Please note that Ellora's

Cave does not endorse any specific brands. You can check our websites at www.ellorascave.com or www.cerridwenpress.com for information we make available to new consumers.)

3. ***Mobility***. Because your new e-library consists of only a microchip within a small, easily transportable e-reader, your entire cache of books can be taken with you wherever you go.
4. ***Personal Viewing Preferences.*** Are the words you are currently reading too small? Too large? Too… *ANNOYING*? Paperback books cannot be modified according to personal preferences, but e-books can.
5. ***Instant Gratification.*** Is it the middle of the night and all the bookstores near you are closed? Are you tired of waiting days, sometimes weeks, for bookstores to ship the novels you bought? Ellora's Cave Publishing sells instantaneous downloads twenty-four hours a day, seven days a week, every day of the year. Our webstore is never closed. Our e-book delivery system is 100% automated, meaning your order is filled as soon as you pay for it.

Those are a few of the top reasons why electronic books are replacing paperbacks for many avid readers.

As always, Ellora's Cave and Cerridwen Press welcome your questions and comments. We invite you to email us at Comments@ellorascave.com or write to us directly at Ellora's Cave Publishing Inc., 1056 Home Avenue, Akron, OH 44310-3502.